Emerald

Chasing Verenathia : I

Madison Noran

The characters and events portrayed in this book are fictitious. Any similarity to real persons, living or dead, is coincidental and not intended by the author.

ISBN: 979-8-9951771-1-1

Cover design by: Joshua Howerton; Madison Noran. At the creator's discretion, the use of artificial intelligence was employed in some capacity for certain design elements.

Printed in the United States of America.

No part of this written story has been touched by the presence of artificial intelligence. Every jot and tittle has been conceptualized, written, and edited by human minds only.

For you, my love. We wouldn't be where we are without your relentless support and grounding. Thank you for being the light at the end of my tunnel.

A note from the author:

Maybe you've felt whispers in your soul that tell you there's more to life than what you've been told. Maybe, just maybe, you've had the feeling that the world isn't as it should be; as if something is irrevocably wrong. Or maybe, it feels like something is missing that you can't quite put your finger on.

If any of this resonates with you, than you, my friend, have come to the right book. Although this story is written for entertainment purposes, I encourage you to never stop questioning, seeking, and challenging.

CHAPTER 1

The world is full of wonder, little bird. I know you can see it too.

The roar of the forge and metal on metal do their best to drown out my thoughts as I watch the dragons through my window. Every day, I watch them. And I listen. The forge blares its inferno in a steady, numbing bellow, twining with the clashing of steel as Markell and I work. It filters out the sounds of the town, but it's not the sounds of the Smithshop that I listen to, no—those sounds have a way of driving you to insanity unless you allow yourself to grow numb to them.

I refuse to shut myself off in order to carry on though, and maybe that's my problem. I'd rather lose my mind bit by bit than accept the jaded existence that so many here on Ra'goramal do. So I listen. That unnamed cry within my soul grows louder by the day.

Some—like my brother—might call it discontent, but I choose to believe it's the ache that comes when color is forced to fade in a monochrome world. It fades slowly, bleeding out over time, until it's nothing more than a muted mass of forgotten desires. Blotted out by the weight of a world that seeks to eradicate any goodness.

But we're not afforded thoughts like that.

Propping my chin with a gloved hand, I gaze out that window. I can't help but watch the dragon atop one of the Loading Platforms. Its wings sparkle, shimmering under the bright mid-morning sun. The wooden crate strapped to its scaled back dips and swerves as it paws the ground impatiently, awaiting the Loading Brigade now swarming around it.

Like a well-choreographed dance, light blue uniform tunics bob in and out of sight as they efficiently transport supplies from the cart they've hauled up the ramp. Heavier and heavier the crate on the dragon's back grows as they work, but the beast doesn't balk under the weight. The dragonhide-clad Verenathian stands by, his red outfit gleaming as he watches the Brigade with a keen eye.

I scan the shifting uniforms on the platform, looking for Ashden, but I can't see my brother anywhere. Trailing my gaze down the platform's ramp, I search the docks and wharf, but to no avail. Only the fishermen, their ships nestled amongst the docks between the platforms, find me. The sea—dark and formidable and so beautiful—glitters beyond for eternity.

"Rae? Did you even hear what I said?" Markell's impatient tone abruptly brings me back to reality. I jerk my gaze from the window to his hulking form over my workstation. Flushed from the heat of the Smithshop, he pushes a strand of damp, gray streaked hair off of his sticky forehead. He's been working hard trying to finish the latest order—we both have—and the strain in his usual calm demeanor shows it.

Looking pointedly at the unfinished weapon in my hand and pile of raw metal beside it, he breathes a sigh of the longsuffering.

I offer him a sheepish grin. "I'm sorry. Do you need something?"

"How's that dagger coming along?" His voice, though gruff, is gentle. Never having spoken a harsh word to me, he's endlessly patient—even when a large part of my time is spent as it has been for the past hour.

"It's coming," I drawl, glancing at the rough-hewn shape. "I'm sorry, I'll have it done before I leave tonight."

His gaze softens knowingly. "As long as it's done by shipment tomorrow. I'm going to head to Rory's for an ale, and I'll be back to finish the lance shortly. I haven't seen a drop of liquid all day."

I nod. "Yes, sir." Facing back toward my workstation, I give another long look out the sooty glass pane as the sound of his footsteps recedes.

Markell let me have this station because he knows I love watching the dragons soar over the Sea of Ashwaroth on their way to and from Verenathia. It's so easy to envision myself floating high above the salt spray, away from my worries and responsibilities. I figure he's regretted it more than once, though he's never mentioned it.

Movement from the platform outside again draws my attention upward. The Loading Brigade begins to pull their now-empty cart back down the ramp, leaving one man remaining. He hands a ledger and quill to the Verenathian, his embroidered navy tunic and flashing auburn hair signifying him as Loadmaster Aurandraya.

After a signature and quick exchange of words, the Verenathian is mounting his dragon. It spreads its massive wings—so deeply green it's as if the earth itself touched it with the vibrancy of spring—and leaps, diving over the edge of the platform. For a breathless heartbeat, they fall before the air catches under its wings, pitching it upward. Both the rider and cargo are secure upon its back as they climb as high as the sun.

I tamp down the ache that blossoms within me at the sight. If there's any one thing in this life that I want above all else—it's a dragon. The freedom to soar whenever and wherever I want… Or maybe it's the freedom that I want.

It's also the one thing in this life that I can't have.

I squint as they shrink, until nothing remains but a speck on the horizon, heading west toward the floating isle. The sun, just past its apex, glides toward the jagged outline that gives the mist body.

Verenathia.

It's almost as if I can *hear* my draw to it; a siren song singing along the threads of magic that tether our worlds together.

Beautiful. So beautiful.

I wish death wasn't the promise for such thoughts.

Sighing, I gaze down at the unformed weapon still in my grasp and turn back toward the forge.

***

I scarcely notice as Markell returns, his arrival announced by the thud of heavy boots on the wooden floorboards. I'm too busy drawing the shape of a dagger out of the stubborn metal to acknowledge him. Blow after blow of my mallet strikes, dampening my body with sweat. Soon, the unruly material begins to look like a true weapon.

Decidedly satisfied, I switch to smoother, lighter, more refining strokes—honing the edge into something deadly.

I can't help but wonder what these are going to be used for. Hathswarden hasn't seen a war in over 400 years. The last—the Great War—was so devastating that the fear of another has been permanently ingrained in the blood of Goramalans.

It doesn't help that our people are constantly taken, serving as the reminder of how we would have been annihilated if it weren't for Verenathia's protection. With them as our ally—our protector—there's peace between our lands. Almost all of our contact with outsiders comes from Verenathia too, save for the occasional shipment from Thrunall—another province three weeks north by ship. I watch, every so often, as Verenathians fly overhead to scope out Ra'goramal's borders but, save for the rare wanderer pandering for coins or food, there's no disturbance.

The requests for more and more weapons leaves me… unsettled, to say the least.

I continue coaxing the edge of the dagger into submission, readying to quench the blade. By the time I'm finished, my arms are aching and new blisters have formed on my palms beneath my leather gloves.

"That's what you get for dawdling," I mutter as I gently slide the gloves off my tender hands. The blisters are still intact, so there's a chance they'll scab tonight without my tearing them open before tomorrow's work begins.

Walking toward the basin of fresh water in the corner of the shop, I pass by Markell, who's now polishing an almost-completed short sword into a mirror finish. Warm evening light filters through the window behind him, streaming onto the rough floor in hazy beams.

"All finished." I dip my burning hands into the cool water, shuddering at the sensation.

He glances up from his work. "Very well. Thanks, Rae." His brown eyes crinkle at the corners as he gives me an approving nod. "We only have two more after this, and the Verenathians never gave a deadline for those, so go ahead and take some time for yourself tomorrow. I'll finish up tonight and then we can both take a well deserved break." The light doesn't reach his eyes in the smile he offers me—it rarely does.

"I don't think I've ever seen you take a day off," I tease, moving from the basin to my workstation. I carefully grab the dagger and bind it in a leather sheath—placing it in the velvet lined crate waiting on the front desk. Something in my stomach tightens at the sight of the other deadly lance already stored there.

"We're gonna work ourselves to death if we try to keep up this pace,"

Markell grunts, returning to his work. The scrape of metal on metal begins ringing through the shop again.

Giving a perfunctory swipe across my worktable to brush off the dust and metal shavings, I grab my leather satchel and make my way toward the door

"Don't do anything I wouldn't do," he calls jokingly after me.

I chuckle, beginning toward the cluster of cottages at the end of the long street. The sun is already sinking behind the floating isle, casting the town into premature dusk. Streaks of red, orange and purple burst across the sky, taking my breath away.

The brilliance of it brings forth that perpetual tugging at the edge of my consciousness. I can always feel it pulsing, pulling—a beating undercurrent of tension that can't be described. I'm usually able to bury it, pressing it down deep where it can be ignored—but that's getting harder lately.

The cry of gulls over the gentle symphony of the sea bathes our town as I pass by the Apothecary and Mara's seamstress shop. Mara is sitting outside, a brocade skirt with needle and thread protruding from her hands.

There's an air of sadness in her dimples and dark circles under her eyes when she flashes me a smile. Her husband was taken for the Culling half a year ago, and I know she misses him terribly.

I offer her a smile of my own. This… sadness, the kind of sadness that hangs like a fog over our town is growing heavier by the day. Yet, through the tension and darkness, are glimpses of perfection. A sunset here, a belly laugh there; always present if you know where to look. It surrounds us, moves within us. It eclipses everything in sight.

And twining through it all, the good and the bad, is the vast yearning for something… what?

More?

Different?

If anyone else feels it too is a constant question running in the back of my mind. But it doesn't matter.

Can't matter.

The scent of fresh baked bread weaves from an open window in Raimy's bakery, making my mouth water. The beloved baker is already hard at work for tomorrow. Part of me is tempted to sneak in right now and snag one of his sweet rolls.

Don't do anything I wouldn't do.

Pulling my bottom lip between my teeth, I chew until it's raw. Markell knows I would never do… anything, really—not that there's anything to be done. I swallow the tension every day, as I'm sure we all do.

Force it down. Ignore it.

Climbing the face of one of the Pulchram mountains to see the petals on a particular flower is about the riskiest thing I'd ever done. Or maybe the time I convinced Ashden and Avice to construct a haphazard boat out of driftwood. We almost drowned in the wake and mother and father scolded us soundly, but it was thrilling, at least.

Everyone knows I'm more likely to be found sketching, legs dangling over the bluffs, or gazing over the sea toward Verenathia, dreaming of lands outside of my own—anything else is treason.

Footsteps come hurtling down the cobblestone behind me and I pause, turning to see Avice jogging from the direction of the Storehouse.

"Wait for me!" she calls, breathless, as she slows to a walk.

I can't help the grin that splits my face at the sight of my best friend. Her brown hair is loose and flowing after being tightly wound in a topknot all day, her cheeks flushed from the apparent sprint from the Loadmaster's Office. Her cream tunic and pants—the uniform of Storehouse Bookkeepers—is still impeccable, even after a long day. I squint at the badge on her uniform as she approaches, noting its change.

"Hey!" Her blue eyes dance.

I gesture toward the scroll gracing her badge. "Are you Head Bookkeeper now?"

"Yes," she beams. "Head Lichera is pleased with my work, noting the 'clarity and accuracy with which the ledgers are kept,"' she deepens her voice to mimic the Head Loadmaster. "Luca and Mirabelle have both been there longer than I have and were staring daggers through me all day," she laughs.

Her excitement is contagious. "I'm proud of you."

"Thanks," she says, scanning my face. "How was your day?"

We walk side by side for a moment as I let the silence lengthen between us. Her soft angles in the tidy Bookkeeper's uniform stand a stark contrast to my curves and thick, sooty smithing pants. I pick at my shirt, noticing it has a few new holes where tiny bits of metal have burned through.

"Good…" I search for the right words. "Speaking of daggers… I was making one for another shipment. Markell and I have been getting a lot of orders similar to this one. I've not seen this amount of weapons requested in such a short amount of time before." A quick glance shows the previous light in her face extinguished.

"I know," she says quietly. "I record most of the shipments from the Smithshop. I've never seen this many either." She works her fingers together as we walk. "What do you think they're for?"

I mull over the question before blowing out a breath. "I'm not sure."

More heavy silence stretches between us like a fog. Nudging her shoulder, I add, "But we can worry about that later. Markell gave me the day off tomorrow."

"Ah, lucky bastard." A hint of a smile returns to her lips.

"I know, I think I might spend some time with Ashden at the Storehouse." A giggle creeps out of me as I watch the rounds of her cheeks go even more pink at the mention of my brother.

"Lucky bastard for sure," she says, a devious glint in her eye.

We reach the cottages at the end of the cobbled path. "See you tomorrow," I laugh, turning toward our door. Her cottage is three down from ours, its stone walls and wooden roof tinted purple in the fading light.

"See ya," she waves and continues down the path.

Facing the thick wooden door, I lift the lever, giving a heave as it creaks on its hinges. The room is dim when I enter, with only the fading light of the sun and soft glow from the stove providing light.

I reach for the oil lamp on the table, glancing at the stove. The fire within stays continuously lit from the magic in the Safeguards—a ward held continuously in place by the Warbearers' magic.

The peaceful flickering of the lamp fills the room, illuminating the cabinet stretching below the window on our back wall, and overpowering the light from the stove.

Two small beds, each with a chest at their foot, grace the wall on the right while a sheet curtains off the corner opposite the stove. Small, practical, comfortable; ours is much like all of the others in the village.

I rummage around in the cabinet until I find a loaf of bread. Selecting a jar of potatoes and a few strips of dried fish, I set everything on the table, suddenly too tired to bother warming them.

Hearing a muffled thud, I look to the door as Ashden walks in. A whole head and a half taller than me, but with the same gray eyes and sharp jawline, I couldn't deny him if I tried. The only difference in our features is his hair—blonde, like our mother's.

There's slow deliberation in his movements as he goes from the front of the room toward the curtained corner, pausing to stoop to the chest at the foot of his bed. He pulls out a fresh long-sleeved undershirt and twill pants.

Stepping behind the curtain, he strips off his uniform and tosses it on the bed. The light blue of the Storehouse uniform winks at me from the folds of cream and brown surrounding it.

"Long day?" I venture, sitting down at the table—not bothering to take my boots or burnt work clothes off. Cutting a slice of bread, I begin nibbling on it thoughtfully.

"Something like that," he says, stepping out from the curtain. Bare chested, he slides the shirt over his head; the muscles in his arms shifting with the movement.

The physical labor of the Storehouse has made him rugged. I remember when we were children running alongside the sea, our mother and father trailing behind us. He was nothing more than a string bean then.

He settles into the chair across from me, grabbing a strip of fish. "There's talk of another Culling soon," he says between bites, his expression blank; tired.

My brows knit in confusion. "Wasn't the last one only, what, two months ago?" I shovel a bite of potatoes into my mouth and watch as he draws a long breath.

"Two and half, but yes," he exhales. "It's just a guess, obviously, but they're requesting so much more from us—we can only assume it'll be sooner than usual." Groaning, he rises, grabbing the canteen resting atop the cabinet and dunking it into the freshwater bucket near the stove.

I chew my food slowly. As part of retribution for Verenathia's protection during the Great War 400 years ago, our people have been taken—handpicked by the Warbearers to serve in their Citadel.

Although we know very little of the fabled structure, whose spires reach high enough to view from Ra'goramal—with the guarantee of a comfortable life in luxury, it looks like it would live up to the promise. The only ones who suffer are those left behind, forced to grow around the absence of the people they love.

To be Culled is an honor. At random and with no regular intervals—age, sex, position—none of it matters. If you're chosen, you go. There is no debate.

The scroll outlining the Accords sits in the library, open and on display for all to read. "*To serve the ones who fought on your behalf. There is no greater position, no greater honor. For Verenathia—the ones who sacrificed all.*"

I stuff another bite of food in my mouth, trying not to think of the second half of it.

We continue to eat in silence, a multitude of thoughts swirling in my head. Markell's weariness with the increasing demand. The slightly bowed shoulders of every single citizen in Ra'goramal. Mara's deep sadness at the loss of her husband, and many like her as they mourn the new gaps in their lives. Still living—just no longer with them.

Part of me is terrified that it will be Ashden every time Lucielle arrives. But the other, quieter half hopes it will be—hopes that maybe one of us will find a better life up there.

There's perfect peace between our lands. We supply their people; we have everything we need, and the Warbearers provide us protection in the form of the Safeguards over Brolithar.

The question of whether it's *true* peace is always lurking around the corner—after all, both parties need to be content in order to call it harmonious.

There's an undeniable tension in the magic that threads through our lands… But it's probably just the weight of life.

Life *is* hard.

I see that green dragon, the salt mist that clouds my judgment, and the inexplicable tug at the edge of my heart.

It's so beautiful.

But I swallow my thoughts. "If anything, we should be happy for them, right?" I probe lightly.

"Who?" he considers, drawing his attention from his half-eaten bread.

"The ones who are taken. Living a life of luxury amongst dragons and clouds doesn't sound so terrible to me."

"Don't be naive, Rae. You may be amongst luxury but you're still a slave no matter how you look at it."

I don't say anything.

"Clouds and all," he adds.

"But have you never considered a life up there, compared to one down here?" I ask incredulously. "That, maybe, there's more?" I've never voiced the words out loud. That invisible tug has been a part of me for as long as I can remember, but I haven't dared speak a word about it. Ashden knows my unrest, though I wonder if he sees the direction my thoughts like to travel. That quiet whispering of *more, more* grows louder by the day and I don't know how much longer I'll be able to block it out.

"As a slave?" he cocks an eyebrow at me.

"Are we not already slaves?" I ask quietly.

He swallows. "We are." A note of surprise touches his tone—at the thought, or my realization of it—I'm not sure.

"All I'm saying is that maybe it would be better to be a slave—*servant*," I correct, "up there, in the Citadel. Swimming in dragons and art and academic exploits. Not to mention living in the sky." I stuff another bite of potato in my mouth.

There's a challenge in his usual gentleness. "How do you know you would have access to any of that, as a *servant*?" He rolls his eyes.

"I think one could easily deduce from 'life of luxury' as being able to at least *look* at the dragons," I say defiantly.

"So you're going to volunteer for Lucielle next time he arrives?" His voice heightens in poor imitation of mine. "Oh great and mighty Lucielle, I would absolutely love to go back with you so I can look at the art on your walls and ride your dragons." Amusement lights his expression. "I don't think that would go over very well."

"That's not what I'm saying," I mumble, glowering. I know I shouldn't be upset. I know the direction of my line of thinking, and it tends toward illegal. Treasonous, actually. Against my will, my mind brings forth the image of the Accords, burned into my memory as it proclaims the latter half in bold, accusing letters.

"*In an effort to keep Verenathian bloodlines pure, no citizen of* Ra'goramal *shall be granted safe passage to the isle. Excluding the express purpose of the Culling, any found trespassing territory lines will be in contradiction of the Accords, and therefore, holy law. Upon discovery, the perpetrator's life will immediately be deemed forfeit. Execution will follow.*"

"They are the enemy, Rae."

"Maybe. Maybe not."

He holds my gaze for a long moment before finally heaving a sigh. "You scare me."

"How so?" I demand, struggling to tamp down my flaring indignation.

He chuckles softly, shaking his head. "You see the world in a way no one else does. And it's terrifying."

Another moment of silence.

"Mom would have understood," I say, dejectedly casting a downward glance at my now tasteless food.

He pauses for a beat, the weight of my words settling like a blanket over us. "I know she would," he says quietly.

Unsure of what to say, I shove my chair back and move to the chest at the foot of my bed, picking out a linen nightdress. I step behind the curtain and unlace my boots, tugging at them with more than a little aggression.

"I have the day off tomorrow," I call, desperately trying to change the subject. "I was thinking about spending some time at the Storehouse with you."

"I would love that." I breathe a sigh of relief at the smile in his voice. "Who doesn't want their obnoxious little sister traipsing about as they're trying to work?"

Smirking, I step out from behind the curtain, placing my soiled clothing on top of my chest. "Precisely."

Having finished supper, we move about the room in routine silence. I turn down the oil lamp and move toward my bed as he pulls me into a hug.

"Everything's gonna be alright, little bird."

That was my mother's nickname for me. One that he calls me by often now that she's gone. She always said I was her little bird with raven black hair.

I lie down on my bed, pulling the covers up around me. Tiredness grips my body and I let my eyes shut.

One day, you'll fly, she had whispered in my ear.

"Love you, Ash," I say sleepily.

"Love you too, sleep well," he replies, settling himself into his own bed.

Darkness overtakes me—my dreams full of dragons and sunsets and questions I can't form.

CHAPTER 2

We spent the day observing the different trades so you would have an idea of your potential future duty. It is hard for me to fathom you approaching your 18th year. I know you'll handle your prescribed responsibilities well, but I do worry about your tendency toward daydreaming. Be diligent, little bird, and you will find life to be much more agreeable.

I wake to the weak morning sun filtering in through the windows by the door. Blinking the sleep out of my eyes, I glance at Ashden's bed to find it empty and neatly made. Judging by the light, he's been at the Storehouse for about an hour already. We're both typically awake at the same time, but having no duties to report to so early in the morning is a welcome change.

Swinging my legs off the bed, I walk to the large window at the back of the cottage, pushing it open to let the gentle sea breeze float through the room. It's my favorite part of our cottage, offering a beautiful view of the sea and sky and… Verenathia. The tang of salt fills my lungs as I gaze out at the horizon. The sunlight faintly illuminates the large body high in the sky, barely visible in the early morning light.

With a wistful sigh, I slip my nightdress over my head and toss it onto my bed. Grabbing a clean pair of soft brown leather pants and white blouse, I dress, tying my satchel around my waist. Leaving my hair loose instead of putting it in its usual braid, I slip my boots on and open the door. I'm greeted with the scent of lilacs that bloom in small clusters between the cottages. The air is thick and heavy with the approach of rain, and a charge tingles against my skin as the sun rises lazily up from the mountains, muted by a haze of clouds.

That invisible weight presses in on me as I start down the path toward the hub of the village, listening as bees drone contentedly between the lilacs. The feeling is almost physical—and not just from the promise of a storm on the breeze. There is an undeniable strain in the Safeguards today. Like the feeling of being underwater— going deeper and deeper until there's no light and no sensation. Nothing other than the weight of the world above you and your heartbeat in your ears.

The isle at the edge of my vision beckons. Breathing deep, I shake my head to clear it; pressing down all feelings of uncertainty.

Walking through Raimy's open doorway, I see him bent over a table, up to his elbows in fresh dough. An open stone oven blazes behind him, ready for the day's baking.

"Mornin'," he says cheerily, giving me a taut smile as he kneads the dough into submission. His rich brown skin is coated in a dusting of flour, giving him the appearance of an apparition.

I bite my lip against a laugh. "Good morning."

Shelves loaded with baskets of baked goods line the walls. Biscuits, scones, and muffins call out to me as I shuffle past. Making my way around the room, I delightedly spot the wildberry jam-filled sweet rolls, and pause to gently remove one from its basket. A carrot muffin and blueberry scone also make their way into my possession on the way back to his table.

I drop a few coins into the leather pouch resting near him and take a bite of the roll, jam deliciously oozing from the soft dough. My eyes close of their own accord as I blissfully savor the tart sweetness.

"These are my favorite," I mumble through a mouthful.

"Why do you think I keep them stocked fresh?" he winks at me, forming the dough on his table into smaller mounds. "No smithing today?" He eyes my clean blouse and pants.

"Just finished a big order," I say around another bite. "Markell said to take the day to myself."

He nods, now dividing each mound into three separate strands. "A beautiful day to spend up to no good," he chuckles.

I lick the sticky jam from my fingertips, considering his expression. Lines feather from the corners of his eyes as he smiles, his strong fingers expertly manipulating the dough as he gently weaves it into small braided loaves. There's a contentedness about him as he works, and, not wanting to trouble him, I decide to keep my concerns about the magic to myself.

I dip my head, holding up the goods. "Thank you." Wrapping them in a small cotton cloth, I place them in the satchel tied around my waist.

He looks up briefly from his work and nods, satisfied, as I move toward the door.

"Be careful of yourself, Rae."

My steps falter at the gentle admonition in his tone, and I turn to face him. He's no longer braiding the dough. Hands paused, he looks at me with eyes the color of well-trodden dirt, understanding dancing within their depths.

Indignation stutters my heartbeat before it races with apprehension. "Of course."

He winks at me and returns to his work, brushing the back of his hand against his floured forehead.

In the fresh air again, gulls cry, diving and swooping to my left as they find their prey among the choppy waves.

What does everyone think I'm going to do, swim out into the sea and never come back?

A twinge of guilt registers. I have considered it. Not swimming out into the sea and going where the current takes me—I'm not stupid and that would be a death wish. But, potentially saving my earnings from the Smithshop and purchasing a small schooner.

The thought of the vast sea surrounding me, the spray and wind through my hair, is enough to send chills down my spine. Enough to potentially satisfy this yearning ache in my chest.

Your father's blood courses through your veins. I can almost hear my mother's words as she had murmured them into my hair, soothing me one night after gasping awake from a nightmare. The fingers of magic had tethered me in their grasp. I could hear the longing in the splash of the wake on the shore; in the whispers of the wind. I could see it in the white expanse of clouds encompassing me.

The magic's desire or mine, I'm still not sure.

Running my fingers through my hair, I pull in deep breaths to clear the haze in my head, the cloying scent of lilac now suffocating. The sweet roll sits like a weight in my stomach.

I look toward Verenathia and envision myself as a weightless petal, the breeze carrying me higher and higher until I'm level with its tallest peak. Borne on an invisible wave, I land and take root; blossoming where the sun has no end.

The thought is soothing as I begin to center myself, straightening my blouse and forcing down the panic that threatens to overwhelm me.

***

The cliffs rising along the bend in the bay tower ahead of me, looming before the Storehouse and shipyard. Moss clings to the damp rock, the foaming water of the sea peaking and breaking against their base.

Nestled against the foot of the steep cliffs, the shipyard is alive as fishermen prepare for the day's catch. Deep voices call out to each other as they load supplies. Many ships sit longways along the massive docks, their masts lowered.

My stomach sinks at the dragonless Loading Platforms rising above the docks, even knowing full well it's too early for Verenathians to start retrieving their shipments.

Skirting a group of men huddled intently over some parchment form, I head toward the Loadmaster's office. The neat wooden building sits primly next to the Storehouse, its face gleaming in smooth, polished planes.

I throw the door open and step into the cool room, spotting Avice deeply absorbed in a stack of parchment.

Six identical desks evenly border the room, with windows taking up the majority of all four walls. A red tapestried rug lies in the center of the room with another, larger desk resting on it. A long stone paperweight faces outward on the edge of the desk, bearing Head Lichera's inscription. Several small, labeled crates, all full of varying levels of documents, sit on its surface.

Each member of the Synod oversees a different section of the town trade, and Head Lichera is in charge of the Storehouse and all that it entails.

The scent of parchment tickles my nose as I approach Avice's hunched form. Three other bookkeepers look up from their work, watching as I cross the room. Two of them feign indifference—Luca and Mirabelle, if I had to guess, as pride wells within me.

Avice doesn't notice my approach. Surrounded by neat stacks of parchment and shipping invoices, her quill bobs as she scribbles something in a ledger.

"For you," I flourish dramatically, setting the scone on her desk. "Madame Breckenwater, Head Bookkeeper."

Her head snaps up at the sound of my voice and she beams.

"Oh!" she reaches for the scone. "I didn't even hear you. Thanks." She heaves a breathy laugh and pops a bite into her mouth. "What are you doing here?"

I spread my arms wide in a grandiose gesture. "Day off, remember? I'm free as a bird and will be doing whatever I please." Sitting on the edge of her desk, I shrug. "How's the life of Head Bookkeeper?"

"Good… different," she stammers, glancing in Mirabelle's direction. "It's still only my first day with the new responsibilities, and it's not even midday yet," she adds. "But I'm enjoying it."

"I'm glad," I grin. "Maybe this elevated position will draw the attention of… certain individuals."

Her face flushes, eliciting a giggle out of me. Avice may be successful in her duties, but her goal has always been to marry. With her calm demeanor, quiet wit, and delicate beauty; she has no shortage of potential suitors. But I know the one she's always had her eye on–and he's blissfully unaware.

"I'm sure Ashden would love to marry someone of such impressive repertoire."

Her eyes sparkle as she taps my elbow, bending my arm and sending me sprawling forward.

"You're right, he'd be a fool to settle for anything less," she preens.

I pull myself back up, giggling like a child. Luca snorts from his desk, and I glance up in time to see him roll his eyes.

"He would," I say, only halfway joking.

The three of us have spent our entire lives together, and Avice has always felt more like a sister than a friend. She and I used to run freely through the grasslands above town, Ashden never far behind. We would scale the bluffs and sit on the edge, looking over the sea toward Verenathia. Her cautious tendencies usually balanced out my rash decisions, and when they didn't, Ashden was there to pick up the pieces of our failed escapades. There was always a perfect harmony between our trio, flowing like a song.

She snickers and tugs on my sleeve. "Come on," she says. "I'll walk you out."

I follow on her heels as we leave her desk. She opens the door and I almost stumble into her as she stops abruptly.

Head Lichera's hulking figure blocks the doorway. Surprise lights his features for a moment as he glances between us, but is quickly replaced by his usual stoicism.

As the head of the Synod, as well as Head Loadmaster, the black uniform he wears is immaculate—not a thread or badge out of place. An impeccably trim mustache rests on thin lips that seem to hold themselves in a perpetual frown. His blue eyes are cold, analytical as they appraise us; scanning me from head to toe.

He offers a curt nod. "Miss Bryorfall." His voice is flat, as cold as his glacial gaze. I reciprocate the acknowledgement, averting my eyes.

"I was just seeing Rae out," Avice says quickly, stepping aside to let him through. I shuffle in behind her, watching as he takes long, purposeful strides toward the desk in the center of the room. He sits down and pulls a pair of spectacles from his overcoat, placing them on the bridge of his nose. Glancing up, he waves a dismissive hand in our direction.

"Do so, quickly," he says uninterestedly.

We step outside and Avice closes the door behind us. The town is buzzing with activity—men's voices boom from the shipyards, squadrons from the Loading Brigade beginning to travel to and from the Storehouse, and below the wharf, children chase each other across the rocky shore.

"I feel like I need a bath," I shudder.

"You get used to it after a while," she says quietly.

I don't know if anyone could get used to the ice that runs up and down your spine when Lichera's around. Something about him has always seemed... different. Slightly enough off-center to be felt, but almost impossible to see when looking directly at it.

I give her a sideways glance. "If you say so. I'm gonna go now—let you get back to work."

She nods, but her expression shifts. Something is on her mind, I can see it.

She inhales, but the door to the office opens and Head Lichera exits, a handful of parchment in his grasp.

"I thought I told you to be quick," he sneers, standing over us.

Avice straightens, casting an apologetic glance toward me. "Yes, sir." She meets my gaze for a heartbeat. "Have a nice day, Rae."

I watch her go, the door slamming as she retreats. Lichera doesn't spare me another glance as he heads toward the loading docks.

In spite of myself, I trace his path and feel a jolt of delight when I notice one of the Loading Brigades standing ready atop a platform; a flying red dragon just a drop of blood in the distant sky.

CHAPTER 3

ASHDEN

Once of age, everyone is prescribed a duty. Determined by the Synod, a duty will be carried out until one either reaches the House of Elders, dies, or is taken for the Culling.

With Verenathia wholly dependent on us for their means to live—as well as sustaining our own people—we run like a fine-tuned clock. Our fishermen, Loading Brigade, textile workers, and farmers all have quotas to fill. Everyone has a responsibility, and when each obligation is fulfilled properly and on time, there is peace. We report when and where we are required, and on days when we have no duties, we're free to do as we please. As long as things continue as they should, we can spend our time however and wherever we would like.

But, unfortunately for me, the Storehouse rarely allows for time off.

I sigh, flipping through the orders that I'm responsible for today. The stack of parchment is thick, and only one of many.

Movement and noise are everywhere around me. The Loading Warehouse is a massive warehouse within the even bigger Storehouse, responsible for sorting, packing, and shipping Verenathia's supplies. Some people are stationary, separating goods or packing them into crates at designated stations, while others—runners—run supplies to and from the different sorting stations.

Loading Brigade squadrons shift about the room, hauling carts laden with fully packed crates out of the Storehouse and to the Loading Platforms.

I weave through the stations, heading toward the back wall of the Storehouse. The massive iron grates that make up the wall are lifted high toward the ceiling, allowing the sea breeze to cut through the thick humidity. More carts—laden with unorganized raw supplies—line the alley behind the building, waiting to be unloaded.

Rod, one of my closest friends, grins as I approach. We were fortunate enough to be assigned to the Storehouse when we received our duties, and it's made the days far more bearable as we trudge through our orders.

"Whatcha got for me?" he asks, eyeing the stack of parchment in my hand.

Flashing him a rueful smile, I rifle through the stack before selecting a handful of orders and hand them over. "Three shipments due by noon. Have fun."

He sighs at the papers and cuts a glance to our right, his eyes taking on a wicked gleam. "Well look who it is."

I follow his gaze and spot my sister, nothing more than a small streak through the bustle of activity as she makes her way toward me.

"Watch yourself, Rod."

His grin widens. "I'm simply an appreciator of the finer things in life."

Rolling my eyes, I begin in Rae's direction. "Get to work."

A green-haired man stops her right as I'm about to call her name—someone she used to have classes with. Arthic, if I remember correctly.

I cross my arms, amused, while I watch her nod curtly, itching to step away from the conversation. She's practically dancing on her feet as impatience radiates from her, and I almost feel bad for him.

Another nod, and she's quickly stepping away, keeping her eyes trained on the floor. She arrives at my side in a huff.

"Trouble in paradise?"

Annoyed, she waves me off and reaches into her satchel, pulling out a muffin.

"Here," she thrusts it at me. "I brought you food."

I laugh, plucking it out of her grasp and take a bite. "Thanks," I mumble.

She mutters a response and glances at the parchment in my hand. "What are you doing today?"

I swallow. "Overseeing the shipments. Making sure Verenathia gets what they've requested. Nothing more, nothing less." I don't hide the hint of bitterness in my voice. "We'll finish here and then we'll take them to the Loading Platforms."

She shuffles on her feet eagerly. I know she's dying to be on the platforms already.

Since working here, being on the platforms with the dragons so high above the sea has lost its luster. As children, we used to sit near the cliffs and watch as the Loading Brigade would take shipment after shipment, admiring the dragons that would come to retrieve the orders. But now, it's just another day. She gets that faraway gleam in her eye, completely distracted now, and sways lightly on her feet as if listening to some undetectable tune.

"Rae?"

She snaps her gaze to mine. "What?"

"You okay? You're doing the thing again." I nod toward her feet.

Her expression darkens, and she stills. "Oh, yeah," she stammers. "I'm fine."

A rush of warmth fills me, and I smile sympathetically. She's always been this way, either lost in her head or pulling me into more trouble than I care to admit. But life with her is so vibrant, it more than makes up for our conundrums.

"You can tell me what's going on, you know. Don't think I haven't noticed you've been distracted lately. Well, more distracted than usual," I add.

She pauses, and I can see the words on the tip of her tongue, and I can see the internal conflict. Her emotions are written across her face like an open book. I *have* noticed that something is on her mind lately. I'm not sure what, but she's even more preoccupied, more distracted, as if whatever it is just won't let her out of its grasp.

"I'm fine," she mutters, seeming to deflate a little.

"It's Arthic, isn't it?" I tease, trying to lighten her mood. "Oh, to be young and in love." I heave an exaggerated sigh, and she punches me in the shoulder.

Out of the corner of my eye, I note the stockers have almost finished loading the last cart. A lanky man with olive skin walks up to me, handing over the order.

"Shipment's ready, Bryorfall," he clips, sauntering back to a different station with a fresh selection of crates that need packed.

I scan the order, mentally checking off each crate on the cart. "Air brigade," I call, projecting my voice above the din.

The individual squadrons of the Loading Brigade are named after the elements: air, earth, fire, and water. With exporting goods our province's backbone, the operation has become militant. The whole of Verenathia and all of our people depend on it.

Three men and one woman materialize in front of me, all coming from the separate stations they were assisting.

"Let's go," I command. They move toward the cart, each grasping one of the rods that protrude from its corners. With a shudder and the creaking of old wood, it starts rolling. Steering clear of the crates and stations and people *everywhere*, they navigate it out of the Storehouse toward the Loading Platforms.

Rae follows at my side as I lead them to the fourth platform. Dragons and their riders rest, ready and waiting, on three of the five.

Darting ahead, Rae makes it to the top and plants herself on the railing, watching the sky. Her face is filled with so much awe that a corner of my mouth lifts.

A dragon, blue gray and blending into the gathering dark clouds, is discernible only by the sharp outline of its wings as it approaches. Shooting toward the platform, it pulls up at the last second and gracefully eases down for a landing. The platform reverberates as the beast lands.

Lowering its head, it allows the rider to jump smoothly from its back. He turns, stroking the dragon between its horns before facing us. His eye catches on Rae, and right there, in that moment, I can see the shift.

I glance at Rae, annoyed. Her expression has changed from wonder to something entirely different, too.

Rolling my eyes, I groan inwardly. *Here we go.*

CHAPTER 4

You will find someone, someday, that will make your heart sing. You won't be able to predict or explain it, but their soul will intertwine with yours and together, you'll create a beautiful harmony. I've found this in your father and it's something I pray the Author gives you; that you'll recognize it when you find it and never let it go.

I crane my head to take in the beautiful dragon now on the platform. Shimmering slate-colored scales run along the length of the beast, ending at its massive webbed wings. Its claws scrape the platform, gouging lines into the already deeply marked wood.

Beholding its size and splendor, it's the ancient wisdom lurking in the depths of its eyes—so blue they're like marbles of lapis lazuli—that I can't look away from. Power and strength emanate from its core while it watches us. Calm, curious.

A wide belt of leather rests just in front of its haunches, securing a wooden pallet where supply crates will be strapped down for the flight back.

Lowering its head, its rider hops off in one fluid motion, stroking it between its horns before turning to face the Loading Brigade.

My heart stutters as he glances at me and begins speaking to Ashden. His lithe body is clad in a red and black dragonhide suit, accentuating every one of the muscled lines that ripple as he takes the parchment from my brother. A dragonhide belt around his waist houses the daggers sheathed there. Black hair, just long enough to start curling on the edges, reaches toward a sharp jawline.

His mouth, held in a way that looks as if it's on the edge of a grin, breaks into a dazzling smile.

And when he does, his dark eyebrows rise confidently over vibrant emerald eyes that crinkle at the edges. Our eyes meet and I tilt my head, squinting slightly.

"And who is she?"

His accent is delicious. I don't think I could ever get tired of hearing it, but I smirk. "*She* is Rae."

He mirrors the angle of my head, looking at me quizzically. Those confident green eyes bore into me, but I don't look away. I could get lost in their emerald depths; I would simply go for a swim and never resurface.

"My sister." Ashden snarls, angling his back toward me protectively. "She's observing shipments today." He tosses an annoyed look in my direction, a clear warning in his eyes.

"Ah, the little sister," the rider muses, an indistinguishable glint in his gaze as he pans it between us. panning his gaze between us.

Ah, the cocky bastard.

The Loading Brigade shifts slightly, waiting to load the supplies and be on with their next task.

"Yes," Ashden bristles. "The little sister." He thrusts another set of papers at the rider, gesturing for the brigade to empty the goods. They lurch into action, efficiently unloading the cart onto the pallet. The dragon doesn't even flinch under the added weight as it calmly considers us.

Ashden—a muscle in his jaw flexing—and the rider face the brigade as they work. Neither of them speak a word. The rider's arms are still crossed easily over his chest, a soft smirk resting on his lips.

As the brigade finishes, the rider signs the stack of papers and seals it with a stamp he produces from his own pocket.

With a nod, he turns and makes a series of clicks with his tongue. Perking its head, the dragon swivels toward him and lowers, allowing him to scale effortlessly up its back.

I can almost taste the annoyance roiling off of Ashden as the dragon shuffles on its clawed feet to face the open sea. I shift, avoiding its spiked tail as it sweeps across the wooden platform.

The rider pivots in his seat to look at us. To look at me. Laughter sparkles in his radiant eyes. Passing a look between the two of us, he winks at me.

"Don't worry." Mischief dances along his words. "I have a little sister too."

"Asshole," Ashden mutters.

He tosses his head back and laughs, the clear sound of his deep voice ringing through the air.

The dragon spreads its wings and dives off the edge of the platform. My heart leaps to my throat as they plummet, but, just as quickly, they bolt high into the sky. Leveling out, they soar fast and far, until they're but a drop in the bucket again.

***

I spend the rest of the day in the grasslands before migrating to the bluff, lost in thought. Ashden had been in a sour mood after returning to the Storehouse, so I'd decided to leave and let him sort himself out.

Now, on my trek back down to the town, there's no sun to signal the end of the day. Just a continual cloudy dimness, ever darkening. The cows lie in huddled groups across the plains while the air feels tense and charged—and not just from the magic pulsing around us. The rain still hasn't come, and the weight of the sky touching the horizon promises a downpour.

What was supposed to be an enjoyable day spent outside of the Smithshop has rapidly declined into abject misery.

I can't stop Raimy and Markell's words as they clang through my head over and over; as if they know something I've not yet been made aware of.

The sea rages, white foam forming as the waves break—looking almost how I feel. I don't understand how I seem to be the only one that notices something is wrong. Verenathia's ever increasing requirement for weapons, more frequent Cullings, and the borderline suffocating oppression of the Safeguards. A hint of dazzling emerald occasionally laces my turmoil, but I push that though far away. Deep, deep down.

I press my hands feverishly into my eyes, trying to rub it all away. My mind is a haze of conflicting thoughts and desires, everything pressing in and ripping me apart all at once.

The sky is too thick and gray to see Verenathia, but I can feel it. Damn me, I can *feel* it as if it were a person standing right in front of me, arms open, drawing me in for an embrace.

Why am I the only one? The thought is a cry of desperation, a plea—unshed tears stinging the backs of my eyes. If my parents were still alive—my mother—maybe they could explain. Help me make sense of what I'm feeling. My mother, with her artist's eye, could always see things nobody else could.

Taking measured breaths, I manage to calm myself somewhat. Maybe there *is* a reason for this madness. Maybe I'm not the only one.

***

Arriving at our cottage raw and emotionally charged, I fling the door open to Ashden, already home and in a fresh change of clothes. I shut the door, wincing as it slams against its frame. He looks up from the book before him on the table, his expression unreadable.

"You're home early," I say flatly as I fall onto my bed, lying on my stomach. Crossing my arms in front of me, I rest my aching head on them.

He closes his book and faces me from his chair. "No, you're home later than you usually are."

"I was at the bluffs." My voice is muffled by the blankets.

"I see."

I want nothing more than to go to sleep. To slip into oblivion, right here, and never wake. My mind is a fog of unfinished thoughts and unanswered questions. Speaking is an impossible effort.

"Are you okay?" He ventures delicately.

I'm tired of trying to find explanations, but I am far more tired of dancing around my turmoil. Maybe I can try again. Ashden is sensible and intelligent; there's a possibility he could explain what's happening. Maybe using math or science, as if this is just a simple equation or chemical imbalance.

Or maybe he feels it too.

"No," I choke out, keeping my face firmly pressed down to prevent the tears burning my eyes from finding a home on my blanket.

His chair scuffs the floor as he shifts away from the table. Footsteps thud softly against the floor as he comes to sit on the edge of my bed.

His voice is calm. "What's going on, Rae?"

Forcing the tears into submission, I prop myself up and sit on the head of my bed. Drawing my knees up to my chest, I inhale deeply, trying to clear the fog that threatens to consume me.

"Do you remember our conversation last night?"

"Of course, what about it?"

I hesitate, unsure of how to voice what's plaguing me. "What if there really *is* more? More than what we have, or more than what we are led to believe?"

He studies me carefully, his expression unwavering. "We have all that we need," he says simply.

I take a deep breath, stuffing down my irritation. "I know, that's not what I'm talking about."

"Then what *are* you talking about?" I can see the thoughts racing behind his eyes, all of them focused on steadying his reckless little sister.

"I can feel it, Ashden."

"Feel what?" A small line creases his brow.

"Everything."

He doesn't say anything for a moment. "You're going to have to be a little less cryptic, Rae."

"Our lands are tethered by magic, right? From the Safeguards?"

"Yes," he drawls.

"Can you feel that magic?" My voice is small, my heart quivering.

There. The undying question.

I can see the weight bearing down on my people—can see the shadows in their eyes. They have to feel it, there's no way they can't.

There's a long pause as he stares at my bed, considering. "I can feel a weight, almost. An awareness that it's around us, but there's nothing definitive."

My shoulders slump. The dichotomy of weightlessness and oppression, of pain and beauty slipping along the tendrils of magic—*why don't you see it?*

"What do you feel when you look at Verenathia? Or Verenathians with their dragons?"

His eyes meet mine for a heartbeat, pain flashing through them before he casts them down again. "Hatred," he says softly.

His admission catches me completely off guard, and I gape at him. "What?"

"Hatred," he repeats, more to himself than to me. "You asked," he says, almost defiantly.

"But why?" I demand.

There's a hard edge to his tone now and he shakes his head slowly. "We *are* slaves, Rae. We spend our whole lives working so they can live a comfortable life of leisure. We're assigned duties simply so things run as efficiently as possible for *them*. There's no consideration for our individual desires or well being."

Because there *is* more.

"Then why were you so argumentative when I said so, myself?" I glare at him.

The words seem to get stuck in his throat. "You can be impulsive sometimes. You don't always think things through. I didn't want you getting any ideas."

Anger sears through me like a hot iron. "I'm not a child."

"I know you're not, but I also know you."

How dare he think he can dictate my actions by withholding information from me. "If you know me so well," I bite. "Then explain to me why I can *feel* Verenathia, the magic—everything." The thick fog I've been trying to swim through reaches a breaking point.

"I have no idea. I don't know how anyone could feel anything other than disgust for them and their land."

I rise, swinging my legs over the side of the bed, and stomp onto the floor, pacing the room like a caged animal. "That land has more to offer than we will ever see here."

He raises his voice a degree to match my rapidly heating blood. "Only because we provide them everything they need while they don't lift a finger. And all we get in return are what, Safeguards?" He sneers.

I try, and fail, to quell my own rising tide of anger. "But that's what I'm saying. There's something we're not being told, and maybe we'd be able to find it up there."

Please, just… understand.

"They will kill you for trying." His voice is eerily quiet now. There is such pain in his eyes it takes my breath away.

"But what if they don't?"

He laughs—a humorless, bitter sound. "Oh, they're going to suddenly disregard 400 years of laws outlined in the Accords?"

"No, I–I don't know." I keep up my furious pacing.

Why don't you understand?

"That's what I thought. It would do you good to stop thinking about these things."

I bite my tongue, trying to get a grasp on my fraying self-control. "And it would do you good to stop being so simple-minded. If you're so angry and so miserable here, then why wouldn't you do something about it?"

"Because I value my life," he says sharply.

"And I don't," I quip.

A muscle ticks in his jaw while he stares intently at the wall, his fingers drumming an incessant rhythm on my bed. "Then go. Go chase after

Verenathian men if that's what will make you happy."

The unnecessary dig breaks something within me. "Is that what you think this is about?" I cry.

"I think I've never heard you talk like this until today. Until you saw *him*," his voice rises in challenge to mine.

The tears that have been burning my eyes threaten to make their appearance. Not tears of sadness now, but tears of searing rage and disbelief at his ignorance. I swallow, forcing the words out hard and cold. "Tell me you're not serious, Ashden."

His gray eyes glint like steel. "I'm beginning to wonder if you've grown so discontent with your life that you've decided to run off and find a Verenathian to live out the rest of your days with."

I shake my head in disbelief. I should have never said anything. Of course he doesn't understand—to consider anything else was wishful thinking.

"Is that really what you think of me?"

"I think you can be incredibly rash," he says with thinly veiled ire.

My voice rises to a shout. "And why is that such a bad thing?"

"Because you belong here," he slams his hand onto my bed, his leash at last snapping. "Why can't you understand that, Rae? There is nothing good or beautiful about them or their home. Nothing." His eyes bore into mine, his jaw clenched. "Why is that not good enough for you?"

My heart breaks at his question. I wish it was enough. I wish I didn't continuously feel this shattering pulse through the world.

"Why can't *you* understand that there is something here that I can't escape, no matter how hard I try." I heave a shaking breath. "It's not my fault; I never asked for it."

He scrubs at the stubble along his chin. "What you're seeing is nothing more than a trick of the light off the sea, and what you're feeling," he pauses. "Is just the heightened emotions of a daydream."

How *dare* he. The pain of everything that has been coursing through me collides with my shock. The tears that have been threatening all night burst my barriers, streaming down my face in hot tracks.

As if realizing what he just said, alarm fills his expression.

"Rae," he starts. Gentle. Apologetic.

"No," I sob. "I'm not doing this anymore." All of my strain and confusion flood out of me along with my tears. Bolting toward the door, I pull it open to the start of the storm that's been building all day.

How poetic.

"Please," his voice falters. "I'm sorry, I shouldn't have said that."

I hate myself; truly hate myself, as I leave my brother's words lingering in the air, unanswered.

The rain drizzles as I walk down to the shore, until it is finally a deluge. Lightning arcs overhead as thunder roars. I'm fully soaked when I arrive, my tears mixing with the rain.

Sitting on the rocky shoreline, I let the roar of the sea and storm quiet the one within me. Lightning shatters off the raging water, the reflection splintering like a starburst.

I don't want to think—don't want to feel anything but the driving rain against my skin.

I know Ashden's afraid of losing me, and I can't be upset at him for that. But he has no right to speak to me and treat me like a child—as if what he does or doesn't say will determine my actions. Although something about what he said does tug at me. A thought worming its way into my heart. One I've squashed and buried and tamped down for as long as I can remember.

Go.

Any Goramalan found traveling to Verenathia will be executed on sight. To attempt anything of the sort is to break the cardinal law between our peoples.

My mother's voice comes floating gently back to me, bringing with it a fresh wave of tears. *One day, you'll fly.*

"What am I supposed to do, mom?" I cry out to the sea.

Even though I know. I've always known. There is so much more and I have to know what it is.

I can remain hidden. I'm sure I can make it to the outskirts of the city. I don't know how to hunt—have never needed to—but if it's that or starvation, what better time to learn? There has to be water there, too. Streams or lakes or something that can sustain me, I'm sure of it.

Guilt shows itself, filling and filling until it threatens to drown me. I can't put Ashden through the grief of losing me, it would probably destroy him.

And yet, staying here with this undying tension will likely destroy *me.*

I'll be executed for treason if I'm discovered—if I can even find a way to get there.

Will it even matter? I don't know if anything can satisfy the aching in my soul.

To stay is a slow, painful decline into insanity. To go is certainly a death wish but the beauty of the world beckons, and I can't ignore it any longer.

I will go. And I'll see what waits on the other side.

CHAPTER 5

You began asking questions today; questions of Verenathia. You're too young to understand, fully, the extent to which it affects our lives, but know this: you will never be able to rid yourself of its song.

I'm tired. Tired of having been damp for so many hours, tired from lack of sleep, tired from our argument, and tired of the constant tension. The rain stopped a couple hours ago, and my bottom has gone numb from sitting on the rocky shoreline. Soaking in the bathhouse and heading straight to my warm bed sounds like bliss right now, but I can't rest—not yet.

Even with that never ending tug and what now lies before me, I relish the small part of stillness in my heart, as if I'm finally on the correct path.

Correct path. The quiet night amplifies my snort. Goramalans aren't allowed to volunteer to take the place of another for the Culling, so that's not even a consideration. The only way to Verenathia is obviously by dragon, but I can't simply walk up to a rider and ask for a ride, not to mention the fact that all of it is still heavily illegal.

Verenathia rests, crystal clear in the freshly washed moonlight. It's so easy to envision myself on the back of a dragon, soaring through the clouds to explore the mysterious isle. A life outside my own is waiting for me.

Again, guilt overwhelms me, rising like the tide. How can I leave my brother? My best friend? My people?

Maybe Ashden is right. Maybe I am just risking my life for a daydream. This could very well be the biggest mistake of my life, one that I can't come back from.

Focus.

The tendrils of magic snake through each piece of me as who I am and what I know threatens to shatter, keeping me somewhat whole—as they usually do.

My undoing, and my lifeline.

If the only way to get there is by the back of a dragon, then on the back of a dragon I will go.

My knees and hips creak as I rise, stiff from sitting on the wet rocks. A rumbling ache fills my stomach as I stretch. I haven't eaten since the sweet roll at Raimy's.

Sighing, I try to run my fingers through my matted hair before realizing it's a futile effort and begin toward town.

My footsteps crunch softly as I approach our cottage and nudge the door open. Ashden is asleep on top of his blankets, still fully clothed. My heart sinks a bit, in spite of the trickle of relief. I halfway expected him to be awake and ready to continue our spat.

Leaving my sodden boots outside, I step through the doorway, pausing to make sure he doesn't stir. My filthy clothes come off until I'm down to my undergarments, and I pull clean ones out of my chest. I know I should make a trip to the bathhouse first, but the silvery light through the window beckons.

I dress quickly, tying my hair into some semblance of a braid. Reaching into the cabinet and pulling out a quill, inkpot, and sheet of parchment, I rest the paper on the cabinet, writing in the spill of moonlight on its surface.

I stare and stare at that note, almost sick with self-loathing.

Ashden deserves the decency of a conversation, at the very least. An apology, even. Yet, I know I won't be able to hide my decision, and he'll likely try and convince me to stay. Or worse. I don't have the strength for another fight.

He'll forgive me—if I live. I know he will. Being able to forgive myself is another matter entirely.

Will he be questioned about my absence? Will Markell? Avice? I couldn't live with myself if something happened to them on my account.

But I wouldn't be able to live with myself—for myself if I don't do this.

I leave the note on the cabinet.

Padding to the chest at the foot of my bed, I select my softest leather moccasins and lace them up my calves. Pilfering deeper, my breath catches when I my fingers brush the cold metal resting at the bottom of my chest.

I've never wielded a weapon before, have never even been taught how to hold one properly. With our territories resting in such peace, there's never been a need for it. This dagger was a practice piece from my apprentice days under Markell. I had only made knives up until that point. One day he told me to make a dagger, and so I did. I could never get them right, the edges always curved and chipped, yet this was the first one I had done correctly and though rough, he let me keep it.

I close my eyes at the rush of remorse. I should have at least said goodbye, especially with the demand right now. He's already overworked and exhausted…

I grasp the dagger, pulling it out and holding it up in the moonlight. The light reflects off the polished surface, accentuating a warp in the shape. I run my fingers along the edge, feeling all of the tiny knicks. The tip is mildly blunted and there's no wooden handle over the tang, but, still deadly.

The weight of the dagger is a brand in my hands. Still crouching at my chest, I hesitate, the weight of what I'm about to do pressing down on me more than the tension in the Safeguards.

Please don't let me use this.

I don't know why I bother—it's not like we have gods to listen to our prayers anyway.

I place the dagger in my satchel. My stomach rumbles as I finish, reminding me again of the last time I ate. Reaching into the cabinet, I pull out several strips of dried fish and a chunk of bread. The smell of the almost-stale bread makes my mouth water, but I doubt I'll be able to get past the knots in my stomach.

The food, a second pair of pants, and an undershirt find their way into my satchel. Double and triple checking, I loose a breath. My gaze sticks on my brother as I take one last look around the room. A pounding sense of finality looms over me as I watch the steady rise and fall of his chest, as if I'll never see him or this room again.

And if I do, it won't be through the eyes of the same person who stands here now.

"Goodbye," I whisper.

I slowly open the door, wincing as it groans on its hinges. But Ashden doesn't stir, his sleeping breaths a far steadier rhythm than my heart. Stepping out into the night, I pull the door shut with a quiet, damning thud.

I move quickly from the safety of the cottages and out into the midst of shops that line the cobbled street. Choosing to take the shadowed alley that runs behind the length of buildings, I dip behind the bakery. The fresh, salt-rain air serves to clear my head and I reach into my satchel, snagging two strips of fish and half the chunk of bread

The food *does* calm my rumbling stomach but helps little in sating my fraying nerves. Aside from the gentle lap of waves against the rocks, it's just me and my footsteps.

The dark, hulking mass of the cliffs approaches as I near the shipyards. Moonlight faintly illuminates their rocky surface, glowing against the dark sea.

A moss-covered stone wall appears to my left. The library. My last line of defense before the openness of the street. I pause at its edge, listening, still hearing nothing other than the whispers of the sea. I pad out from the safety of its shadow and continue toward the Storehouse, my heart beating harder with each step. My mouth is impossibly dry—from the bread or my anxiety is debatable.

My eyes are drawn to the sea, shimmering under the gaze of the moon. Light dances across its surface, rippling; the whole of it waving and pulsing with calm energy.

And there, resplendent in the silvery glow—Verenathia. She sits beautifully high in the sky, perfectly visible, reaching for me. This time, instead of resisting, I embrace her. Reaching forward with all my might, the energy around me crackles with desire.

I'm coming.

My breaths come unevenly as I approach the Storehouse. The massive grates on the back of the building are impossible to raise by myself, so I make my way toward the front, carefully choosing the set of double doors closest to me.

The doors open easily, as nothing is locked in Ra'goramal. Everyone has a given purpose—food to eat, comfortable homes—everything we need for a sufficient life. With our sole responsibility being the supply of both our provinces, everything must run as smoothly and efficiently as possible. We don't have time for criminal activity of any sort. With everyone adequately taken care of, there's no lack, and therefore no need for theft. Sitting so far from any other province, we also rarely see wanderers come within our borders. There has never been a need for any of the public spaces to be locked down.

I bite my lip, trying to ignore how dangerous my decision is and how many laws I'm about to break.

Stupid stupid stupid.

Cracking the door just enough, I slip into the Storehouse. Only the faintest of light comes through the grates, barely illuminating the space as I ease the door shut again, and pause to let my eyes adjust.

I give myself time for three deep breaths before heading deeper amongst the crates and workstations. Grateful for having visited Ashden enough to know what I'm looking for, I pick my way to the area that houses already-filled crates destined to be on the next day's shipments.

A wave of lightheadedness washes over me as I scan the neat rows of crates. I swallow, taking measured breaths to quell my rising panic, then resume my search.

Coming across a crate that looks just large enough to house my body, I reach into my satchel for my dagger. Using the flat part of the blade, I pry the lid off of the crate.

Oranges. The crate is full of them.

Everything is tracked so precisely here that acquiring an empty crate to hide in and adding it to the next day's shipments can't even be a consideration.

My racing heart threatens to give out as I search and search for something that will work.

I dig my way through the rows and stacks, at last coming upon another crate that should serve me well. A sigh of relief escapes me as I pry it open and see several bags of salt and sugar. I can work with this.

My face heats and my arms start to burn as I lift the heavy bags one at a time from the crate, emptying it. Prying open more already—filled crates, I stash the bags amongst cartons of eggs, vegetables, and bags of dried fish—cramming them into every gap and hollow I can find.

Pounding the last one into a too-small crack among several large sacks of flour, I stand back, eyeing the now-empty crate.

The Verenathians will be irritated at the unchecked items and crude packing. Lichera will likely receive a good tongue lashing, but it's a small price to pay for my safety.

Setting the lids back on each of the tampered crates, I climb atop, giving a firm bounce to settle the lids securely in place.

My palms are damp with sweat when I return to my own crate. Staring into its emptiness, I force myself onward and ease into it. Crouching down, I grab the lid and pull it over me.

A vice squeezes my chest. I have no way of sealing it. Someone will notice it's not secure and open it to double check the contents. The walls feel like they're pressing in on me and there's not enough air—

Breathe.

Shifting the lid, I pop up above the lip of the crate, searching for something, anything, and notice that the one I'm in is next to a stack three crates high. I crawl out, setting the lid back in its place and climb on top of it, reaching for the topmost crate on the stack next to me. Grasping both sides, I wiggle it, an idea forming in my mind. It barely moves—much heavier than I anticipated. Good.

I wiggle the topmost crate side to side, alternating pushing and pulling with each arm until my muscles are burning all over again. Slowly but surely, it creeps forward. Once it rests precariously on the edge, I stop.

Climbing back into my crate, I replace the lid and crouch with my head cocked from the height of the proverbial ceiling.

Facing the stack of crates next to me, my neck starts to cramp as I collect myself. With one last breath before I talk myself out of this completely, I throw myself forward, thrusting all of my weight into the wall of my crate.

Pain blossoms through my body as the side of my head and shoulder collide with the wood. I catch myself on my hands in an awkward, half-crawling position, but it's working—I felt the crate move, even if just the slightest bit. I return to my crouch and repeat the process, harder this time, shifting my weight toward my shoulder to absorb the brunt of the impact. The sharp blow of the wood throbs, but is manageable.

I throw myself forward again and again, forcing all of my will and weight into the movement. My shoulder bleats in pain as I throw myself forward again, but meet a sudden, hard stop on the outside. I hold my breath as noise explodes around me, the crate above crashing down on top of mine. My crate shudders under the impact as wood splinters. A rain of dull thuds sounds all around me as the lid of the fallen crate breaks off under its own weight.

I blink into the darkness, the weight of what I've just done settling over me like the weight of the crate above, sealing me in my tomb. I ease myself onto my bottom, pulling my knees into my stomach, and try to breathe as the walls of the crate press in on me, the air growing more stifling by the second.

I shouldn't have done this. This is the biggest mistake of my life and the only thing I'm going to get out of it is my execution.

My breaths grow ragged from panic, sucking the remaining life out of the cramped space.

I know I'm fine. I know I'm fine. The crates are produced for quantity, not quality, and though not slatted, the rough hewn boards are thrown together quickly, providing for small gaps. I know there's enough air for me to survive; I just can't panic.

In through the nose, out through the mouth, I pull in deep breaths, fighting a swell of nausea.

I will survive. I will be okay. I have to be.

Stupid stupid stupid.

CHAPTER 6

ASHDEN

Rae isn't home when I wake the next morning. Her bed is still made, the blankets disheveled where we sat. I rake my fingers through my hair and let my arm rest over my eyes, blocking out the empty room.

I shouldn't have fallen asleep. I didn't mean the things that I said and meant to apologize, but I know she needed her space. Going after her would have sent her completely over the edge.

She can be so reckless. I didn't want her to consider anything that would put her in danger, but I know her too well. She was already fully aware of what I'm most afraid of, and now I may have pushed her to the point of fulfilling those fears.

Rising, I ease myself over the edge of the bed and drop my face into my hands.

I've failed her. I should have just been honest with her. I know she's not a child to be shielded. I was only trying to protect her. The things I said—I didn't mean any of them. I was so afraid she was going to leave, so afraid she was going to get herself killed; that fear presented itself as anger. I lashed out.

Though rash and reckless, she's incredibly intelligent and insightful.

Good. Rae is good. Everything she does—there's always a deeper reason. Many times it's one that I don't understand, but she rarely does things out of spite or anger.

Fear drove me to the awful words that I said to her.

I *do* feel the increasing tension in the Safeguards. I doubt there's anyone that can't. But, unlike Rae, I can't seem to grasp the beauty and good she sees.

Life is black and white. There is good, and there is bad. The two don't intermingle.

We live *our* life, and they live *theirs*. The only difference is our lives revolve around provisioning theirs while we get nothing in return, our people taken to serve them—as slaves. But maybe she's right. Maybe there's more we can't see.

I lift myself out of bed, feeling as if I'm trudging through mud, my body is so heavy. It's barely dawn, the room only lit enough for me to make my way around without stumbling into things.

I need to report to work in half an hour—I have until then to find my sister and make sure she's alright. I know she's probably at the bluffs or the shore; those are her two favorite spots.

Some of my favorite memories are those of us running freely through the grasslands while our parents looked on from the bluff. Rae was always right on my heels, and then she got older. We would race side by side until we were breathless and aching. I never told her I slowed, just a bit, because the light in her face when we kept pace together was worth it.

There had been joy in the world then, the scales tipped more heavily toward good than bad.

But now, the weight of grief threatens to crush me at the situation I've found myself in. And my parents… Since their passing, I've done my best to be the older brother Rae needs, although I know I'll never be able to replace either one of them—nor do I want to.

We're all the other has now.

I breathe deep, shaking off the sorrow that clings like cobwebs. There is a time and place for it, and right now there are tasks at hand.

Wanting to leave as quickly as possible, I slough my uniform on.

A piece of parchment resting on the cabinet glares at me as I pass, its cream surface catching what little light there is. Dread settles heavy in my stomach.

That little paper wasn't there before I fell asleep.

I walk slowly toward the cabinet, already knowing what I'm going to find and trying to swallow the pain it brings.

Sure enough, Rae's handwriting greets me as I pick it up, the delicate loops and lines on the page searing into my mind.

There are things I need to do. I told you I can't explain how or why, but I'm hoping I'll be able to find some answers. Please don't come looking for me, I will return when I'm ready. I love you.

I read the letter until I'm numb, over and over and over again.

I knew she was going to do it, but seeing her admission of it almost brings me to my knees.

I've failed her. I've failed mother and father. I'm the one who pushed her to her breaking point. I should have just listened. That's all she was looking for; someone to listen and understand.

Anger pierces through the guilt clouding my mind, hot and sharp. Balling the letter up, I toss it back onto the cabinet.

If she wasn't so rash, so immature, she would have come back home and we could have had another conversation. I would have apologized for antagonizing her and let her know that yes, I do notice something is off but I don't know how to fix it. Maybe fear of the unknown is what's preventing me from doing anything about it.

If I know Rae, and her mind is set on leaving, she's already formulated a plan—likely is well underway with it. She wouldn't stick around long once the decision is cemented in her mind.

The realization stings as the weight of everything unsaid lingers in my chest.

I can't go looking for her, that would only raise suspicion. The last thing we need is the Synod on alert and Verenathian patrols on the hunt for her.

With nothing but time to kill until I report to the Loading Warehouse, I open the front door. I need some fresh air—this room is stifling.

The moment I step foot outside, a warm body thuds into mine and a muffled cry sounds near my shoulder.

"Sorry," the voice cries, fumbling aside. I peer down into Avice's eyes, her face warming when our gazes meet. She's in her bookkeeper's uniform already, heading to start on the day's invoices before shipments start loading.

I plaster on the most convincing smile I can muster. "That was definitely my bad."

She cocks her head, searching me in that way she's always had, as if she can read all the things I keep hidden.

"What's going on? It's way too early for you to be reporting."

A wave of fresh guilt courses through me. I can't tell her about our argument; she'll see right through it.

"I, uh, I wanted to go for a walk," I stumble over the words.

"Right now?" The smallest line creases her brow.

"Yes, I," I search for the right words. "It's really nice out after the storm, and I thought it'd be good to get some fresh air before work. You know how the Storehouse can get and—"

Her blue gaze is piercing. "What's going on, Ash?"

Frustration eats at my stomach. This woman—the woman who has adopted the role of my second sister, who we've spent our entire lives with, who loves Rae just as much as I do—has a right to be told.

Regardless of whose fault it is.

"Rae is gone." The words are flat and lifeless, all anger and guilt bleeding into weariness as I drop my gaze to the ground.

"What do you mean, *gone*?"

"To Verenathia," I wince.

She blinks, stupified, before her eyes widen in horror. Saying the words out loud sounds so absurd that anger prickles through me again at my sister's stupidity.

"But she…" Avice trails off, eyes darting and unfocused as she scans for listening ears. "How? Why?"

Closing my eyes, I groan, rubbing my temples where the beginning of a headache is forming.

"I don't know how," I admit. "But it doesn't matter. She left me a letter. We had a… discussion last night. She got really upset and left, and when I woke up she was gone."

"I don't understand," Avice mutters, her features framed with worry. "What did the letter say?"

"There are things she needs to do and she doesn't want me going after her." I paraphrase the words that are now burned into my mind.

"And you're just going to bow to her wishes?" She asks indignantly—sarcasm dripping from her tone. "She'll die up there. What was she thinking?"

"She might, but we can't do anything."

"But—"

"Listen, Avice. If you and I disappear as well, then the Synod will get involved. They'll alert Verenathian patrols. If a Loading Brigade member or bookkeeper goes missing—or both— it's far more likely to get noticed, and a lot faster, than a blacksmith's apprentice. The longer before the authorities are alerted, the more of a chance she has of finding what she's looking for and coming back."

"They'd send patrols to scour the isle as well as our territory," she says, more to herself than me. "And they'd start questioning people."

I nod. "I'll tell Markell what happened." Markell was my father's friend, and has always been a sort of like an uncle to us anyway. I trust he'll keep her absence to himself.

I can see the same conclusions I've come to click into place in her mind, but she shakes her head. "This is insane. No one has ever done this before, Ashden."

"I know." Author above, she doesn't have to rub it in.

She looks up at me, resolve settling in her expression. "So you know what you do now?"

"What?" I mutter, dazed at even having to have this conversation.

"There's only one way to get to Verenathia. Go find her in the Storehouse."

The Storehouse. Of course. There's hundreds of crates in the Storehouse, but I can try to find her and convince her to stay.

If I *do* find her, getting her out unseen would be… Well, that's something I can figure out when we get there.

If we get there.

And if I don't find her… I swallow the sickness that rises in my throat. "I—"

"Can't believe you didn't think of that right away? And should have been there the instant you read her letter?" Her eyes gleam. "I know."

"Right."

She straightens her shoulders, not needing to voice what we're both thinking. "Rae is smart. She knows the laws. She made a really bad call but she'll figure it out. We will figure this out."

I nod, looking up at the brightening sky. Streaks of pink spread across it from the approaching daylight.

"You need to get to the office," I say.

"I know." She gives me a quick hug before pulling away to head into town. "It'll be okay, Ash."

I don't respond, instead watching her retreat, my thoughts darkening with each of her footsteps.

CHAPTER 7

I am sitting here, resting your small form in my lap. You are sleeping soundly, wrapped in a linen blanket. I cannot take my eyes from you, my firstborn. Your eyelashes are so long and your nose is a perfect imitation of your father's. There isn't anything like you in this world. I love you, my son.

The air in the crate is stifling, heavy with moisture from my breath and suffocatingly warm. I must have fallen asleep at some point, though I don't understand how with all of the adrenaline coursing through me. I recall, faintly, a flash of emerald eyes in what must have been some sort of half dream, but I shove the memory down.

Rubbing my gritty eyes, I blink, realizing I can now make out the outline of my hands and legs. No longer floundering through the thick darkness.
Voices are carrying softly, as if behind a wall of cotton. They're most likely outside the Storehouse, readying to enter for the day's work as their voices float through the grates.

I wait anxiously for something, anything to happen. My bottom is numb from the lack of movement, my joints aching from being bent so tightly, and my stomach pressed against my thighs makes it hard to draw a full breath.

And then there's the thought of the crate on top of me, sealing me in, trapping me—and I try not to panic all over again.

The wooden doors bang against the wall as they're thrown open, followed by a trickle of footsteps. It's not the entire team—only a handful if the footsteps are any indication, but they'll all be here soon enough. These are most likely the Loadmasters as they arrive early to go over the day's intake and shipments.

Footfalls ricochet from the opposite end of the Storehouse, and I'm grateful. I'm dying to get moving but terrified of being discovered. I doubt they'll check my crate, but the thought of them being so near sends a heavy shiver of weight into my stomach.

I listen as crates scrape and bags of provisions thud around me, the team going about readying for the day.

"Hey, you got five loads in D section?" a man calls from across the Storehouse. Clopping bootsteps begin, growing louder as they head this direction, and my heart practically flies out of my chest.

They grow closer, stopping once they sound like they're on the opposite side of the stack I'm against.

"Ay, five in D."

The footsteps pick back up, and I can see a shadow block the faint light leaking in through the gaps in the crate.

"Dammit Jer," calls a whiny voice from above me. "That whole crate of potatoes fell off the stack."

Two more sets of thudding boots saunter over. My heart reaches a fever pitch at their nearness, right outside of my crate. The air diminishes, and my throat threatens to close in on itself.

"Well, shit. Looks like you got some extra work to do before sendoff," another man's voice quips. Through the banter, I hear the commanding stride of yet another person approaching.

"Get this straightened up, Ackles," a familiar voice booms, the rat-like timbre of it sending chills down my spine. "Now. And make sure the crate below it isn't damaged."

Head Lichera. Even the soles of his boots reveal cold assurance as they retreat. Ackles groans as he starts to pick up all of the potatoes, and I can hear him stuffing them aggressively into their burlap sacks, grumbling something about incompetent overseers.

Ackles braces himself against my crate, and I stifle a cry as he tugs on the fallen one above me. Clearly still heavy leaden, he mutters curses under his breath as the crate shifts the lid of mine just slightly before crashing to the floor. I bite my lip and breathe deeply while he finishes the job, loading the potatoes back into the empty crate. I don't calm down until I hear the crate shuffled back toward the stack. His footsteps retreat, leaving me in the silence of my thoughts.

There's no way I'm getting out of here without getting caught. They're going to search my crate, or drop it and bust the lid off, or I actually was wrong and my crate won't be shipped out today. Maybe I'm stuck, maybe I won't be able to get the lid off and I'll starve to death in here—

I can't keep my thoughts from spiraling out of control while I wait mercilessly to be either hauled away or discovered. I squeeze my eyes shut and rest them forward on my knees, making my already cramped breathing room borderline unbearable.

Breathe.

I'm not wrong. I know I'm not. I may not be an expert, but I know enough of the procedures here to know that these shipments have been double checked and organized for sendoff. The Loading Brigade will retrieve them and take them to their designated rider on the Loading Platforms.

Once we get to Verenathia… I swallow a wave of nausea. I haven't gotten that far in my planning.

With nothing to do but sit and wait uncomfortably, I listen to the spattering of voices grow into an ever loudening clamor of activity.

CHAPTER 8

ASHDEN

"Get it together, Bryorfall," Aurandraya snaps after receiving word that a shipment went to the incorrect rider.

I inhale, trying to clear my head. I'm far too distracted to be of any use tracking the items going out. Every single crate I pass, I scan for signs of tampering. A loose lid, a crate shifted out of position, anything.

It's now early afternoon and I haven't been able to find anything amiss. Searching desperately while trying to remain inconspicuous is maddening, and if I haven't found something by now, she's likely already gone.

My sister is at risk of execution now. I close my eyes for a heartbeat, trying to bury the agony tearing me apart.

I can't do this right now. I can't keep track of anything worth shit.

Mindless physical labor is what I need today.

I spot the flash of Aurandraya's red hair as he moves about the Storehouse, barking orders. Approaching him, I stand at attention. He acknowledges me with a stern dip of his head.

"Permission to switch to Brigade Runner, sir," I say.

"Granted," he sneers with a wave of his hand.

I move back to my station, informing Rod that he'll be overseeing for the rest of the day. He eyes me warily, but I ignore it.

My muscles start to burn as I lift crate after crate, trying to force thoughts of Rae aside.

I've failed her. I've failed in finding her. I've failed my parents. I've failed myself.

Having almost fulfilled another order, I heave the last crate—this one loaded with fresh fruits from our orchards, onto the cart.

Scanning the orders, Rod shouts, "Water brigade!" The brigade members appear and move to a corner of the cart for transport.

The air in the Storehouse is too stuffy. There are too many people crowding my already crowded mind. I need fresh air and the openness of the sea around me.

Moving up to the short, ruddy woman at the back corner of the cart, I reach for the pole in her hand. "I'm going to take this one, go start sorting at B station."

Looking to Rod I ask, "That okay, boss?"

He smirks. "You're the boss, boss."

I toss him a halfhearted grin. Aside from the Loadmasters who oversee entire sections of the Loading Warehouse, we all hold the same level of authority. The positions rotate on a weekly basis—this week I was assigned Shipment Overseer.

"Move out!" Rod calls.

I strain, pushing into the pole with all my might. With a groan, the cart starts moving forward, and we're soon navigating through the different stations and bodies.

I squint against the bright springtime sun as we make it through the grates at the back of the Storehouse, a bead of sweat already trickling down my temple.

Gulls cry overhead while the sounds of the town clang through my head. I focus on the crash of the waves against the docks ahead of us and push the cart even harder.

Reaching the Loading Platform's ramp, we give a mighty heave, forcing the cart upward. It tries to roll back, but we dig in. My legs begin to burn, and the physical discomfort is a welcome distraction from the mental hell I've been in all morning.

There's no rider on the platform yet, but I can see them in the distance as we level out, the dragon's orange body stark against the blue sky. It pans slightly to the right, revealing another on its tail. A massive dragon, black as death. They're both heading for our platform.

A glimpse of white flashes from atop the black dragon, sending my heart beating hard and fast.

No.

The dragons slow as they near the platform, pitching upward before they descend, claws outstretched. Coming to a graceful landing, the black dragon doesn't have enough room to stand on the platform, so it perches effortlessly on the railing—a feat for its size.

A rider jumps down from the orange dragon, her light purple hair gleaming against the backdrop of her dragon's body. She's wearing an iridescent gray dragonhide suit, a longsword sheathed across her back.

Her presence is notable, but it's the rider behind her that has my attention. My racing heart almost sinks as low as his dragon's head as it allows him to step onto the platform.

A tall figure clad in a white, flowing robe glides across the platform to stand in front of us. His face is fully hooded by the robe, but it's his lifeless gaze that I can't look away from. The whole of his eyes are a milky blue-white, no pupils visible. Black scrolling tattoos crawl up the sides of his face, curling in and reaching toward his eyes as if trying to pluck them out of their sockets. And although I can't see fully, I'm almost certain he has no hair—those scrolling, twisting tattoos covering his entire head instead.

No.

No. The only word I can think of. The single syllable cutting through the chaos of my head on an endless loop.

The female rider clears her throat, standing tall, and gestures to the man beside her. "Pay your respects to Lucielle, Verenathia's Talebearer."

I want to wrap my hands around her throat and squeeze the air of superiority right out of her, but we bow at the waist, as is custom for Goramalans in the presence of Verenathian Clerics. Anger heats my face as I stare at the ground in front of me.

"You may stand," she says after a long pause.

Rising back to my full height, I stare defiantly into the unearthly eyes of the Talebearer. He gazes down his pointed nose at the Brigade, his movements slow, wraithlike. The smooth folds of his robe ripple as he reaches into its depths, producing a scroll. He unrolls the parchment, his bony fingers working carefully.

"In agreement with the Accords between our lands," he begins, his deep voice booming across the platform. "Verenathia requests the servitude of Raimy Therim. Please inform him of his duty immediately and proceed with farewells. A Verenathian rider will arrive at this time tomorrow to collect."

And with that, he turns. No goodbyes, no words of departure, as if we are below even the most basic of human decency.

His dragon quickly lowers its head to receive the Talebearer. Instead of climbing up its back like all of the other Verenathians, he steps onto the dragon's head, walking the length of its neck.

A shiver creeps through me as the robe gives him the appearance of floating across the dragon, looking like something otherworldly. An apparition. Meeting the dragon's gaze, I'm taken aback to see the anger and pain in its eyes as it begrudgingly bears the indignity.

Once settled, Lucielle shifts subtly in his seat, informing the dragon it's time to depart. The dragon pivots and dives off the edge. As they plummet, part of me hopes they'll keep going until the Talebearer is far below the surface of the sea. They reappear, ascending before disappearing into the clouds.

"I said to begin loading, Bryorfall." Rod's tone is terse, but there's a touch of sorrow shadowing his eyes as he meets mine questioningly.

Giving a slight shake of my head, I bring my mind back to the job before us. The other members of the Brigade are already unloading onto the back of the orange dragon, its rider eyeing me with disdain. I snap my attention back to the crates.

We finish and head down the ramp, my mind now numb at the events of the day.

I look up at the sky, toward the isle, cursing it and all who occupy it.

CHAPTER 9

We took you two to the mountains today. I thought you were simply going to fly away. We stopped on top of a bluff for midday meal, your father and I had packed a basket of bread and fruits. Ashden was very protective over you, always by your side and gently guiding you away from the edge when you strayed too far.

Time drags on, more slowly than I ever miserably thought possible.

My legs have gone numb now, a faint sensation of pins and needles tickling my feet. My joints throb, and I'm so thirsty my tongue feels like a bone buried in the sand. The air inside my crate is reminiscent of a damp work boot after a long day, and my back and neck are aching to be stretched—hours of being hunched no doubt taking several inches off my height.

Around me, the din of voices and activity never lulls. Carts groan, crates shuffle, and sacks thud as shipments are packed and sent off.

I can occasionally make out conversations among the commands of overseers and Loadmasters, if they're near enough, having heard Ashden once or twice. Each time has brough a jolt of guilt and pain.

"You hear about ol' Raimy?" A male voice pipes up.

"Ay," another responds. "What a shame. I'm gonna miss his blueberry pies. He makes 'em better than my wife." Laughter crackles through the air from multiple directions but I hardly notice.

The Culling. My breath catches in my throat, and I know without a doubt that is the only explanation.Tears prick at the back of my eyes at the thought of the caring baker.

Maybe the Verenathians will use him to keep their people supplied with treats. I have no doubt he'd rival any baker they have.

"Laugh all you want, but his poor wife's gonna need help now trying to run the bakery without the baker there," a woman's voice calls.

"Well Neola, sounds like you'll need to put in a request for a duty transfer," another voice says, arousing more snickers.

The woman, Neola, scoffs.

I'm so miserable with my thoughts I don't even notice the two sets of footsteps approaching until they're speaking right beside me.

"There was a delay, but the issue is resolved now," a woman says. "Section D is ready to go, sir."

Parchment shuffles as the second person double checks the orders. Giving a confirmational grunt, the man's voice calls out, "Fire brigade!"

Several more sets of footsteps approach, along with the creaking of a wooden cart. The sound is enough to snap me out of my fog.

"Five loads here, just take the second. Third platform."

Please be me. Please.

People surround me, and my heart lurches as my crate jolts. I can feel myself hoisted into the air before my crate is dropped unceremoniously into the cart. My weight shifts, and my bottom takes the brunt of the impact. I wince, carefully readjusting.

"That felt awful light for a whole bunch of flour," a voice, now even with my head, says.

"Don't know what to tell you. Consider it your break for the day," another quips.

More crates crash down next to me, landing heavily in the base of the cart.

If I want to get out, now is likely my last chance. Terror locks my body. How can I get out now and successfully explain why the hell I'm in here?

I suck in deep breaths, willing my heartbeat to steady. Even if I could get out, I will never find peace here. If I back out now, there won't be any chance of getting to Verenathia ever again. They'd no doubt lock all of the trade buildings down, or even post a guard—after I had already been executed.

I grit my teeth, resolve washing over me. I will go.

"Move out!" a voice to my left calls. And then we're moving, the cart creaking and groaning as it rolls under the weight of the load. The hum of activity grows quieter as the faint tang of the docks begins to drift through the cracks in my crate. The tangible closeness of the sea calms my racing heart, each lap of the waves sating my fear.

The cart pitches upward, pinning me back against the wall as it creaks and creaks.

A memory flashes through my mind. I couldn't have been more than five years old. Our father took us all on his boat for a day. The sea was wild that day, the waves towering over us as we climbed and climbed. Ashden spent most of the day with his head hanging over the railing, but I was with my father at the helm, the wind and waves inciting a feral sort of energy in me. The sea was wild and untamed, the waves towering over us as we climbed and climbed. There was a moment of stillness at the peak of each wave we crested; a heartbeat of unparalleled, infinite sea. And then we would drop, my father grinning mischievously every time I squealed.

The drop is much less dramatic here, and when we level out atop the Loading Platform, my weight shifts back squarely onto my bottom. The snuffle of a dragon greets us as the order is confirmed and papers are exchanged.

Finally, finally, the command to unload is given, and my heart threatens to stop. There's a slight dip and bounce as I'm borne along between the brigade members before being set, much more kindly this time, on the back of the dragon. My stomach flutters as I sway over its haunches, wishing I could see the beautiful beast below me. I want to touch its shimmering scales, feel the power rippling below their surface.

A semblance of that power echoes through me now as the dragon dutifully accepts its cargo without so much as a shudder.

The rustle of a rope net rubs against the load as it's put securely in place, signifying the end of loading. The fear pulsing through me peaks as I realize my tomb is sealed and I'm about to be lowered into the ground, buried beneath the weight of my decisions.

"I will survive," I breathe. "I will return."

The brigade is finished, announced by the fading sound of the groaning cart down the ramp. The scratch of a quill and stamp of a seal on parchment signals our departure. Excitement crackles through me despite my apprehension.

I'm going to ride a dragon.

The beast leans forward to accept its rider, throwing me into the wall of the crate. Gently, I right myself, just in time to pitch sideways over its rotating haunches as it pivots.

I know we're looking toward the sea now, toward Verenathia. I can feel it singing, beckoning to me, calling me into her depths.

I can't breathe, the air around me tight, knowing we're hovering over the edge of the sea—over the edge of my life. I close my eyes, preparing for a brand new one—or the end of it—at the hands of the Verenathians. I have no idea what awaits me, or what I'm even looking for; all I know is the delicate tendrils of magic snaking through the Safeguards are pulling me into their grasp, and I will face whatever comes.

I hold my breath, and the dragon leaps.

My stomach rises as we drop, then I'm slammed into the back of the crate as we pitch upward. Tears begin to flow freely down my face in joyful streams as we level out and soar through the sky—something I've dreamed about since I was a little girl coming to fruition. I may not be able to see the dragon below me or the sky stretching endlessly, but to be airborne nonetheless is enough to send the thrill of adrenaline pulsing through me.

A never ending cerulean glow surrounds us. Every fiber of me wishes I could pry the wood apart with my bare hands to feel the wind in my hair and sun against my skin.

I can't hear anything but the wind buffeting the crates, except for what occasionally sounds like snippets of a conversation between the rider and her dragon.

I know very little about dragons, as Ra'goramal doesn't keep any records on them. Nothing, except that the bond between a dragon and its rider is unbreakable. More than a pet—no, considering such a magnificent beast to be a pet would be an insult. They're more of a partner; one to be revered and respected.

The yearning for such a bond hits me so hard it takes my breath away. No Goramalans have ever bonded a dragon, so I bury that thought deep and focus on what lies before me.

Fear crackles through me anew. I would assume the Verenathians have something to the effect of a Storehouse, or at least an unloading area—somewhere I can slip out unseen. But if they don't…

I reach into my satchel and clutch the cool metal of the dagger, clinging to the comfort its weight holds.

CHAPTER 10

You asked question after question as I painted with you in the grasslands today. What I was painting, how I was painting, why I was painting it. I did my best to explain that the world is full of light and color, and it's our duty to capture it as best we can. To commemorate and remember it. But I know you, little bird. Your heart understands these things whether you're yet aware of it or not.

The air grows more charged the further we fly from Ra'goramal. Like the energy in the atmosphere before a storm, it tingles along my skin, growing stronger by the minute. That heaviness I always feel, that sensation of something… off presses in on me, suffocating me.

With the song in my heart drawing me to Verenathia, the weight threatening to crush me, and that tingling, crackling energy crawling along my skin—it's as if I'm being ripped apart and pressed back together all at once.

Tingling grows to stinging which quickly becomes burning. My flesh is alive with it. A crackling sort of burn that devours me from the inside out; no longer just licking my skin. The very air in the crate becomes heavy, like drawing in lungfuls of syrup. I squeeze my eyes shut and suck i want to crawl out of my own skin. This is too much, it's too heavy and… I'm drowning. I'm drowning and it aches and consumes and something is wrong. Something is so so wrong—

A line of fire sizzles across my body. The hair on the back of my neck rises, electricity skittering across me.

And then it stops. I gasp, scanning my arms, hands, legs—but there are no wounds. My skin is still the same shade of ivory, not a scratch or burn in sight.

And that weight, the oppressive vice I've never known a day without, is gone.

The Safeguards. We must have crossed over the edge of the wards.

My body is light and airy and alive. Alive in a way I've never experienced. Verenathia's magic is no longer a song calling to me, but a roar.

Energy crackles at my fingertips, raw and free and delicious. Is this what the Verenathians feel all the time? This… clarity? This raw freedom? The breeze coming through the cracks smells saltier, the sun brighter and I notice each wisp of air as it caresses my skin.

My hearing is sharper too, as if plugs of cotton have been pulled out. The sound of voices and dragons and—

Without warning, we dive forward, our speed pressing me back into the wall of the crate. My stomach rises to my throat, though the shift is somewhat of a relief on my aching body.

We fall for several long moments before the dragon starts to slow. I'm abruptly thrown forward as it thrusts its wings out, bringing our fall to an almost complete stop. Its booming wingbeats keep us bobbing in the air while it waits to land.

Up and down and up and down, we hover. Then we're lowering, if the angle of my crate is any indication.

The landing is far less jarring than I would have expected, considering the load the dragon carries.

I pitch forward again as it leans forward, and the thud of boots follows as the rider dismounts. A din of activity hums around me, so similar to the Storehouse that, for a second, I swear I'm home.

Except for the dragons. Snorts and snuffs sound all around me while claws scrape the ground in staccato shrieks. And the voices… The accent of the Verenathians. A lilting clip of words; an educated upturn at the end of syllables. Slight, but noticeable.

Definitely Verenathia.

A female voice rings out from right below me. "Hey! Can I get some help over here?" There's a creaking and sighing of rope, then the rustle of the net as it recedes over the load.

Panic stabs through me. They're going to unload the crate and I realize now that I have no idea if they check their contents. I force my breaths to steady, straining to hear against the blood roaring in my ears.

Multiple voices carry like they're in open air—air that is still flowing gently through the cracks in the crate. The lighting hasn't changed either.

Good. We're still outside. That much I can tell, at least.

The clipped footsteps, the scraping claws… It sounds like smooth stone, and if it's stone, maybe that means we're at the Citadel. I don't know where and how they unload their supplies, but the Citadel seems like a reasonable guess

How little I know of these people and this place sinks heavier in my stomach. This was a horrible, horrible mistake.

I press a trembling hand to my mouth as three sets of footsteps jog over. My breaths are coming hard and fast, my racing heart unwilling to calm. Do I fight? Do I run?

"Come on, Misha. Can't lift a couple hundred pounds of potatoes? Someone needs to spend more time in the gym." The three newcomers snicker as the rider, Misha, laughs.

"Whatever, just help me unload so I can report the order. I'm starving." The emphasis reminds me that I haven't eaten in hours and will need to find food at some point.

The crates around me shift and creak as they're removed from the dragon. A dramatic round of groans arises when they lift the one that is, evidently, full of potatoes.

A bud of hope springs in my chest. I haven't heard any of them opened, which heightens my chances of getting out of here before they are.

I'm lifted yet again into the air, and, just like before, am little more than tossed to the ground. My jaw snaps shut with the impact, filling my mouth with the metallic taste of blood. I run my tongue over the bite in my lip, wincing.

"That was way too light for all the sugar and salt that was supposed to be in there. Damned Goramalans."

My heart stops.

"Eh, they'll catch it at the Warehouse."

The Warehouse? I release my pent up breath when none of the crates are checked and the group saunters off, wholly engaged in conversation. I don't hear any more crates being unloaded, which could potentially mean I'm the final shipment of the day. The only sounds now are the booming wingbeats of multiple dragons as they depart.

I wait, not daring to move—listening as even more dragons take off, and the number of voices diminishes. Misha's dragon is still standing beside me, clawing at the ground as its serpentine tail swishes across the stone.

Suddenly, it pauses its pawing, its breath growing louder as its head nears my crate. My heart flies into my throat. Hot puffs of breath blow through the cracks as it snorts all along the crate's exterior. It stills, a faint growl stirring in its throat, and I begin trembling.

I can get away or get out of situations with people, but a dragon? I'm as good as dead.

A long inhale, as if the dragon is memorizing my scent, and resumes the swishing of its tail. After several too-tense moments, I don't know if my heart can take it anymore.

Footsteps approach in the distance, coming closer. My savior and my terror in this moment. The dragon's head shoots up as it cries a greeting, to who I would assume to be Misha. She makes a series of whistles and clicks as she approaches, laughing as the dragon moves in response; an act I can't make out from sound alone.

"Hey girl," she coos to the dragon, coming to a stop. The dragon utters a soft growl, the sound incredibly different from the one she gave me.

"Let's get you back," Misha says. Scales rustle as she mounts, the sound of wingbeats following as they leap to their ascent a few seconds later.

Once they're gone, the area is silent. There's only the beating of my own heart to keep me company as I strain for any signs of life. I wait fifteen minutes, counting each one to be completely sure I'm alone, but there isn't so much as a single footstep.

Taking a deep breath, I shift my stiff legs and pull them into a squat beneath me. Pushing up, I rise, pressing my hunched back into the lid with all my might. My skin barks against the rough wood, but I strain, my legs burning.

The lid doesn't budge. Cursing, I shift forward, leaning toward a corner of the crate and try again. This time, the corner breaks over, pulling the nail up but leaving half of it within the crate.

Shifting again, I give one final heave, and the nail frees itself, coming completely undone. I crouch again, peering through the gap to take stock of my surroundings.

White marble pillars rise up high to my left, their tops out of sight above the lip of my crate. I scan along the smooth stone ground until my gaze stops on a wall that seems to encircle this unloading area—sealed crates lining its base while more rest in neat rows across the ground.

Nothing and no one stirs.

I hold my breath and count to five.

I press up until the other three corners are released, and remove the lid fully. Setting it gently on the ground, I stand to my full height, my back screaming at me for having been bent for so long. Every muscle tenses—all my joints creaking—unwilling to yield. Blood rushes to my legs, sending pins and needles from my toes to my thighs.

Waiting for the discomfort to subside, I take a real look around me, quickly forgetting about my pain as I behold the sight before me.

The pillars stretch high into the sky, far above the vantage point of my crate, and support a vast vaulted ceiling that towers over the space underneath. I stare in awe at the open air concept, the stone of the courtyard flowing seamlessly into the sheltered area underneath the pillars. Beyond those pillars are white marble walls that meet to form a wide corridor. A grand marble staircase ascends into its belly while more entrance ways are spaced evenly across the wall, each leading to a corridor that disappears deep into the Citadel.

The Citadel. Yes, I know without a doubt that that is what I'm looking at right now.

The courtyard—forming a rough half circle—is enormous, the stone wall encircling it far too tall to scale.

I bring a hand to my mouth, breath caught in my throat as I look beyond that wall.

We're among the clouds, the blue-white hazy expanse stretching out endlessly before me. It looks to be early evening, with the sun beginning to slip behind the wall—so close I feel like I could touch it.

Everywhere I look is grandeur. The gleaming white stone walls, the polished floor, the intermingling of the clouds.

But there's no time to reflect; not yet.

Blinking rapidly, I ease myself over the lip of the crate and softly set the lid in place. My heart rate kicks up again as I scan the entryways.

Going up the stairway in the center would likely mean a swift capture—no chance of escape—after getting caught on an upper level. Each of the other corridors lead deeper into the Citadel, and I'm not sure of their direction. I *am* sure I can find my way out, though.

Or at least find somewhere to hide.

Terror tries to overwhelm me, but I breathe through its waves. I don't know anything about the Citadel, Verenathia's land, how her people operate. Nothing. Nothing other than the assurance of an execution if I'm caught.

Making, more or less, a wild guess, I head toward the corridor furthest to the left. The space between my crate and the wall yawns before me. I'm too vulnerable in the open like this, with nothing in between me and every single entrance into the Citadel; like a fish caught in the sight of a fisherman's spear. I try to find a balance between speed and stealth, grateful for choosing my soft moccasins.

The corridor approaches too slowly. Every second I'm exposed is another second closer to discovery. Damning the consequences, I sprint toward the corridor, years of running through the grasslands coming to my advantage as my feet light across the stone floor.

I reach the entrance and stand with my back against the wall, pulling in long, deep breaths. The white marble is smooth as glass under my fingertips, not a scratch or pore on its surface.

The vaulted ceiling crests high above me. Skylights open in each apex of the marbled architecture, allowing for minimal shadows and an airy feel under its protection.

Leaning over, I peer into the corridor and swallow a gasp of both dismay and wonder. The marbled corridor stretches so far that I can't see the end of it. It gleams radiantly under the warm gaze of the sun as sunlit alcoves dot its length. The light coming from the floor to ceiling windows gives it an ethereal glow.

I hesitate for a moment, unsure now that I'm staring down its face. There has to be intersecting halls or rooms—the thought of tearing blindly down it is utterly terrifying.

Is it even possible to remain undetected? To find my way out of this place? Having followed nothing but a tugging at the edge of my consciousness, I don't even know why I'm here or what I'm looking for. I'd liked to think I could avoid the Verenathians, but that hope is very quickly fading.

There's nothing to do but press onward. I made this decision and now I have to face whatever comes.

Steeling myself, I make my way into the corridor, stepping lightly and sticking close to the wall. I pause every few feet, listening for voices or footsteps, but all I hear is the roar of blood in my ears.

I continue padding along until I reach what, from a distance, looked like another set of alcoves, but is actually another corridor. Intersecting the one I'm in, this next one is just as large and as long. Apprehension trickles through me, trailing goosebumps across my skin as I hesitate.

The sound of brisk footsteps almost makes me jump out of my own silent moccasins. Coming from ahead and to the… right? It's hard to tell from the way they echo through the massive corridor. I dive into the alcove nearest me and duck against the wall, the footsteps getting louder with each strike. My heart feels like it's going to explode in my chest as I take shaking breaths, bracing myself for discovery.

The footsteps continue until they sound like they could be right next to me, then begin growing quieter again until they fade completely. I stay crouched for another minute, steadying my trembling hands, feeling more vulnerable than ever. I would easily be spotted from any distance, the brown leather of my pants painting a streak of mud against the glowing white.

The only way out is through.

I exit my alcove and peer around the corner to find the next corridor empty.

Letting out a pent up breath, I make my way forward and slip into another connecting corridor. This one is shorter with a definable opening at the end.

The sunlight warms my skin each time I pass under the gaze of the alcoves, and I can't help but glance out of the spotless glass every time, still awestruck by the nearness of the sky.

Nearing the opening, I realize with a start that it's a stairwell—a broad set of flowing marble stairs descending to the floor below me. My feet brush the top step, but I can't see the bottom as the stairs spiral downward against a rounded pillar, their base hidden from view.

I take a tentative step forward, hesitation leadening my feet, but the heavy silence of the Citadel continues. Another step, and I tighten my satchel around my waist, feeling the reassuring weight of the dagger through the leather. I round down the staircase, sticking close to the pillar, and crane my neck to see what awaits.

Nothing.

Reaching the bottom of the stairs, I stare ahead into yet another vast corridor. A flicker of irritation warms my blood, replacing the fear there. How big is this place?

This corridor, like the others, is empty, and there's a gap in the wall ahead.

Another intersection.

I walk for what feels like forever, taking random turns at every change and going down another spiral stairway. Frustration fuels my steps now and all pretense of stealth is abandoned. I just want to see something or someone other than the never ending maze of corridors that lead to nowhere.

I glance in disdain at my white surroundings, the stone seeming to have lost its luster.

Verenathia's population rivals Ra'goramal's; how have I only heard one person within this hell? Where have they gone?

Maybe this is a nightmare. I dreamed of escaping to Verenathia, and now that I'm here, I'm being punished—sentenced to roam these halls for eternity with no escape in sight.

I run my fingers through my hair, coming to yet another descending set of marble stairs. A murmur of activity softly drifts up through the stairwell. Fear and excitement meet to send my heart racing, and I tiptoe down the steps, eager to see what's around the corner.

A strong arm wraps around my shoulders, the other quickly stifling the scream tearing its way up my throat by placing a cupped palm around my mouth. Pure, white-hot panic knifes through me, and I fumble for my satchel but my assailant easily removes it, holding me pinned to their body by the hand around my mouth. I thrust my elbow back and into the person's abdomen, but they easily dodge my pathetic attempt before grabbing my arm and twisting it behind my back. I cry out at the sharp pain, the sound muffled by their hand. They release their grip on my arm, keeping it pinned against me with their body, and effortlessly switch their grasp around my mouth to secure my other arm. With both of my arms restrained, they drop their head forward until I can feel their warm breath in my ear—a woman's voice.

"What do you think you're doing here?"

CHAPTER 11

I braided a crown of field lilies for your hair from the bunch you found on the bluffs. You were so delighted. We spent the day out there, and you and your brother were both too tired to walk back. Your father and I carried you back to the cottage, where you now rest. Your tiny, sleeping breaths fill the quiet as your father repairs his nets. Never forget our love, little bird. Sleep well.

My abductor doesn't allow me to speak as I'm shoved through corridor after corridor. I try to pay attention to the direction we're taking, but my mind is overridden with panic, and I find it impossible to remember our way.

My heart beats so fast I think I might pass out—the fear pulsing through me and the hand stifling my words threatening to send me over the edge. My shoulder winces as my arm is twisted high behind my back, and I stumble as the Verenathian shoves me mercilessly forward.

Despair cuts through the haze of my panic. I haven't been here more than a few hours and I'm already being led to what is most likely my death.

I'm never going to see Ash or Avice again.

We come to another set of descending stairs as the hum of noise that has been running through the air heightens from the stairwell.

I almost collapse at the thought of facing more Verenathians, especially if all of them are as aggressively unfriendly as the one restraining me. On the verge of hyperventilating, tears begin to prick my vision and I hesitate.

She shoves me forward, forcing me down a step.

My frustration resurfaces. No, I will not cry. I force the tears back and start fighting, trying desperately to free myself from her iron grip.

"Oh, no you don't," my attacker says, her voice cold. She thrusts me down the steps, and I fumble to catch my footing. Facing the Verenathians sounds like hell, but doing so sprawled across the floor? A fate worse than death.

We round the marble pillar, coming to the base of the stairs. In spite of myself, my eyes widen at the great expanse before me.

We're in what appears to be some sort of vast commons area. The polished walls rise high with even more corridors opening into them. The whole of the vaulted ceiling is made of what looks to be crystal—not a shadow to be seen as soft sunlight shines down through the entire space.

Red, blue, and purple tapestries hang down the far wall. Tables are set throughout the room while chairs and benches comfortably surround them. Several circles of chaise lounges face each other in loose semi-circles.

Clearly, this place is for socialization and leisure.

That thought is confirmed as all of the eyes in the room turn toward me as we step off the stairs.

More Verenathians than I could even bother counting stare at me. Many are gathered around tables, cards now held halfway in their grasp. Others lounge together on the chaises, and still more stand frozen, like statues planted throughout the room. Every one of them looks to be about my age, no children or elders in sight. They all wear some form of dragonhide outfit, many of them even brandishing larger scales as a sort of armor over their chests and arms. The outfits shimmer as they move, the radiant material catching the light from the crystal above.

It's a sea of glittering color that stands starkly against the pure white backdrop, and I am the grimy streak against their opalescent perfection. Their confusion and shock taint the air, suffocating me.

After a moment of standing for their perusal, the woman speaks.

"Look what I found," she calls out. Finally releasing me, she gives a swift kick to the back of my legs that sends me to my knees.

Members of the crowd snicker, some of them coming forward to get a closer look while others start calling out insults.

"Goramalan pig!"

"Look, she can't even stand on her own."

"She's so dirty."

"She broke the Accords. Why is she here?"

"I found her sneaking through the Citadel," the woman says. "I followed her for a good while. Damned fool didn't even notice me."

I stare at the floor, my mind going numb to the hostility around me. I don't know what I expected coming here, but it wasn't this. I could handle a fair trial before my inevitable execution, but to sit here—hungry, sweaty, and reviled—is almost an indignity more than I can bear.

And I have no one to blame but myself.

What you're feeling is nothing more than the heightened emotions of a daydream.

The woman drops my satchel beside me in an outright show of arrogance. Still, I reach out and clutch it to my lap, pressing the weight of the dagger against me.

A man—no more than two years my senior—saunters forward, his bulky shoulders swaying confidently. A predatory sneer twists his face as he kneels in front of me, his green suit catching the light as he reaches a calloused finger under my chin. Cruel hazel eyes peer into mine when he tilts my head up.

"At least she's pretty," he calls out. Some of the men jeer as anger flashes through me. I jerk my head sideways and away from his touch, glaring defiantly.

The woman slaps my head from behind, sending me staring at the cold stone of the floor again.

"Lose the attitude," she spits. "What do you think you're doing here?"

Her question goes unanswered as a clear, deep voice rings through the air.

"Nobody touch her."

The woman steps back at the command, the man in front of me giving one last smirk as he rises and makes his way back to his friends.

My heart rains a drumbeat in my ears. I know that voice. I don't know how, but the sound of it sends a nervous shiver into my stomach.

Movement ripples through the crowd as people begin shuffling apart, making way for someone striding toward the front of the room. The drumbeat in my ears is now a deafening roar as I catch a streak of midnight hair. One of the groups moves aside, and the rider I met that day on the platforms emerges, standing before me. His dragonhide suit is black as night, cutting an impressive form against the wall of bodies behind him.

"What the hell are you doing, Laurel?" He addresses the woman behind me, his green eyes flashing.

"Didn't you hear?" There's not a trace of concern in her voice. "She was lurking through the corridors—came from the supply field."

"And that gives you all the right to treat her like an animal?"

My face heats as I continue to train my eyes at his boots.

Laurel scoffs. "It gives us the right to treat her like a Goramalan infiltrating our land."

"If you were half as smart as you think you are, you would know that she, in fact, is not infiltrating, and has just as much right to be here as we do."

The room goes silent as a grave before a hushed murmur rises.

Part of our initial education on Ra'goramal was teaching of our relationship with Verenathia: they provide our defenses, and we stick to our own land. It's wholeheartedly illegal for a Goramalan to travel here; outlined in *both* of our Accords.

And as far as I know, it's never happened before.

"What are you talking about, Kieran?" There's a note of hesitation in her voice now.

I glance up at the man in front of me, rolling his name over in my mind—feeling all of its sharp edges; lingering over the fluidity of it.

A challenging light glints in his eyes as he glares at her. "She is allowed to be here," he says, without a hint of wavering. Laurel holds her tongue in response to the command lacing his tone.

The room is utterly silent as Kieran walks forward to kneel in front of me. I can't stop the blush that spreads from my neck to my cheeks at his nearness. I peer up at him, setting my expression defiantly, steeling myself against his gaze. I wonder if remembers me.

"Are you okay?" His demeanor shifts ever so slightly as he addresses me, a subtle gentleness softening the hard edges of his countenance.

I grit my teeth. "Yes."

I can't help but notice his perfectly angled jawline, sitting softly with a shadow of scruff on its edge. There's a small crease between his dark eyebrows—of irritation or concern, I can't tell.

"What's your name?" he asks quietly.

"Rae," I snap.

He nods. Rising to his full height, he calls out, "This is a matter for the Court of Elders, not you dumbasses. Go back to playing cards." He beckons to me with an outstretched arm, and I stand shakily, refusing his support.

"You," he points at Laurel. "Come with me."

I glance for the first time toward the woman. Her hair is bright purple, glowing in the sunlight against her shimmering gray suit. Fine features decorate her face, which is now bearing a contorted look of hatred.

I look away quickly, following on Kieran's heels as he begins to leave, and almost stumble into him as he stops abruptly in front of the man who threatened me. His glare is all flint and daggers, not a hint of kindness or mercy to be seen.

"If you lay a finger on her," he begins, his quiet voice as hard as the stone around us, "I'll slit your throat while you sleep."

The man doesn't respond, giving Kieran a look of cold indifference. I swallow hard, trying to dislodge the weight in my throat.

Kieran leads the way to the corridor on the left side of the room, Laurel trailing behind us. I can feel the stares of every single person in the crowd as they weigh my presence. My whole body burns under their speculation, and I want to float away through the crystal ceiling and never return.

I don't know why I ever thought this was a good idea.

My heart is beating like a war drum, loud enough that I'm sure everyone in this room can hear it. The physical incarnation of the fear shredding me apart—it's the only thing I hear, the only thing filling all of my senses as I follow Kieran into a corridor.

I inhale deeply, trying to clear my head and force myself toward whatever is waiting at the end of this trek.

Stupid.

CHAPTER 12

My dear Rae, do not be afraid of trouble when it comes. It has its way of finding those that look into the deep, inevitably knocking on your door. Know this, little bird: you are stronger than you know and possess a light that cannot be extinguished.

At this point, I'm convinced the Citadel was built to confuse whoever didn't have a structural diagram of the place in their bedroom chest. I don't even bother tracking our turns, defeat raining over me as I accept that I will never know how to escape. Not that it will matter in the end, as I'm going to die anyway.

I don't know what part of the Citadel I was in before I got caught, but, clearly, these are the more populated areas. My skin heats as more than one wide-eyed, slack-jawed look is cast in my direction.

Similar to the one I was taken to, several more common areas open into the corridors through large entryways, each room filled with a shimmering sea of bodies. Some of the Verenathians stare as we pass by, craning their necks to see, while others outrightly gape.

Kieran leads us down turn after turn, the marble now a golden hue as the sun begins to set. The color shift turns the gleaming expanse into something truly ethereal, and I wonder if maybe I have already been killed and am walking the halls of the afterlife.

Neither one of the Verenathians speak, although Kieran occasionally darts a side-eyed glance back in my direction. I try to keep my eyes on the floor, the walls, the sky—anywhere but him—yet his emerald gaze is intriguing, and I find it harder to look away each time. His expression remains unreadable, although a faint hint of curiosity glints there.

Finally, we approach a doorway that leads us into a dim antechamber. A massive, dark paneled door looms on the far wall.

Kieran leads us to the door, crossing the windowless room in a few quick strides. It groans as he opens it, and I follow as we take a few steps down past the doorway, lowering into a chamber that's slightly smaller than the common areas.

But this room… Something about this room is different. The light filtering through the antechamber from the corridor stops abruptly at the entrance, as if the sun itself wouldn't dare show itself here.

Stone benches form a semicircle line, facing what appears to be some sort of tribune. The whole of it, including the floor and ceiling, is paneled in polished wood, so dark it's almost black. Sconces evenly line the walls, their yellowed glow casting an eerie warmth about the dark space.

On the tribune at the back of the room are four high-backed chairs. Six smaller chairs, three on each side, spread out from them, overlooking the orderly benches.

I squint in the dim light and realize that those aren't chairs… They're thrones. Thrones with gold runes inlaid along their backrests. Black velvet cushions rest in each of their seats, while the base and feet bear intricate, scrolling carvings lined with various precious stones I can't name.

A weight settles in my stomach when I see the swords plunged into the back of each throne, the hilts burning with blue fire.

I really am going to die.

We walk further down the center of the room, toward the tribune. Kieran motions to one of the benches beside us.

"Have a seat."

I obey, grateful to be off my unsteady feet as my heart races.

I don't know what he was talking about back in that room, but I am definitely going to die. This is my trial, and I'm about to be sentenced for treason.

Laurel chooses a seat straight across from me on the opposite bench. She doesn't even glance my direction, keeping her eyes firmly trained in front of her. Tension is written in the hard set of her shoulders, her hands planted firmly to her sides on the seat of the bench.

Kieran continues toward the front of the room, the heels of his boots echoing around us. He walks confidently, as though having done this a hundred times over.

A brass horn-like instrument is attached to the wall by a chain, hanging to the right of the tribune. Kieran reaches for it, bringing the unrecognizable instrument to his mouth. Inhaling sharply, he purses his lips, and blows into it. A low, ominous moan bellows from the mouth of the instrument as the sound echoes through the chamber—if not the entire Citadel. The sound rattles my teeth with its prolonged eerie groan. My chest constricts, and I can't control the trembling that grips my body.

Please just kill me now, I want to beg as Kieran takes a seat on a bench near the front of the room.

We wait for what's probably only a couple of minutes, but may as well be hours. My stomach churns as I sit with my hands folded tightly in my lap, staring at the wooden floor—polished so clear I can almost see my reflection in its depths. Like the sea on a moonlit night.

The thought is somewhat comforting.

The dull thud of footsteps and swishing fabric issues from ahead of us, and I snap my gaze forward, a vice squeezing my chest. In the dim light, six people—men in cream colored cloaks—emerge through a doorway hidden behind the bulk of the thrones.

With hoods pulled high over their heads, they spread—three on each side of the tribune. By some undetectable cue, they simultaneously take their seats next to the thrones.

A man with deep bronze skin follows, his white robe trailing behind him. My stomach twists when I see his eyes beneath the hood—milky blue-white and unfocused. He stops, standing to the left of the thrones, and folds his forearms together as he gazes out at us.

Lucielle.

I've never seen him up close, only from afar when he comes to the loading platforms.

Starting to feel faint, I wait for who will claim the thrones in front of me.

I almost vomit when I see four hooded figures glide slowly from behind, their black robes blanketing their bodies entirely. All four of them bear eyes dark as night, no whites to be found. Their smooth, pale grayish skin suggests that they haven't seen the sun in years, if at all. They make their way to the thrones, and, like the cream-colored figures, sit as if one mind.

Cold, lifeless gazes pin on me, and I feel like I might combust. Yet, I'm drawn to the fine black tattoos that swirl up from their fingertips, covering the backs of their hands until they disappear under their robes.

The Warbearers. No Goramalan has ever laid eyes on one, but I know it with a certainty I can't place.

The air holds the heavy weight of something forbidden—similar to the tension of the Safeguards over Ra'goramal, and I shift uncomfortably at the murkiness.

One of them clears his throat, almost sending me flying out of my skin.

"Kieran Trymera." His voice, dripping with the smoothness of aged leather, booms through the air.

There he is, sitting in the center of the set of chairs on the right of the thrones. Tufts of sparse white hair spring from his head, trailing down into a thick, full beard. His skin bears the wrinkles of a long life, with deep set creases webbing from the corners of his eyes.

Kieran stands, bowing low before them.

"You have summoned the Court of Elders. Explain the reason for this gathering, as you know our time is valuable." None of the others speak as they wait for Kieran's response.

"We have a Goramalan in our midst," Kieran gestures to me.

Not mincing words, evidently.

All of their expressions remain calm, unsurprised, even. As if I'm nothing more than an incomplete shipment—merely an inconvenience. Lucielle still stands silent, unfocused eyes gazing into nothing.

"A Goramalan…" another says. "So you say. Bring this foreigner before us, immediately." His time-worn voice is commanding, but not harsh.

Kieran reaches back, offering me his arm. This time I take it. He may be the enemy, but the thought of standing before this unfamiliar court of my own will is too much to handle.

He leads me forward as I take hesitant steps, not daring to look them in the eyes as we are now so near, I can smell the scent of parchment clinging to their robes.

"Laurel found her wandering our halls," Kieran says.

I force myself not to flinch under their appraising gazes, even as my knees tremble. They remain silent for several long moments before speaking.

"Reck," a voice like the crunch of gravel on the shore speaks, but I don't look up to see who it is. "Is this true?"

Laurel's suit rustles as she stands behind me. "Yes, my elder. She was coming from the direction of the supply field before I restrained her."

"Ah," the white-haired man speaks. "So she was."

Fear and confusion cast a dream-like haze over my senses; dulling them, muddling my thoughts.

"This is true," the second man says. "Why have you brought her before us, Trymera? You know our laws and customs." He says the last word with a knowing look that turns my blood to ice.

"Yes, my elder," Kieran begins. "And I would like to speak with the Court"—he turns a cold glance toward me, then Laurel—"alone."

My legs almost give out from under me. Was his kindness in front of the congregation a facade and he really does plan to have me executed?

I don't know what I was expecting. I'm not undeserving. I knew the risks, knew the punishment. I have no one to blame but myself. But even so, I can't help the sinking feeling of dread as one of the Elders nods, waiting for our departure.

Laurel stands, irritation evident in every one of her fine features, but turns and stalks out of the room without another glance toward me.

I watch her leave, willing my legs to follow—to move even a step—but they're frozen, rooted to the spot. My mind, overridden with terror, is numb.

Kieran lets go of my hand, beckoning me in the direction of the doorway, and gives me a quick wink before turning his attention back to the Elders.

Somehow, my legs move. Focusing on one step at a time, I make my way out of that dark and terrible room and into the antechamber. The door closes of its own accord with a finalizing thud behind me.

With my back against the wall, I slide down its smooth surface and sink to the ground, wrapping my arms tightly around my knees.

Just earlier today, I wanted nothing more than to get out of that cramped crate and stretch, to never have to curl myself into safety again. But now, the thought of being pressed between its confining walls is comforting. Standing alone, with no barriers between myself and these strange people is far too vulnerable.

Kieran's low voice sounds from behind the closed door. I can't make out any of the words spoken, but his tone sends my heart hammering again. The Elders respond, and his voice starts again.

This back and forth continues for a while. I lose track of time while I wait, taking deep breaths to steady my nerves. To my relief, the corridor ahead remains abandoned, with no sight of Laurel's return.

By the time Kieran emerges, I've managed to calm myself into coherency, my heart no longer punishing itself against my ribs. Still, I jump when the large door groans and he steps across the threshold.

My expression must be horrified because he takes one look at me and smirks, amusement decorating his bright eyes. "Welcome to Verenathia, Rae. I'm Kieran."

"I'd gathered," I say. "Did you come to take me to the gallows?"

"Of course not; that's an outdated practice. We just use swords now." Something wicked dances in the smile he flashes me.

I force the tremor out of my voice. "Well then, let's get it over with." I stand, stretching my back in what, I hope, is a relaxed gesture; wincing when my bones protest.

That same amusement still clings to the slight lift in the corners of his mouth as he shakes his head. "No need for that. You'll be staying here for the immediate future."

My jaw slackens as shock registers and I stare dumbly at him. "But… how, I—"

"Should be getting executed as we speak? Yes, yes you should. You're welcome."

I blink. "I don't understand."

"The Elders were feeling generous." He picks at a fingernail. "And I don't feel like seeing anyone die today."

I stare and stare, not grasping what he's saying. "So… what? I'm just going to get away with breaking the Accords?"

"Yes," he says wryly.

I should be grateful I'm not dead right now but the urge to slap the arrogant smirk off of his face is so strong I curl my fingers into fists at my sides.

"You'll be with me for the duration of your stay," he says, sketching a bow.

"Which is how long?" I ask incredulously.

He shrugs. "As long as you like."

"And then what?"

He raises a singular eyebrow. "If that's unsatisfactory, we have a few trained warriors on standby who will gladly uphold our end of the Accords… Right now."

The terrifying words render me silent.

He adds quietly, all teasing in his tone gone, "I hold some sway with the

Warbearers. I asked them to let you stay, and so you will, albeit temporarily." Resuming that same self-assured amusement, he scans me from head to toe. "You need some food." Scrunching his nose, he adds, "And a bath."

Indignation flares through me, extinguishing itself when my air-dried blouse crunches as I move. Hours spent in the hot crate have done no favors to my rain and sweat-soaked body.

"Let's get you taken care of," he says, guiding me out of the chamber. I breathe a sigh of relief as we enter into the open air of the corridor, the sunset now casting a purple tint as it bounces off the walls.

Out here, the crushing weight of something forbidden feels lighter, almost unnoticeable. My pulse quickens at the thought of that dark chamber, the soulless eyes of the robed figures. I hope I never have to be in their presence again.

No more words are spoken as Kieran leads me through the Citadel. I'm tired, hungry, and confused; setting my nerves on edge.

His suit gleams over shifting muscle as he walks. The way he easily carries himself—without any cares or the weight of worry that plagues every Goramalan—sends irritation prickling through me.

He really has been nothing but kind, albeit in his own, unorthodox way. I have no reason to feel such a sense of contempt toward him; my being alive at this very moment is proof enough of that. But the spike of my heart rate, unrelated to the very real possibility of death, only serves to fan a growing flame.

"Look," I snap, breaking the silence. "I know I shouldn't be here right now. I also know you probably have one hundred other things to do rather than deal with me, but there is no way I was allowed to go free when the opposite has been pounded into my head my entire life. So, if you would be kind enough to give some sort of explanation—an actual explanation—of what happened in that room, I would be eternally grateful."

He pauses abruptly and whirls, stopping when his face is mere inches from mine. I almost run directly into his chest, but I catch myself, my face warming as my stumbling steps come to a halt. His eyes, so close to mine I can see they're rimmed in blue, dance with curiosity.

No smile tugs at his mouth as he leans forward. I struggle not to flinch while trying to find my breath, breathing in his scent. Something like salt rain and… wind tickles my nose. Like the feeling of endless sky and freedom.

"I would love to answer all of your questions, even though yes, I do have at least one hundred and *one* things that require my attention at the moment.

But you look like you haven't slept in two days, or bathed in at least double that. So while you may feel entitled to my answers, I can assure you they will remain the same whether I decide to share them now, or a week from this moment."

Anger and embarrassment sear through my body at the truth in his words.

He raises a dark eyebrow, challenging. "Is that explanation satisfactory?"

"Perfectly," I say through gritted teeth.

"Good. Let's carry on, then."

***

There are even more people populating the halls the closer we get to the front of the Citadel. I keep my head down to avoid the questioning looks I've already seen on several, my body burning as I'm reminded over and over of how I stand out.

We come to a large, circular entryway at the end of a corridor. Massive glass doors stand commandingly to one side, and a domed skylight rests high above us. My breath catches on the view through the doors.

The Citadel was built to touch the sky. A vast colonnade stretches across its face before blending into marbled steps that extend down, down, down the hill it's built on. Below, spreading out from the base of the grand stairway, are paved pathways that branch out like spokes on a wheel. White stone structures dot the pathways in neat, semicircular rings, continuing to the edge of the isle.

Everywhere I look is gleaming order, all of it white as snow and perfectly designed. A sense of inferiority settles deeply within me, weighing on my chest and dampening my awe.

"Over here," Kieran breaks through my thoughts.

He gestures to an entryway on our right. Entering through, we come to a stop at a wall in front of us. Two more openings stand on either side of it, stretching ahead before they turn, leading further into the Citadel.

"Ladies on the right," Kieran says. "Uniforms are kept with the towels."

My breath stutters as I envision myself in the telltale attire of a Verenathian. Begrudgingly, I thank him and quickly make my way forward.

The bathing chamber is almost identical in design to the ones on Ra'goramal, and a bit of the heaviness in my stomach lifts when I see it's unoccupied. I unlace my moccasins and place them in a corner of the room, unsure if I'll be able to find another pair of shoes. Removing my soiled clothing, I place it in a chute I find built into the wall.

I swallow. Someone is going to find it. There will be more questions and more gossip and—

Stepping into the steaming pool, a sigh escapes me as the water embraces my tired body. I scrub quickly, not allowing myself to linger. My heart races at the thought of someone finding me in here.

With soft red skin and no trace of grime in my hair, I leave the safety of the water and race to the armoires lining one side of the room.

I rifle through two of them, my breaths beginning to tighten, before I find the one housing the towels. My naked body drips as I pull out a plush swathe of fabric, far different from the thin linen towels we have at home, and dry quickly. Wrapping the towel tightly around my body, I begin picking through the stacks of uniforms.

Selecting a deep red one with a metallic cast, I hold it up to my body, the length close enough to my height that it will suffice.

Made of the more delicate areas of a dragon's hide, the uniforms are all one piece. I dip my feet into the legs, pulling it up over my hips, and shiver in delight as the cool, smooth material glides onto my body like silk. Reinforced with larger, more protective scales at the knees, hips, elbows, and chest, it cuts in at my waist, clinging comfortably to my curves. I reach behind me, hooking the small metal clasps lining up the back, only to realize that I can't grasp the ones in the center.

Cursing, I strain, reaching my arm as far as it will go—first from the top, then the bottom. Then the other arm.

The small, exposed section of my back remains cool against the air.

My irritation blooms into tired rage as I yank my hair into a braid and toss it behind my back. Rolling the legs of my uniform up slightly, I reach for my moccasins and lace them up my calves.

Storming through the bathing chamber, I make my way to the hall that leads out of here when a section of floor to ceiling mirrors catches my eye.

I don't recognize the woman staring back at me. Aside from my moccasins, still spattered with mud, I couldn't be picked out from a room of Verenathians.

Bringing shaky hands to the scales at my hips and chest, I run my fingers across their hard planes and onto the softer scales below. Closing my eyes, I take a deep breath, trying to collect myself before leaving the relative safety of the secluded room—away from the prying eyes and questioning looks.

A Goramalan in heart and soul; I will need to become something else entirely now if I wish to live. Ashden and Avice, mother and father… all that

I've known and loved rest across the sea.

I force myself forward, shaking off the regret that threatens to sweep me off my feet.

CHAPTER 13

Today has been a long one. Your father has been out to sea for three days now, and the storms continue to rage. You are getting very tense with Ashden and I, as we are all stuck in the cottage until the rain lets up. You do not do well staying confined for any length of time. Your brother has been so patient with you as you do everything in your power to be the petulant little sister, but don't fret, the sun will come out soon enough.

Kieran is leaning against the wall, gazing out the glass doors when I emerge from the bathing chamber. Arms crossed over his chest, he must hear the pad of my moccasins because he turns to face me as I approach. I can't place the expression that flashes across his face, but it's quickly replaced by look of calm indifference. His eyes dart up and down my body, coming back to rest on my face.

Something stirs within me under his gaze, but I dismiss it.

"Feel better?"

The air tickling my exposed back seems to be taunting me. "I can't finish the last clasp," I grit out.

His lips tighten as he tries not to grin. "Would you like some help?"

Glaring death straight into him, I say sweetly, "If you would be so kind."

Frustration and embarrassment burn hot through me as he makes a swirling motion with his finger. Rolling my eyes, I turn, exposing my back to him.

The brush of his fingers against my skin sends a shiver through me, but I squash it beneath my doneness with the day.

"The trick is," he says into my ear as he finishes clasping the hook. "To do them halfway up the back before stepping into it."

Of course. Shame begins in my chest, crawling up my collarbones and staining my cheeks. He probably thinks I'm mindless, or that I wanted him to help me. The thought almost makes me choke.

"We don't have anything like this on Ra'goramal," I snap, turning to face him.

"Clothes?" He doesn't bother disguising his amusement.

"*Dragonhide*." I narrow my eyes at him. "And it's been an extremely long day. Forgive me if I'm not functioning at full capacity."

"Unsure of how to dress herself and likes to play the victim in situations she creates." He's barely containing the laugh in his grin now.

I don't give him the satisfaction of a response.

"Hungry?" he asks.

My stomach rumbles uncomfortably at the thought of food. "Yes," I say flatly, wanting nothing more than to be done with this conversation and eat.

"Come on." He leads me down the hall in front of us, speaking as he walks. "There's a mess hall in this wing."

His statement incites a flurry of new questions, and, irritated or not, I can't help myself.

"So do you all live here, in the Citadel?"

"No, only the Warbearers and Elders do. The rest of us live in the city bordering it," he says. "We spend most of our time here though."

"What do you do here?"

He shrugs. "Study; work; train."

"Study?"

"Our primary education classes are held here. All of our classes are, for that matter. The Court places huge emphasis on academics, so… it's all in here," he gestures widely.

"Why were there so many people in that first room, not doing… anything?" I ask.

He laughs, the bright sound ringing through the corridor. "That was one of the common areas. It's one of the places we can spend our free time. Do you guys not know how to have fun down there?"

The question leaves a bitterness in my stomach. "We don't really have time for fun."

He nods slowly, letting silence stretch between us, until we arrive at the mess hall. Thankfully, this room is empty as well.

I'm surprised to see the white marble that has become characteristic of the rest of the Citadel end, and the room made up of wooden planks instead. Fading sunlight filters down from windows near the vaulted ceiling, casting shadows on the gray stone floor. Bench-lined tables dot the room while a long wooden one runs the length of it.

My mouth waters at the sight of the table, stocked with fruits, cheeses, baked goods, and dried strips of meat. Kieran leads me to it and I greedily make my selection.

"Don't expect any full course meals here. It's mainly stuff like this. We're still responsible to feed ourselves in our own homes. This is for training and studying hours," he says.

I grab two sweet pastries, a roll, an apple, several chunks of hard cheese, and five strips of dried mutton. Sitting down at the nearest table, I start to devour my food, brushing all pretense of awkwardness aside as my hunger takes over.

Kieran grabs an orange and several strips of beef before striding over to sit across from me.

"Breakfast is always available, though. Between classes, training, and supply runs, this place is full in the mornings," he says, peeling the orange.

My mood begins to lighten with each bite. Cocking my head, I ask, "What do you guys train for?"

He doesn't miss a beat as he responds. "We're a defensive territory; it's in our blood."

"So," I pause, trying to recall all that we're taught of Verenathia. "Combat training?"

"Yes. Combat, patrols, strategic defense, survival techniques, airborne attacks—all of it."

I chew my food thoughtfully. "Does that mean all of Verenathia is one massive army?" All of the weapons Markell and I have made; the increasing demand…

He pauses for a moment, considering my question. "Essentially, yes, if the need arose."

I nod slowly. Verenathia was the defensive powerhouse during the last war, so it makes sense that they would stay on top of their training—being the only territory within a several-hundred mile radius capable of defending Ra'goramal. And themselves, I suppose. Goramalans have no military training and a thorough lack of weapons; all of them are sent here.

"And the Warbearers?"

He pops a slice of orange into his mouth. "What about them?"

"Well… they hold the Safeguards in place, right? With their magic?"

"Yes," he drawls.

"Do they… well, are they, uh—"

He tilts his head, his eyes gleaming mischievously. "What's that, little raven?"

The cheese turns tasteless in my mouth. "What?"

"A little bird who flew away from home." He inclines his head. "And your hair—"

"Don't call me that." Grief rears itself, threatening to crush the air from my lungs.

That amused, wicked expression doesn't leave. He opens his mouth again but I cut him off.

"Don't," my breathing becomes uneven. "Call me that. You don't know me, and I sure as hell don't know you. We are not friends. The only reason we're here right now is because I made what was likely the biggest mistake of my life, and you were unlucky enough to get stuck with me."

He watches me intently, his amusement finally having faded before silently finishing his orange.

Brushing the peels into his hand, he stands. "Are you ready to go?"

I glance down at the crumbs and apple cores on the table, trying to find my composure as I wipe them into my hand.

"Yes." Dumping the remnants into a bin near the door, I decide to grab another pastry on our way out. I linger a heartbeat longer than necessary as I make my selection, if only to regain some semblance of control, then meet him in the doorway.

A curious glance, and then he leads me back into the maze of marble halls. With my small outburst, the unknown looming before, and the distinct lack of distraction that our meal provided, my palms start sweating nervously. The pastry in my hand unfortunately takes the brunt of my emotions, and I wince when I realize I have it clutched in a death grip.

Kieran doesn't seem to notice any of this as he guides me away from the mess hall. "The Citadel was built with extra quarters for housing military aid and the like. The rooms are rarely used now—usually for those who are displaced—but they're fully stocked with anything you'll need."

I nod, keeping an eye on our direction, mentally mapping my way back to the food. The sun has finally dipped below the horizon, and the fading light casts a cool glow over everything.

A sense of empty finality settles over me as I watch the Verenathians make their way in the direction of the glass doors. They stroll casually through the corridors, laughing and chatting all the while. I draw less attention now in my suit, but have still garnered more than one confused glance as my onlooker tries to place me.

A shudder crawls its way down my spine. I'm going to be left in this endless place with only the Warbearers and Elders. What wing do they reside in—how close is it to where I'll be staying?

I do my best to repress the thought. Kieran has promised my safety, and though I may not trust him, if I were to be executed, it would have happened already.

We come to a great room, larger even than the commons. A wide marble staircase rests in the center, extending down from a mezzanine that runs the perimeter of the room. Gold winks at me from where it's inlaid along the railing of the balcony, while a domed crystal ceiling blankets the openness above me. I blink once, twice when I see the doors lining the mezzanine—each empty and waiting for inhabitants.

Kieran continues to the foot of the staircase, glancing back when I hesitate. "Are you coming?"

My body is leaden as I try to push myself forward, the striking beauty before me doing nothing to calm my racing heart.

Taking a deep breath, I stride past him, unwilling to give in to my mounting panic. Behind me, a snort of… amusement? Derision? I can't decide, but he follows on my heels, gesturing to a door when we reach the top.

"Here. I'll be in the mess hall at first light."

I nod, swallowing.

"There's always food there, and you remember where the bath chamber is? Your room should have everything else you need."

The words are unexpectedly gentle, and the touch of concern in his eyes sets me on edge. "Thank you."

Dipping his head, he turns and stalks off without another word. I almost call out to him so I won't have to be alone in this foreign place, but instead open the door before me.

The room is bathed in dim light, and relatively simply furnished considering the luxury of the rest of the Citadel. A large bed with a plush comforter and several plump pillows sits in the center of the room. To its left, a wooden vanity, its panels polished to a mirror finish. An armoire, identical to the ones in the bathing chamber, sits beside me near the door. And the window… that window; the *sky*.

A deepening shade of lavender—the sky is the only thing visible through the window from where I stand. I shut the door quietly and hurry across the room. My jaw drops—actually drops—at the sight before me.

Lush greenery veils the rolling expanse outside the walls of the Citadel. The landscape itself looks like the undulating sea, climbing and dipping; continuing on and on before eventually bleeding into the sky. Flowers I don't recognize populate the distance in multicolored clusters, but there are no trees, only massive dark boulders that rest across its rolling face, leading to mountains that tower along the edge of the isle.

White stone bricks reinforce the hill that rises high to my right. Far above, atop that hill, I can see the wall that encompasses the supply field.

The setting sun casts the land into deep shadow, beginning to blend the land and sky into one celestial body as the heavens reach their fingers around us.

I close my eyes and rest my forehead on the cool glass, all the questions of the day rushing at me in a flurry.

I'm alive.

I'm alive.

I'm alive.

Amidst the headache, the only thought—the realization—that loops itself through my mind.

I am alive.

I stare out over the isle until long after the sun has set. Stars blink into view one by one, so close I could pluck them right out of their homes.

Turning away from the window, my body heavy with exhaustion, I move to the bed. Not bothering to undress, I fold back the thick comforters and plop down. The plush bed absorbs my weight, caressing my tiredness in luxurious comfort.

I close my eyes, but a flash of black immediately startles me out of my stupor. I glance quickly around the room, making sure I'm still alone. The air crackles with tension, and for a moment, I feel like I'm back on Ra'goramal. My chest tightens.

It's just exhaustion.

Squeezing my eyes shut, I'm unable to shake the weight pressing in on me, as if it's trying to say, "*You're here. I know you're here. I can feel you.*"

Taking deep breaths to calm my racing heart, I try to force the thoughts out of my mind. My palms are sweating again as the tension reaches a peak.

Another flash of black streaks through my mind, this time in the form of soulless eyes. I suppress a cry as the weight breaks around me, leaving me shaking on the bed.

The moment is gone just as quickly as it arrived, and I'm left wondering if I imagined it.

***

My body is rejuvenated as I walk to the mess hall, but my mind is just as weary as when I fell asleep. I'm only halfway sure I'm taking the right turns. I slept dreamlessly, but that darkness lurked at the edge of my consciousness all night, just out of view.

Somehow I make it to the final corridor before the mess hall and snap back to alertness when I hear voices and movement. I've been too deep in my thoughts to think about the fact that there will be others here besides Kieran.

My mouth goes dry as I approach the entry, hoping I'll be able to slip in unnoticed.

As if on cue, all eyes turn to me when I step into the room. My cheeks heat as my gaze darts around, landing on faces I don't recognize.

I finally find Kieran and my heart sinks when I see him sitting with a man and woman I've never seen before.

His gaze meets mine, drawn by the attention of the crowd. There's a playful glint in his eyes as he looks at me, slowly bringing a tumbler to his lips and taking a long, slow drink.

A surge of determination fills me at the challenge. Flicking my braid behind my back, I stride to the food table, dodging other breakfast goers. Making my selection, I move to their table and sit down right beside Kieran; stuffing down the spike of adrenaline at his proximity with a bite of my muffin.

The two sitting across the table exchange glances with each other and Kieran, clearly waiting for an introduction. Not deigning to have him speak for me, I clear my throat.

"Hi, I'm Rae."

"Hi. I'm Sebastian," the man says, his warm bronze skin reminding me of Raimy. "Kieran's boyfriend."

Before I can react, the woman starts laughing, and Kieran reaches out and smacks Sebastian on the side of the head.

"What?" Sebastian dramatically raises his arms against his head. "I didn't know her romantic affiliations. I had to clear the air." His comment garners another laugh from the woman, and an annoyed look from Kieran.

"I'm Opal," she smiles kindly. "Kieran's sister… You don't look like you're from around here." Her long blonde hair is pulled up into two knots on each side of her head, soft tendrils falling down around violet eyes. She pauses, cocking her head to the side. "I honestly never thought I'd say that."

"Oh, please," Sebastian says. "Everyone and their dragon has been talking about a Goramalan sneaking in on a supply shipment. That takes some balls."

I shrug, smiling in spite of myself. "It's me, the crazy Goramalan."

"Why did you do it?" Opal asks. I'm surprised by the question, but I respect her directness.

"I honestly don't know." It's not a total lie—I'm still not fully sure what I'm doing here or what I'm looking for.

"Man, balls but no brains. Can't have it all," Sebastian sighs. Opal jabs him in the side, and he laughs, wincing. "I'm just kidding. I can't imagine being stuffed in a hot crate for hours, especially when it's inconceivably illegal. It was honestly genius. I probably would have died."

Opal takes a massive bite from a scone and casts a side-eyed glance at him. "Don't hurt yourself with big words," she mumbles.

Kieran, who hasn't spoken a word since my arrival, grins. Sebastian follows my gaze toward his friend.

Has he told them of his conversation with the Court of Elders? Does everyone here know of the exception made for me? And if so, do they question how, or why?

"What's on the agenda for today, boss?" Sebastian asks.

A devious grin spreads across Kieran's face. I blink as he drops the biscuit to his plate and rises, stepping onto his seat.

"Everyone, eyes on me!" His voice projects through the room, clear and confident. Every gaze in the room turns his direction, first noticing him before settling on me.

Oh, no.

"This is Rae from Ra'goramal. Before any of you ask any stupid questions: yes, the punishment for coming here is execution and yes, she should be dead right now. I've already spoken with the Court and Warbearers; she's going to be allowed a temporary stay here so as not to strain relations with Ra'goramal. Laws are laws, but this particular one has never been broken before. The Goramalans are fully aware of the repercussions, but still wouldn't take kindly to the death of their own."

I want to dissolve into the floor. Many of the expressions facing me are confused—some outrightly hostile.

"You are to treat her as one of your own. If you can't, you can deal with me. You are not to breathe a word of it to the Goramalans on your supply runs. If you have a problem with any of the decisions made, feel free to take it up with your Elders and Warbearers." He says the last two words as if it's not really an option. "Do I make myself clear?"

Furious whispering rips through those gathered as they process. Heads dart my direction, scanning me up and down.

"I *said*, do I make myself clear?"

There's not an ounce of doubt in him—not a trace of fear. He's completely at ease up there, dozens of eyes on him.

The whispering hushes.

"Good." Kieran hops down from the bench and takes his seat beside me again.

"What was that?" I hiss.

"That was me ensuring you don't get harassed. You're welcome." He pops a bite of sausage in his mouth.

"I can take care of myself."

Sebastian rubs the stubble on his chin. "Against fully trained soldiers? I mean, no offense, but Kier did you a favor."

All he did is make me public enemy number one, but I roll my eyes and resume eating, ignoring Kieran's attention even as it warms my skin.

"Nobody made you come here, you know. That was all you, and if I were you, I'd be grateful to not be dead right now."

"Or soon-to-be dragon feed," Opal adds.

They're right. All of this was my choice. They don't owe me anything.

Motion draws my attention from across the room. Peering over Kieran, my heart starts to race the moment I spot Laurel. She's dutifully ignoring us as she downs her breakfast, sullen amidst her talkative group. But another man—the one, I recognize, who approached me yesterday—stares right at me. A sneer is written below eyes burning with hatred. Smirking, his gaze pointedly travels up and down my body, slowly.

I shudder, feeling as if I've bathed in oil, and turn my attention back to my half eaten muffin. "I didn't know dragons ate people," I mutter.

"They don't," Sebastian chuckles.

"Maybe you could visit the library," Opal bursts out. "You can learn all you want or need to know about us and this place. Assuming that's why you came here, I guess." Her brow knits together.

I give her an appreciative smile while eagerness, though timid, flickers inside me. I can only imagine the wonders a Verenathian library holds.

Sebastian adds over a mouthful of food, "If that's your thing."

Opal rolls her eyes. "We all know it definitely isn't yours."

I give them both a perplexed look. "What, reading?"

"Reading, writing, studying," Opal drawls. "Basically anything that requires a functioning brain."

Sebastian feigns a hurt expression. "I'll have you know I've passed all of my courses with flying colors."

Kieran snorts.

"What courses do you have?" I ask.

"History, math, science, literature—the usual," Kieran responds. "Once you complete those, you get to move onto the good stuff."

"What's the good stuff?"

His eyes gleam as he angles himself toward me. "The arts, astronomy, music… magic."

Sebastian dips his head solemnly toward Kieran. "A man of culture," he says reverently, earning him another nudge in the ribs by Opal.

I stifle a grin before eyeing Kieran, and ask hesitantly, "Do you enjoy that sort of thing?"

"What thing?" His head tilts ever so slightly.

I avert my gaze, my cheeks warming. "Studying, reading—any of it."

"It's all he ever does," Sebastian sighs.

Kieran smiles, and his left cheek dimples in a way I haven't noticed before. *Author above.*

"Yes," he offers. "If I'm not working, I'm usually in the Library."

I cock my head. "When you say work, do you mean retrieving shipments from Ra'goramal?"

Opal responds brightly. "Yes. This place, the Citadel, is kind of like the hub for all of us. All of our shipments… from you guys," she adds, somewhat awkwardly. "Come directly here, where they're sorted and dispatched. That's why, aside from academics, you see so many people here."

I nod, beginning to piece it all together. Not entirely unlike Ra'goramal. My newfound distaste starts to soften.

"Speaking of," Sebastian drawls. "Duty calls." He and Opal rise from the table, clearing their breakfast remnants, and head out of the mess hall.

"Good luck," Opal calls over her shoulder as they depart.

Our table falls into stunted silence, Kieran and I sitting so close I can feel the warmth radiating off of him. I try to eat more but the muffin has turned to sand on my tongue and I find I can't swallow properly.

"Supply runs?" I venture lightly as I take a sip of water to dislodge the anxiety in my throat.

"Yes," he says casually. His broad shoulders take up most of my view from this distance, and I politely disregard the perfect cling of his suit to his biceps.

"Do you get out of your duties while I'm here?"

"Yes, I'm out of rotations for now. Can't trust a foreigner lurking about on her own."

"Interesting," I mutter. "Now that we're both in better moods, can you tell me what was actually said yesterday in the Court?"

His gaze shifts for a moment. "Well," he starts. "The Accords state that any Goramalan found trespassing on Verenathia is authorized for immediate execution and—"

"I know."

"I was getting there," he drawls. "But, no Goramalan has ever been crazy enough to dare come here."

I fight the urge to squirm in my seat.

"Because it has never happened, the Elders were lenient in bestowing punishment—said they didn't want to strain relations between the territories. Apparently, that clause was more specifically geared toward interterritorial travel to prevent Goramalans from settling on Verenathia and 'polluting the bloodline.'" He rolls his eyes. "They felt it best to let this one incident slip, as long as you return home. Don't expect it to happen in the future or with anyone else, though. Laws are written for a reason."

I don't miss the low note of warning in his voice. And while the Court of Elders may have felt like allowing an exception, I know the Synod back home will be less… understanding. As far as anyone on Ra'goramal is concerned, I've broken the Accords—in effect, committing capital treason.

"How long do I have here?"

"As long as you need." I can see the question in the quizzical look he gives me and know what he's going to ask before he even opens his mouth.

"So…" he levels his curiosity on me. "Why *did* you come here?"

"The threat of execution sounded like a thrill," I quip, pulling in a long breath as I try to buy time. Mentally preparing myself for the dismissal or judgment I'm sure is to come.

He only waits. Calmly; expectantly.

I decide to dive in head first—no point in veiling the truth. "Okay, this is going to sound ridiculous, but, bear with me." His emerald eyes practically glow in the early morning light. "Have you ever watched the way a mother looks at her child? Truly watched? The way her eyes sparkle, almost like she's glowing from some invisible source within? And in the smallest interaction, she'll give a part of that light to someone else, offering them hope or joy or… whatever it is they need in that moment?"

"Yes," he says quietly, a contemplative look on his face.

"Or the way the lightning splinters across the sea, fracturing and shattering into a million pieces? The way it paints the sky? Or a clear sunset, the goodness to be found in new life, or at the end of a long one." The words come faster now, flowing from a well of emotion. "Take bees, for example. They simply exist. All they know is to collect nectar to take care of the hive. And by doing just that simple action, they pollinate our plants—providing life and sustenance for us. The smallest of creatures, and they keep life flowing in an endless cycle. They give us life. And then there's the joy we'll find in admiring the flowers they helped to grow, or even the honey they provide." I look at him insistently, hoping for understanding, fighting against the fear of rejection. "There's a song inside everything. The grass, the sea, the mountains—in the heart of every person I've ever met. Every single laugh and tear and… It's always there, but it gets drowned out by all of the noise of, of…"

I shake my head. "I don't know. I can't help but feel that that's the way things are supposed to be—how it's meant to be. Such harmony and beauty in everything as it all works together perfectly. Every thing beautiful in its own right, existing for the purpose it was created for.

"It's art," I breathe. "A masterpiece." I'm surprised to see no judgment in his expression, only a quiet interest that asks for more.

"But it doesn't," he murmurs, quietly enough that I wonder if he's talking to himself.

"But it doesn't," I repeat. "Something is wrong. I can't explain how or why, but something is wrong. Everything is almost…" I pause, searching for the correct word. "Muted, if that makes sense. Like we're all being crushed under an invisible weight, forced to step out of that seamless perfection into something… wrong."

He watches me with an unreadable expression. My stomach clenches under that masked gaze, the hope that I had for understanding quickly dying.

"What did you think you could gain by coming here?" he finally asks.

I hesitate, knowing I'm going to sound like a fool. "I don't know," I say quietly. "I've always felt drawn to this place. I can't explain it, but there's something different here. Almost like the magic in the Safeguards was calling to me. I've never been able to tell if it was actually the magic, or just me."

Fool. Daydreaming fool.

Maybe this was a mistake. Coming here and now trying to explain something that has been burning in my blood for as long as I can remember. I ready myself for his laughter, his judgment, and glance toward the entrance to the mess hall so I can make a quick escape from the shame that is surely coming.

"I understand," he says simply. I dare a glance through lowered brows and am shocked to find him sincere.

Stabs of pain beat in time with my heart. All I had wanted in sharing these same thoughts with Ashden was to be understood. I know my brother tries his best, but I don't know if he was able to grasp the ceaseless chaos in my heart.

"Thank you," I whisper.

A spasm of butterflies flutters in my stomach when I realize how close we now sit to each other. I shoot to my feet and begin hastily clearing the table.

This man is an almost perfect stranger—and one who could still have me executed at any moment, technically. I can't let my guard fall from one conversation.

He joins me in gathering the leftovers. "We better start looking."

"For what?"

That beautiful dimpled grin shows itself. "We're going to find you some answers."

CHAPTER 14

Life is much like a painting, my precious daughter. From a distance, it's beautiful, breathtaking, potentially awe-inspiring. But when you get closer to the canvas, you begin to see ridges in the brushstrokes. Small sections may not be blended properly, and some colors will blot out others. Something that seemed flawless from a distance will have uneven lines when you become intimately acquainted with it, and you may find imperfections in the canvas itself.

My heart feels a little bit lighter as Kieran leads me to the library, but begins to falter at the looks given by almost everyone we pass in the corridors—all of whom do a double take or stare in wide-eyed shock.

Either word travels fast here, or they can sense I'm not of the same blood. Can smell it in the fear now radiating from me, or can see it in the way I shy from their stares, clinging close to Kieran.

We pass under a lofty arched entryway and into the library. The room is only about the width of two corridors, extending far ahead, where it ends in a floor to ceiling arched windowpane. It's designed like a corridor as well, with alcoves dotting the walls down the length of it. Bright sunlight spills onto the white marble floor in gleaming puddles. The entirety of its walls are covered with built-in bookshelves, stacked from floor to ceiling.

Looking up at the glass ceiling, I'm unable to halt my gasp. Another floor of the library lies atop this one, the same bookshelves lining its walls. I look closer and see another above it, and yet another above that one, on and on—the library towering up the Citadel on planes of glass.

"Here we are," Kieran gives a dramatic flare of his hand as we enter.

"This is amazing," I whisper, absorbing every detail. I inhale the scent of parchment, surprised to find no hint of dust or mildew, nothing to denote its age.

"It really is something," he says as his eyes rove about the room. "I love it here."

"I believe you mentioned that already. Maybe that's where the insufferability comes from; the scholarly type usually has heads too big for their bodies." I'm shocked at how easily the words find their way out of me.

He laughs, a genuine laugh, the sound of it bouncing mirthfully off the marble.

I follow him deeper into the library, marveling at the beauty of it all. Two comfortable looking leather chairs sit in each bright alcove, separated by a small stone table.

Drifting to one of the shelves near me, I slow as I run my finger along the spines of the books that rest there.

"These are all about fishing."

"Don't look so surprised," he says, sauntering over. "We've been known to grace the waters every so often."

I snort.

We make our way down the rows and rows of books. I'm not sure what I'm looking for, but the enjoyment of being in the library is good enough for me in this moment.

Kieran was right—every topic and subject I could ever want or need is here. Books ranging from cooking to masonry; basket weaving to poetry. Stories of romance and tragedy, adventure, horror, all of it.

Reaching the far end of this level, I find a ladder built into the wide frame of the window. I give Kieran a questioning look, and he nods encouragingly. That's all the confirmation I need. Hand over hand, I pull myself up the ladder while Kieran follows on my heels.

We reach the second story, the glass beneath our feet crystal clear as I gaze down onto the first floor. My head spins for a moment as I orient myself—countless levels spanning above us.

This floor is set up identically to the one below it, down to the same chairs and tables in the alcoves.

I could do this forever. Walking down the sheet of glass, I feel as if I'm floating along some ethereal plane. I graze the titles of books like I'm picking berries from a bush—selecting the juiciest ones and mentally tucking them away for later.

Reaching the back wall, I find a stone lectern set in the corner. An aged parchment rests beneath its milky translucent barrier.

Magic.

The whole thing is so similar to the one we have in the library on Ra'goramal, a weight settles in my stomach.

The Accords. I briefly scan the document, although its contents are already imprinted in my memory. But as I skim, I notice where ours ends, this one continues—a second page resting behind the first.

My brow knits together. I reach out to flip the browned page, crinkled and faded with age, but Kieran's voice calls from the row of shelves he's retreated to.

"What are your thoughts on the art of undergarments?" he asks, holding a ridiculous book in his hands—a very intricately illustrated set of women's undergarments on the cover.

I roll my eyes and turn my attention back to the Accords, but something tight grips my chest.

"Where are my people? The ones taken for the Culling."

He leans against the shelf beside him. "They're here, in the Citadel," he says easily.

"I know *that*, but how come I haven't seen anyone?" This place is massive, but surely I would have crossed paths with someone by now.

His eyes meet mine for a moment before wandering to the shelves behind me. "You've read the Accords. They spend most of their time in the Inner Sanctum with the Warbearers."

"Oh..."

"What?"

"I just thought they would have been given a little more freedom, is all."

Amongst art and dragons and academic exploits, my ass. The tightness in my chest turns to shame.

"Residing in the Inner Sanctum doesn't equate to a lack of freedom. The Warbearers need assistance with menial tasks; performing the magic that holds the Safeguards in place is very energy-consuming."

Tucking away that berry of information, I allow myself to be distracted by the gilded spine resting at eye level near him. *Field of Stars* scrolls down it in bold, golden letters.

I close the gap between us, running my finger across the cool gilding as I slide it from its shelf. The ornate patterning continues, feathering across its olive-green cover. "What's the Field of Stars?"

To my shock, Kieran snatches the book out of my hands. "Wouldn't you like to know?" he says, his eyes flashing playfully.

"Yes, I would, actually."

He shrugs. "Dragons and such."

My breath hitches. "Dragons?"

"Maybe," he says cryptically.

I roll my eyes, stalking back toward the Accords. "You don't have to be such a prick."

"But why wouldn't I? It's so much fun."

Ignoring him, I've almost reached the lectern when he calls, "You're not going to find anything you want to see there."

I pause. "What do you mean?"

He nonchalantly flips through the *Field of Stars*. "Wartime treaties typically aren't a very riveting read."

"Coming from the history scholar."

He sighs—such a long-suffering sound. "Why don't we find something that will help you now, instead of a document I'm sure has already been forced down your throat. And maybe, if you weren't so difficult, I'd show you the dragons."

"Because *I'm* the one with the problem right now."

He gives me a look as if to say *aren't you*?

I blow out an exasperated breath. Resolving to read it at a later date, I start scanning the rows, searching for answers to the nagging questions in my mind. Finding a book on the history and development of the Citadel, I run my hands across its worn leather—smooth from age and use.

"That's a good one," Kieran nods as I tuck the book under my arm.

"Yeah?" History has never been my subject of choice, but what better way to gain some insight than to read how the very building we're in came about?

"Yes," he responds, starting back toward the opposite end of the room. "Have you never wondered why there's so much glass in a structure built for wartime defense?"

The question catches me off-guard. I assumed the Citadel was built as a display of power and wealth. "I hadn't," I say, "but now that you mentioned it, I suppose I need to know."

A smile cracks his handsome face. "It was originally built to be impenetrable, made out of stone and wood, and was used to house the wounded during the war. After the war—and the Accords were signed—our masons and glassworkers set about redoing it to showcase Verenathia's emphasis on beauty rather than power."

Interesting. "Well it *is* beautiful."

We leave the second floor and make our way through to the beginning of the first. I hesitate at the ledger used for recording book loans, but Kieran takes the quill and puts my book under his name.

"Thanks," I offer him a half-smile.

He winks, striding easily out of the library. An overwhelming sense of loneliness creeps over me as I follow him out into the corridor.

I wish I had someone here I could process everything with—someone who could help me start to make sense of all the things swirling through my mind.

Everyone I've ever known, everyone I love, rests miles across the ocean. If Avice were here, she would offer advice and insight in her quiet way, and snicker when I tell her how Kieran's cheek dimples when he smiles.

A pang of regret hits me so hard it almost takes my breath away.

And Ashden. My chest constricts, making it hard to breathe.

"Are you okay?" Kieran looks back, not breaking his stride. Genuine concern clouds his eyes.

I shake the thoughts off and exhale a sharp breath. My voice is as bright as my smile as I say, "I've never been better."

***

"Tell me about yourself." Kieran has himself draped across the sofa next to mine, his leg dangling over the arm.

This room—unlike the commons, which was mainly filled with tables and benches—*this* room was designed purely for comfort. Couches, chaise lounges, and large reclining chairs are spread haphazardly over exotic-looking, colorful rugs. The walls, which are the same paneled wood as the mess hall, are set off by the technicolor patchwork.

Most of the seating has been arranged to face the back wall, which is comprised entirely of a single glass pane. Orange-hued rays filter in through the floor-to-ceiling window, warming the colors of the rugs.

"Why?" I laugh.

When we arrived, I had gaped at the view beyond the windows. They overlook the same broad, lush lands that I saw from the window in my own room; the green so rich and vibrant it holds a dreamlike quality. The glass is polished so clearly—not a streak or imperfection in sight—that standing before it feels like falling into a field of oblivion. As if there's nothing between me and the sea of green, going on and on until it fades into the sparkling sky.

"*Why*?" he parrots. "Why not? We're going to be spending a fair amount of time together over the duration of your stay. I feel it's only fair that we do so as something more than vague acquaintances."

I level a blank stare at him. "Where has that kindness been this whole time?"

"Well, typically, it's proper to respond with gratitude when someone saves your life. I happen to think I've been quite chivalrous."

I smirk. "I wouldn't say I've been entirely ungrateful."

His eyes dance with amusement. "I wouldn't say you've been entirely great at showing it, so let's start over. Hi, I'm Kieran; it's nice to meet you."

"Hi," I fight my smile. "I'm Rae. Thank you for saving my life."

"That's better," he says, clapping slowly. "And you're welcome. Now, tell me about yourself."

Inclining my head, I watch two dragons soar distantly, no more than two black shadows against the glowing backdrop.

"Well," I begin. "I live with my brother. I was assigned, back home, to work at the Smithshop, so that's where I spend most of my time now."

"Mmm," he hums. "But what do you do when you're not forced to sling mallets? Or do you enjoy bending things to your will?"

I cast him a sidelong glance. "Would you find it fascinating if I did?"

He shrugs. "Possibly."

"Then, no. I don't particularly enjoy my duties. I'd much rather spend my time in the grasslands. Or at the cliffs, the shore. Pretty much anywhere but there."

"I see."

I narrow my eyes at him. "What about you?"

"What about me?"

"Anything."

He's quiet for a moment, a contemplative look on his face.

"I don't particularly like it here."

I cock my head, caught off-guard by the admission. "What's not to like? You have everything you could ever want or need. Try living in Ra'goramal for a day, then tell me you don't like it here."

His burning emerald gaze finds mine. "But do I—do we—truly have everything we want? Need, yes. But want?"

I chew my bottom lip. We've only known each other for a day and he's already complaining about his life?

"I know those things aren't actually important, though, in the grand scheme of things."

A part of me does understand, though I won't admit it. Yet, maybe I already had when I tried to explain my reasoning for coming here. The bone-deep ache for something beyond my understanding. I don't, however, see how he could possibly be struggling with similar thoughts and desires when he's surrounded by such ease.

I want my parents on this side of reality with me and would give anything to see them again.

It's probably just Verenathian arrogance.

"They aren't, especially when someone's biggest concern is what they'll choose for breakfast," I retort.

He chuckles, but there's an unexplained sadness in the sound. "You're right, it would probably do all of us some good not to focus on the things we want, but can't have."

I consider asking him what it is that he wants, but there's still a tightness in my throat over the thought of my parents.

"Do you have a family?" I venture.

"I do," his face softens. "You've met Opal, and my mom is a healer on the outer ring. And you?"

I give a slight shake of my head, unable to push past that tightness. And noticing the absent mention of a father, I again decide to leave some things unsaid. "What's the outer ring?"

He seems to understand my hesitation. "Our residential sector. The city of Verenathia is built in rings that spread out from the Citadel."

The Citadel sits so grand, so commanding from its home atop the hill it crests. I imagine it looming over the city, Verenathians living under its shadow. "A bit pretentious, don't you think?"

He grins. "I do, indeed. It's a shame I wasn't around all those years ago to give my input on the design."

A smile tugs at my lips. The setting sun has deepened into richer shades of amber, rose, and a touch of violet as it sinks to the horizon. Everywhere the light touches gleams with a soft warmth–the colors on the rugs dance under it; the walls as rich as molten chocolate.

"Can I see the city?" I ask.

He nods. "Of course. We can go tomorrow."

Tomorrow. Here, in Verenathia. A day promised in a forbidden land.

I let his words stretch between us while a comfortable silence fills the room. The warmth of the setting sun eases me into drowsiness.

Not for the first time, I'm shocked to find myself so at ease. This man is still practically a stranger, and could very well be disguising the same feelings as Laurel. Yet, here I am.

Straightening, I pull my heavy-lidded gaze away from the window. Kieran's eyes are already on me, and a warmth unrelated to the setting sun starts to creep up my neck. "I'd like to go to my room now."

He smiles lazily at me. "Are you sure? It's not even the best part yet," he gestures toward the sunset.

"Yes." I rise to my feet.

He follows, stretching as he stands. "I'll walk you back."

"No," I say quickly, a bit breathlessly. "I-um, I mean no, thank you. I can find the way myself."

A wickedly dimpled smirk. "Are you sure? It's no trouble."

I turn to leave, trying to escape the raging heat under my skin. "Yes, I'm sure. Thank you, though. I'll see you tomorrow."

Without giving him the time to respond, I quickly exit the room, feeling his eyes on my back as I leave.

CHAPTER 15

ASHDEN

Wood shavings from the piece I've been absentmindedly whittling litter the table. I've spent the past few days half-present at the Storeouse, only to come home and mindlessly carve bits of driftwood until I fall into a fitful sleep. The loss of both my sister and Raimy feels like an infection, slowly poisoning me. So I whittle, my body itching for a distraction.

A knock sounds at the door.

"Come in," I shout from my spot at the table.

Avice appears behind the opening door, her cheeks flushed, pausing while she fidgets with the hem of her uniform.

"Oh, hey." My knife—one Rae made for me when she first started at the Smithsop—flashes in the candlelight as I set it down. "Why did you knock?"

"I, um… no reason." She practically bounces from foot to foot. "I need to show you something."

In spite of my self-inflicted mood, I can't help my curiosity. Her excitement is contagious. "What is it?"

Slamming the door shut, she rushes to the table and carefully reaches under her shirt. I avert my gaze for a heartbeat when the skin of her stomach flashes.

Slipping out a book I've never seen before, she sets it reverently on the table.

I glance up at her, my brow pinched. "I don't understand."

"I know," she says, wincing. "I found it hidden in Lichera's desk."

A laugh escapes me. That's why she's acting so odd. "You mean you stole Lichera's personal property? Innocent little Avice?"

She blushes bright pink now. "Technically, yes."

As if unable to restrain herself any longer, she caresses the face of the book. I watch her slender fingers run over the time-worn leather. It's old—very old—and I can't find a title anywhere on it.

I lean forward. "Can I see?"

She sits in the chair opposite mine, sliding the book to me.

Running my hands across its surface, I note the fine lines and grooves in the leather. It's black, and there's some sort of pattern. A line here, a raised spot there, a curve in the—

"This is dragonhide!" I cry in a hoarse whisper as realization erupts through me.

Avice's eyes widen and she carefully snatches the book out of my grasp. Tracing her fingers along its front and back, she gapes.

"Author above," she breathes. "It is."

"Open it," I say, hardly able to contain my burning curiosity.

Spreading it out before us, she gently opens it. The inscription on the inside, faded by time, is barely legible. One by one, she flips the pages, each creaking with age.

It's older than anything I've ever seen.

The ink is nothing but the color of tea-stain on the yellowed parchment, and in a language I don't recognize. I cock my head as she slowly flips through the strange pages.

"What is this?" she breathes.

She flips again but there—finally, a page that has been well protected from light and prying eyes. Darker than the rest, neat words line the page from top to bottom.

In *our* language.

I lean forward, scanning the words. "This is just an in depth account of Verenathia's history."

Avice chews her bottom lip, nodding her head in agreement. "Mmhmm," she hums.

We read in silence for several moments until I ask, "Why would Lichera have this?"

She furrows her brow, her head tilted contemplatively. "I'm not sure. What language do you think it's written in?"

"One I've never seen before, that's for sure." I grab my piece of chunked-up wood and began carving again. "And why has part of it been rewritten?"

"Or written over," she muses.

Wood shavings begin falling on the table again as my mind wanders. Verenathia's establishment and development affect us little. From what I remember… Ra'goramal didn't have a strong relationship with them before the War. Neighboring territories in proximity, but they sourced their provisions elsewhere—or provided for themselves.

Our history on them is murky at best. The fact that Lichera is in possession of this book is nothing short of baffling. It's clearly something significant, but why wouldn't we have studied it during our education years?

Avice sucks in a breath. "It's at least 1,000 years old."

I blink. "That's not possible. Most of our oldest manuscripts were destroyed in the War."

Everything was destroyed in the War. Our harbors were invaded by outsiders, and the smoke of Ra'goramal's pillaging rose high enough to alert the Verenathians. It isn't recorded why, but they swept in to fight tooth and nail. Thrunall involved themselves, then Pulrye, and the battle wasn't won until the Warbearers stepped in, obliterating everything with their magic. The Verenathians fought hard, but it wasn't enough. Without the Warbearers, we would have been wiped out completely. Much of the town was burnt—the library and all official offices included—which resulted in us losing most of our ancient texts and manuscripts. Something like this shouldn't exist.

"Unless it was kept somewhere safe," she suggests.

"Maybe." I eye the book warily. The use of dragonhide binding, along with the fact that it's been hiding in Lichera's desk have to be the only way it's still legible, and in one piece. It's a marvel and a mystery, and…

"Whatever the reason," I slice a long, satisfying sliver off of the wood. "We shouldn't keep it too long. I think it's best to take it back as soon as possible."

"But don't you want to find out what it means?" she asks, her eyes still glued to the pages.

I smirk, in spite of myself. "Of course I do, but I don't want Lichera to have your head for snooping around in his stuff."

She glares at me.

"Why were you snooping?"

Holding up her hands, she reveals ink-stained fingertips. "Not snooping. Cleaning."

A laugh, an actual laugh—the first since Rae left, huffs out of me.

"There was a hidden compartment underneath his desk," she says, eyes trained on the pages in front of her. "I only found it because I dropped a bottle of ink."

I snort.

Her face, bright with excitement, now begins to dim—confusion and concern taking its place.

"What is it?"

Pursing her lips, her brows continue to knit together until a stark line has formed between them.

"Avice," I demand.

"I don't understand," she murmurs.

I restrain myself from snatching the book out of her grasp. "What's wrong?"

Her distant gaze meets mine. "It's not just about Verenathia's history. It talks about the Warbearers and the type of magic they use to keep the Safeguards. It also speaks of the source of their magic…" her voice trails off.

"Which is?"

"I don't know," she shakes her head. "It-I… I think it's referencing another book."

"Was there another book in his desk?"

She shakes her head. "Not that I saw. Granted, I didn't look very hard, either."

My mind runs over everything I know about such things. Slowly, her eyes begin to widen as they scan the rewritten sections.

"Avice?"

She brings a hand to her mouth. "There's an island," she whispers. "The rest of the information must be in this… other book, but the island—" her eyes dart across the page. "The source of the Warbearers' magic—it's from an island."

"An island?" I can't help but feel useless as I say, again, "I don't understand. Like Verenathia?"

"No… I don't—no, not like that, I don't think. It's name—*Edrealle*—it very clearly says it supplies the magic. But here…" she trails off again, running a finger along a line of text.

"Avice," I drawl.

"The magic—the magic the Warbearers possess—it speaks of it. And there's a temple...

"Here," she whispers. "There was a temple somewhere. I don't know what it's for, but..."

"But the Warbearers are the only ones capable of any of this. Maybe this is meant for them," I offer, even though the thought of a temple here when the Warbearers are from Verenathia makes almost no sense.

"I know." She blows out a breath, swiping away a fallen tendril of hair. "I'd be curious to find the other book. Maybe it will help translate this one; like a key."

"I don't think you should go poking your nose around trying to find the other one. It feels... off. Like we're not supposed to know it exists. Why else would it have been hidden?"

"That's exactly why I want to know what it's for," she glares. "Why would it have been hidden? And why here, when the Warbearers are up there?" She gestures at the sea outside the window.

"You're starting to sound like Rae," I mumble, more than a little unease rumbling in my stomach.

"No," she says simply. "I'm just curious what could be so important that it's remained hidden this long. Maybe Lichera didn't even know it was there—his desk is pretty old."

"Doubtful."

She shrugs, drawing her attention back to the ancient manuscript.

I leave her to her reading, moving to the cabinet below the window. The sky is purple, darkening to dusk as the sun slips behind the isle.

Maybe Avice is right: Lichera may not be aware of the book's existence. Her being in possession of it for a day or two can't hurt. She can glean what little information there is before returning it.

History on Ra'goramal is free for everyone to access, after all. Lichera would technically be the one in question if it's something of significance and intentionally hidden.

The tension in my gut, coiling ever since Rae left, tightens, but I ignore it and return to my whittling.

CHAPTER 16

Something different courses through your veins, my beloved. In you is the song of the wind; the melody of the stars. Listen for it.

Warm beams of sunshine gaze at Kieran and I as I follow him down the Citadel's grand stairway, my stomach fluttering nervously as we make our way into the city.

Emanating from the base of the hill that foundations the Citadel, white buildings are laid out in neat, semicircular rows—rings, Kieran explains. The innermost ring, the Provisioning District, pertains to sorting and distribution of supplies. Warehouses and storage buildings rest here while dragons swoop down from the supply field atop the hill, finishing up the day's retrievals.

Wide paths spread from the first ring like spokes on a wheel, intersecting through all rings of the city—the centermost path forming a straight line from the Citadel to the edge of the isle. The paths themselves are ornately patterned white stone that gleams in the sunlight, and I can't help but take a moment to admire the intricate designs. Lush, green grass stretches all around the city, expanding into the rolling hills I've seen from the Citadel.

Leaving the Provisioning district, we pass by a ring humming with activity.

"The Commercial District," Kieran says.

Storefronts line the street as far as I can see down the curved path, with people bustling about everywhere, many of them lugging metal carts laden with various items.

I don't know what I expected, but I'm surprised to see Verenathia is a fully functioning city—a lively hub of activity. Guilt twinges in my stomach at the times I thought less of them, while Ashden's almost-outright hatred sits heavy in my heart as we continue on.

A small child darts in front of me, her friends racing after her as they all chase some sort of glowing sphere. Squinting against the glare of the sun, I try to make sense of the object. Grabbing the sphere, one of the children throws it. It floats through the air before bouncing delicately on the ground.

"What is that?" I ask, unable to take my eyes off of it.

Kieran smiles. "The magic here on Verenathia is strong, giving us the ability to manipulate and imbue any object."

My confusion must be written across my face because he adds, "Imbuing… it's a lesser magic, but children are more sensitive to its presence than we are. That's an inflated pig bladder one of them has poured light into."

I blink, at a complete loss for words. We watch as the group tumbles over each other in an effort to catch it.

"You're telling me you can and do use magic? Like the magic the Warbearers use?" I wince at the pitch in my voice.

He eyes me sidelong. "Yes. You didn't know that?"

"No, I didn't know that!" I cry, dropping my voice to a rough whisper. "Since when?"

"Since… always," he shrugs. "When I say the magic the Warbearers use, I mean that in the loosest of terms. We only know the basics—lesser magics. What they possess is far beyond the scope of what we're taught."

One of the children catches the sphere, holding it up triumphantly before he's tackled to the ground.

"My favorite was always the little wooden people my father carved for me. He would make them dance and walk and… I loved it."

Glancing up at the unexpected edge in his voice, I catch a glimpse of such intense pain my breath pauses, but he stares straight ahead.

"How do you do it?" I ask, trying to drive the conversation away from whatever is causing that depth of misery.

There's a couple heartbeats of silence before he answers, and when he does, he does so slowly; as if reeling himself back from some faraway place. "Think of the elements: air, water, fire, earth. Those are the basis for everything around us, but below even that—frequencies. The basest level of the elements themselves. You learn to feel them—the frequencies; let them flow through you. Once you've found them, you can begin to isolate and manipulate them."

He holds his hand out, and I watch, shocked, as a small orb develops. A soft, golden-white sphere of light—it hovers neatly above his palm.

Overturning his hand, he lets the orb go, directing it toward the ground where it breaks against the stone path, shattering into hundreds of tiny stars.

"Show me how to do it." The words leave my mouth before I think better of it.

He cocks his head, watching me contemplatively—a slight, wry smile cracking his beautiful features.

"Alright. Let's get to the Edge first."

"The Edge?"

He only inclines his head, gesturing forward as he leads me on.

Passing through the Dining District, the smell of fresh bread and something warm and spiced drift to me on the breeze, making my mouth water. Small tables and chairs rest under awnings that emerge from cafes and restaurants; beautiful, foreign flowers sitting in vases atop each table.

There are people everywhere—milling about, eating together, strolling through the city rings. The rainbow of dragonhide suits before me is so different from the earthen colors of Ra'goramal that I pause for a moment just to admire it.

Houses similar to the cottages back home appear before us as we make our way out of the dining district. Made of white stone bricks, the cottages radiate the light of the sun, casting that same glow that seems to blanket the entire isle. Elderly women rest between the shade the cottages provide, working on small projects together while children dart in and out of view.

"Does everyone our age work up there?" I ask, noting the stark difference between the city and Citadel.

"Yes. I believe on Ra'goramal, you guys receive a duty once you come of age?"

I nod.

"It's similar here. We study, and once we're old enough—we train, work the supply field, and maintain the Citadel."

"And the businesses down here?"

"Run by the ones who dedicate themselves to a trade."

"You have the freedom to choose a trade?" I ask incredulously.

"If someone desires, yes. There's a lot of pressure put on our military training and maintaining the Citadel, not to mention quotas to fill, so, not many go that route. Enough to keep our businesses running, but no excess," he shrugs.

Pressure or no, they still have the choice. That freedom has not been taken from them.

I glance at him from beneath my lashes. "What path are you on now?"

"I'm where I need to be." He remains relaxed except for the almost imperceptible tick of his jaw.

I cock my head at the ambiguous answer. "By choice?"

"By necessity."

I don't miss the finality in his tone.

He glances sideways at me. "I chose the path of a soldier because that's where I felt I would be most needed." A loose bit of gravel flies ahead when his boot knocks it.

Though mildly annoyed at his elusivity, I can't ignore the underlying threat in his words. All of the weapons demanded from Markell and I come flashing back through my mind.

"For war?" I ask hesitantly.

He sighs. "Not necessarily."

A trickle of relief flows through me along with the irritation of his dodging my questions. If he doesn't consider the possibility of another war, then maybe those weapons were being used for something else. In either case, his tone says he's done with the topic.

"If you weren't forced to choose a path out of necessity," I roll my eyes. "What would you have done?"

I focus on the clip of our steps and happy sounds of livelihood while I wait for his response. Something in my stomach warms at the soft smile that's taken over his face, replacing the former hardness.

"Wait, let me guess," I cut in the moment he opens his mouth. "You definitely wanted to be a baker."

The deadpan look he gives me is entirely unimpressed, and I laugh. "What? I could absolutely see it. Up to your elbows in dough every day, making breads and cookies and such. You'd have to make a good berry tart though, those are my favorite."

He pauses. "Berry tarts are your favorite?"

"Oh… Yeah."

"Intriguing."

"You haven't answered my question," I grouse.

He smirks. "Only because the insufferable Goramalan won't let me speak."

I toss a glare at him and he chuckles.

"I would have been a librarian," he says, relenting.

A line pinches between my brows. "A librarian?"

He nods. "Think about it. You're surrounded by all the knowledge in the world, right at your fingertips. Anything and everything you could ever want to know. And if that's not your thing, there are countless stories to choose from. Love and loss, life and death, heartache, betrayal, adventure; whatever you're looking for—right there, ready to take you to another world."

"Kieran Trymera," I giggle—actually *giggle*. "Are you telling me you're a hopeless romantic?"

He rolls his eyes. "Of all that I just said, that's the most important thing you gleaned?"

"Possibly one of the more interesting things, yes."

"Maybe I am, although I think traveling to other worlds to be the more fascinating aspect of literature." His expression is neutral, but there's a hint of amusement in his eyes. "Is that such a bad thing?"

I give him a wicked grin. "Not at all."

Leaving the safety of the cottages, the path begins disintegrating into broken stone bits and gravel. The land spreads as far as I can see on either side, and in front of me? The open sky. The path and grass just… stop. Peering over the edge, I stare down at the calm sea far, far below.

He gestures grandly to the unending openness before us. "The Edge. Brilliant name, when you think about it."

"No wall?" I ask.

"You learn from a pretty young age not to go near the edge of the isle. That's not to say a few unfortunate ones haven't heeded the warning, but it's rare. We're people of the sky and partner with dragons—we don't need boundaries."

"Arrogant ass."

He chuckles. "We are, aren't we?"

I meet his gaze, doing my best to ignore the heat under my skin at his focus. "Now. Show me."

Crossing his arms, he stands, unyielding. His deep voice is a sultry caress when he says, "That's no way to ask."

I paint my most innocent expression, looking up at him through lowered brows. "Please?"

"Better."

Huffing, I join him as he lowers himself to the Edge.

A fitting name, indeed.

"Close your eyes."

I eye him incredulously. "You're not going to push me off, are you?"

"If that had been my goal, you'd be at the bottom of the sea already."

"Prick," I mutter.

"Close your eyes" he says again.

I do, this time. With eyes closed, feet dangling off the edge of the isle—no sensation but the wind against me and grass beneath me—I feel like I'm at the edge of my own existence.

"Good. Now feel the wind on your skin. Picture the way it moves through the air—the shape it holds—how it touches you."

I imagine the breeze, soft as a whisper, as I feel it brushing against me. Translucent featherlight streams grazing the air around us, almost like a river. Pushing forward, flowing, intertwining with itself—always moving as it continues in its coming and going.

Nodding, I ask, "Now what?"

"As you visualize it, allow yourself to *feel* it. Let its energy flow around you and through you. See it for what it is—each individual particle. Each layer of energy. Find the deepest one—the base."

Focusing hard, I begin to imagine it as he's describing. And soon, I *can* feel it. More than just the breeze itself, I can feel its energy—its soul. I allow it to dissolve and flow through me, picking it apart and putting it back together again where it leaves my body.

My breath whispers past parted lips as I nod again, slowly.

"Now, do the same with the earth beneath you."

I press my palms into the ground at my sides.

This feels different. Richer, bolder, more… alive. It's warm and cold and unyielding, yet,forgiving. Vibrant. It's a technicolor wave of life at its source. Pure; undiluted.

Shapes and images of the energy begin to fill me. I relish every sensation, feeling as it ebbs and flows.

"Feel and see the light; the energy from the sun."

I obey, opening myself to the warmth and strength of its beams.

Without meaning to, I begin to see and feel Kieran's presence, too; his warmth and strength—like a steadfast rock that bears the crashing of ceaseless waves. And… something different. Almost as if his energy is amplified, yet cloaked; like he's trying to minimize it.

"Feel it all, Rae. See it."

I shake my head, trying to clear it of the distraction and focus on my own energy. The people of Verenathia. The essence of our being curls up into the atmosphere like tendrils of living smoke.

Awed, I nod.

"Now, open your eyes."

I do, and gasp. The image I had in my head now lies before me. I blink to clear it, but it stays.

Translucent streams of wind float through the air; golden particles beam down from the sun—swirling and flowing together. Earthen wisps of vibrant life rise from the land below us.

I gape at the scene, squinting at the water particles sparkling in the air. Glowing particles of light intertwine with orange-hued radiant bands.

The sun.

Energy from the growing green things around us rises up to meet the sun, intermingling with the earth, the water. All of it pushes and pulls and blends so seamlessly. A cacophony of pulsing color, and yet, it's perfect. A beautifully balanced give and take.

"What is this?" I breathe.

Kieran's voice holds a touch of reverence as he says, "Everything has energy. Every single living thing in this world. Whether it's flesh and blood, or plant, water, light—all of it has energy. Once you know what you're looking for, you can see it."

How can this be real?

"As it flows through you, grab onto something, whatever you want. Grasp it, and don't let go."

I watch as the glittering streams of energy move through me. Focusing on a tendril of light, I reach for it with my hand. To my shock and delight—it remains in my fingertips, warming them.

"Good," I can hear the smile in Kieran's voice as he watches. "Now manipulate it. Bend it; shape it to your will. Whatever that looks like to you."

Concentrating on the small section in my grasp, I focus on the scintillating particles and grasp them with my free hand. Grabbing them, scooping them up and pinching them together, I begin to form a ball—much like what I saw earlier.

Soon, a rough orb of pure light rests in my palm. Looser, not as smooth as the one Kieran had created, but still. A laugh of hysterical delight escapes me.

"I can't believe this is possible," I cry.

"It's incredible. And this," he gestures to the light in my hand. "Is just the basics of it. Not even a scratch on the surface. Pretty much anything you can imagine, good or bad, can be done by manipulations like that; manipulating the energy and frequencies around you. It's how the Warbearers control the Safeguards. The foundation of Verenathia's magic. I've been studying it in my free time for years." A pause. "I've taught myself how to do things nobody else here knows."

Maybe that's why his energy feels untouchable. I nod softly as I turn my palm over, watching the orb drift delicately off of it. Getting caught in a breeze, it dissolves into glittering mist.

I start laughing—a touch of bitterness lacing my tone at the sheer wonder, amazement, and shock of all of this. The streaming energy around me vanishes from my vision.

"What?"

I shake my head. "I don't understand why we haven't been taught any of this."

He scratches the back of his neck. "The Safeguards contain a binding that prevents Verenathians from speaking of the magic when on Ra'goramal, and you've read the Accords… they've tried to teach us Goramalans are inferior and incapable of magic."

I've always believed that the bloodlines Verenathians set out to protect was simply that—a bloodline. I never realized it was because we were seen as inferior and would dilute the magic coursing through their veins.

But I'm not Verenathian, and here I am, tampering with magic. Something about that doesn't settle well within me.

"Why did you even bother?" I can't help but ask.

He leans forward, resting his elbows on his knees. "Bother with what?"

"With this—showing me how to use it. If your half of the Accords describes us as a sickness to your bloodline, and incapable—why did you show me?"

Gazing out at the sky, he scrubs his jaw softly, contemplatively. "Because I never believed it. I guess I never realized its existence was kept from you entirely."

My face warms, but the questions worm their way deep into my soul. Why has this been kept hidden from us? What good does it do?

He nudges me in the shoulder, pulling me from my thoughts while almost knocking me off balance. "Maybe you can show your people when you go back," he winks. "Start a revolution."

Smirking, I shake off my lingering unease and shove him back. "Maybe."

CHAPTER 17

Some say the world is full of darkness, and though they may be right, in part, you know better, little bird. There are always good things to be seen, touched, and experienced. Sometimes you just need to seek them out.

Dreams of magic and sunshine and wonderful, mysterious things bombard my sleep—and with them, a nameless dark that lurks at the edges of my subconscious.

I wake from the haze of my dreams, my mind foggy. Blinking against the sunlight streaming through my windows, I pull myself from the warmth of my blankets and grab the suit draped over the foot of the bed. My body heats as I hook the clasps up the back before stepping into it, remembering the brush of Kieran's fingertips against my skin.

No.

I frown at the leather moccasins waiting for me. I may be Goramalan in heart and blood, but remaining unidentifiable here would serve to ease some of my anxiety.

Lacing them up quickly, I leave the safety of my room and dart through the corridors to the bathing chamber, keeping my head down to avoid the looks of the Verenathians.

Thankfully, it's early enough that the place isn't fully populated. I scrub my face and see to my needs quickly before slipping out, making my way to the mess hall.

Padding through the corridor that joins the housing wing with the mess hall, a flash of midnight hair draws my attention upward.

Kieran is headed in the opposite direction, toward the housing wing, pastry in hand.

"Hey," I call out, wincing as my voice echoes off the marble.

His eyes meet mine and he pauses, flashing a dimpled grin. "I was just coming to find you." He extends the pastry toward me.

I ignore the rush his words send through my body, and instead focus on the proffered treat as I reach his side.

"For you."

I accept, eyeing him under an arched brow. "What's the catch?"

"Can a man not bring a beautiful woman breakfast?"

Fumbling for words, my body becomes a living, burning flame. I blink, inclining my head. "Thank you."

"Ah, there are those manners," he winks. Turning on his heel, he begins back down the corridor.

Scowling, and with no choice but to follow, I nibble on the pastry.

Berry.

"Where are we going?" I force over the butterflies swirling in my gut.

He shrugs. "Nowhere in particular."

Wonderful.

***

We spend the morning exploring. Kieran leads me through the Citadel, explaining the history and purpose of each room we pass. The whole place is a maze, and I'm soon dizzy with all of the floors and turns, but I do my best to mark each change. The Verenathians eye me warily, but none offer any comments on my presence.

Still, I stick close to Kieran's side.

Rounding a corner, we arrive at an open air courtyard. This courtyard—though smaller—is similar to the supply field.

And packed with people.

Some lean against the stone wall that borders the space, while others sit on the ground around large mats that mark each corner of the courtyard. Racks attached to the wall near the back hold all manner of weaponry—swords, daggers, axes, maces, clubs. My mouth goes dry when I see the gleaming tip of a spear as it hangs, its tip pointed menacingly to the sky.

The breeze running through the courtyard does little to cool the heat of my face when more eyes than I'm comfortable with turn to Kieran and I.

"What is this place?" I whisper.

The mat in the center of a group to my right holds two men locked in combat, backs bared to the bright sun.

"Where we train," he says easily, as if the weapons lining the walls are as commonplace as the food in the mess hall.

Which for them, I guess, they are.

"The training you were telling me about? Combat?"

"Mmhmm." He scans the crowd. "Classes are held here. Combat and weaponry and self-defense."

I swallow. "Oh."

A trickle of relief sneaks its way down my spine when I see Opal among a cluster of people on the ground. Deeply involved in conversation, she's gesturing wildly, but I manage to catch her eye. Hers widen in surprise as she smiles and jumps to her feet, heading our direction.

"What are you guys doing?" she asks cheerfully as she approaches. A sheen of sweat glistens on her face—her side knots loose and disheveled as wisps of hair fall over her neck and ears.

"We were exploring, and… here we are," Kieran drawls.

"Oh, how *convenient*," she crosses her arms, glancing sidelong at me before turning her attention back to Kieran. "Frellan isn't here today,"

I dart a look between the two of them. "Who's Frellan?"

She grins. "Our training headmaster. He leads three sessions a week here. We're required to attend ten each month, but other than that we're free to train as we see fit." She gestures broadly to the courtyard.

I scan the crowd, landing on a man and woman stuck with daggers angled at each other's throats. Faster than I can blink, the woman pivots, flipping the man and sending the dagger toward his heart.

I shudder. This is what they do for fun?

Following my line of sight, Opal shrugs. "Come on." She grabs my wrist, tugging me toward the group she was with.

My heart pounds in my ears as they watch us approach, all eyes on me. Kieran's presence behind me is like a brace, and I draw a deep breath, letting it steady me.

"This is Rae." Opal settles onto the mat, pulling me down with her while Kieran follows suit. "She's the one who snuck in on a supply shipment."

No shock registers on any of their expressions, as I'm sure everyone on Verenathia has heard of me by now. But I breathe a sigh of relief to see there's no animosity either—mainly just curiosity.

"I'm Eva," a beautiful redhead states, her fiery tendrils loosely tamed by the band in her hair. "I think it's incredible you had the guts to come here in a crate knowing you were going to die." Her comment earns hearty murmurs of agreement from the rest, and my heartbeat starts to ease.

"Look," Opal whispers to me, drawing my attention to the men running through maneuvers on the mat before us. "You see the taller one? That's Gabe."

I stifle a smile at the longing in her tone.

"Isn't he stunning? He was going over some techniques with me before you got here." She sighs. "I would love to be hot and sweaty for so many other reasons right now."

Grinning, I glance at Kieran, who's studying the fighters intently.

Our bodies, locked together as he forces a dagger to my heart—

Nope, absolutely not.

Gabe blocks a blow from the other man, grabbing his wrist and spinning him around in a heartbeat. *That's* exactly how Laurel was able to sneak up on me without so much as a whisper.

As if my thoughts summoned her, my heart leaps to my throat when I spot her amidst a group of people. She's sitting at the edge of a mat where two men, shirtless and slick with sweat, are trading punches. A bubble of panic rises up when I see one of them is the same damned man who has a burning, lustful, hatred for me.

A few in their group are watching me, drawing the attention of the man on the mat. He turns my direction, a cruel grin spreading across his face as he punches the man in front of him; *hard*. He throws another punch, and another, even harder. The other man takes it, giving another of his own, but the hazel-eyed bastard dodges easily. His eyes don't leave mine as he tosses blow after blow, hard enough to make the man stagger.

Finally, he sweeps his leg out and into his opponent, knocking him to the ground. I swallow rising dread as he keeps his eyes trained on me, and, wearing a devilish grin, walks to the downed man, placing his foot atop his chest.

You, he seems to be saying. *You're next.*

Opal nudges me. "You alright?" she whispers.

"Fine." I draw my attention away from him and to Gabe, who's now beckoning Kieran to the mat.

Kieran hesitates, the stiffening of his shoulders hardly noticeable, before rising to his feet.

"Weapons?" he asks.

"Always," Gabe grins fiendishly.

Together, they move to the wall of weapons. Kieran selects twin daggers, while Gabe opts for a shortsword. They return to the mat and begin circling each other.

Gabe bounces on his toes, rolling his shoulders before angling the shortsword toward Kieran—who sways easily on his feet. Kieran's daggers are expertly held in hands that remain loose at his sides, ready to strike at any moment.

It's Gabe who strikes first. Kieran dodges with practiced swiftness, feinting right and sliding in behind him, but Gabe reacts just as quickly, and the two face each other again.

Kieran lashes out with a dagger, forcing Gabe to block the blow. On his exposed side, Kieran strikes again, slamming the handle of the dagger into Gabe's ribs.

A death blow.

Gabe lets out a grunt before dropping his sword arm. Kieran takes advantage of the retreat, and slams his fist into the side of Gabe's face—hard enough to hurt—but had this been an actual battle, the blow would have left him unconscious.

"Ugh," Opal huffs.

"What?" I ask, not taking my eyes from the mat.

"Kieran's the best fighter we have," she whispers. "He may as well just get it over with so I can watch an actual fight."

My stomach lurches as Gabe thrusts toward Kieran's stomach with the sword, but he jumps back before sweeping out a leg to knock Gabe to the ground.

Kieran… every move he makes has been honed into nothing short of deadly, practiced until it's become second nature. His battle-readiness is worn like a suit—one that he dons easily to become the weapon he's trained himself to be.

Gabe grins as they dance in and out of each other's range, and while Kieran wears a twin smile, something lurks beneath the surface of his gaze.

Each jab with his daggers, every blow and skillful kick, holds something like reluctance—as if he's using every ounce of willpower just to go through the motions of the fight.

Gabe should be down within the first few seconds, and yet, they continue.

Everyone watches intently, all eyes pinned on the match with glee, but no one seems to notice. Not even Opal, whose attention is now locked on Gabe.

Kieran is holding back, allowing Gabe to toy with him. Restrained in the sense that, yes, it's a training match, but there's that hesitation; that weariness.

In a blur of motion, steel flashing in the sunlight, Kieran's daggers are knocked from his hands. The match ends with Gabe holding a sword to Kieran's throat.

Cheers go up around me as Gabe, still grinning, releases Kieran and clasps him on the shoulder.

"Well done," he pants.

Kieran matches his grin. "Always a pleasure."

They return the weapons to the rack before Gabe, head held a little higher, saunters back to the mat, calling on another opponent.

Kieran skirts the mat and eases himself down beside me.

"Why did you let him win?" I whisper.

His eyes widen innocently. "Who said I did?"

"Oh, come on," I keep my voice low as Gabe calls another to the mat. "I know nothing about this stuff and even I can see he's no match for you."

He shrugs nonchalantly. "Maybe I'm having an off day."

I pull my legs in, crossing them underneath me. "If that's an off day, I'd hate to see you on a good one."

Gabe and his next opponent undo the backs of their suits, shrugging off the top half before tying them behind their backs. Kieran watches as they face each other, and lowering his voice, says, "Not right now. Later, okay?"

"What—"

He gives me a look as if to say *no more*, and I let the words fall from my tongue.

Chewing my lip in confusion, my attention is again drawn to that man on the other mat—just in time to see him slam his opponent into the ground.

"Could you show me some self defense techniques?" I whisper.

"Of course," he says, quickly masking the flash of surprise on his face. "Right now?"

I glance around the courtyard at the number of people present, unease squeezing my stomach. "Maybe later, when everyone's gone."

His eyes glint mischievously. “Consider it a date.”

CHAPTER 18

My love, how I do worry about our children. You know well it's growing stronger by the day. I don't know what this world is going to look like for them; especially after we're gone. I have no doubt they'll be strong enough to face whatever comes, but how I wish I could keep them from it.

"Connect with your knuckles, you don't want to break your hand." Kieran demonstrates, emphasizing the correct position while my bruised hands hang uselessly at my sides.

In the distance, the dark forms of dragons dive and soar through the air among the dying rays of sun, while its fading light paints soft pink brushstrokes over the courtyard.

"Like this?" I mimic the move, trying to hold myself the way he's explaining. Whatever I'm doing must be several different shades of wrong because the crease between his eyebrows grows deeper by the second.

I'm beginning to think combat may not be my strong suit.

"Yes… mostly." He grasps both of my wrists. "And when your opponent moves in again, send your knee directly into their gut."

His eyes, mere inches from mine, glint deviously. "Or their balls, if it's a guy. It'll send them to the ground in a heartbeat."

I take in a deep breath, fighting to steady myself against his nearness—and instead inhale a lungful of his salt rain scent.

Fresh, clear, soothing.

"Let's go again." He pulls his fists up, his forearms in front of his face.

Our suits graze cleanly off of each other as I pathetically throw punch after punch. Sweat trickles down my back and temples, but I can't tell if it's from the exertion or my rapidly fraying nerves.

I blink, panting, and he's behind me—the movement so deft it's almost like he's stepped through thin air.

"If someone comes from behind like Laurel did, never reach backward." He reaches his arm around my shoulders, pinning me to him. I fight the urge to run my fingers along the lines of his forearm.

"Okay," I breathe, hoping he can't feel my heart pounding under his palm.

"What do you do in this situation?" His breath tickles my ear as he secures both of my wrists in his grasp.

The world dissolves as I'm borne along a wave of warmth and strength. One that smells like the sea and fresh air and everything I've never wanted. I try to recall anything he's shown me so far but I can't think beyond the feeling of him around me.

"I don't know," I whisper.

Stop. I need to stop right now.

I strain, wriggling against his grasp until he releases me. My chest heaves as I take a step back, trying to regain my composure.

His expression is unreadable; or maybe I don't want to define the emotion flickering alongside the amusement there as he watches me.

"Why did you let him win?" I blurt, trying desperately to ease… whatever it is that's dwelling in the space between us right now.

A weight falls, crushing that flicker—so heavy that I may have made a mistake in asking

He holds my gaze for several long moments before his shoulders slump. "I don't like fighting."

I pull on the material over my stomach, lifting the clinging suit from my body. "That's not a very good answer."

"I'm serious." The previous amusement in his eyes is gone, replaced with a solemnity I've not yet witnessed.

I pause, weighing my next words. "But isn't that the path you chose—what you've trained your whole life for?"

"Maybe." He crosses his arms before moving to the back of the courtyard, eyeing the weapons hung on the rack.

"What is it you don't like?" I ask, coming to stand at his side.

He keeps his focus straight ahead. "I don't particularly like being a weapon."

"For Verenathia?"

"Yes," he sighs. "I don't want to fight—I hate it, actually. I don't want to hurt anyone, and yet, I've been created into a weapon for a people I'm not sure I want to be a part of."

I don't know how to respond. This deep vein of discontentment… What could have possibly transpired that lead him to this?

"What about your people is so bad that you don't want to be a part of them?" I ask quietly.

He flicks his gaze toward me. "Would you consider yourself a slave?"

My heartbeat falters, and I swallow, the words lodging in my throat.

"It's okay," his shoulder brushes mine. "I won't tell anyone."

A breeze glides through the courtyard, lifting the hairs stuck to my neck. After a few moments, I blow out a long, long breath.

"Yes."

He inclines his head, turning his attention back to the weapons lining the wall—weapons that Markell and I have made. There's such a sadness, such a deep weariness in his expression that I almost reach out to brush my hand along his.

"There you have it," he says flatly. "It's not their fault; what we've become. I don't blame them for it."

I let his words settle over us, the questions forming in my head burning like acid on my tongue. "And what have you become?"

He shakes his head. "A people so caught up in their own lives and ideals that they don't even question what they've been taught, and all the while, others—ones they've deemed less-than—are suffering. But they don't care. They have all they could ever want or need, so why should they?"

I nod slowly, allowing his words to fill in the gaps of who I thought him to be.

"Is that all? The enslavement of my people was outlined 400 years ago. It has very little to do with you now."

He runs a hand through his hair. "Is that not enough, Rae?"

"It is," I concede. "But you can't take on any sort of responsibility for the decisions of our forefathers—or for your people. That's incredibly unfair."

"I know, but I think I'm allowed to be appalled by the current attitude of my people toward yours."

I hadn't realized we meant so little to them, but now, it's beginning to dawn on me like some creeping sort of rot.

We're not the province that provides for them, not the province their Warbearers spend day and night protecting, no—we're just a means to an end. Heat begins to inch up from my collarbone as shame sours my stomach.

"If I could change it, I would. Believe me—I would change it in a heartbeat." His eyes burn—insistently enough that I believe him.

"Why are you telling me any of this?"

He turns that breathtaking gaze on me, and a corner of his mouth lifts slightly. "Because you asked. No one has ever asked before."

"And you trust me enough to tell me?" I can't help the question, the deep well of unknown within me. "Are we not enemies?"

He cocks his head, eyeing me warily. "Do you believe we are?"

I don't know how to answer. Tyrant and dictator seems like a relevant way to describe Verenathia—but are we slaves or… providers? I'm not sure what the relationship is between our peoples. They may view us as dogs, but my people dislike them equally as much. Does that make us enemies? They couldn't survive without us, but we would be defenseless without them.

This man before me… no, he's not the enemy—that much I'm beginning to believe.

"No, I don't think we are."

He runs a finger along a dagger hanging on the rack. "Good. It'd be really awkward if I thought we were becoming good friends, only to find out you were waiting for the right moment to slit my throat."

"Considering—"

Sebastian and Opal breeze through the courtyard, their hair windblown and eyes wild.

"What'd we miss?" Sebastian drawls, wiggling his eyebrows.

Opal glances between Kieran and I and grins. "Looks like we missed out on all the fun."

Kieran looks skyward and sighs—pausing as if he's counting for patience. "Don't you two have more important things to be doing right now?"

"Than watching Rae kick your ass?" Sebastian flops to the ground. "I don't think so."

Joining him, Opal stretches out her long legs on the stone ground. "How is our little friend doing?"

"There will, unfortunately, be no kicking of the asses today. Or any day, for that matter," I wince.

Sebastian snorts. "That bad, huh?"

"Terrible," Kieran sighs.

"Forgive me," I smile sweetly at him. Waving a hand at Opal and Sebastian's disheveled hair, I ask, "Where were you two?"

Sebastian offers a coy smile. "Out playing with Stoney."

"Stoney?"

He wiggles his eyebrows again. "My dragon?"

"Your dragon."

"My dragon," he winks.

I gape. If there's one thing above all else that has sent a burning wave of jealousy through me—it's the fact that Verenathians have the capability of bonding to dragons. Watching them on the Loading Platforms, soaring to and from Verenathia, has always filled me with such indescribable longing. One I knew I would never be able to fulfill.

"Where?" I demand.

"You haven't told her about the Field, Kier?" Sebastian levels a flat look at him.

Kieran shrugs. "We were going to get there eventually."

As if I hadn't asked him directly in the library.

"Asshole," I narrow my eyes at him.

"Look who's talking," he smirks.

Restraining the urge to bolt to wherever this Field of Stars is, I say, "I've seen your dragon before; that day on the Loading Platforms."

"Oh I know," he chuckles. "She remembers you, too."

"She?"

He steps away from the weapons rack. "Cinder—we've had each other for five years now."

"That's incredible," I breathe.

His eyes soften. "It is. She's one of a kind."

"And Stoney?" I ask Sebastian, noticing now that Opal has gone quiet—sullen, even.

"A bastard. Always. But I love him."

Crossing my arms, I lean against the wall. "Takes one to know one."

He blinks, entirely unimpressed. "I'm right here, you know."

I smile apologetically while Kieran snickers.

"He's just a young thing—still practically a teenager," he continues. "Thinks he knows everything and doesn't want to listen. But we're getting there."

Opal huffs a wisp of hair out of her face, tossing me a sidelong glance. "Don't bother, I don't have one yet."

Okay, clearly a touchy subject.

"Well, how do you get one?" I venture; for my own sake—hoping not to rub any salt on the wound.

Kieran brushes a tendril of midnight hair out of his eyes. "Verenathia is full of magic, as you're now well aware. Every living creature is affected by it, and has their own affect on it."

"We all have our own magic," I murmur, tucking the thought away.

"We do, and certain types of magic are drawn to each other."

I run my finger absentmindedly over the purple bruise spreading across my knuckles. "So you look for the dragon that's drawn to you?"

"No," Sebastian and Kieran answer simultaneously.

I blink.

"You have to feel it." Kieran tilts his head, as if studying me. "If you look for it too hard, it has a tendency to evade you. It has to be drawn organically. No forcing."

"Probably why Opal here hasn't found hers yet," Sebastian nudges her. She shoots him a dirty look, shoving his arm away.

"She hasn't been told no a day in her life," he whispers—earning another, more severe, shove.

Kieran sighs at the sky again, and I bite back my smile.

"You'll find one eventually," he says to his sister, offering a small smile.

"I know," she snaps, then pins her violet gaze on me. "Anyway, would you like to go?"

I've never wanted anything more. To see the dragons, up close and in their home—my blood sings at the thought.

"Yes," I breathe.

Kieran pulls an arm across his chest, stretching. "We'll go first thing in the morning, then."

"You really are trying to torture her, aren't you?" Sebastian asks, rising to his feet.

"No," Kieran drawls. "The view is better when the sun is up, and we still have some training to do."

CHAPTER 19

ASHDEN

The Loading Warehouse is hot. Really damn hot. Tempers are short as we sling crates, track shipments, and heave the heavy carts out into the sun. Sweat runs down my back, down my temples, stinging my eyes. I squat, lifting a loaded crate with Rod, and toss it into the awaiting cart beside us.

"You alright?" He eyes me warily.

"Fine," I grit, straining against the next crate.

He snorts, his face reddening with the effort of lifting. "You've been acting off for awhile now."

Oh, because my sister is at the mercy of the Verenathians? Because she might be dead right now and there's no way for me to know for sure? Because I pushed her to leave, and had I just reigned in my frustration, we could have had a productive conversation? Yeah, I've been a little off.

But I only shake my head, offering him a half smile. "Just been thinking about my parents is all." It's not a total lie, they have been on my mind a lot, and not because of my utter failure in dealing with Rae. We're coming up on the one year anniversary of their deaths.

"Oh." His face turns contemplative. Slapping a hand on my shoulder, he grips it, looking me in the eye. "A few of the guys and I are going to Rory's tonight. Come with us."

"Maybe," is all I can offer him.

He nods, satisfied enough, before sauntering over to the next station in waiting. "Let me know if you need anything," he calls over his shoulder.

I scrub my face with my hands then run them through my hair, willing myself to focus. I can't think, can't eat, can't sleep, and to make matters worse—Avice won't take the damned book back.

I don't think we're supposed to know it exists, let alone have stolen it. So many questions swirl around it with no answers, along with something that I can't place but simply doesn't feel right. I'm glad that Avice is thrilled, but I have the sickening feeling it's going to get her into trouble and I just can't bring myself to care about its purpose anymore.

I leave the now-loaded cart and head to the basin of water resting in the corner of the Storehouse.

The water soothes the heat rising inside of me and washes away some of the stinging sweat when I dump a cupful of it over my head.

" ...that's what Markell said."

I pause, eavesdropping on the two women gossipping near one of the loading stations.

"Must be a lot to keep up with," one of them says.

I stroll over to them as casually as I can, though my blood begins roaring in my ears. They incline their heads as I approach.

"Have either one of you seen today's crate from the Smithshop?" I ask easily.

They exchange a glance before the brown-haired woman speaks—one of the brigade members but I can't remember her name. "No, haven't you heard?"

A weight settles in my stomach, but I keep my expression neutral. "Heard what?"

The older woman—Mayabelle—looks me up and down. "The Smithshop's apprentice hasn't shown up for several days. No one knows where she went and ol' Markell's starting to fall behind."

"He hasn't said where she went?" I fight to keep the tremor out of my voice.

"No," the brown haired woman answers. "Claims she didn't show up after her day off, just disappeared without a trace."

A beat of silence. The brown haired woman narrows her eyes at me.

"Say, Bryorfall—isn't it your sister who apprentices there?"

"Yeah," Mayabelle cocks her head. "I remember it being a Bryorfall."

I fight the urge to fidget. "No, you're probably thinking about the Baidenforths." A stupid lie—anyone can easily check the records. "And I've not heard anything, but I'll keep my ears open."

I dip my head and retreat before they have a chance to respond.

***

The evening light has faded as I stumble against the dimly lit door to our cottage, the half empty bottle in my hand sloshing some of its contents out and onto my boots.

Is it our cottage or… just mine now? I blow out a breath, shaking the thought out of my head. Waiting until the world stops spinning, I linger in the doorway before pushing the door open.

It felt like a soft push, but the door flies open and slams against the wall. Oops.

Avice shouts, shooting to her feet from her spot at the table. Lichera's book is spread open before her, a notepad and quill resting next to it.

"What are you doing?" she demands, glaring.

I shut the door and fumble with the latch before finally managing to lock it. "What am I doing? You er in my house."

She crinkles her nose. "Where were you?"

I cross the room and fall into the chair opposite hers, clattering the bottle onto the table. "Rory's. I mayyy have had a drink or two?"

The room won't stop spinning and swaying. Closing my eyes only makes it worse, and when I open them again, she's watching me with an unreadable expression.

Or maybe she's angry. It's too hard to tell.

"Are you drunk?" she huffs, snatching the bottle from me. She opens the door and pours the rest of the vile liquid out onto the cobbled path.

"Meee?" I blink.

She shuts the door and sets the bottle on the cabinet. "Yes, you. What are you doing?"

"I was simply having a goood time."

She levels a look I can't quite place on me. "Since when do you drink?"

Since I decided I don't want to live with the reminders of it all, damnit.

I lean back in the chair, trying to orient myself in the tilting room. "Sssince

I wanted to relaxx. Rod invited me."

She scrubs her face with her hands. "I get it, Ash."

"Mmm what?"

"A year since your parents' passing, and now…" she swallows. "Rae."

My stomach churns. "Damn, Avice. Can't a guy enjoy a drink with friendsss?"

"Of course. But this isn't you."

I scoff. "I'm grown… I do what I want."

Her eyes burn holes into my soul. She casts them to the table, her voice quieting. "You can't forget Rae, no matter how hard you try."

I don't want to forget. I just don't want to feel it.

"I, but, it, I—" Irritation flashes through me—at the accusation and the fact that I can't get my mouth to work right.

Settling back into the chair at the table, she raises an eyebrow at me. "You can't kill reality, no matter how much liquor you try to drown it in."

I snort, swallowing the liquid attempting to revolt in my stomach. "Since when er you so wise?"

She ignores the question but again, her voice softens. "She might still be alive, Ash."

I shake my head, regretting it as the world sets to spinning again, almost sending my entire night right out through my mouth. "I don't… want to talk about it."

"Well you're going to have to at some point," she snaps. "You think I don't notice how you drag yourself through your day? How irritable you've gotten?"

Where did that bottle go? I need another drink.

"I miss her too," she whispers. "Every day."

Holding her gaze, I keep my breathing steady, trying to keep from slipping away on the dizzying wave bent on taking me under.

"People… at the Storehouse. They're starting to notice. The weaponsss…"

"Markell," she mumbles, absentmindedly flipping through the book. "If he's starting to fall behind, it's only a matter of time before the Synod gets involved and starts an investigation."

I know. I know I know I know I know.

"Part of me wonders why she didn't say something to me," she continues. "If she was thinking about it, contemplating it—why wouldn't she have told me? She's always told me everything…"

Probably because she tried to tell me first and I made her feel like a fool.

"We could have figured it out," she says quietly. "I don't know why she felt the need to try and get herself killed."

"Enough," I say, rising unsteadily from the chair. My head is spinning, the floor shifting beneath my feet and I almost fall on my ass.

"What?"

"I told you, I'm not talking about… this." Bile rises in my throat.

She waves a disgusted hand at me. "So is this what you're going to resort to? Is this who you are now? A drunkard who can't face his problems?"

It's just one time, damnit.

"Avice—"

"No," she snaps. "I won't let you do this."

"Aviiice," I insist, my stomach roiling.

"I've already lost Rae," her voice cracks. "I'm not going to sit by and watch as I lose you too."

The tentative hold I had on myself breaks, and I vomit. All of the alcohol and bile in my stomach spews onto the table, the chair, the floor. Avice gasps and snatches up Lichera's book as I heave again. I blink away the watering in my eyes as the bitter liquid stings my nose and throat.

When I'm finished, I drag myself over to my bed and fall onto it. My mind feels a little bit clearer, but I can't bring myself to look at Avice.

Silence spans for a few minutes until she finally moves. She goes to the bucket on the cabinet, pouring a cup of water before sidestepping the mess and coming to the side of my bed.

She thrusts the cup at me. "Drink."

I take the cup and down it in one gulp.

Without a word, she begins to unlace my splattered boots. I try to protest, but she keeps a firm grip on the laces, her face set with determination. One by one, she undoes my boots and pulls them off.

"Lay down."

"But—"

"Lay. Down."

Reluctantly, I obey. She covers me with my quilt, tucking it around me.

"Avice, I—"

"Go to sleep."

"Avice—"

"Go to sleep, Ashden." There's no anger, only grim determination and a stubbornness I could never possess.

Realizing it's hopeless to try and argue, I close my eyes, getting lost in another wave of dizziness.

The sounds of her cleaning and, occasionally, gagging, are the only things I hear as sleep claims me.

CHAPTER 20

Ashden, it's your twentieth birthday today. How I have adored watching you grow into such an honorable young man. You are cautious, analytical, tender-hearted, and a joy to be around. If there is one thing I can share with you as you go into your twentieth year: it is to be bold, my son. Hold fast to what you know.

I practically fly out of bed at the first ray of sun through my window. Grabbing the shimmering suit thrown onto the vanity, I slip into it and toss my moccasins on. I'm still lacing them up as I stumble out the door.

And right into Kieran.

"Whoa," he chuckles. "The Field isn't going anywhere; I promise."

My body becomes a living flame as I shuffle backward, looping the leather lace through its final hole before tying it.

Rising to my full height, I try to ignore his broad chest mere inches from my face. "Sorry."

A mischievous smile plays on his lips. "Don't be" —and, glancing down at my feet— "We should really get you a new pair of shoes."

"Yes, but it can wait." I slip past him, ready to go search for the Field myself if he doesn't hurry.

Amusement dances in a sea of emerald. "I'll race you," he says with a wry grin.

"You'll… what?" I blink. Did he really just say he would race me? This highly trained, poised, fully grown man?

"To the entrance of the Citadel. You remember how to get there, right?"

"I don't—"

He doesn't give me a chance to respond before taking the stairs two at a time down to the main floor and sprinting out of the housing wing.

I sputter, fumbling down the stairs and race after him. He's already halfway down the first corridor by the time I make it out.

Damn, he's fast. But I've spent my entire life flying through the grasslands. My feet light across the marble floor as I pick up my pace. The handful of Verenathians in the corridors gawk; first at Kieran, then me as we rush past.

My legs begin burning as I gain on him, rounding the corner to the next corridor. I can't tell if I'm faster or if he's slowing for my sake. He reaches the end of the corridor and takes a right.

Definitely for my sake. I was going to go left.

Light from the Citadel's massive glass doors appears ahead, filtering into the chamber at the end of the corridor. I pump my legs as hard and as fast as they'll go until Kieran and I are side by side, matching each other's every stride.

We burst into the chamber and I slam to a halt, leaning over my knees as I pull in gulps of fresh air.

"You're… insane," I heave, unable to stop the smile spreading across my face.

"And yet," he pants, pure joy written in his expression. "You followed."

I pull myself up, still panting, and make my way toward the doors. "Where are Sebastian and Opal?"

"Likely sleeping—Opal was, at least." He comes to my side and opens the door, gesturing me ahead of him. "They'll get there eventually."

The fresh morning air, laced with the scent of sea and honeysuckle, greets me when I step through. "No supply runs today?"

Letting the door glide shut behind us, he crosses the colonnade in a few quick strides. "They work this afternoon."

"How do they always manage to have the same shift?"

He glances sideways at me, eyebrow raised. "I'll let you draw your own conclusions on that one."

Oh.

We begin down the wide marble stairs, turning off the intricate path and into the grass when we reach their base.

Leaving the rings of the city behind, we trek into Verenathia's grasslands, following a well-trodden footpath. The boulders from the windows of the Citadel are absolutely massive up close; towering far, far above us. A deep black, there are glittering, golden veins running through them.

Scattered all across the rolling plains, the boulders and rocks stand stark—commanding. A firm presence in the midst of delicate flowers and soft, swaying grasses.

We head toward the side of Verenathia opposite that of Ra'goramal. The waist-high grass along the footpath is warm from the sun as I run my fingers through it. The excitement coursing through me is a force that sends me practically skipping along the path.

The sky blossoms around us, a brilliant blue, stooping to touch the land on every horizon. Grabbing a cluster of unfamiliar orange flowers, I inhale their scent. Something delicately sweet, but with a crackle of energy and wind.

Eventually, the land begins to slope downward. Down, down, down, until, like the Edge, it stops. Like stepping off of the bank at the water's edge, the land disappears. Only now, there's no water, but endless openness. The sky, boundless and free, lies before us.

And rocks.

So many rocks.

Suspended in the sky are thousands upon thousands of rocks. Gravel, stones, boulders—some are as small as my fist, while others are easily as big as the Citadel.

Hundreds, if not thousands, of small, brightly colored figures weave in and out among the dotted masses and clouds. Waterfalls flow freely from many of the larger boulders, shattering into mist and rainbows as they catch the light of the sun. A dragon bursts through a waterfall, a sparkling, misty cloud dancing around it.

My heart is thundering so loud it's all I can hear.

Kieran leans down, his soft breath tickling my ear. "Welcome to the Field of Stars."

Dragons of every color swoop and dodge and glide. Groups of them are scattered throughout: flying, diving, playing, and resting—gathered together on the bigger boulders. Others, so small I can only assume they're babies, bounce from rock to rock—plucked out of the air by the adults when they slip.

An iridescent black dragon calls out before plummeting off of a rock above us. It seems to fall limp for a heartbeat before spreading its wings, catching itself before soaring to another rock nearby. I stifle a giggle as it lands gracefully and preens at us.

There's a flat boulder suspended close enough to us that the urge to jump becomes an itching in my bones. My heart falters when Kieran takes a running leap and does just that.

He lands effortlessly on the rock, turning back to face me with a taunting grin. "Scared?"

I eye the gap between the mainland and the edge of the rock. Maybe three feet? But the sea churning so far below sends my head spinning.

Not giving any more room for thought, I sprint to the edge and leap. Time stops for the second I'm suspended between worlds. My feet hit the rock and I land squarely beside Kieran.

"Well done," he claps slowly. "I'm impressed."

"What would you have done if I fell?" I ask, watching as a deep purple dragon swoops gracefully through a misty rainbow, shattering it into a million prismatic shards.

He shrugs. "I suppose I would have mourned the loss of the Goramalan that came here illegally and should have been dead the first day."

"I would shove you right now if it wouldn't kill you."

"What an honor to be left alive," he says, hopping to a neighboring rock. Following, I squint into the distance.

"Are those people?"

"Yes. Once you have a dragon, you can go as far as the world will take you." He looks at me with that perpetual amusement. "Or you could just jump from rock to rock and pray you don't fall."

I toss him a wicked grin and take another running leap, landing on the nearest boulder.

Then the next.

And the next.

Soon, Kieran and I are bounding across the sky, lighting across the surface of the boulders. One after another, we go, until the mainland is far, far away. Dragons come alongside us, chortling and roaring with glee—a wing or tail somehow always right where I need it if I land wrong.

The wind is wild and free up here, untamed and unkept, tearing through me. Each jump sends my heart hammering—a delicious sort of adrenaline pumping through my body. A feral laugh rasps out of me as I burst through a waterfall, the water beading off of my iridescent suit.

I am free.

This is freedom.

I take another running leap, and a blue dragon to my right matches my pace, diving under the rock as I land on it.

There's so much energy out here, pure and raw and beautiful. I want to drink it all in, let it fill me and envelop me. I want to become the wind and sea and stars.

I wish Avice and Ashden could see this.

That familiar tug in my heart returns out of nowhere; stronger than ever. Beckoning me, calling me into the unknown. Somewhere, some magic is pulling on a thread intertwining with my heart.

Is it here, on Verenathia?

I halt on a large, flat rock, staring out at the Field of Stars. Droplets from a waterfall far above me catch the light of the sun, glinting and shimmering.

Kieran stops at my side, a concerned pinch in his brow. "Everything okay?"

"Everything is perfect," I whisper.

Just then, a green dragon shoots up from the open sky below our rock and banks left. I follow its trail, gasping as it lands several rocks away from us and two figures dismount.

Sebastian and Opal.

"This is Stoney," he calls out, his voice almost lost against the backdrop of wind and water.

I cry out in amazement, then start when Kieran makes a series of clicks and whistles.

A pulse of blue-gray comes soaring from a distant rock—the same blue-gray I saw that day on the Loading Platforms. Anticipation sends my heart racing as Kieran watches the sky expectantly.

The dragon lands evenly on the smooth surface of our rock, eying me suspiciously before turning to nudge Kieran with her snout. He rubs her cheek gently, resting his forehead between the dragon's eyes. "Easy girl," he murmurs, stroking her snout.

Stepping back, he gestures. "This is Cinder."

I swallow at the sheer size of her. With her slate scales and lapis lazuli eyes, she's absolutely magnificent. She watches me curiously, her tail swishing lazily from where she stands at Kieran's side.

"Does she breathe fire?" I whisper, and immediately feel like a fool for asking such a question.

She gives a gruff snort, flicking her head defiantly.

Kieran chuckles. "She can hear you. And yes, she can, if she chooses. She's just being on her best behavior right now." He strokes her chin. "Aren't you?"

Cinder snorts again as she paws at the ground.

I tentatively reach out my hand. "Can I?"

"Up to her," Kieran inclines his head.

Cinder edges closer, squinting her large eyes at me while she sniffs my hand. Her nostrils flare as she breathes in my scent, and a moment later, she thrusts her nose into my hand, nudging it gently.

A thrill pulses through me at the feeling of her smooth, scaled nose under my fingertips. I rub gently down her snout and along her jaw, and she leans into my touch. When our eyes meet again, thousands of years worth of collective wisdom shine in their depthless pools.

That tug reignites within me, pulling beyond the here and now.

"Am I allowed to have one?" I ask as I trace my finger around the edge of her cheek.

"A dragon?"

"Yes," I glance at Kieran, allowing myself to feel a small trickle of hope.

He considers, chewing on his bottom lip.

That trickle fades into some sad, shriveled thing before disappearing completely as a line appears between brows that have crept together while his gaze remains trained on the ground.

When I don't think I can bear the silence any longer, he exhales a long breath. "I don't know," he admits.

I try to hide the crushing disappointment. Cinder snuffles softly, leaning into my hand once again as I rub a particularly troublesome spot.

"I'll take that as a no."

"You," he starts slowly. "Are allowed to do whatever you want. But something of this significance," he gestures toward Cinder. "I don't know how well that would go over."

I raise a questioning eyebrow. "With the others, or the Court?"

"Both."

Running a finger along a single scale, I marvel at how it catches and reflects the light. Not flashy, but a subtle, magnificent opalescence that makes Cinder look as if she's made of stardust. "Why?"

He steps closer to us, resting a hand on her snout. "Because having a dragon is one of the most sacred bonds a human can have, next only to that of a spouse."

I shift, ignoring the warmth that heats my core.

"It's the final part of our formal training. There are exceptions, of course—

people finding their dragon before they're finished—some, not at all. The connection will come to you; you can't seek it out. And when it does, you need to grab onto it. Fight for it. Once the bond is found and accepted on both ends, you'll be paired for life—bonded by Verenathian magic."

My mouth goes dry at the importance—the implication—of such a bond.

"Verenathians take it very seriously," he says quietly, his face pinched with distaste. "The bonds belong only to us—only to those with a Verenathian bloodline. Part of the reason for the blockade on Goramalan travel..."

"I know. It's been pounded into my head my entire life. I don't need to hear it again."

He gives me a sympathetic smile. "I know you know. And..." a muscle in his jaw ticks, his eyes shadowed, as if he's fighting a war within himself. "From all of my reading and studying, I would be inclined to think you could. Damn them and their rules—the magic flows through everyone. I don't see why it'd be kept from you based on your blood alone."

Maybe he's right. The thought of the magic—so open and accessible once you know it's there—for it to only allow Verenathians to bond dragons... Something about that doesn't settle well within me.

"So..." I nibble my bottom lip until I taste the tang of blood. "Your dragon is determined by the one you feel the strongest connection to? And that bond is through the magic?"

"Yes," he says, eyes gleaming.

"Say I found a dragon and we bonded, no one would have the right to do anything about it because it was determined by the dragon and the magic itself; Verenathian blood or no." Holding his gaze, I add, "Those laws seem to transcend the ones of your people."

"One would think," he murmurs.

Crossing my arms, I face the sea of rocks suspended before us.

"How do you initiate a bond?"

Following my gaze, he smiles wryly.

"You jump."

I blink. Cinder chortles, as if laughing at me.

"Jump?" My voice is barely more than a squeak.

He grins deviously. "You'll know your dragon when you see them. I can't explain how, but you'll know. And then yes, you jump. Hopefully landing on their back, but it's not unheard of for someone to miss completely and fall."

I gape at the nonchalance in his tone, knowing a fall from this height would undoubtedly kill a person.

"Oh, don't worry," his deep voice is smooth as honey. "If that happens, the dragons aren't cruel. One of them will save you, but the one you initially tried bonding will most likely reject you. After that you'll probably not be able to find another one."

Silence falls as the weight of his words sinks in.

"Come on," he says abruptly, climbing up onto Cinder's back. He leans down, offering me a hand.

I look at the hand in front of me, then at the emerald eyes gleaming behind it as my stomach clenches and unclenches in anticipation.

His hand is warm and strong around mine when I take it, and he heaves me up. My feet scramble for purchase against Cinder's side.

"Sorry," I whisper as I finally make it to her back and settle in.

She gives a high-pitched chirp, wriggling underneath us.

"She forgives you," Kieran pats her head. "Are you ready?"

He doesn't wait for me to respond, instead, nudging Cinder forward off the rock and into open air.

We plummet.

My stomach flies into my throat before Cinder thrusts her wings out, catching the air and sending us upward. The force of her ascent drives us backward, and panic bursts through me when my ass slips. I wrap my arms around Kieran's waist tightly and squeeze my eyes shut, the wind whipping my braid until, finally, she levels out. I inch forward in my seat, not daring to loosen my grip around Kieran.

Feeling somewhat more steady, I open my eyes and gasp at what I behold.

The open sky stretches endlessly around us. An azure infinity.

We glide through the air until Verenathia is but a distant memory. Other dragons swoop from the stones near us, calling out cheerfully to Cinder in chuffs and mewls, matching her wingbeats as they soar alongside us.

I can't deny how good Kieran feels against me. Warm and solid and unwavering. He leans gently into me, not at all seeming to mind our closeness, either.

He guides Cinder downward, dipping underneath a well-populated rock. It's so close above us that I could reach out and run my finger along its surface, but we shoot back up abruptly as we exit from the other side. I slip again at the force of the incline, leaving me no choice but to grip Kieran and Cinder with my legs, my arms—squeezing so tightly it's a wonder either one of them can breathe.

Laughing, his head thrown back to the sky, Kieran relinquishes control of Cinder, allowing her to fly freely. My stomach somersaults as we duck and weave and corkscrew through the sky, dodging the rocks suspended there.

Soaring for… minutes? Hours? I've entirely lost track, but other than the sun beaming down to note the passing of time, there's nothing; nothing else that matters. It's the most beautiful thing I've ever seen or felt and I never want it to end.

If running through the Field of Stars was freedom, then this is paradise. More than free—I'm the very wind itself. Limitless. One with the sun and sky. Tears stream across my face in the wake of it all.

Too soon, Kieran circles back and leads Cinder down to a large white stone below us. We land lightly, her legs effortlessly absorbing the energy of the impact before she kneels, allowing Kieran to hop down.

"What did you think?" he asks, offering a hand as I clamber down her side.

Alive. He just looks so… *alive*. With hair wild and windblown, distractedly brushed away from bright eyes, his smile is the broadest and happiest I've seen in the short time I've known him.

For a heartbeat, treaties and rules broken; deception and confusion and things far outside my realm of understanding cease.

"That was amazing," I choke, hastily swiping at the trails of tears down my face.

His smile breaks and he reaches toward me before letting his hand fall to his side. "What's wrong?"

"No—nothing," I rasp. Taking a deep breath to steady my voice, "It's just… when you spend your whole life dreaming of something you know you'll never get the chance to experience—" the lump in my throat blocks the rest of my words. A shaky, blissful laugh shudders out of me as I press my palms into my eyes, forcing the tears into submission. "I'm fine, I promise I'm fine. I'm more than fine."

Understanding glints in his eyes. He knows exactly what I'm feeling.

A corner of his mouth tilts upward. "I'm glad you enjoyed it," he says quietly.

Cinder sneezes loudly beside us, her head shaking violently. We both laugh as she looks at us, confused, before giving an indignant chuff.

This rock we're on is so high in the sky, the only thing I can see are the clouds below us and dragons dotting the air.

And again, that relentless pull threatens to tear me apart just like it did back home. Out here, among the wind and sun and sky, it rages, pulling me toward something unseen.

All of my levity and joy falls away, dissipating like steam.

What do you want?

Kieran comes to my side, easing himself down over the edge of the rock. Letting all my weariness bleed into a long sigh, I follow, dangling my legs over the edge. Cinder comes to rest her snout between the two of us, snuffling.

He nudges me with his shoulder. "Something on your mind?"

I stare out at the vastness and shrug. "It's nothing, really."

How do I explain something that has been a part of me for as long as I can remember; something I, myself, don't yet understand? Neither good, nor bad—it's simply there. Always whispering that there's more.

More.

So quiet, yet all encompassing.

More. There's so much more.

"*More*," I told Ashden. "*Maybe there's more.*"

Yet here I am, amongst the more, and there's still no rest from it. I would give anything to drown it out. If it's not sated by coming here, there's nothing more I can do.

"Well, if you decide you want to talk about it—whenever—I'm here."

A soft smile pulls at my lips and I lean into him, just slightly; appreciative of his quiet strength. "Thanks."

He doesn't pull away. "Anytime."

CHAPTER 21

A basket of kittens showed up in town today. One of them is gravely injured, but you spent your time seeing to its needs and tending its wounds. I'm beginning to hope for its recovery now because of your love, little bird. I pray you never lose that part of you.

Thoughts of Ash and Avice continuously float through my mind. I can't help but wonder if they're okay; if my disappearance has brought suspicious whispers and looks… or worse.

Even if I wanted to go back home, I can't. I'm a fugitive now. Though I've found temporary acceptance here; I broke what is, essentially, the only law in the Accords that actually matters. Returning home will, without a doubt, result in my execution.

I should be there right now, soaked in sweat at the Smithshop—doing my duties like a responsible citizen. Swallowing my lot in life like the rest of them.

"One would think," Kieran's deep voice cuts into my thoughts as we meander through the atrium—yet another wing of the Citadel. "That someone kicked your dragon, considering how pouty you are right now."

I continue inspecting the flower in my hand, wondering if he can see the dark, brooding cloud swirling above my head. Its petals are like frost—lacy and light and frilled into an intricate pattern.

Weighing the words pummeling my head, my heart, I venture, "Have you ever done anything you regret? Real, actual, soul-sucking regret."

His eyes match the vibrant green bursting from the foliage around us. "Of course, hasn't everyone?"

"I guess so," I mutter as I run my hand along the wispy frond of a fern-like plant. Its green tendrils turn bright blue and curl inward, caressing my fingers as I move across it.

"What is it?" he asks, lightly brushing his hand against mine. The touch leaves my skin burning. The touch that I'm beginning to love—beginning to want more of the moment it leaves my skin.

"My brother," I sigh. "I shouldn't have left him the way I did. I shouldn't have left at all. I just…"

"Talk to me."

Plopping to the ground amidst a cluster of sweet-smelling bushes, I smile softly at the wandering salvia that follow. The small, light blue flowers delicately stretch their roots across the ground, propelling themselves forward until they form a rough semicircle around me. They had uprooted themselves the moment Kieran and I walked past earlier, having trailed us through the atrium this whole time.

Now, sinking their roots back into the dirt, they rest contentedly as Kieran eases himself to the ground beside me.

"You've met him, I'm sure you remember." I doubt he's forgotten about that day on the docks.

"Oh I remember," he smirks.

I swallow a surge of defensiveness. "His heart is in the right place, he can just be a bit… much, sometimes."

Snippets of our final argument loop through my mind. "He never understood. I couldn't escape it. I had to know what else there was—what was wrong." My chest aches with the hurt and anger from the memory of him just… dismissing me. My thoughts, opinions, questions.

Me.

"He was so afraid of losing me that he tried to make me believe I was imagining things—nothing more than an irrational child. The things I was feeling, seeing… it didn't matter." The words are as bitter on my tongue as they were the night they were spoken.

Kieran nods, his eyes never leaving me.

I raise my face to the glass ceiling, bathing in the warmth that filters through. Unlike the other frosted rooms in the Citadel, the glass here is transparent to let in the life-giving sunlight.

"I'm not angry with him for being afraid. I probably would have been the same if it was the other way around. I just wish he would have given me some credit."

The weight of the memories burn the backs of my eyes and I blink, clearing them away.

"The last time I saw him, we were screaming at each other. I said things I shouldn't have, and," I pause, hearing Ashden's soft voice as I was stepping into the rain like clanging bells through my head. "I didn't speak to him again. Didn't apologize. I should have—I knew I was going to be killed when I left—and still, I left anyway. Can you imagine what that would have done to him? How could I have done that to him?"

I pluck another frost-laced flower. "I didn't want to. I wanted to leave, I mean—but I didn't want to leave him. He's all I have left, besides Avice, but I couldn't stand another second there.

"Maybe he was right. Maybe I really am as selfish and immature as he believed I was." The realization stings, more than I'm willing to admit.

Kieran shifts closer to me, lightly pressing his knees into mine. He grasps my chin in his fingers and brings my gaze directly to his.

"Stop it."

I only give him a blank stare.

"I'm serious, Rae. If you never do something that keeps you awake at night, that makes you sick with self-loathing, are you really alive? Feeling things like that—like this—experiencing these things; it shows that you're alive. Truly alive. Imagine not giving a damn enough to feel. To care. To have a conversation like that in the first place."

"Sounds an awful lot like justification for being a shit person," I mutter.

"No. I'm not saying that what you did was the right call, not by a long shot. But I'm sure Ashden hates himself—probably even blames himself—just as much as you do."

I groan, dropping my face into my hands. "Don't remind me."

He taps my head with his finger and I raise my face just enough to meet his eyes. "Don't do that," he says gently.

"Don't do what?"

"Let yourself slip into that pit. One moment you're the most vibrant, beautiful thing I've ever seen, and the next… It's like all that light and life leaves you. I can see you slipping into the pit."

I swallow the well of emotion rising within me, my heart stuttering over his words. "And what is that pit?"

A tight smile. "Depression, despair, emptiness—whatever you want to call it."

My heart would have taken a full dive into those words, except now, I feel it cracking. He's seen the feelings I've tried so hard to hide. It takes one who's experienced such things, someone who's been to the depths of hell and trudged their way back out again, to recognize it in someone else.

It's as if all the foliage around us leans in, drawn to the calm strength he exudes. "You know that, whatever comes, you're going to do everything you can to make it right. You can't undo what's already been done, but focusing only on the regret that came from those decisions is just a downward spiral that leads you to unravel yourself."

"And what if I'm never able to?" I whisper. I don't need to voice the death that waits for me if I return home.

He winces. "If it comes to that, it'll be a hell of its own. But if your brother is half the person that you are, he'll learn to process and grieve what could have been."

Tell me, I want to beg. *Tell me what has made you this way.*

"He'll learn to forgive you, no matter how badly it hurts and how angry it makes him."

Forgive me? When I am inevitably executed for what I've done, Ashden will have to learn how to forgive me for leaving him in the most permanent way.

But he would. I know he would.

I don't think I can learn to forgive myself.

I swallow the knot in my throat. "You're right."

"I know I am," he says lightly.

"No need to be a prick," I mumble.

Some of the light returns to his expression. "I just gave some of my best advice, asking nothing in return, and that's how you talk to me?"

Forcing aside my guilt, I give in to the heat his gaze ignites. "What would you ask for, if it came at a price?"

No. No no no no.

His gaze rakes up and down my body, lingering wickedly on my mouth. He chuckles, low and deep. "I don't think you're ready for that, my dear Rae."

Try me.

The response is almost rolling off the tip of my tongue—almost. But I bite it back. This is not what I came here for.

He leans in closer. "Focus on right now. You're not going to be here forever and there's no use in spending it miserable. Need I remind you you're in the sky?"

***

Kieran leads me out of the atrium, through the Citadel, and to the Field of Stars. My heart races with giddy anticipation when I see Cinder waiting on a large boulder near the edge of the isle.

"Ladies, first," Kieran gestures to the large gap between us and the boulder.

I don't hesitate this time, sprinting before leaping onto the suspended mass. Cinder chuffles as if amused. Tentatively, I reach my hand out and let her sniff it before stroking along her neck and sides.

Cool and slick, the feel of her scales sends a shiver of delight down my spine. Kieran reaches my side and mounts her, offering a hand down to me.

"Shall we?" he winks.

"Oh, absolutely."

His touch sends a warmth of pleasure into my core as he pulls me atop Cinder's back. I wrap my arms tightly around him, nestling into his back when I feel Cinder's haunches bunch.

A breath-stealing leap, and then we're free. One with the wind and sky.

Bliss reigns over me as I pull in lungfuls of crisp, fresh air, interwoven with Kieran's salt rain scent. The hard edges of his muscles fill the material beneath my fingertips. I don't think I could ever get tired of this.

Dragons swoop down from neighboring rocks, racing alongside Cinder as she ducks and weaves and dives. Pumping her wings hard, she takes us higher and higher, until I'm staring directly into the sun. The dragons at our sides fall away as she climbs higher still.

And then she dives. Tucking her wings in tightly to her sides, she plummets straight toward the sea.

A wild laugh tears out of Kieran as he ducks, pressing himself into Cinder's back. I cling to him, the roar of my blood and wind filling my ears as I squeeze her so tightly my legs begin to cramp.

She cries out, a cawing shriek that I can only assume is a dragon's version of a laugh, before effortlessly leveling out. Approaching a flat rock, she eases down, landing gently.

My hands are trembling as Kieran slides down. Reaching up, his hands find my waist comfortably to help me down. I brush my windblown hair out of my eyes, tucking it roughly back into the braid down my back.

"That was…" I have no words. Perfection seems to be the only adequate description.

"I know," he grins.

I avert my gaze at the dimple flashing in that grin. Staring out at the vastness before us, I let the freedom and contentment of this moment settle over me.

"Look at it, Rae," Kieran breathes, coming to my side and gazing out at the Field of Stars.

"Trust me, I am."

"No. Try looking at the magic."

Cocking my head, I close my eyes and envision the energy from the sun, the wind, the sea—let it envelope and flow through me unabashed. It's easier this time—more natural—I simply open myself to that inner ache and let it be soothed by the force of the world.

Opening my eyes, I gasp. Calm, cool bands of watery resistance rise up from the sea, meeting the sun in a cacophony of starbursts. Streams of wind curl and cut through everything, directing the light from the sun and shaping mist from the sea.

This time, though, hundreds of technicolor streams rise from the life of the dragons. Earthen bands of solid might flow from the rocks, playing with the dragons' energy.

It all moves and pulses, ebbing and flowing in a dance. Interacting in ways one would never know if they weren't taught to look.

A masterpiece.

My awe must show on my face, because Kieran takes one look at me and smiles softly. "Can I show you something?"

He doesn't wait for my response. Using his hands, he begins to manipulate the salt mist floating around us. Breathless, I as he pulls in its energy, driving it toward himself. Like plucking an apple off its branch, he reaches into the wet air near him and grabs tendrils of wisping energy. His touch is so gentle, so careful, as he shapes it.

A perfect rose forms in his hand, made entirely of water. My chest aches as he hands it to me.

"For you."

A rose.

I gingerly take the flower out of his hands, admiring the water as it flows within the shape. It's perfect.

He flicks a finger, and the rose bursts, spilling water all down the front of me. I cry out, startled.

"Asshole," I mutter, unable to stop myself from grinning as I wipe the droplets off my suit.

"It's wonderful though, isn't it?"

I brush a droplet off my nose. "No, I'd much rather be dry."

"Not that." The look he gives me is equal parts deadpan and wickedly delightful. "The magic."

I nod. "It's incredible." It truly is unreal.

He inclines his head toward the energy flowing around me. "Try it."

My eyebrows flick upward. "Me?"

He smirks. "No, the voices in my head."

"You really are insufferable, you know that?"

"Most definitely," he winks "You don't seem to mind too bad, though."

Chewing my lip, I ignore the comment. "How do I do it?"

"Just like that light you made before. Find an element, isolate it, and manipulate it."

Nodding slowly, I squint out at the endless forces of life. Multicolor strands rise up from people out on the floating stones, a soft purple tendril wisping up from a dragon resting on a rock below us. I reach out, brushing my fingers against it.

I'm met with a roar of outrage before the dragon shakes itself off and dives off the rock.

"Keep in mind, tampering with someone or something's life force is usually… unwelcome."

"You could have told me that beforehand," I retort, my face warming.

His eyes sparkle. "I know."

Huffing, I return to scanning the sky. "Did I hurt the dragon?"

"Oh, no. It's more of a poke into their subconscious. Think of when someone is watching you. You know they're there—you can sense them without having to see them. Messing with someone's life force is like inserting your own presence directly into theirs."

Interesting. "What if your intentions were… less than ideal?"

He contemplates this for a moment. Maybe deciding if he can trust me with whatever the answer is.

"You can do wicked things with someone's life force if that's your desire."

My brow furrows. "Then how are you guys still alive?" I can't imagine living amongst an entire population with the knowledge to do… whatever you can do with someone's life force.

"Because nobody knows," he says quietly.

I whip my head toward him. "What do you mean?"

"I mean," he avoids my gaze, instead looking out over the Field. "That nobody knows how to manipulate the magic in that way."

"And you do?" The question bubbles its way out of me before I can think better of it.

"No," he says quickly. "But I know that it can be done."

Nodding slowly, I mull over his words. "It's probably best that no one is taught things like that, right? It seems more like a liability."

"And training with swords and daggers isn't?"

I blink, unprepared for the bite to his voice. Unsure of what to say, I return to searching the elements.

He blows out a breath. "Sorry. I just… I don't agree with the way things are done here."

"Then why don't you do something about it?" I snap.

I did, after all—stupid or no.

A pained shadow flickers across his face. "I can't."

"You can't, or you won't?"

All of a sudden, a rock grazes my shoulder. I whirl, the view of the magic disappearing. Kieran's body tenses as he surveys the surrounding area.

Another rock hits me in the stomach with enough force that it had to be thrown. Hard. Cinder growls, stalking in the direction it flew from.

More pelting—a volley of them, this time. I spot the group on a boulder several yards away.

"Pig!" someone shouts.

"Go home!" another yells.

"You don't belong here!"

Any more questions I had for Kieran, the joy of simply being here are gone—replaced by a burning shame and overwhelming sense of alienation.

Surely none of them saw me on Cinder's back?

Kieran's steadying presence warms my side, bolstering me. He places a comforting hand at the small of my back and glares at the group.

"Unless you want an audience with the Court," he shouts across the gap. "I suggest you find something else to do with your piss-poor excuses for lives".

His gaze softens on me. "You don't have to prove yourself to anyone."

Maybe not, but their words cut deeply. My insides feel like they're bleeding.

Cinder perches on the edge of our island and roars at them, spit flying from her mouth. The group wears a uniform smirk as they turn, losing interest in me. I stand, dumb, as one by one, they leave on their dragons.

"We should get back to the Citadel," I say quietly.

I'm so drained, so empty. Reminders of what I've done, what I've left behind, all come crashing back in a torrent of reality and heartache.

"Hey," Kieran says softly, tentatively cupping my face in his hands. "I'm serious, don't let them get to you."

"You know why that's so hard for me," I whisper.

He reluctantly removes his hands from my face. The space where they were feels naked against the breeze. "I know, and if it wouldn't cause more trouble for you, I'd beat them into the ground." He says it with enough steel that I believe him.

"I know," I mutter. "But, please, let's go."

Another shadow flickers across his expression, but he quickly conceals it. "Alright."

Our flight back to the isle is significantly less enthralling than before. The sky has lost its luster and the safety of my room sounds wonderful.

Cinder brings us to the edge of the isle and Kieran dismounts, helping me down again. Wordlessly, I begin toward the Citadel, but the brush of his fingers against my shoulder stops me.

"I'd like you to come have dinner with my family." The words are tentative. "If you want, that is."

I swallow. "Your family?"

"My mother, Opal." He sighs and reluctantly offers, "Sebastian."

Return to my room and dwell on my sorrows, or learn more of the Verenathians, even if they reject me?

"I think I'd like that," I say softly.

A wide grin splits his face. "Perfect. Tonight?"

"Tonight," I smile.

CHAPTER 22

ASHDEN

The work day is almost over, and I want nothing more than to lie in bed and think about nothing. I'm tired. I'm so tired. This whole town could burn up in a blaze at this point and I don't know if I'd care.

Every day that I wake up without Rae in the bed next to mine is another day that pounds the reminder of my failure into my head. It's beginning to be too much to bear, so the flask in my pocket is quickly becoming my best friend. I should thank Rod—I never knew numbness could be such a blessing. Better than neverending grief.

That's the hardest thing about all of it—the feeling of grieving someone who's lost without knowing if they actually are. For all I know, she could have found a way around the Accords and is now thriving; beginning the rest of her days where she's always dreamed.

I know that's wishful thinking at best. What she's done is completely illegal. Treason. She knows that. I know that. I just can't bring myself to dwell on the alternative. But the not knowing for certain is what's tearing me apart.

The small stack of papers in my hand rustles as I head back from the Loading Platforms, trying—and failing—to swallow the bitterness that comes every time I have to look a Verenathian in the eye. Every time I have to hand over crates of our hard labor.

I hate them.

I *hate* them.

Entering the Storehouse, I stiffen at the immediate tension. Voices carry in a murmured frenzy, but unlike the usual controlled chaos, something about this is different.

"Bryorfall!" someone shouts.

I scan until I find the source of the voice. Rod.

Closing the gap between us in a few quick strides, I demand, "What is going on?"

His eyes are bright with concern. "Lucielle just left. Lander said he gave Aurandraya a scroll and now the Synod's called a meeting for the whole town tonight."

The Storehouse tilts around me as his words sink in.

"What do you think it's for?" he asks. "I'm hoping it's not a higher demand, granted, I don't think the Synod would call a meeting just for that. But if it's for all departments, it would make sense—"

"I need to go," I interrupt his rambling. Nausea surges within me.

He pauses, clamping his mouth shut. "You okay? You don't look so hot."

I blink, trying to clear my head; fighting the dread that threatens to pull me to the ground. "Tell Aurandraya I went home sick."

"I…" his brow creases. "Alright. Let me know if you need anything."

Nodding, I fumble my way toward the doors without another word.

Rae. I know without question that's what this meeting is for.

Rae has been found.

Rae is dead.

***

The Meeting House is hot and cramped with so many bodies. People stand shoulder to shoulder and spill out into the street, all whispering in confusion and speculation.

Are the Verenathians demanding even more materials and weapons?

Are they going to alter the Accords?

Are they going to send some of their people here to monitor us?

All of these and many more float in the air around me. But I know.

I know.

And I wish I didn't.

My eyes are swollen and gritty, my mouth dry while I wait for them to officially get this meeting underway. Avice squeezes my hand, looking up at me with wide, red-rimmed eyes.

Finally, Lichera climbs the platform at the head of the room, a Verenathian scroll in hand. The rest of the Synod is seated behind him, their faces tight with anger.

He clears his throat before his voice booms through the room. "It has been brought to the Synod's attention that there have been some… misunderstandings amongst you, and, in response, our Verenathian friends have felt the need to reinform us of some very crucial rules outlined in the Accords." He shakes his head. "The fact that this meeting has to be called is a testament to the failure of every person in this room. When rules and instructions are followed, there is peace and prosperity. It really is as simple as that."

Not a whisper or murmur stirs as heavy silence falls over the room.

"Shall I read?" He sneers. Unrolling the scroll, he adjusts the spectacles on his nose. "To all peoples of Ra'goramal: there has recently been a grave infringement of Verenathia's boundaries. It should stand to reason that the laws put in place between our lands exist for explicit purposes, and the ramifications of disobedience are terminal in nature. The perpetrator in question has been found guilty of treason, and has been treated accordingly. Any such further instances will not be tolerated, and may result in the punishment of those deemed innocent."

Bile rises in my throat.

He lowers the scroll, scanning the gathered crowd. "Signed by Verenathia's Court of Elders, Warbearers, and Lucielle." Rubbing the bridge of his nose, eyes closed, he sighs. "Now… do we understand why we don't go to Verenathia?"

Murmurs ripple through the crowd. *Who did it? Who did it? Who did it?* The question they're all asking. Everyone wants to know who committed treason. Who was brave—or stupid enough to try. Who left and got themselves killed.

Lichera scans the crowd, letting the murmuring rise to a cacophony of outrage and fear.

I don't need to hear any more. I shoulder my way through the crowd, desperate to get out of the clustered bodies and heat.

My parents, gone.

And now my sister.

Lichera didn't name anyone… Maybe he doesn't know who. The Verenathians sure as hell didn't ask her name before they executed her.

The Synod is going to begin questioning everyone now. If they've had any rebellious thoughts; if anyone they know has questioned these things; has anyone tried to do anything questionable and do they *really* know the implications of this?

I don't know why they would even bother. The ramifications are clear. No one is going to leave. Rae was the only one desperate enough to try, but she's gone.

Given a nameless death.

I leave the crowd behind and keep walking. I don't stop until I'm miles down the shore, away from it all. Until my mind is quiet enough that I hear the soft crunch of footsteps behind me.

Whirling around, I find Avice. Tears run in silent streams down her face.

I've hardly turned to her, opening my arms before she crashes into me, sobbing. Holding her against me, I sink to my knees, the gravel on the shore biting into my skin.

The weight of what we're forced to endure, and now the very real death of my sister breaks me.

My sister.

My parents.

My *sister.*

My chest feels like it's caving in on itself.

"It's my fault," Avice cries. "Lichera probably noticed the book was missing and he started questioning people and noticed Rae was gone and" —she sucks in a shuddering breath— "it's all my fault."

I hold her tightly, splitting into two. She knows why this happened—we all do. It's law, outlined in the Accords. Always has been, always will be.

But that doesn't make it right.

"Shh," I murmur through the tears wetting my lips. "It's not."

"But it is," she shrieks.

"It's not," I whisper. "She's a grown woman. She made her own decisions."

It's not yours. It's mine.

I've always been able to find my way out of tight situations. My mother used to say it was my father's mind that I inherited—always able to fix things that are broken.

This is something so broken I don't think I'll ever be able to put it back together again.

CHAPTER 23

I'm sitting at the window in my favorite chair, watching out the window as you play. You continue to stumble on the shore, the rocks too cumbersome for your small legs. Ashden follows as if your shadow, picking you up every time you fall. Your spirit travels faster than your legs can take you, and I can see the adventure in you every time you gaze at the open sea.

The afternoon sun beats down on us as we make our way through the district rings of Verenathia. Nearing the end of the residential sector, we come to a stop in front of one of the cottages. Stone pots rest by the front door, filled with vibrant red flowers. Intricate carvings etched into the stone around the windows catch my eye, and I marvel at the delicate hand that formed the soft lines. A jeweled symbol, similar to the ones I saw on the Warbearer's thrones, rests in the frame above the door.

Kieran follows my gaze, landing on the jeweled rune. "It's mandatory for all healers to mark their homes with an imbued rune, signifying their abilities."

"Oh," I whisper, my stomach churning.

He smiles. "Come on."

The door opens smoothly—no creaking hinges, and he leads me inside.

I stand on the threshold as my eyes adjust. The house is similar to ours, but there are two bedrooms instead of a shared common space. Vials and bottles line the countless shelves along the walls, filled with liquids and powders of various colors. Amber jars housing mysterious concoctions take up the tops of the cabinets, and I blink at the herbs hanging from rafters in the ceiling, tied together in stacks and fluffy bundles with colorful ribbons.

"Why doesn't your mom open an apothecary?"

A warm, subdued voice sounds from one of the doorways. "I find it to be much more personable to help those in need from my home."

Kieran's mother emerges, smiling. Petite, but lean with muscle, she watches us with glimmering green eyes. The patina of copper to Kieran's glowing emerald.

She sweeps into the room, rising on her tiptoes to kiss Kieran's cheek. A familiar ache blossoms in my chest at that kiss. Turning a lovely, well-lined face to me, she runs her gaze head to toe.

My skin heats under her appraisal, but there's no animosity in her eyes. The kindness and acceptance there eases some of the tension coiling in my gut.

"I'm Rose Trymera. Kieran and Opal's mother, as I'm sure you know. And yes, I'm a healer, but I choose to do so out of my home. What good is profiting off of others' misfortune?"

The air is sucked out of me, like I've been punched in the gut.

My mother's name was Rosalynn, but my father would always affectionately call her Rosie. I've been careful to avoid the flowers since their passing—never bringing them into the house, doing my best to rush by when they're available in the stands at the market. I can't bear their colorful petals, their scent. It's as if their thorns are memories that puncture my heart, and I'm left bleeding out for days afterward.

I breathe slowly, forcing my breath to remain steady; my vision clear.

A ready smile finds its home on her gentle face; framed by age-streaked auburn hair. She clasps my hand in hers, surprisingly warm and soft despite their leathered appearance. "It's wonderful to meet you."

The silence stretches as I collect myself, and I take another calming breath. "As it is you. I'm Rae—the Goramalan, as I'm sure you know."

Her eyes twinkle playfully. "I've heard some talk, here and there. It's an honor to have you in my home."

A squeeze, and she bustles away, pulling out the chairs at the dining room table. "Come, sit. I'll get supper started."

Kieran steers me toward a doorway. "We'll be back in a minute."

"Okay," her voice is a sing-song pitch as she gives Kieran a knowing look.

The clanking of jars sounds from the main room as Kieran softly closes the door. Books line every possible surface of what I'm assuming to be his room. The desk, several shelves, even part of the bed has a handful of books—all dog-eared and opened in various places.

"You alright?" he asks, watching me intently.

"Mmhmm," I mumble, scanning the room. "You weren't kidding when you said you like to read."

He chuckles. "I told you."

A shelf above his neatly made bed holds wooden figurines, hand carved. I swallow the tightness that finds itself restricting my breath, and look away.

A text rests open on the desk, and I run a finger along the worn pages. The language is clunky and unfamiliar; I don't even recognize half of the characters.

"What is this?"

He peers over my shoulder at the odd book. "Ah, the Ancient Language."

Swiveling my head up to him, I furrow my brow. "What ancient language?"

"The language of the world before the War."

"Hmm," I hum. "I didn't know there was such a thing."

Moving beside me, he surveys the stacks of books on his desk. "And that surprises you?"

I scoff. "No."

A leather-bound tome with yellowed pages lies atop a stack of others—that same unfamiliar language scrolling down their spines. With frayed binding and a cover almost worn through in spots, it looks like it's being held together by sheer will alone.

Old. Very old.

Kieran follows my gaze. "*The Covenant*," he says, almost reverently. "Very old magic. And what I can't seem to figure out," he gestures toward the numerous books, "is its translation. Not fully, at least. There's an addendum at the beginning written in our own language… It speaks of another book like it, but I haven't been able to find it. I wonder if it could be the key."

A book not found in the endless Verenathian library? Something deep, deep within me perks its ears at that—listening.

"Can I look?"

"Of course."

Running my fingers along the cover, I instantly recognize the pattern of dragonhide. Carefully, so carefully, I flip through the faded pages. Nothing stands out among the unfamiliar characters.

"Why do you have this?" It's unreadable, nothing of the characters or structure recognizable.

He's silent for a moment, chewing his lip. "I've been looking—"

"Hey!" Sebastian's voice calls. He barrels through the cottage before swinging Kieran's door open.

"Oh," his eyebrows meet his hairline before he wiggles them at Kieran. "My bad. Don't mind me, just..." he slowly backs out of the doorway, easing the door shut.

Kieran rolls his eyes, yanking the door out of Sebastian's grasp, and we emerge into the main area. Rose's cheerful humming fills the room as Opal closes the front door behind her.

Her eyes light when she sees me. "Hi, friend." She strides to Rose, placing a kiss on her cheek. "Hi, mama."

I take a seat at the table, the rawness in my chest sharpening, ever so slightly.

Opal sits across from me. "I didn't know you were going to be here tonight."

"If I had known," Sebastian tosses me a wink as he flops into the chair next to her. "I would have worn my favorite suit. Green really makes the blue in my eyes pop."

I stifle a giggle as Opal gives him a sidelong glance.

"Ms. Trymera, can I help you with anything?" I ask.

Her voice is as bright as the sun as she says, "Please, call me Rose. Life is too short for formalities. A friend of my children's is a child of mine."

I offer a tight-lipped smile, swallowing hard. Kieran's attention on me eats into my soul but I avoid looking at him, unsure if I can handle the questioning concern I know will be there. Instead, I busy myself with the jars lining the wall, finding them to be very, very interesting.

Rose brings a large pot of potatoes and plops it in the center of the table. Handing each of us a knife, she says, "You can all set to work peeling these."

A grumble from Sebastian, but soon, merry chatter fills the room while we painstakingly pare the skins. Between muttered curses and slipped potatoes rolling across the table, the number of unclean ones in the pot slowly dwindles.

Laughter floats through the air. The room is filled—full to the brim with more than just the bodies gathered.

Kieran's deep, clear laugh reverberates around me, pulling me back to the present. A delicious, warm scent has begun to waft through the room—making my mouth water.

"Well would you look at that," Sebastian smirks. "The man does have a sense of humor." Kieran slugs him in the shoulder, prompting a wide-eyed gesture of innocence.

"What? It's not my fault you've been so distracted lately."

The faintest warmth creeps up Kieran's smooth, creamy skin. "I have not," he starts, but is cut off by Rose when she leans in, an unreadable expression on her face. She takes the pot—now full of peeled potatoes—to the stove.

"If you boys are going to start tussling, take it outside," she reprimands.

Sebastian smiles sweetly at her. "We would never, Rose. Kieran is too afraid I'd mar his pretty face."

Quicker than I can process, Kieran has Sebastian removed from the chair and pinned to the ground in a maneuver I could never even hope to attempt. Full of satisfaction, he grins as he presses Sebastian into the ground. "I'm sorry, what was that, again?"

I laugh when Sebastian grunts. "That wasn't fair; I wasn't ready."

Opal rolls her eyes at the two grown men on the ground. Kieran rises to his feet, offering a hand to Sebastian—who takes it, but only to pull Kieran down beside him.

Rose shoos them out as Opal sighs. "You'd think they were still twelve years old."

I laugh again, truly laugh.

"Rae, would you be a dear and put these in serving bowls?" Rose calls from her place near the stove, gesturing to the jars at her side. The clip of metal on the wooden cutting block rings through the room as she deftly chops carrots.

I rise. "Of course, can you show me where they are?"

She points with her knife to a shelf across the room filled with plates and bowls, but my attention snags on the one right above, lined with an assortment of concoctions. I scan the menagerie of jars and vials, wondering at the strange substances they contain.

A pale blue, effervescent liquid catches my eye as it… swirls? Yes—*moves* of its own accord within the jar.

My breath hitches. Tiny, twinkling lights, like the smallest of fireflies, dance throughout. The pale, shimmering liquid is borderline translucent—almost a mist, and yet, as thick and viscous as syrup; if its movements are any indication.

Wide-eyed, I ask, "What is this?"

Rose looks up from her chopping. "Ah," she muses, her eyes shining. "Of all the substances in my possession, that is the most valuable. You're looking at liquid starlight, my dear."

My eyebrows practically reach my hairline as I gape at her, dumbfounded.

"Long ago—so long ago that it has passed from memory, there was an island; abounding in the magic we now possess. Legends say the Author himself resided on this island, writing the story of the world from amongst its brilliance and plenty.

"According to these same legends: once a year, the stars would fall—attracted to the magnificence of the land and the Author, himself. They would collect in a pool at the center of the island where they would then diffuse. In the process, the water absorbed their essence."

She gestures to the shimmering jar. "It's unknown how or by whom it was collected, but at some point, someone was able to. It's been passed down in my family for many generations. Slowly, very slowly, dwindling with each healer it's bestowed upon."

"What does it do?" I breathe.

Her eyes, still twinkling, crinkle at the corners. "It does whatever you need it to. Bind up a wound, resolve mental maladies, cure an infection; even heal a broken heart."

I don't know if I'm breathing.

"It is to be used sparingly, only in the most dire of situations—and even just a drop at a time, at that."

"That's…" I falter. "That's amazing. I've never heard of anything like it."

"Most haven't," she winks. "Folklore and stories and all."

I swallow. "Do you believe that this… this island—that it was real?"

The knife in her hand goes still as she turns to me, her expression soft but an unmistakable fire in her eyes. "If you are looking, my dear Rae, for something to believe in; something deeper and more meaningful than what you've found yet—I will not have the answers you seek."

Casting my gaze down, I nod.

She moves gracefully to the shelf, selecting an empty stone bowl. Placing a warm hand on my shoulder, she hands it to me, whispering.

"But I do. Never stop looking."

Chapter 24

It's a dark, stormy night. You and Ashden are peacefully asleep as the rain and wind batter our cottage. I can't help but watch you, little bird. You are so peaceful when you sleep. It is the only time I can see the storm quieted within you.

The sun has set by the time Kieran and Sebastian return, disheveled and panting, right as I'm helping Rose and Opal set bowls of steaming food on the table. Roasted carrots, mashed potatoes, baked lamb and chicken; a large bowl of gravy, and sweetened peach preserves to go with the fresh bread. The sight of it makes my mouth water, reminding me of the lack of food I've had today.

"Man, it smells amazing in here," Sebastian says, falling into his seat. Opal swats at him as he leans over her to claim a piece of bread.

"A feast," Kieran agrees.

Rose beams. "I had to make sure our guest was well taken care of."

Kieran casts me a questioning glance, eyes darting to Rose as she bustles cheerfully about the room. I offer an encouraging nod of my head, which seems to satisfy him enough.

We take our seats and begin passing around dishes laden with the steaming fare. Sebastian heaps his plate full, commenting loudly on how delicious it is.

He's not wrong. I close my eyes, savoring the flavors dancing on my tongue. The joy and love put into the food is evident in every single bite.

The last time I tasted anything like this, my parents were still alive. I hadn't realized how much I missed it.

"I just can't get my form quite right," Opal admits, speaking of some advanced combat maneuver she's been practicing. I drag myself out of my thoughts.

"Maybe it would make more sense if I showed you, granted you'd be too distracted by all of *this*," Sebastian gestures grandly to himself. She only levels a blank stare at him.

"I'm sure Frellan could help you when he's outside of classes," Rose offers.

Opal shrugs. "Probably."

Sebastian stabs a carrot as big as my finger. "My offer still stands."

"Thank you, I'll keep that in mind," she smiles sweetly at him. Glancing at me, wicked amusement dancing in her eyes, she says, "Rae came to one of our sessions too."

"Oh?" Rose rests her fork on her plate, dabbing a napkin to her chin.

My face heats when I remember that specific session, Kieran's body so close to mine. His hands on me, around me, guiding me through the movements. I almost choke on the lamb in my mouth.

"Yes," I take a long drink of water. "It's very different from anything we've been taught on Ra'goramal. I don't think it's my strong suit."

"That's okay." Opal's voice is muffled behind a mouthful of potatoes. "Everyone has something they excel in. Kieran can't paint to save his life."

I quirk an eyebrow at him.

"The arts are not my specialty," he concedes.

Sebastian snorts. "Isn't that the truth. One time, we were instructed to make clay dragons in class. Kieran's abomination was the stuff of nightmares. I still think about it," he shudders.

"And yet, no one is talking about your attempt at the alchemy experiment that almost blew half the Citadel up," Kieran retorts.

Sebastian stutters while Opal's bright laugh bubbles around us. Rose is beaming, the softness in her eyes when she gazes at Opal and Kieran not lost on me.

Joy, a kind of joy I haven't felt in too long, floats softly through the room—a sense of delighted contentment. My stomach and chest and heart are warm, aching, and not because of the delicious meal. Laughter punctuates the lively conversation, which has moved to a debate between Opal and Sebastian on whether they would rather have blueberries in the form of pies or muffins.

I wonder if they realize how privileged they are to have their mother. The question of their absent father gnaws at me, but I know better than to mention it.

Each meal Ashden and I now share has become a reminder of what we've lost. While we sit with the two empty chairs across from us, eating what's easily available, no longer is the comfort in the multi-course meals my mother would make. Richly layered scents filled our house each evening as she carefully and lovingly prepared our meals. Neither Ashden nor I inherited her talent.

Rose brushes my hand from her place on the side of the table next to mine, asking, "Is everything to your liking?"

"Oh yes," I agree heartily, "Everything is perfect." I return her smile, hoping she doesn't notice the slight quiver to my lips.

And everything is perfect. So perfect.

I can feel Kieran watching me from across the table again. Not a judgemental or scrutinizing gaze; only gentle contemplation. And again, I avoid it.

Too quickly, the meal is finished. I help clear the table, trying to ignore the ache in my chest. My heart is too raw, too exposed; its protective layers stripped away by the quiet joy of this evening.

Kieran comes to my side and asks softly, "Are you ready to go?"

"Sure," I say, realizing only now how late it is.

I follow him to Rose's side at the wash basin, wrist deep in soapy water. Opal waits nearby with a rag, drying the dishes while Sebastian puts them away.

"I'm going to take Rae back to the Citadel," he says, planting a kiss on his mother's cheek.

"Of course," she flings her arms around his neck, careful not to place her wet hands on his back. Turning to me, her face creases with a smile. "Thank you for coming, Rae. If you need anything while you're here, you let me know, okay? You're always welcome in our home."

"Thank you," I say hoarsely.

Her eyes are still crinkled by her smile, but now hold a level of understanding I didn't notice before. Knowledge that could only be gleaned from a healer—or a mother. She throws her arms around my shoulders the same way she did Kieran, and I find myself wrapping mine around her, holding tightly. I breathe in, steadying myself, inhaling the scent of earth and spice, and… roses.

She retreats, holding me at arms length. I don't even care that my shoulders are now soaked from the dishwater on her hands.

"Thank you," I say again, blinking rapidly. She nods, squeezing me in response.

***

We walk silently through the now-still city rings. The moon is high overhead, bathing the world in pale, silvery light.

I try to sort through myself as each memory from tonight, each clip of a moment, stings; chafing at my already raw emotions. Try as I might, I can't swallow the gaping ache in my chest or the burning in my eyes.

Kieran doesn't speak. Holding the gentle silence and space I need. No expectation, never demanding an explanation.

As we reach the first inner ring, nearing the Citadel, he breaks the silence by asking, "Can I show you something?"

A large part of me wants to return to my room and dissolve into oblivion. But some other, smaller part of me quietly says yes.

"Sure."

He takes my hand and leads me off the path at the great stairway leading up toward the Citadel; instead, cutting a diagonal line through the lush grass, away from civilization and into the silvery unknown.

***

We veer inland off the footpath. Lush grasslands give way to stones reaching toward the night sky. Pillars of stone—some are only as high as my waist, while others tower over us. Most are like trees, tall and narrow, and grow more tightly packed the further we go.

A forest of stone. There are no branches and leaves providing a blanket of cover, but rather, tendrils of a wispy, smoke-like substance weave through the tops of the pillars above us, casting the forest floor into an ethereal milky glow.

A soft murmur begins at the edge of my hearing as the rocks grow closer together. Soon, we're sidestepping and squeezing in between the spaces to get to our destination—that murmuring growing louder with each step forward.

I'm surprised Kieran is able to find his way, as I'm scarcely able to fit between them—or even see in the moonlight, dimmed by the smoke-like substance swirling above us. He hoists himself onto a waist-level rock and climbs higher, now a layer above me, and picks his way across its surface before reaching down to offer a hand. I hesitate only a moment before taking it, allowing him to pull me up with him.

Carefully, we make our way across the tops of the pillars—now a plain stretching on and on around us. The forest floor below disappears, that smokey substance swirling about our feet.

We come to a wall of pillars so closely packed that they form, what seems to be, an impenetrable barrier. Curiosity burns through me, pressing my sorrow into an almost-memory now as Kieran wordlessly leads me along the wall. In the low light, I can make out a small opening straight ahead of us.

He goes through first, leading me through after him. The scales on my suit graze cleanly off the stone as I squeeze through.

Emerging on the other side, my breath catches at the sight before me.

That murmuring is a waterfall; roaring over a bed of stone pillars and tumbling into a pool.

The water is unlike any I've ever seen on Ra'goramal. It practically glows, effervescent in the moonlight as its mist shatters into rainbows with no sunlight to do so.

Looking down into the shimmering pool, I'm shocked to find no reflection on the water. But every color imaginable swirls within its depths; glowing, pulsing, shimmering. I blink hard as twinkling lights seem to dance among the rainbows, blinking in and out of view.

Just like that jar of starlight.

I take a step back, absorbing this strange and wonderful place. The foliage around the pool is such a vibrant green, even under the light of the moon. More flowers than I've ever seen at once seem to burst from every bush and vine and rock.

I stoop down to a flower growing near the edge of the pool, fingering its petals delicately. It looks as if it's made of glass, transparent and gleaming, but is velvety smooth under my touch. Panning my gaze around the pool, I find them all glass with drastically different shapes and colors and sizes.

"What is this?" I breathe, spinning in a slow circle to take it all in.

"We call them Ethereal Ponds. There's several of them." He gently plucks a flower from its resting spot and places it between my fingers. "But this one is my favorite." Its stem is so delicate, this small pink flower with its bell-shaped petals.

Kieran moves to the edge of the glimmering pool and lowers himself, reaching out his hand to run it lazily through the water.

My heart lurches when I see a slither of movement below the surface, casting ripples throughout the colors. I lean down, peering closer.

"You might want to—" Kieran's voice is cut off by my shriek as a creature flies out of the water and into my chest. I brace myself, but it thuds softly against me before flying away, perching on a nearby outcropping.

The unusual creature cocks its head, watching me curiously with large brown eyes. It has the lithe, scaled body of a fish, but with wings instead of fins.

"What?" I choke, squinting in disbelief. They are fins, trailing delicately around the sides of its body. It hops from the rocks in a bundle of orange and white, propelling itself off of paw-like feet.

Another one glides out of the water and into Kieran's lap. He chuckles as it wriggles around like a puppy, nudging his hand for attention.

"What are these?" I ask, dumbfounded.

Two more fly out and into the air, delicately swooping above the pool before coming to rest beside me. I ease myself down and hesitantly hold my hand out. One of them comes forward, nuzzling its face in my open palm.

"Canipis," Kieran says. "They're very friendly."

A giggle escapes me as more emerge and clamber onto my lap. Their bodies are surprisingly warm rather than the cold I was expecting. Curious, I reach my hand into the water, only to find it as warm and light as the night air.

"This is incredible," I laugh. The canipis curl up against my outstretched legs while the ones in my lap nestle down, closing their eyes as if ready to take a nap.

"They're pretty amazing." Kieran gently strokes the canipi that landed on him, now sound asleep. My aching heart softens at how tender he is with the little creatures.

He glances up, catching my eye with the brilliant green of his own. I look away quickly, heat prickling under my collar.

The moment soon passes, and I revel in the roar of the waterfall while the canipis sleep against me. The moon watches us quietly, none of the smokey wisps weaving among the stones on the other side of the wall to be found.

Kieran says gently, "I know you're missing your home. If there's anything bothering you or anything you want to talk about, I'm here. And if you don't, that's alright too. I'm here either way."

The suffocating grief at the reminders of my parents come flooding back to me. The pain that I've worked so hard to hide, suppressed in a dark corner of my heart, threatens to spill over—threatens to drown me.

Ashden and I never discussed their passing; it was always too painful. The only conversations we've shared have been about logistical issues: when to have the funeral, what to do with their belongings, whose beds we now sleep in. Avice was always there with open arms when I needed it, but I mostly avoid the topic. It's easier that way.

Yet, something about the way he talks, the gentle understanding, prompts me onward.

I give him a small smile. "I know what you're asking, you don't have to dodge the question."

"I didn't want to push," he shrugs. "Doesn't feel right. But, that's an open invitation. Anything you do, or don't want to share, is completely up to you. I'm simply here."

Bolstered by his openness, his sincerity—I take a deep breath, steadying myself. "My parents died in a shipwreck a little over a year ago."

And there it is—that never ending sorrow given a voice.

Blinking against the moisture in my eyes, I focus on the peaceful canipi in my lap, on the steady rise and fall of its scaled side.

"I'm so sorry, Rae." His deep voice is rough, tinged with something deeper than sympathy.

A watery laugh escapes me. "It's okay. It's okay. My mother kept a diary my whole life and I had no idea. I don't know what she intended to do with it, but most of the entries were addressed to me. A handful are to my father and brother, but... It's almost like it was her last secret to me. I've been reading through it slowly," my voice falters. "It's almost too much to bear, some days."

That precious book; one I haven't even told Ashden of. And maybe it's selfish, but I don't regret it. He'll read it, one day.

A tear sneaks its way down my cheek, but I quickly brush it away, hoping he doesn't notice.

"The last time I saw them, they were leaving for my father's boat. My mother and I had spent that day together, buying our favorite things from the bakery and exploring the grasslands above town. She had found a cluster of wild indigos and pocketed a handful of them—told me she was going to paint them later." I smile at the memory. "She was an artist. A seamstress by trade, but it was painting that she adored. You could see the passion in every single brushstroke. She taught me to see all the color in life—the good and the bad—and to appreciate the beauty in all of it."

Kieran's warm hand rests gently on mine. "She sounds wonderful."

"She was," I whisper, not trusting my voice to remain steady. A heartbeat of silence passes as I collect myself. "Her name was Rosalynn."

Another heartbeat.

"She called me her little bird. I think she was always afraid I was going to fly away."

"Well well…"

"I know."

And here I am. Was it fear with which she thought of me flying away, or expectation?

"I would have liked to meet her," he says lightly; sincerely.

"She would have loved to meet you, if things weren't the way they are."

"Well, you could have introduced me as your lover," he says wryly. "Maybe the Synod would have been kind enough to make an exception. Love knows no boundaries, after all."

I nudge him in the arm. "You wish."

Even as I say the words, I'm hoping he can't see the question burning within me. Is that really how he feels? With this—whatever this is—between us?

He chuckles, returning his attention to the sleeping canipi in his lap.

I'm surprised at the ease with which I can talk to him—sharing things I've never shared with anyone. We may have only known each other for a short time, but already—in ways I can't quite fathom, yet—he feels like he's becoming a part of me.

"I don't see my father anymore," he says unexpectedly. "I know it's not the same as if he were truly gone, but…" his voice trails off, the rigidness in his body breaking as his shoulders slump.

"What happened?" I ask softly, regretting the words the moment they leave my mouth. "You don't have to answer that," I wince.

Several moments pass in silence. "It's a long story," he says eventually, sighing heavily. "But there's time for that. I just wanted you to know you're not alone."

I nod, offering him a tight-lipped smile.

He returns my pitiful look. "Pain for pain."

A sad laugh barks out of me. "Well Kieran—life is full of pain, isn't it?"

"Cheers to that."

The canipi in my lap twitches, its long fin flopping over its head.

"But there's good too," he says quietly.

His strong hand envelops mine, and I savor the warmth and tenderness of his touch.

"Always," I murmur.

He eases himself down to his back, lying in the soft grass. A smile tugs at my lips when he pats the ground beside him.

With an unceremonious groan, I join him. We lay like that—side by side in companionable silence while the stars keep watch.

CHAPTER 25

Never fear the unknown, my dear. Be aware, be cautious, but never afraid. Approach it willingly, and learn from it.

The feeling of Kieran's body lying next to mine lingers against my skin. The soft words spoken between us in the seclusion of the Ethereal Ponds—my stomach warms at the memory. A different sort of warmth, though, then what lights there at the sight of him in his skintight suit. A more… tentative warmth. A softer one. One that offers small pieces of myself with the hope that they'll be accepted, understood. A warmth that grows stronger with every pain shared.

And although his nearness is distracting right now, I push the thoughts and memories away, focusing on the magic in front of me.

In spite of the negativity I dealt with last time, I can't get enough of the Field of Stars. We've been sitting here for hours among the islands of rock and wind; practicing magic, enjoying the openness. It's the only place I feel the most… me, even if that insatiable ache rears itself.

If I could live out here forever, I would.

And if I could just perfect this damned sphere, I would.

A tiny bead of sweat trickles down my temple as I focus on the illuminated shape in my hand. I keep bending bands of light around it, willing it to hold its shape, but it's sloppy at best.

"Ugh," I huff in frustration, sending the light off the edge of the rock we dangle from. A sky-blue dragon darts in front of us, catching the rough-hewn sphere in her mouth before disappearing.

Kieran stretches a line of fire between his open palms. "It's okay, these things take time."

Eyeing the flame, I visualize the energy flowing around it—allowing it to move freely within and through me—until I can see it right in front of my face.

I reach for a bit of Kieran's fire, and feel no pain when it licks my fingers.

I gasp. "How does that work?"

He flicks his fingers, shaping the fire into one of the glass-like flowers of the Ethereal ponds, and hands it to me. "You were grasping its energy—its essence. Let go of the magic and you'll see very quickly what it does."

Carefully taking the flaming flower from him, I begin to release my hold on the magic, allowing the physical world to take back over.

Immediately, my hand begins burning. I drop the flower off the edge too, shaking the heat from my fingers.

That same dragon appears, shooting a streaming jet of fire at the flower from where she's landed on a rock near us. Just as quickly, she takes off when the two flames meet.

Inspecting my palm and finding no damage other than reddened skin, I again pull myself into the magic and begin trying to manipulate water droplets.

"You know, it's easier if you focus on one element at a time—mastering it before you move on to the next."

I let go of the magic and look at him. "You want to know what's infuriating?"

He lifts an eyebrow. "Oh no—Rae is angry about something again? I, for one, would have never seen that coming."

Ignoring the comment completely, I continue on. "The fact that there's a world of magic and possibilities at our fingertips, but it's been kept hidden from an entire people for an age—and taught to another that those people are inferior and incapable of it."

A dragon roars from nearby, as if in agreement.

Kieran rests a comforting hand on my thigh. "Rae… you're capable of so much more than they've led you to believe—so much more powerful than you've probably ever thought possible. What's been taken and kept hidden from you and your people is nothing short of the greatest crime known to our world. It's your birthright. Your power to behold."

"I know."

"You want to know what I think?" he asks, now absentmindedly stroking his finger up and down my thigh. "I think that if you knew—if all of you knew—what you're capable of, they couldn't control you. Once that knowledge and purpose is written into your identity, they can't take it away from you. Letting you believe you're nothing more than another body is exactly what they want to keep you from realizing you're worth so much more."

The sky-blue dragon appears again, swirling and flipping in front of us before diving toward the sea.

I can't help the frustration leaching into my voice. "Who are you talking about? Who are they? You act like you know something else I don't."

That same dragon darts across the sky again, but this time I notice it.

A pause.

No. I *feel* it.

Kieran opens his mouth to speak but I hold up a hand.

"Hold on."

He falls silent, his brow furrowed. I keep my eyes on the sky: watching, waiting for her to appear again.

Her.

That's impossible—there's no way for me to know who or what she is.

She appears again, swooping gracefully among the others, and I just know. Her scales are a beautiful, shimmering mix of blues and whites, seamlessly blending her into the sky.

Cinder lands behind us and chortles to Kieran.

"Be right back," he whispers, rising to his feet.

I murmur something to him but I can't take my eyes from her, mesmerized as she hops from rock to rock, beating her wings playfully with the others.

She lifts her head and my heart stops. Her deep blue eyes dance as she stares right at me, gracefully bobbing her head. I motion to her, but she only continues to watch.

She's saying something, I know she is, but I can't quite make it out. As if whatever it is—it's just out of reach.

A small chirp, and with a flick of her snout, she dives off the rock, blending into the sky.

I almost cry out as she disappears. I can't explain why but I need to see her again. What was she saying when she looked at me? The bobbing of her head as she watched me… beckoned me.

To what? What do you want?

I catch a glimpse of the tip of her wing below.

She wanted something from me. Could it be a piece to the puzzle that's been plaguing me?

I glance back at Kieran, who's murmuring something to Cinder as he strokes her neck.

What if I never see her again? Whatever she was saying, whatever she wanted—I can't let that go.

I only give a moment's contemplation before I know what I need to do. Taking a deep breath, I close my eyes—counting to five before I thrust myself off the edge of the rock.

Into oblivion.

Kieran's screams are lost in the howling of the wind as I fall.

Writhing, my limbs flailing uselessly, the wind buffets my body and stings my eyes as I try to make sense of the undulating clouds around me. Terror seizes me, forcing the air from my lungs.

I've made a mistake, completely misreading the situation—letting my emotions get the better of me.

Again.

Rocks. Hundreds of them. Blocking my path to the sea—which falling into would alone kill me. One is rising up to meet me far quicker than I'm comfortable with as I continue to fall, helpless.

Squinting against the ripping wind and sunlight, I search for the dragon, but I can't find her. Everything is falling and spinning so fast, the only thing I'm sure of is the large rock drawing ever closer below me.

Ashden.

"I'm so sorry!" I cry, panic throwing me headlong into the yawning abyss of incoming death.

I'm going to die.

I'm going to die, not because I broke the Accords; not because I was executed. No, I'm going to die because I jumped off of a floating rock.

"You idiot!" I scream. I'm a Goramalan. Goramalans can't have dragons.

My breath comes in choked gasps as the wind pushes the air from my lungs, and I reach for something, anything to grab onto. Something to stop my freefall—a lifeline.

Unable to see anything against the wind forcing my eyes half shut, I flail my arms and legs out blindly, knowing it won't do me any good. Even the smallest of rocks at this speed would end in something broken—or worse.

I see a glimpse of sky-colored movement out of my peripherals, and a primal scream tears through my throat. The only sounds I hear are those of the wind and the scream shredding my vocal cords.

There it is, I see it again.

I cry out, begging for her to save me. Fear grips me entirely, locking my body as I face the rock coming up below me, uncomfortably close and only getting closer. I let out one more long, pleading cry before my voice gives out, but she's disappeared from my view again.

Acceptance settles over me, leadening my bones and drawing me faster toward the rock as I surrender.

I'm sorry. I cast one more apology to Ashden, wishing with my whole heart I could tell him in person. I know the pain my death is going to cause him, and it's all my fault.

The smooth surface of the rock comes into view, clear from the mist of clouds. I close my eyes, not wanting my last memory to be that of stone before my body smashes into it.

The breath is knocked from me as I collide with something.

Hard.

I groan in pain while every bone in my body screams as they bear the impact.

I must be dead now.

The sound of the wind—that I would have expected to be absent in the afterlife—continues to batter me. I open my eyes quickly, a cry tearing up my throat as I realize I'm not falling through the air anymore, but flying.

The dragon is supporting me, sprawled across her body. Horrified, I scramble to my hands and knees on her back, struggling to keep my balance as she keeps up her speed through the sky.

Slowly crawling forward, tightly gripping the protruding scales along her back, I find the natural dip behind her forelegs that serves as a seat.

My thoughts are a jumble of terror and confusion, but she gives a little flick of her wings, nudging me into that dip.

I lift off of her for one horrifying second before clutching her scales, desperately trying to keep my hold as I ease my legs over her.

She accepts me there, craning her head to look at me with ancient, midnight-blue eyes. They seem to hold approval as she watches me closely. My hand is shaking as I reach out to stroke her neck, which draws a soft chortle from her.

"Thank you," I pant. She eyes me again, curious. This must be one of the times Kieran told me about. When the dragons have mercy on foolish humans who fall out of the sky.

"What's your name?"

But even as I ask the question, I realize I don't need to. I know her name, and have always known it—much like I've always known I was going to leave the only home I've ever known to come to this strange and wonderful place.

A trickle of… something—something I can't isolate—but feels as if it's a part of me runs through my mind; my heart; my very being. A part of me, and yet, something entirely different—a soft, shimmering vein, intertwining. I can feel her. Her presence, her life.

Her. The vein is a connection that translates itself without my trying.

"Boreal," I say, breathless. Wriggling underneath me, she chirps joyfully. My heart is still trying to beat its way out of my ribcage but I force myself to take measured, even breaths.

I grasp her horns tightly as she starts to beat her wings harder, thrusting us higher into the atmosphere. The large rocks we were soaring alongside now shrink into pebbles as we ascend.

She banks hard to the right, and I almost lose my seat. Squeezing my legs as hard as I can around her midsection, I don't ask her to stop.

She chortles, and I swear she's laughing at me.

We soar for several minutes—giving me time to find my seat. I settle in, reveling in the natural fit of her below me. Relaxing my body, I begin to move with her—leaning as she banks, bobbing fluidly as she beats her wings. But when she attempts a barrel roll I cry out, almost losing my seat. She levels out, again giving that chortling laugh.

Tears of joy—not unlike my first flight with Cinder—begin to stream down my face.

A dragon. What is happening?

Is this really my dragon?

She can't be. I'm a Goramalan—dragons don't bond with Goramalans. This can't be real.

Traitor.

She gives a roar as if to say "How dare you?"

"I'm sorry!" I shout above the wind.

Something settles deep within me—clicking into place as if it's a missing puzzle piece.

This is my dragon.

Traitor.

A torrent of guilt tries to overwhelm me but I block it out, not daring to ruin this moment.

A blue-gray dragon joins, soaring alongside us. The figure on its back, wearing an unreadable expression, levels his emerald eyes on me.

"Oh shit," I whisper. "I think Kieran's mad at me."

Cutting through the sky together, we arrive at a wide, flat rock, gliding down and coming to a smooth landing.

Well, smooth for Boreal. The impact almost jars me from my seat, and I shuffle myself unceremoniously from her back before thudding to the ground.

"I'm gonna have to work on that," I mutter.

I take a step back, admiring her. This can't be real. I have to be dreaming right now. Maybe I did die on that rock and this is some blessed afterlife.

She's slightly smaller than Cinder, and her sky-colored scales almost make her appear wraithlike; all sleek lines and smooth edges as she shimmers in the sunlight.

She cranes her neck, peering behind me, and begins to wriggle and paw at the ground. I hear a greeting chirp, then the scrape of claws on stone from Cinder as she saunters over.

I wince when I turn to Kieran. His expression is closely guarded, but the churning emotion behind his eyes is evident as he walks slowly toward us, his arms crossed.

"I thought you fell," he says evenly.

I shake my head, my voice a raw, broken thing now that I'm no longer whispering. "I'm sorry. I just—I felt something." My eyes search his, pleading. "I couldn't ignore it."

He sighs heavily, shocking me as he pulls me into a tight hug. I can't think, can't even breathe over the sensation of his arms around me, the side of my face pressed perfectly against his heart. I breathe in the salt rain scent of him, letting it wash over me.

"Maybe give a little more warning next time," he murmurs against my hair.

I pause when he releases me, wishing I could stay in his arms forever.

"You came after me?" I ask, realizing now why he was on Cinder.

He gives me a look, as if to say that that's the stupidest question he's ever heard. "Of course."

Gently holding his hand out, he steps toward Boreal while she lowers her head. Resting her snout against his palm, she snuffles loudly. I hold my breath, waiting, and then she nudges her head into his chest. He chuckles, and reaches to stroke behind her horn.

"You did it, Rae."

A wide grin splits my face as pride and joy bloom through me.

We did it.

Boreal rises to her full height, easily more than double mine—and looks down at us, chirping. She seems equally as proud.

"She's young," Kieran muses, running his hand along her side. "She's perfect."

Cinder snuffs. Tossing her head indignantly, she shuffles away from Kieran, placing herself behind me.

He smirks. "Perfect for Rae, you little brat."

She relents and returns to his side, but it's me he's watching.

"What?" I ask.

He shakes his head as if to clear it. "Nothing."

I watch with disappointment as the wonder in his expression fades to concern.

"You're afraid of what everyone is going to think of a Goramalan taking one of your dragons."

Blowing out a long breath, he crosses his arms. "No, not afraid. I just don't want you to draw any more attention to yourself." He pauses. "I don't think you should tell anyone."

I start, my temper flaring.

I've always dreamed of having a dragon. Longingly watching the Loading Platforms from the bluffs, I would envision myself on the backs of all the dragons that I saw—how it would feel, what I would do with that amount of freedom. No more responsibilities weighing me down, no bleakness.

I know I don't deserve it though. Alongside the dwindling excitement of finding my own dragon, is the niggling, sickly-sweet whisper that's started driving through my thoughts.

Traitor.

A traitor to my people. A traitor to my brother. To Avice.

Seeming to read my thoughts, he says, "All I'm saying is maybe don't go parade it around. It's probably best if you stick to the outskirts of the Field; don't let everyone see you on her."

As much as I hate to admit it, he's probably right. "Can I tell Sebastian and

Opal, at least?"

He smiles wickedly. "Of course. Opal might have your head though."

I smirk and step toward Boreal, breathless at the way her iridescent scales display every color of the rainbow within their sky-blue hue. She spreads her wings and chortles, as if to show them off. The sun catches on the webbing between her spines, illuminating it in a glowing pinkish-blue.

I cup her snout in my hands, peering into the wisdom her eyes hold. She blinks slowly.

"This is going to be our little secret," I whisper to her. Bobbing her head, she grunts.

I swear that's a nod.

I trail my fingers over the tiny, delicate scales along her face. Blues, greens, and pinks form an intricate, glimmering pattern. So beautiful; she rivals Verenathian sunsets.

"Boreal," I whisper, speaking her name just to marvel at the way it sounds. Already I can feel that vein through me settling even deeper, sinking into the fabric of my being.

I am hers, and she is mine.

CHAPTER 26

ASHDEN

The sun is beginning to set behind the isle as I head back to the Storehouse from my final shipment of the day.

Ever since Verenathia's declaration, people have been speaking in hushed whispers, eyeing each other suspiciously. I've gotten my fair share of side eye as conversations fall silent when I walk by.

Everyone knows Markell's assistant has been missing now, and it doesn't take a genius to put the pieces together. The town is in a panic—half expecting Verenathia to up demand as punishment or send soldiers to monitor. The tentative peace we held has now crumbled, and the fear thickening the air is palpable. Tempers flare in the Storehouse, Loadmasters watch everything with an eagle's eye, and the Synod has been breathing down everyone's necks.

All I have left is Avice, and as much as I love her, I can feel myself slipping further into a yawning abyss by the day. The only thing keeping me from falling completely is the bottle of liquor I keep under my bed. Avice would kill me if she found it, although I'm sure she can see it all over me.

The commanding clip of boots on the cobbled street issues ahead of me, and I drag my gaze from the ground to see Lichera peering at me across his rat's nose. The glass on his new spectacles is narrower than his last, causing him to squint even harder into them.

Surprisingly, I haven't seen him for a couple days. He's usually around somewhere in the Storehouse, barking orders and generally making himself a nuisance, but he's been absent from duties. Most likely responsibilities of the Synod, especially with the chaos now. But still, odd.

He nods cordially, but I see the hint of undisguised suspicion in his eyes. The hair on the back of my neck prickles.

"Head Lichera," I incline my head.

His gait slows as he approaches me, his eyes searching as if he's looking for something and will find the evidence on me.

"Evening, Bryorfall."

I stare back, unfazed. "I haven't seen you in the Storehouse for a few days." A casual question.

He stiffens slightly. "I've been on official business of the Synod," he says cooly. "I was just making my way there now, having been in my office all day, taking care of shipment paperwork. Not that it's any of your business, *citizen*."

I do my best not to bristle. "Understood. I hope things have been running smoothly?"

He scoffs and makes a pointed sweep of the town along the shore. "How do you think things have been running, Bryorfall?"

I really don't want to do this right now.

"I assume they've been easier," is all I offer.

"Mmm," he hums, again searching me.

Something is off. "Is there something I can do for you, sir?"

He cocks his head. "Funny you should ask. Do you happen to know where your sister has been?"

My stomach sickens.

"We've been falling behind in that department, so, naturally, I looked into the need and found that your sister hasn't shown up for her duties for quite some time now. I, myself, have been too busy to be keeping tabs. I would hope that most citizens would be capable of carrying out their duties properly, but..." he sighs dramatically. "That does not appear to be the case. Do you have any idea of her whereabouts, Bryorfall?"

I cannot believe we're having this conversation right now. My sorrow is spooling itself into a tight coil of rage, and it's only a matter of time before I snap completely.

He says, icily, "Mr. Arman requested a new apprentice at the Smithshop. So to me, this seems to be a more… permanent type of disappearance. Would you be willing to help me out, Bryorfall?"

Dread races through my body, fury on its heels, curdling in my stomach.

Damnit, Markell.

I fumble for a response, but Lichera beats me to it, filling in the silence. "There are only three plausible explanations in this scenario. Would you like to hear them, or would you rather save us both the time and tell me where Ms. Bryorfall is?"

At a complete loss for words, I hold clenched fists rigidly at my sides, wishing I could send one of them flying into his face.

With smug satisfaction, he launches into his presentation as if he's practiced for this very moment. "Seeing that you refuse to relinquish information, I will give you three options to pick from that happen to be the most likely causes of your sister's absence. Can't you tell I'm feeling generous today?" He flashes a cold smile before continuing.

"The way I see it—she could have been taking a swim and got caught in the wake, drowning before anyone was able to get to her. And although you had your theories of her whereabouts, you may not have even been aware that this is what happened. In which case, my condolences."

I fully glare at him now, clenching my jaw so tight my teeth might crack. He still wears the same cruel smile, his eyes chunks of ice in their sockets.

"The other option would be that she has attempted to leave the province. You are well aware Thrunall is the closest point and is a three week's journey by ship. We don't think that's very likely, now do we?"

I have never hated anyone more than I do in this moment.

"And lastly," he sighs. "I find this to be the most realistic hypothesis, but you'll need to let me know your thoughts." He gestures skyward, toward the mass on the horizon. "Your sister has somehow found her way to Verenathia, and was the unnamed traitor they so graciously shared with us. What do you think?"

I think he's lucky I don't wrap my hands around his throat and squeeze until the life has drained from his already lifeless eyes.

I grit my teeth, willing myself to hold his gaze. She's already dead, what does the truth matter now? Throw me in the brig for questioning—I don't care anymore. I don't care about anything at all.

"What do you think, Lichera?" my voice is low, an acidic warning. "You seem to be a rather intelligent man."

His expression hardens. "I'll give you the mercy of benevolence for speaking to your Head with disregard; because this is such a trying time, isn't it, Bryorfall? My condolences on your sister's pointless death. What a fool she was to believe she would get away with it."

That spooling rage coils so tightly it breaks. Every ounce of self-control I was using shatters, and I grab his neck between my hands.

"Don't you dare call her a fool," I spit.

His face reddens, his eyes bulging as I squeeze and squeeze. He rakes at my hands, but to no avail—working in the Storehouse has made me far stronger.

Oh, how satisfying it would be to hold on until he stops struggling, to rid us of his horrid presence. Maybe afterward I can take a long walk… straight off the cliffs at the edge of town.

But as much as I'd like to, I know I can't kill the damn man.

I release him. Gasping and sputtering, his face is red with fury, his eyes burning with hatred.

"How dare you," he pulls in another breath before lashing out and grabbing my shirt. I brace myself as he jerks me forward, close enough that I can smell his rancid breath.

"You are out of line, Bryorfall," he growls, low and cold. "Watch what happens when you interfere with interterritorial relations." He throws me away from him, a look icy enough to freeze hell darkening his face, before spinning on his heel and stalking away.

I don't care. Let him threaten. I have nothing left worth living for.

CHAPTER 27

There are those in this world who will seek harm toward you. Because of who you are, you will attract it. Know that it is never a reflection of you, but of their hearts.

Kieran wasn't in the mess hall this morning. I knew he wouldn't be—he told me last night he would finally have to go back on rotation for supply runs—but still, I hate the enveloping fear without him by my side. The corridors of the Citadel loom menacingly around me as I pass through them alone, searching for anything to take care of the telltale pain beginning low in my stomach.

The scrutinizing looks and whispers still follow me, but the outright hostility within the Citadel has seemed to fade—at least a little bit. Most have been accepting of my presence, but some—like that group in the Field of Stars—want me gone. I can't say that I blame them, though. Hundreds of years of laws shouldn't bend for just one woman.

I tread carefully, softening my footsteps as much as possible with the Verenathian boots that mysteriously showed up in my room the other day.

Slowing at an intersection, I pause to listen for others as a wave of pain stabs my gut. Hissing through clenched teeth, I check for any visible signs on my suit before carrying on.

There has to be an infirmary near me somewhere. I know we've passed them before—I should have been paying more attention.

Corridor after corridor, the pain in my gut intensifies. Commons, storage rooms, classrooms, and more than enough side eye from the Verenathians… maybe I should have just stayed in my room and made do with a pillowcase.

More doorways, more rooms that I don't need.

Finally, I find the infirmary storage and slip in, scanning the well-stocked shelves. Bottles of antiseptic, various metal tools that make my throat constrict, and…

I snatch a handful of fabric bandages out of a small crate and tuck them under my arm. Ducking back through the doorway, I shuffle down the corridor, beginning the trek back to my room.

I pass another classroom, this one empty, save for the small group standing near the doorway. I barely make eye contact with the woman facing the door before snapping my gaze forward.

Shit. Laurel.

Shit shit shit shit.

Head held high, heart racing, I take quick, purposeful strides. Footsteps begin pounding down the corridor behind me.

One second of being followed is enough to send me bursting into a run down the marbled floor, and I almost cry out in terror as the pace of the ones behind me increases.

My legs start to burn as I sprint down corridor after corridor, breaths coming in great gasps.

Strong hands grab my shoulders, jerking me to a stop before wrapping around my body and pinning my arms to my sides. All of my bandages scatter to the ground. Fear unleashes through me and I try to remember the training Kieran gave me, but the man—if his massive forearms are any indication—is too strong.

I inhale deeply to scream but he clasps his hand around my mouth.

"Say one word and I'll gut you where you stand, pig." The familiar voice crawls down my ears and into my stomach, making me feel sick. I swallow hard. "It would be such a shame to see you die though, I'd rather have you in my bed."

Anger and disgust sear through me, and I thrash, futilely trying to escape his grasp.

"Hey guys," he calls loudly in the direction of the classroom. "Look what I've got."

Terror ices my veins as he spins me around, facing the group of people that emerge from the room. Laurel watches me closely as she saunters toward us, a cruel look of satisfaction set in her beautiful face.

The man releases me and shoves me, hard, onto the ground. I lose my footing with the force of the thrust and fall onto my bottom, my arms doing little to soften the blow.

The rest of the group arrives, leering over me with looks of disgusted pleasure. I glare into the hazel eyes of the man who trapped me, wishing I knew his name so I could spit it at him like a curse.

Laurel lowers herself to my level, her smile sickly sweet. "What are you doing here, all alone? Are you lost?" Her eyes flick to the ground, to the bandages scattered around us. The mock kindness immediately shifts to cold venom. "We let you live and this is how you repay us? By stealing our supplies?"

Rage cuts through my fear like a forge-heated blade. "Funny, you wouldn't have them—or anything—without us."

She sneers and lashes out, striking the side of my face. White bursts across my vision at the pain and I blink back tears of anger. Licking my lip, I wince as the faint metallic taste of blood lingers on it. The others snicker.

"Pig," she spits, and rises to her feet.

"I've never seen a pig with a set like these," the hazel eyed man reaches down, grabbing my breast.

"Don't touch me," I bark, shoving his arm away with as much hatred as I can muster.

With a twisted look of contempt, he pulls his arm away and rears back, kicking me in my stomach. The impact knocks the breath from me, and I fall forward to my hands and knees, gasping. Pain and anger swirl together, casting me into some distant nightmarish haze.

They laugh, watching me struggle. Someone grabs my braid and yanks it back, forcing my head upward. Laurel's face appears in front of me.

"Pretty," she sneers. "Too bad you're one of them." She spits the word as if it's the worst form of curse and strikes me across the face again, harder this time. "Go back to where you came from."

I see stars as I fight to remain on my hands and knees. A bright drop of blood falls to the marble in front of me, spreading in crimson curls on the white marble.

Like a trail of blood on freshly fallen snow.

Someone kicks me and I almost collapse at the blow. They begin to take turns now, each trading kicks as I retract lower and lower to the ground. I cry out as a foot strikes me sharply in the ribs.

Their taunting and laughter grow dim as I imagine myself back at home, sitting in the cottage with my mother. We would likely have the window open at this time of the year, letting in the pleasant sea breeze.

A sharp, enraged voice cuts through the fog, silencing the clamor around me. "What the fuck are you doing?"

Sebastian.

The blows mercifully cease, and I slump in relief, a puddled mass on the floor.

Sebastian's footsteps echo in sharp clips as he approaches. I can't see his expression, but the anger coming off of him is almost palpable.

"Relax, it's just the Goramalan," the man states.

"I know who it is. I'm not fucking blind, dumbass," Sebastian snaps. Trying to preserve even a shred of dignity, I pull myself into a sitting position, biting my lip at the pain in each movement.

"She doesn't belong here," a woman I've never seen before retorts, no hint of remorse in her tone. "There's no reason for an exception now."

"She needs to die," Laurel says simply, daring anyone to defy her.

Sebastian shakes his head in disbelief. "She's been given permission to be here. Bodily harm toward anyone on Verenathia is strictly forbidden and you know it." His voice lowers ominously, so quiet I almost strain to hear him. "Kieran is going to know about this, and if you don't want to get reported, I suggest it doesn't ever happen again."

Laurel scoffs. "He doesn't hold near the amount of influence he thinks he does."

"No?" Sebastian asks, wide eyed. "Then how about he tells the Court? It'd be fun to see how that would play out."

The rest of the group shifts nervously as Laurel considers his words.

"Tell her little boyfriend to get her out of here." She spins on her heel and strides back down the corridor, passing the commons. Her friends follow, that man giving me an icy look before shuffling after them.

Sebastian eyes him warily. "Fuck off, Barrett."

Barrett.

Once they're well away, he crouches down in front of me, his eyes roving over my body. Worry lines his face. "Are you okay?"

I inhale, attempting to steady what I know will be a shaking voice. "I think so."

"Come on," he reaches out his hands. I take them, allowing him to slowly pull me to my feet. My ribs scream in protest, but thankfully, the rest of the kicks fell over muscle. All of that will bruise—nothing broken. My cheek is swollen and raw, my lip not faring any better. I run my tongue over the split, tasting fresh blood.

"You know how to tell if someone broke a rib?" I offer a weak laugh, which comes out as more of a grimace.

The look he gives me is flat and worried. "Do you think it might actually be broken?"

"No, probably not. I…" my voice trails off. "Bad joke. I'm fine."

"We should probably get you to a healer," he says, raking his eyes over me once more to make sure there are no injuries he's missed.

"No, really. I'm fine, I promise." The thought of walking these halls alone now terrifies me. "If you wouldn't mind going back to my room with me?"

"Of course, I wasn't going to let you go by yourself anyways." He offers a smile, but there's a certain unease in the rigidity of his shoulders—the tightness in his jaw.

"Hold on." I bend over, groaning, as I gather my bandages.

He cocks an eyebrow. "Were you anticipating a beating?"

"No. This is why I was out here in the first place."

He doesn't ask any more questions. We head through the corridor in the opposite direction of the others, the pain in my ribs numbing with each step.

"I don't understand why they hate me so much," I murmur, with no less than a pathetic amount of dejection.

He looses a long breath. "The rules have been pounded into people's heads for so long they can't think for themselves."

I can't blame them, honestly. It's no different on Ra'goramal. No one there would dare question the status quo, either.

"What am I even doing here?" I mutter, more to myself than anyone. Never before have I felt so out of place.

"Hey," Sebastian drapes an arm around my shoulder. "Don't let a few sadistic fucks get you down."

I level a blank stare at him.

"Too soon?" He winces when I offer him a sad smile, splitting the crusting blood at my lip and drawing a fresh trickle.

He tightens his arm around my shoulder, nodding. "Too soon."

***

Uneventfully returned to my room, I spend the rest of the day alone and absolutely miserable. Starving, but in too much pain to eat, my stomach is a mess by late afternoon. Knotting anxiety from my encounter does nothing to help the churning nausea.

I'm sitting on the vanity stool in front of the window, overlooking the lush Verenathian fields, doing my best to breathe through the waves of nausea. A fight I'm quickly losing.

A surge stronger than the rest barrels over me, making my mouth water. I inhale deeply—but to no avail. Lunging for the wastebasket beside the vanity, I clutch it tightly as I'm thoroughly sick.

A knock sounds at the door.

Kieran. No one else would come to me here.

"Hold… on," I pant in between heaving. Nothing but water and bile come out of my empty stomach.

"Rae?" his tone is concerned, but insistent—demanding.

"One second." I cough, the force of it sending my swollen cheek pulsing. I can't even pull myself away from the wastebasket long enough to find something to clean myself up with.

He gives me a few more seconds of gagging before saying, "I'm going to come in now, okay?"

I don't respond as another wave overtakes me. The door creaks open as he peaks in, and, finding me not naked or otherwise indisposed, slips in. The door snicks shut behind him as he immediately comes to my side and kneels down, gathering my hair in his hands. His touch is gentle, but I don't need to look at him to feel the wrath rolling off of him.

My stomach now completely empty, I begin dry heaving. He rubs soothing lines up and down my back as I retch over and over again.

When the heaving subsides, I haul myself up and toward the bed on unsteady feet. Flopping unceremoniously onto it, I curl into a miserable ball. He sits at the foot of my bed, stroking my leg. I don't have the energy to broach my bruised face, nor his thinly veiled fury.

Blowing out a breath, he rises to his feet. "I'll be back."

I can't bring myself to be embarrassed as Kieran grabs the wastebasket and leaves me alone with my thoughts.

Dozing in and out of consciousness for what seems like an eternity, I crack open an eye as my door opens again. Kieran returns with two covered plates and an empty wastebasket.

Tossing it near the vanity, he sets the food on the bed. Groggily, I prop myself up and reach for a plate, surprised to find that it's warm.

"Where did you get these?"

He kicks his boots off and crawls onto the bed with me, crossing his legs underneath him. "My mother had dinner ready."

I gape at him. "You went all the way home for this?" For me?

He shrugs. "It's not too far."

Swallowing the emotion welling inside me, I uncover the plate. Roast pork, a generous pile of whipped potatoes, green beans smothered in butter, and a slice of pie—all still steaming.

"Thank you."

He inclines his head, dutifully pushing the food around on his plate while I stuff my face—my stomach now decidedly more content after purging itself.

We eat in silence for several long minutes, and I relish every single bite. *Thank you, Rose.*

Kieran sets his fork down softly—too softly. "What happened?"

I swallow a mouthful of flaky apple pie.

"Laurel," I poke at the final piece with my fork. "And Barrett." It's the first time I've spoken his name, and it tastes terrible on my tongue. I hope with everything in me I never see his despicable face again. "And… whoever else."

"Damn it, Rae," he breathes, leaning in and running his finger along my lip. My heart pauses at his touch, lightning jolting through my battered body.

"I'm fine."

"I'll kill them." Something about the dark glint in his eyes tells me he's not joking.

I look up at him through lowered brows. "You'll do no such thing."

"They can't do that and think they'll get away with it. Attacking Verenathians is a punishable offense."

"I'm not a Verenathian," I say bluntly.

"We're all trained warriors." A muscle in his jaw ticks. "Do you really think we don't have rules of our own for infighting? Unless it's wartime, attacking anyone here is a punishable offense, Verenathian or no. Not to mention the fact that it's just wrong."

"Which is why you're going to drop it. Okay? I told you—I'm fine." I hope he can't see that I am, indeed, very much lying. My cheek throbs with every little movement, and last I checked, was a multitude of blues and purples and browns.

His eyes glint with cold steel, and there's an undercurrent of malcontent running through them. "I don't want everyone seeing you've been attacked. There's no need to draw unnecessary negative attention. They already consider you an inferior—if they see you like this"—he gestures to my face—"and that they got away with it? They might just start using you as a punching bag. Or worse."

"So what?" I challenge. "Let them look." I say it with as much arrogance as I can muster, but the thought is nauseating. I can't have Kieran putting himself at risk for my sake, though.

"I can't have you getting hurt, Rae."

The way he murmurs those words softens a small part of me. "I'll be fine. I can train with you more so I'm not entirely helpless."

"That's not good enough. They can't get away with this."

"If you're worried about drawing more attention," I meet his gaze, unflinching. "Then that is sure as hell a good way to do it. I didn't die, so let it be."

The muscle in his jaw continues to tick.

"I didn't know you were such an overprotective bastard," I mutter.

"And I didn't know you were such a masochist."

"Are you kidding? Getting jumped by a group of people who want me dead is the most fun I've had all week."

He rolls his eyes, relenting. "Well you obviously can't be left alone anymore."

Indignation flares within me. "I can take care of myself just fine."

"Clearly."

"When did you become such a prick?" I glare.

He blinks. "When you were jumped by a group of people who want you dead."

Another round of cramping pain begins again, and I groan. "Can we move on now?"

He rubs the bridge of his nose before leveling a flat expression on me. "Stubborn ass."

"Hey," I smack him on the arm. "That's not very nice."

He lifts a brow. "Even if it's true?"

"Especially if it's true."

He sighs, watching me with something akin to yearning.

If I dared… I could close the tiny gap between us, putting me right in his arms—which, if I'm being honest, is truly all I want right now. I want the day to fade away in the comfort of his steadiness and strength.

"Well," he drawls. "I'm not going to be able to sleep now knowing you're in here alone."

I know he's still a writhing tempest on the inside—I can see it in the shadows in his eyes. But, for my sake, he's making an effort.

So this—an offer. A question within an unspoken request. My heart picks up its pace, beating erratically. There's a chasm opening up before me, and taking the leap across will leave everything changed. Do I dare jump and risk falling? Or do I throw myself at it unabashed, accepting the shift that awaits on the other side?

I sweep my eyes quickly across the bed, breathing in a little unevenly. "You can stay here if you're going to be so dramatic about it."

"Well, I couldn't have you thinking that about me, now could I?" He makes to leave, stooping down toward his boots. I let him, knowing that in his current state, he won't be able to leave.

Finishing with his laces, he heads toward the door. "Let me know if you need anything," he says.

"I will."

He opens the door to my room, and my heart stutters. I didn't think he'd make it this far.

"Wait." *Asshole.* "Stay… please." The thought of being here alone after the events of today is suddenly too much to bear.

He stops, a satisfied smirk playing upon his lips. "But only for my sake, right?"

"Precisely."

He grins a wicked grin, his eyes darkening—and not because of the troubled shadows within. Crawling up beside me, he lays down on his side, patting the space in front of him.

I swallow, and, deciding to take the leap, lie down, nestling tentatively against him. He wraps an arm tightly around my waist and pulls me in close to his chest. A shiver ripples through me at the feel of his muscled form against my back.

The arm he has draped over me begins to shift, lightly roving up my stomach, gently following the curve of my waist to my shoulder, then my collarbone.

His touch is soft, curious—nothing heavy or lustful in it. No question behind it, no insistence; only quiet exploration. I find myself relaxing, melting against him as he draws lazy lines up and down my body.

His fingers stroke delicately up my neck, feathering my swollen cheek. He tenses as they graze over the crusted scab on my lip, but lingers for only a moment before traveling back to my waist.

My eyelids grow heavier by the moment, lured into rest by his steady touch.

A satisfied sigh escapes me as the suffering of the day fades, and I can't remember the last time I felt this safe. As if nothing and no one can touch me, hurt me, ever again.

I drown in the sensation, letting it envelope me completely. Thoughts of the assault, of the pain, the poisonous undercurrent of life—all of them fade, borne along a wave of contentment and security.

In my last moments of wakefulness, I grasp his hand in mine; stopping his exploration. Pulling it toward my chest, I grip it unrelentingly. His hold tightens, pulling me in even closer.

The room fades, and I slip into oblivion.

CHAPTER 28

You and I went to the market today. I bought you a bouquet that now rests on the cabinet. Your cheeks simply glowed with joy when I showed you the bundle of peonies. I love the time we spend together, as I know it's fleeting. You are almost old enough to begin your duty, and I will miss your fiery spirit lighting the air around me.

"Again."

Despite our night together after yesterday's attack, Kieran has been on edge, his usual calm and teasing demeanor replaced by a tension that's started to get on my nerves.

Though we've crossed an invisible line together, dissolving some crucial boundary between friends, this side doesn't feel as different as I expected.

Maybe it's because he's decided to be an insufferable prick today.

I thrust forward, holding my fist the way Kieran has shown me too many times to count now. This time, it connects solidly with the padded board he's holding up, sending a resonant shock through my arm. I gasp, letting it fall loosely to my side. I've not managed a solid hit like that this entire time.

Something akin to pride lights his expression. "Perfect."

I shake the soreness from my hand, keeping my eyes trained on the ground as a satisfied flush creeps up my cheeks.

"Again?" He asks this time.

Nodding, I bring my clenched fists close to my face, adopting the stance he's spent all day drilling into my body.

I throw a punch, then another, and another. Each one connects perfectly. I fall into a rhythm, allowing my body to flow fully through the movement. Faster and faster, my blows begin to land with a satisfying thud, thud, thud.

Faster. Harder. Punch after punch lands, reverberating through my entire body. I let all of my fear over the assault, my guilt from leaving Ashden, grief over losing my parents, and the unending tension pulling at me pour into each and every hit. My arms begin to burn as air comes in pants, but I savor the pain, relish it. Spending the past several years pounding on metal has evidently given me a strength I wasn't fully aware of.

I go until the ache in my arms becomes a quiver and sweat is pouring down my back, my neck, my temples. Throwing a final blow, I draw back, panting.

Kieran lowers the board, a questioning eyebrow raised in surprise. "What was that?"

My face is hot from exertion and the soft intensity he meets me with. "I don't… know," I pant. "I just… needed that… I guess."

Brushing the back of my hand across my forehead, I move away from his penetrating gaze and into the lukewarm shadow of the wall lining the training courtyard. The space is empty right now, which I know was an intentional consideration on Kieran's part, and I'm grateful for the privacy.

I plop to the ground, leaning back and letting my head rest against the cool stone wall. My breaths calm as my heart rate slows, and I let my eyes close against the brilliant blue above me.

A moment later, a twin thud sounds as Kieran lowers himself beside me.

"You're actually pretty good at that," he muses.

I shrug, blinking against the brightness. "Smithing, I guess. I use my arms a lot."

He squints across the courtyard, his gaze faraway. "With some more training, you could be pretty good. I don't know what was going on that first time."

I couldn't think around his presence. That's what was going on.

I toss him an irreverent glance. "You mean I could be like all of you guys?"

"No—just an observation. You're strong."

Again, I shrug. "Like I said, I'm a blacksmith. It comes with the territory."

He picks at one of the scales on his suit. "You guys are done such a disservice." The words are murmured so quietly that, for a moment, I wonder if he's talking to himself.

"What do you mean?"

Shaking off whatever lingering thoughts, he stands and offers me a tight smile. "Nevermind. Let's get some more training in while we still have time."

Raising an eyebrow, I concede, groaning while I pull myself to my feet.

Dodging and ducking and kicking and holding proper form for punching—it's exhausting.

"Let's try some sparring."

Adrenaline jolts through me. "You mean… with you?"

He scans the courtyard. "I don't see anybody else here."

I narrow my eyes, trying desperately to hide the blood roaring through me. "Fine."

"Fine." His eyebrows lower, a wickedly delicious smile dancing on his lips.

A fire heats low in my core, but I ignore it, instead focusing; trying to recall all that he's shown me thus far.

We face each other—neither of us moving—hands held loosely at our sides, bouncing lightly on our feet. I keep my eyes on his chest, his feet, his fists; anywhere I can to avoid meeting his gaze.

He sidesteps, and I move in the opposite direction. Again. One step at a time, we circle each other, and I wait for him to make the first move.

But he doesn't. Step after step after step, and nothing but his near silent footwork.

I flick my hair impatiently, skimming over his body. If I go for his head, I'll be down in two seconds flat; same with his sides. Anywhere, really.

Ducking low, I sweep my leg out but he easily dodges, and I'm left spinning on my heel, my face burning.

Rising back up, I narrow my eyes at him. His are gleaming with pure amusement.

I don't give him another second of gloating, and again duck. This time, I reach out with a fist, aiming for his ribs.

He has my wrist in his grasp and is pulling me against him before I even realize what's happening. My face is pinned against his chest while he wraps his other arm around me—trapping me.

His voice is a sultry caress against my neck. "My dear Rae, never look where your next blow will land. I knew what you were going to do before you even did it."

My body is burning, burning, but he releases me. I leap away from his distracting solidity, sputtering. "Maybe you should keep your eyes to yourself," I snap.

His lips twitch with barely contained laughter. "And miss all of this?" He gestures to me, to the body that is ready to combust under his gaze. "I wouldn't be a very good combatant if I didn't study my opponent."

"Well your opponent has had all of two training sessions." I begin circling him again.

"And whose fault is that?"

I widen my eyes. "Surely not mine. The poor, unlearned, oppressed Goramalan?"

He chuckles. "Playing the victim again, are we?"

My voice is like honey as I pause in my circling. "Never."

His eyes darken, roving over every inch of my body as I stand before him, wholly still.

"And if I was, preying upon a woman like that says a lot more about you than it does me."

There it is. A slight hint of annoyance. Enough so that his impenetrable exterior cracks a fraction.

I throw myself at him, reaching for the dagger he had me sheath in a belt at my waist earlier. My full body weight slams into him as I drive forward into his chest, and he topples backward. We land with a thud. I immediately dig my knees into his arms, pinning them at his sides before I sit up, straddling him. Holding the dagger to his throat, I grin triumphantly down at him.

Every point our bodies touch is electric, searing my skin under the dragonhide.

"Not bad, Goramalan."

He thrusts up with hips, knocking me off balance. I fall forward, dropping the dagger as I seek the ground for balance, but in that same movement, he grips me with his legs—our bodies now locked at the hips.

He twists, throwing me to the side and snatching the fallen dagger as we roll. His weight settles on me, pinning me underneath him. The cold metal meets my throat in a hairline touch.

Leaning close enough I can feel the brush of his jawline against my bruised cheek, he whispers, "Don't call the fight until you're sure your opponent is down."

I strain against him, struggling to move under his considerable weight. Everywhere I'm pressed into the ground is gentle. Firm enough to keep me trapped, but soft enough not to hurt.

I know he can feel my racing heart beneath him. I know, too, that I can see an uneven edge to his breathing.

I want to push, want to take it one step further and see where we land, but I force my breaths to steady, force my heart back into submission.

"Don't worry. I have a lot of years' worth of practice on you." His tone is light, teasing—belying the intensity in his gaze.

"You don't have to rub it in."

"Oh, I don't have to. There's a lot more I could hold over your head, don't worry."

"Shut up." His face is so close I can't help but admire every inch of it—of the lips that are so dangerously close to mine.

"We have dragons, magic—"

"I don't care," I breathe.

"Oh, don't you now? What was the reason you came here, again? Something about—"

I grip his legs the same way he did mine and heave, rotating with all my strength. Ignoring the fact that he's allowing me to, I flip on top of him and pin his arms beneath my legs again.

Pressing myself against him until we're almost cheek to cheek, I whisper in his ear, "Something about that magic you mentioned." The scent of salt mist on his skin threatens to overwhelm every ounce of logic I possess. "The dragons are just a bonus."

I swear his breath catches.

The low timber of his voice reverberates through my chest. "And what about the people?"

"Assholes, most of them."

He shoves me off of him as I laugh; a little breathlessly.

"Takes one to know one," he grins.

"Indeed." I move back to the cool relief of the wall, trying desperately to pretend that the thing burning between us didn't almost just consume me.

Smoothing my hair down, I ask, "What now?"

His midnight hair ruffles in the breeze that trails through the courtyard. "I suppose we can work on kicks next…"

"No more training." I need space between us before I end up doing something I'll really regret. "Something else."

"Something else…" he rubs his chin thoughtfully, looking completely unruffled in spite of the past few minutes. Another reason I need to distance myself. "What about those bonus dragons?"

I roll my eyes, though a thrill pulses through me. The dragons—my dragon. I have my very own dragon. My blood begins to sing for an entirely different reason.

"I'd say the dragons are a good place to start."

***

The wind tears past Boreal and I as we shoot through the sky, Sebastian and Stoney close on our tail. The roaring in my ears drowns out every other sound, save for Boreal's shrieks of both joy and indignation—aimed at the two dragons behind us.

With each flight Boreal and I take, I find it easier to hold my seat, and hold it well. She soars higher and faster, taking us through sharp turns and rolling maneuvers—purely for her enjoyment.

Each time I fall, she's below me before I can scream—ready to catch me and carry on. There's a certain thrill to falling too. The weightlessness, the freedom without the fear of plummeting to my death, the knowing that she's going to be there every time. It's ecstasy.

She banks hard to the right. I grip her horns so tightly the whites of my knuckles show, my legs aching from clenching around her midsection. Above the roar of the wind, Stoney, cut off by Boreal's sharp turn, shrieks in protest.

Suddenly, Cinder's lithe form cuts across the sky directly in front of us. Kieran's rakish grin is all I see for a heartbeat before Boreal cries out and pulls up, sending us straight into the sun. She pumps her wings hard, carrying us higher and higher before leveling out. We coast for a moment, and when her nose dips forward, the rest of her body follows.

We dive, Cinder and Stoney mere streaks below us. I force my stomach back down where it belongs as my bottom begins to lift from Boreal's back. Squeezing with my thighs until they tremble from the exertion, I settle deeper into my seat, tucking myself low into her neck.

A wisp of a cloud breaks, revealing a large, smooth rock floating ahead of us. The finish line. I keep an eye on Cinder and Stoney as we dive down, down. They beat their wings furiously, each stretching into a sleek line from nose to tail, but they don't stand a chance. Stoney overtakes Cinder and jets forward. She shrieks, snapping at Stoney's tail as they soar so close it whips her face.

Boreal cranes her neck, pinning her wings to her sides. We are a lightning bolt, shooting to the ground. A wild laugh escapes me as we race through the sky, aiming for the ever-shortening gap between Stoney and Sebastian, and the massive rock looming before them.

We plummet, getting closer, closer, until Stoney's head is so near I could reach out and touch him. Another halfway feral laugh tears from me when Sebastian, eyes wide with shock, gapes as we drop like a wraith in front of them; careening to the right and skimming over the surface of the rock.

Boreal thrusts her wings out wide, bringing us to an abrupt stop. I fly forward over her neck, my bones groaning as they slam into the rock's surface. The air is forced from my lungs, and I scrape and slide across the rock, coming to a rolling stop.

I lay, stunned, staring up at the bright blue sky. My lungs ache as I try to force air down them.

Kieran's face appears above me. Even shadowed by the sun behind him, I can see the concern etched into his brow. His hair is wild from the wind, sticking up at odd angles all over his head, and a wide grin splits my face.

"We won," I croak.

"Yes, but you didn't stick the landing, so it doesn't count." He smiles, offering me a hand.

I take it, groaning as I pull myself to my feet. Sebastian is leaned against Stoney's side, arms crossed over his chest while he cocks an eyebrow at me.

"I've never seen that one before."

"Oh, shut up. You're just upset you lost."

Boreal's head is held high, preening at the other two dragons.

"Sure," he winks.

Boreal chirps, prancing between Cinder and Stoney now. Laughing, I reach for her snout, resting my forehead against hers.

"Good job, girl," I whisper. Her eyes—sapphire pools of wisdom that belie her age—close as she leans into my touch. A moment later and she's back to preening. Cinder and Stoney exchange twin glances of annoyance.

I can't help it as I beam. I can't remember the last time I felt this light, this happy. And maybe it's the adrenaline coursing through me, but my heart is full to bursting.

Joy doesn't come this easily on Ra'goramal. Not this… this joy that's *alive.* More of a muted contentment back home, I suppose. But it hurts. This type of joy aches and chafes because it's temporary and I wish I've discovered why, *why* things are the way they are. Not just the demands of an entire separate population to support, but something else.

I truly don't know what I want—what I'm looking for,but I feel an itching in my bones; like some deep, silent part of me knows something that my mind has not yet been made aware of.

Knowing I'm most likely banished from Ra'goramal, there's no reason to return so soon, but I can't ignore the sense of urgency that pulses through me. The part of me that is still screaming something is wrong, *wrong.*

And there I go. That must be what Kieran meant about the pit. Damnit.

Shaking the questions off, I peer down at the sea far below. "Do you guys think I should jump?"

"No," they answer simultaneously.

"Why in the world would you want to do that?" Sebastian eyes me with concern.

I shrug. "For the thrill of it." Because Boreal would catch me, and spending that long in weightlessness seems exhilarating.

"You're insane," he muses.

"Oh, but we've already established that," I smirk.

He returns my grin, his brown eyes dancing. Turning to Kieran, he asks, "You tell her about tonight, yet?"

"What's tonight?"

"The Night of Parallel Flame," Kierean says, giving him a heavy dose of side-eye.

Something like realization seems to settle in Sebastian's features. "Oh… Right. Well, I definitely didn't say anything." He holds his hands up, backing away toward Stoney.

"What's the Night of Parallel Flame?" I ask, my skin practically tingling with curiosity.

Those emerald eyes dance with light. "Once a year, the dragons that have reached maturity seek out a mate. They leave the Field of Stars and go out into the open sky, searching for their match. Remember how every living being has its own magic?"

I nod.

"Two dragons will be drawn to each other through their own. When they mate, their bond will create an entirely new type of magic—one that belongs to both of them, and the land. They'll no longer be two separate beings, but one, tethered eternally to Verenathia. Think of it like a holiday… A celebration. Everything we are and do is tied to the dragons. We celebrate because the mated pairs will produce offspring, and without them, we're nothing."

I don't think I've ever heard anything so wonderful in all my life. But as I mull over his words, beginning to understand Sebastian's meaning, my stomach flutters.

"And you wanted me to go with you?"

He rolls his eyes. "I wasn't going to leave you in your room while it was happening. It's a sight to behold."

I ignore the ambiguous response. "Kieran, are you asking me to go with you?"

He hooks his thumbs over the belt at his hips. "Yes, Rae. I'd love nothing more than for you to go with me, but if you don't—I understand."

The fluttering in my stomach turns into a full-blown swarm. Dragons soaring through the sky, diving and cleaving to one another as they find their mates. Lights and colors and magic and… Kieran.

He watches me closely, undisguised earnestness in his expression.

"I think I would quite like to see this Night of Parallel Flame."

Chapter 29

ASHDEN

Shit. That's the second order I've sent out wrong… this morning.

Aurundraya is going to kill me.

I know I need to get a grip and stop sipping from the flask in my pocket, but I'm finding I really don't care to.

I should.

But I don't.

I also know I'm being selfish. Though I've lost my entire family… I still have Avice, and dammit, she's been too good to me. It honestly makes me hate myself even more.

Rae was always the one to find the color in life, even when everything was gray. I've always anchored myself to more tangible aspects. Reason, logic. Although only concepts, they give me the vision to keep going. A purpose.

After our parents, I know Rae kept going because she knew one day the color would return to life. Slowly, fading in and out in parts, but overall—filling back in. She pressed forward, looking for that good.

I kept pressing forward too, for her. On the days it hurt so badly I couldn't breathe, I kept going for her.

And now that reason—that purpose—is gone.

Which leaves me with this colorless life that I can hardly bear. I don't want to slosh through my days, with every thought that crosses my mind muddling into an incoherent jumble… but maybe I do.

Maybe it really is easier this way.

I snicker to myself—a broken, crooked sort of sound. Being the town drunk was never the goal I had in mind for myself.

Sighing, I rub the bleariness from my eyes and force myself to focus on the stack of papers in my hand.

Words… So many words. So many orders, too many instructions, too much demand—not enough grace.

It's all too much, really. I turn toward the grate, acting like I'm getting a breath of outside air, but I press the flask quickly to my lips.

"BRYORFALL!"

Shit.

Aurundraya's sharp voice cuts through the clamor of the Storehouse, finding me stuffing the offensive object back in my pocket.

His auburn hair flashes a head above most of the workers as he barrels his way from the direction of the loading docks. His skin is mottled and angry, his eyes gleaming.

"Bryorfall!" He barks again, nearly about to plow me down.

"Sir?" I straighten. Aurundraya is a decent man. Demanding, precise, but usually kind. I've always respected him for it. The anger in his expression coils my stomach with even more self-loathing.

"I've received reports that multiple orders have been incorrect, and they've all been signed by your hand."

I blink, unable to deny it but hoping he can't smell the alcohol on me. "My mistake. It won't happen again."

"You're damn sure it won't. Until further notice, you're demoted to brigade runner."

I do my best to look chagrined, but it's a relief. No orders to track, no supplies to delegate—just mindlessly heaving crates.

"Understood, sir."

His sharp eyes narrow on me, cutting right through my bullshit. Lowering his voice, he says, "I know things have been a bit of a challenge lately." He doesn't need to mention my sister or Verenathia's incessant demands. "But you're going to have to get it under control. We all depend on it."

I scan the room, full of people each trying to do their part to keep Verenathia appeased. To keep them from breathing down our necks. People who feel the never ending weight bearing down on them too, who are only trying to get their part done in order to go home to their families at the end of the day. People trying to stay unnoticed, hoping their name isn't the one on Lucielle's scroll when he arrives.

More people for me to let down.

I grit my teeth. "Yes sir."

He nods stiffly. "You're a good kid, Bryorfall. Always have been. We'll get through this." And with that, he's striding away, finding someone else to bark orders at.

I'm good at nothing and *for* nothing, but I appreciate the sentiment.

Moving to my station, I breathe a sigh of relief at the cart almost ready to head out. Until I find one of my running partners—a green-haired man who used to be friends with Rae.

Were they even friends? I can't remember. And what was his name…

I blink away a wave of dizziness while the green-haired man cuts me an awkward glance.

Arthic. Oh, yes. How could I forget?

We move in and out of each other's way, lifting the last few crates. Each time I make eye contact with him, his lips twitch as if he's deciding whether or not what he has on his mind is worth saying.

I try to give him my best look that says it's definitely not.

We linger around the cart while it's double checked by an overseer before being given the go-ahead.

"Move out!" the woman calls, and I wordlessly move to a corner of the cart, waiting for the rest of the brigade.

Arthic takes up the post straight across from mine. I keep my eyes straight forward, feeling his all over me.

We heave the cart forward, straining to get it moving under the weight of all the crates. Gaining momentum, we keep our pace steady as we guide the cart out of the Loading Warehouse and into the bright midday sunshine.

I close my eyes for a heartbeat, relishing its warmth even though it's hot as balls in the Storehouse.

I hear a quick intake of breath across from me, and groan inwardly.

"I'm sorry about Rae."

I open my eyes, blinking slowly, welcoming the growing burn in my legs. The two in front of us at the other posts both stiffen, doing their best to act like they aren't listening.

"Me too," I mutter.

He opens his mouth again, but I say quickly, "I appreciate it, but I don't want to talk about it."

He shuts his mouth, his face reddening. "She was a real cool girl, is all."

The ground seems to shift below me, maybe from the alcohol, maybe not.

"I said," through gritted teeth, "I don't want to talk about it. Just shut your mouth and put your head down like the rest of us."

Because if there's one thing that's worse than the whispers, the quiet side eye and judgmental suspicion—it's sympathy.

Call me an accomplice, question if I'm a traitor, have your conspiratorial conversations around the dinner table—but do not look at me with that pathetic, sorry look in your eyes. I'm glad you're happy it wasn't you, and you're so sorry for the situation I'm in, but keep your damned pitiful words to yourself.

An uncomfortable tension falls around us as we heave the cart up the loading ramp. I ignore it, throwing myself into the strain on my body.

Too soon, we've reached the top, ready to unload onto the awaiting dragon. Its rider watches us with more smugness than what's typical for the Verenathians. Maybe he got to watch Rae get beheaded or burned alive by a dragon.

Was it a public spectacle, or did she get taken to the dungeon? Was it quick? Did they make her suffer?

My stomach churns. I shove the thoughts away, pushing them into the warm, muddled tide flowing through my mind. A sense of peace settles over me as I let them get swept away into wherever that stream empties into.

I don't hear any of the words exchanged, nor the orders. My mind and body are numbing to the motions of the day. I begin unloading when the others set into action, and only stop when I see the cart is empty.

I make my way to the beginning of the loading ramp, not bothering to wait for the brigade or finalization, but something in the sky catches my eye.

Squinting into the bright blue, I find a black dragon heading toward us.

My churning stomach coils itself into a knot and sinks at the sight of the white-robed figure sitting calmly atop the beast.

Author above, help us.

Lucielle. Lucielle is coming.

CHAPTER 30

We spent the day on your father's boat. Your poor brother was seasick the whole time, but you, my little bird, you were so alive with the wind in your hair and sea before you. I think these days are going to be the ones I look back on most fondly—our family, together on the open ocean.

Black or gray? Or blue? Or… maybe red?

I'm picking up each dragonhide suit, chewing my lip, trying to figure out why I care so much which color I wear. The black one is a full body suit, long-sleeved and all. The grey one is sleeveless, cut off right at the neckline, which would leave my shoulders and entire arm exposed. The blue is the same as the gray, but the red; long-sleeved like the black, the entire back is cut out, swooping dangerously low down the backside.

The standard full-coverage uniform is what I've seen day-to-day, but, clearly, the Verenathians know how to have fun. I hadn't realized my wardrobe was stocked with such a variety. Or if Kieran had a say in any of them.

My stomach clenches when I finger the delicate scales, the movement jarring my aching ribs. The memory of heels and fists on my body is too new, too fresh. Part of me wants to stay in this room and never come out, while the rest of me sings its never ending cry for freedom. I'll be damned if I cower when I'm surrounded by such an opportunity, such magic and life.

The black one. Unassuming enough—no flesh on display; maybe I'll go unnoticed for the night.

I slip it on, relishing the silken cling of the hide. Finishing the buttons, I run a hand over my hair. Reaching back to begin braiding it, I let my arms fall to my sides at the sharp pain issuing again from the bruises at my ribs.

Peering at myself in the mirror, I run my fingers through the thick waves of my hair. I pull a few strands out, tuck some behind my ear, frame my face this way and that, and heave a sigh of frustration as heat begins to creep up my neck.

It doesn't matter. I smooth it all back down and leave it loose.

A knock sounds at the door. Tossing one more look at my reflection, I groan at the purple splotching along my cheek before opening it.

"Are you ready, my…"

Kieran falls silent. He's decked in a blood-red and skintight suit. The dragon that owned these scales was not iridescent, but rich and velvety. The red is so deep it's as if he's soaked in blood, accentuated even further by his onyx hair. Every one of his muscles is outlined in stark relief as they tense, and his eyes…

Author above. Words are almost impossible to find.

"You should wear your hair down more often," he says, voice low.

Heat begins in my core, warming the rest of my body. "Oh, should I now?"

His darkened eyes don't leave me as I cross the room and grab my boots.

"Yes."

I flick my hair over a shoulder before leaning to lace the boots up my calves. "Well, unfortunately for you, I've never taken suggestions from a man before."

Only because I've never cared to—never had a man I cared enough for to even consider it.

He crosses the room in two strides and kneels before me. My skin tightens over my bones, pulling me taut.

He takes the laces out of my hands and begins looping them through the boots. "Well, maybe you should consider it."

I swallow, leaving my feelings caught in my throat.

Tugging on the last tie, he stands and extends an arm to me.

"The Night of Parallel Flame awaits, my dear Rae."

***

Our footsteps echo through the corridor as we make our way to the largest commons in the Citadel. Verenathians are everywhere—milling about, chatting. Most are dressed in vibrant colors, with glitter or striking cosmetics painting their faces and skin.

I glance at my sleeve, the plain black hide, and sigh. So much for blending in.

As if the thought tugged on some tether between Kieran and I, he leans down.

"I think you look absolutely ravishing," he whispers.

I bite my lip. "Thank you."

Weaving in and out of people who don't seem particularly concerned to let us through, Kieran leads us into an intersecting corridor, away from the throng.

Immediately, the air grows heavy, holding the weight of something dark and forbidden. Tossing a glance over my shoulder, I can't shake the feeling that there's someone watching me, but Kieran's expression remains calm, neutral.

That weight continues to press in on me. Tighter and tighter, my chest constricts, and my steps quicken. Faster and faster, I try to make it to the end. Kieran's hand brushes mine, his steps unfaltering; though now, there's a mild warning in the touch.

A thudding procession of footsteps sounds ahead of us. Steady and uniform, the steps hold a monotone form; unlike the light, energetic ones of the riders.

We're only halfway through the corridor when a group of black-hooded figures rounds the corner in front of us. My heart jumps to my throat as the Warbearers make their way through the marbled hall.

All four in straight line, they don't speak, their cold eyes focusing straight ahead; not even giving us a second glance. Nearer and nearer they draw, not a footstep out of rhythm. Each second has us drawing closer, until we're passing each other side by side in the wide corridor.

I try to press myself as close to the wall as possible without them noticing. We're so close I could reach out and touch their thick black robes if I wanted to.

I wonder if they can see fear with those black, soulless eyes.

My blood chills when the last one in line slowly turns his head toward us, unfaltering in his march. His eyes are a depthless void like all the others, but there's something within them that I can't place—a flicker, some form of emotion… of something.

Kieran goes rigid beside me. Tension practically rolls off of him in waves, but he keeps his focus trained on the end of the corridor, squeezing my hand tightly.

That Warbearer is no longer looking at me, but intently at Kieran. No words. No expression. Just that glint of… something.

I flit my gaze to Kieran. His chest is heaving now, as if he's trying to gain control over himself—or maybe hold something back.

My mouth goes dry as I finally place the Warbearer's expression.

Recognition.

But no, it's more than that. It's the familiar look of someone once intimately acquainted. My eyes dart between the two, my palms starting to sweat. Kieran continues to stare straight ahead and I drag my attention there as well—struggling to ignore the Warbearer's piercing gaze.

Another cursory glance, and I take in all of the features beneath the shadow of his hood. He looks familiar, and something twists deep inside me. His brows are as dark as his eyes, and that jawline—

Understanding hits me. Hits me so hard I almost stumble.

I force one foot in front of the other, not daring to make eye contact again for fear that the Warbearer would see, would know that I now know.

Slowly, too slowly, the space between us grows as we each reach opposite ends of the corridor. The sound of their footsteps fades before disappearing altogether as they round the corner.

Scanning ahead, I grab Kieran's hand, pulling him into an open doorway on our right. I scan the room quickly, breathing a small sigh of relief when I find it's empty.

I whip around to face him, accusation burning on my tongue, but I pause. He's trembling slightly, his jaw hard set; tension written in ever line of his body. A storm rages in his eyes, a storm he's trying, and failing, to conceal.

"Kieran," I whisper.

Staring at the ground, he exhales a shaky breath. "I'm sorry."

"Why didn't you tell me?"

He raises his head, running his hands through his hair. "I didn't know how to."

The Warbearers… I know next to nothing about them, aside from the fact they keep our Safeguards running. They're disturbing, yes, but he didn't know how to tell me?

"I don't understand."

"I know you don't."

My mind is a confused jumble of memories and images as I try to piece it all together.

"So," I begin tentatively. "He *is* your dad?"

The look he gives breaks something within me. "Yes."

I can feel there are many layers to the situation. I don't want to pry, but the questions are burning inside me.

"What happened?" I ask quietly. "Unless… unless you don't want to talk about it."

He brings his gaze reluctantly to mine. No longer trembling, but his shoulders are still hard set. His jaw clenches and unclenches, his eyes glistening.

Finally, he lets out a long breath.

"I had a brother. I was 18 when he was born.

"I'm sure you can tell that with such an age gap between him and Opal, he wasn't exactly… planned. There's things my mom could have done to do away with him before he was born but she was so excited. She wanted him. Opal and I were just excited to have a baby sibling." He shifts his unfocused gaze to some faraway place, his arms crossed protectively over his chest.

"The months after he was born were some of the happiest of our lives. Then one day he got sick. Really sick. My mom is a healer, but even her magic and remedies couldn't save him."

"Kieran," I breathe.

"A week after he died, my father disappeared. With nothing more than a note on the table telling us he was going to join the Warbearers, he just… left. No warning. No goodbye. One day he was there with us, the next, he was gone." He looses a shuddering breath.

"When someone joins the Warbearers, you don't see them again. They commit to lives of solitude and celibacy, only interacting with each other and holding presence in the Court when need be. Which is rare."

"When you took me to them…" My voice trails off, I can hardly form the question.

"Yes. That was only the second time I've been in his presence since he left."

"I'm so sorry," I whisper. I hate myself for making him tell me, hate myself for putting him through this. Hate myself for coming here in the first place and forcing him to bring me before his father.

"It almost killed my mom to lose her baby and then my father almost immediately after." He drops his arms to his sides, clenching his fists. "It almost killed me, Rae."

I gently grab his tight fists, surprised by his vulnerability. My thumbs work in smooth circles over the tops of his hands as I search for the right words.

His lip quivers slightly as he blows out a puff of breath. "There's nothing else to say. Now you know."

"I'm sorry," I whisper again. I know it's pathetic but there's nothing else for me to say. I could tell him I understand, that I know what it's like to lose a parent. But do I really understand what he's gone through? My parents died of natural causes; we never doubted their love for us. I've never had to question if every act and *I love you* was genuine. It's something I just simply knew, and never had to question. I don't know what it's like to be abandoned by the only people in my life who are never supposed to leave. And to have to experience that in the midst of grief from a lost sibling—a *baby.* My heart breaks for him.

He unclenches his fists in my hands, grasping mine lightly as he does so. "Don't be. It's in the past."

I nod, understanding that although in the past, this matter is far from healed. Holding his penetrating gaze, I ask quietly, "Do you avoid him intentionally?"

"I think most people do. You learn their habits and tend to stay out of the way when you know where they're going to be. It's easier that way—easier to pretend I don't have a father when I never see him. Seeing is the reminder that keeps me up at night." A muscle in his jaw ticks, but he exhales, running his thumbs along the sides of my own hands now. "I… didn't expect them to be out tonight."

I imagine him now, planning his paths, his days, away from his father's presence.

"Earlier, when you spoke of regret…" I let my words trail, unsure of the question I'm trying to ask.

"Partially," he looks down at our clasped hands, his expression softening. "But that's a story for a different day."

"What?" I ask.

"Nothing," he says quietly.

Seeing the pain my questions have already put him through, I don't press any further. But there's an unexplainable weight in my stomach now, only squeezing tighter at the thought of the Warbearers and the dark, creeping cloud that seems to surround them everywhere they go. I do my best to shake it off.

He raises our hands to his lips, pressing a kiss gently into the top of mine. My breath catches at the feel of his soft lips.

"I'm sorry I didn't tell you sooner."

I swallow. "You don't owe me anything; I should have left it alone."

"No, you have a right to know." His breath lingers on my skin.

"How so?"

His eyes are gentle when he looks at me, the grief that showed so clearly in them a moment ago now carefully concealed. "You shared some of your pain with me; it's only fair that I share some of mine with you. Pain for pain, after all."

A tingling shiver runs down my back, barrelling past the hesitation that beats from somewhere deep inside me. "Pain for pain," I murmur. Then, repeating his words from earlier, add, "If you never get the chance to make things right, you'll learn to process and grieve what could have been."

"I still stand by that," he says.

"Maybe you should start taking your own advice." I don't mean it as an insult, but wince when it comes out.

"Fair enough." His mouth tilts upward. The short distance between us feels as if the whole of Verenathia's magic has been concentrated to the small space between our bodies.

Footsteps sound in the corridor, and Kieran's eyes slide to the doorway. "We should probably go."

"We definitely should." I return a kiss to his hand before letting it go.

We walk out side by side—the nearness of Kieran creating a warmth that almost, almost drives away the uncertainty writhing inside me.

Chapter 31

I just arrived home from a fishing trip with your father. Ashden tells me you fell ill the day we left. Had I known beforehand, I would have never gone. You have been well taken care of by your brother, though, who put in a request to the Synod for time off and has spent these past days by your side. Your fever has broken now as I lay beside you. Rest well, my dear.

The Citadel is filled with working-age people, the children and elders opting to watch and celebrate from the residential sector—leaving us to a night of revelry and drinking.

That is precisely what I find myself doing now, drink in hand, as we weave in and out of the bodies gathered in the commons. Although almost everyone is smiling, more relaxed than I've ever seen them, I stick close to Kieran's side. Groups sit at large tables, engaged in boisterous conversations or playing cards and tabletop games as the alcohol flows freely.

There's a lightness in the air—laughter ringing across the expansive space. I let it seep into me, let it try to purge the sorrow that's lingering after Kieran's confession.

I've spotted Laurel and Barrett a handful of times, but one glance at Kieran and they look the other direction. It's grating, but I'm not going to let it ruin my night.

A genuine smile splits my face when I find Sebastian near a table, the laugh that's always ready on the edge of his lips crackling the air around him as he tosses his head back.

He spots me as I approach, raising the drink in his hand high toward me.

"Well, if it isn't our little friend." His eyes dance, his friends raising their drinks along with him.

Shouts and cheers erupt from his group at our arrival. I leave the safety of Kieran's shadow and sidle up to him, leaning in as he wraps an arm around my shoulders.

"Well if it isn't my fourth favorite acquaintance," I tease, tapping my drink against his.

He draws his cup back, sucking in a dramatic gasp. "Fourth? And only an acquaintance? And here I was thinking you were at least my third favorite friend."

I laugh. "Wow, must not be a very impressive list if I hold third place."

He brings a hand to his chest. "You wound me."

A giggle creeps out of me, a comfortable warmth spreading throughout my body, evidence of the substance in my cup already at work.

"Well Rae, these are my friends." He gestures to the men around him. "You've already met Kieran."

A corner of Kieran's mouth tilts up. Sebastian's friends all grin, expressions open and nonjudgmental as I dip my head. "Hi."

He points to each of them individually, "Jansen, Thresh, Byron, and Carden."

"You ever played fang table?" The tall, dark-skinned one asks. Thresh.

Matching amusement ripples through them at my confusion. "No, what is it?"

"Your mistake," Sebastian nudges me in the ribs with his elbow.

Kieran chuckles as he leans in, his breath tickling my ear. "I'll be right back." And then, louder, "Go easy on her, Seb."

I scowl at him as they lead me to an empty table, each choosing a side to stand on. I stay by Sebastian's side, my curiosity piqued.

"Oh hey, I want in on that!" A lilting voice calls. Opal materializes on my other side, eyes glowing. Her skin shimmers as if she dusted it with the iridescence of dragons themselves—which, maybe she has. Her light pink suit is sleeveless, and our arms brush as she turns to me, white teeth flashing. "Hi."

"Hey," I return the smile. Her energy is infectious.

"Your hair looks good," she fingers the ends of the black strands, darting a playfully dirty glance in the direction Kieran left.

I take another drink, my cheeks flushing. "So I've been told."

"Oh?" She raises an eyebrow high above eyes dancing with mischief, so much like her brother's that I force myself to look away.

The game is ridiculous, but fun, and I'm apparently good enough at it that I don't take too many sips of the strong liquid swirling in my cup. Sebastian, on the other hand, doesn't fare as well—unsteady on his feet by the end of the third round.

Laughter bounces from our group at a mistake Jansen just made when Kieran's low voice caresses my ear. "Glad to see you're having fun without me."

Sebastian claps a broad hand onto Kieran's shoulder. "Glad to see you're finally back," he drawls. "Rae was working herself into a fit, started to think you weren't going to show." He gives me a pointed look while I glare at him. A lazy grin is his only response.

"Well, I certainly wouldn't want you to think that," Kieran says.

I say, loud enough for our friend to hear, "Don't let it go to your head. Sebastian just likes the sound of his own voice."

"How can I not when it's this tantalizing ?"

Opal rolls her eyes. "There's a lot of words that describe you and I don't think *tantalizing* is anywhere on that list."

He straightens, puffing out his chest a little. "I'm happy to hear I'm such a dynamic individual."

Opal groans as she casts her eyes to the high ceiling. "Author, help me."

As I lift my cup to my lips, a shift occurs in the air around us, the ground below—in something soul deep. It's not heavy or tense or taut like the usual sensations tearing at me… No, this is light and airy—like a fresh sea breeze coming through an open window. Like the whisper of sunlight in the predawn sky. The raucous voices quiet as everyone notices the pulse within the world.

I shoot a questioning look at Kieran, his face serene, but expectant.

"Come with me," he mouths, tipping his head to the entrance of the commons.

I do, grabbing the hand he offers as he leads me out. Opal and Sebastian exchange knowing glances as we retreat, hand in hand. Excited murmurs ripple through the crowd as they, too, start to make their way toward the exit.

The corridor is a few degrees cooler and far quieter as we head down its length in the direction of the Supply Field. Moonlight is pouring in through the glass, casting the white stone in a gleaming silver sheen. Between the games and lights in the commons, I hadn't realized the sun had set.

My body hums with a contented buzz as the alcohol courses through it. It also heightens my senses—touch, particularly—while I savor the feel of my hand enveloped in Kieran's gentle grasp.

"Was what we felt in there, was that the dragons?" I ask, keenly aware of his nearness.

"Yes," he says, squeezing my hand.

"And we're going to see them now?"

He grins. "Yes."

I look ahead to the open covered expanse that lies before the Supply Field. "Will we be able to see them from there?"

"Shhh," he murmurs. "No more questions."

I bristle at the command, but hold my tongue. We enter under the pillared roof before it opens into the massive courtyard that is the Supply Field. We're the first to arrive, but voices and footsteps echo behind us, ensuring that our solitude won't last long.

"This way," Kieran gestures toward the western wall of the covered expanse. I furrow my brow in confusion as I stare at the empty wall, but follow dutifully behind him.

What the darkness hadn't revealed, but I can see now as we near the wall, is a narrow set of stairs built into the stone itself—leading up to the top of the wall.

I look between Kieran and the stone steps. They're only about as wide as my shoulders, jutting out as if they and the wall are one piece. No railing to be seen, even as they rise higher and higher.

He inclines his chin upward. "Ladies, first."

I swallow the butterflies starting to take flight in my stomach, and take the first few steps tentatively, now very aware of his eyes on my backside. And my slightly unsteady footing. I watch the steps as close as I can in the dim light, gasping when I misjudge a step and my foot catches on the next. Only a step behind, Kieran reaches out and places a hand on either side of my waist, steadying me. My skin burns each place our bodies touch, and I take a deep breath as I continue up, up, up the towering wall.

I dare to look down and almost tumble over the edge as the world tilts. Kieran's steadying touch at my waist balances me, guiding me upward.

At last, we reach the end, emerging onto a parapet that leads to a turret standing commandingly in the corner of the intersecting walls.

Wordlessly, Kieran steps beside me and offers his hand. I take it, and we walk along the wall as I gaze at the stars. The twinkling lights are so close I feel like I could reach up and pluck one right out of the sky.

Glittering bands of a wispy, flowing liquid seem to float through the heavens, suspended in place by an invisible force. Large orbs of infinite colors rest among the wisps and stars, declaring their beauty.

This high in the sky, without a cloud to be seen, I feel like I am a star. I weave in them and among them, becoming a part of them while they fill the air around us. Kieran's hair blends seamlessly into the night, but his eyes reflect the shimmering lights with a glow of their own that's almost ethereal.

It's all so beautiful that my chest aches, the air becoming too full to pull into my lungs.

We come to the edge of the turret and step onto its surface, pausing between the battlements. Cocooned in stone safety while the endless, glittering sky stretches out before us, I peer down into the courtyard below to see a dark mass of bodies as they all gaze upward. The air holds an expectant charge, as if we're collectively holding our breath while waiting for the dragons.

Kieran draws my attention back to the sky with a whispered "look," as he gently guides me to the outer battlement. I squint into the shimmering obsidian, searching and searching.

"Where?" I ask breathlessly—and then I see it. Faint at first, but once I find it, it's the only thing that matters. A lithe, dark form tears across the sky, blotting out the stars in an inky black streak as it passes. My eyes burn until I remember to blink. The dragon swoops in large, graceful circles weaving in and out among—

My breath catches as I notice the rest of them all dancing among each other. Hundreds of dragons, visible only by the void of starlight in their wake. As my eyes adjust to their moving forms, I can see that they're not only dark spots, but shimmering bolts through the air as their scales reflect the moonlight. Dichotomies of light and darkness, they glide through the sky as they search for their mate.

Smoke-like, glowing tendrils begin to form among the undulating dragons, encircling them in a bright haze. Golden wisps emanate from each of them, reaching through the sky; probing. The tendrils intertwine, continuing their coming and going as they search for their true match; their equal and opposite.

Magic tendrils cobweb across the sky, illuminating the dragons while they continue their dance.

I spot a streak that, although so far away, is so familiar that I gasp.

"Cinder," I whisper to Kieran, pointing to his dragon.

His eyes are already where mine are, and a smile softens his face. "That it is."

I probe for the shimmering vein of Boreal's presence in my mind and realize she's not here—still tucked away in the Field of Stars. Maybe next year.

The filigreed web they've woven around themselves is so bright that the dragons' colors are now visible. I see one, a little orange thing, break away from the golden haze. She flies far away from the group, the wisps of her magic trailing behind her.

A larger green one jets across the sky after her. His magic encircles him in a cocoon of delicate gold while sending out probes, stretching out its fingers as if to grab ahold of her. It reaches, reaches, almost translucent as he shoots across the sky, and latches onto a single wisp of the orange one's presence as she continues her flight.

I watch in awed silence as the two life forces grasp each other, intertwining like the fingers of lovers' hands. All of their magic weaves itself together—each glowing wisp feeding itself into the ever brightening bond between them.

The bond, like a rope, grows stronger with each strand of magic added. Brighter and brighter and brighter as the green dragon gives its desperate chase, until finally, they collide.

The impact has them clinging to each other, both scrambling to orient themselves as they plummet. Golden-white fibers writhe around the mass of claws and wings as the dragons continue to try and get their bearings. The dragons are falling, falling, and then suddenly, the wisps blend into a singular haze, combining seamlessly together. They stop their fight, now fully embracing their free fall as the milky gold solidifies around them, ensconcing them.

A few heartbeats later, there's a bright, glittering flash as streaks of light and color explode from their center like a starburst. The two dragons burst apart, gathering themselves before soaring high into the sky and meeting each other again.

Tears trickle down my face as they soar and dive through the sky in tandem now, never leaving each other's side.

More flashes burst across the sky as other dragons find their mates. The golden haze that filled the sky is now a technicolor ethereal cloud.

I look down, blinking away the wetness, but gasp at the ground far, far below me. Tiny, twinkling lights are slowly leaking from the ground, rising up to meet the magic of the dragons.

The magic of the land.

"It's really something, isn't it."

I nod, quickly brushing the tears from my cheeks.

"You never really get used to it," he whispers.

I let his words settle over us, watching as Verenathia's magic reaches the dragons and weaves together. Delicate, swirling strands of magic span the distance between land and sky, thousands of tendrils tethering the dragons.

"What happens now?" I ask.

"All the mated pairs will go back to the Field of Stars to physically solidify the mating bond. The other unpaired individuals will try again next year."

I nod, feeling a bit sad for the unmated pairs, but I realize a bond like that would be worth waiting for.

We watch for another hour. The colorful, glittering cloud dissipates as the last of the dragons find their mates, evaporating like smoke. Mated pairs glide through the sky, sharing in their dance of celebration.

And here, as suddenly and surely as I've ever decided anything, I realize I don't want to return to Ra'goramal. Whether I can or can't, I don't want to. Right here, right now; one with the stars, I can't imagine leaving.

I can't stay, I know I can't. But now the thought of leaving Kieran, someone who has become such a genuine friend to me—maybe more, if his presence against my back is any indication—hurts almost as much as the thought of being away from Ash and Avice.

And here I am, caught between two territories, unable to dwell in either. A traitor. A fugitive; with people I love and care for in both, yet still not having found what I'm looking for.

My heart is being torn in two while the unknown continues its ceaseless beckoning.

I close my eyes and lean into Kieran, savoring his warmth as he wraps his arms around my chest, pulling me closer.

These thoughts are too much for my inebriated mind right now. I'll revisit them when I'm sober.

Even still, something twists deep inside of me.

Probably just the alcohol.

CHAPTER 32

When life gets so dark that you cannot see, hold fast to our love for you, my dear.

Bright, unfiltered sunlight pours from the open window in my room. At night, I gaze out at the crystal clear obsidian sky before falling asleep with them open for this very reason. The light gently pulls me from my sleep, then keeps me suspended in hazy wakefulness while its warmth seeps into my bones.

I yawn, stretching my body in the massive bed. Memories of last night come filtering back to me on the sun's rays.

We had celebrated long into the night, returning to the commons for games and companionship after the dragons had left.

Doing my best to ignore the twinges in my heart, I allowed myself to enjoy the night. The games, each one more absurd than the last, grew more boisterous as drinks flowed and the night wore deep.

I spent the whole night with Kieran, Sebastian, and Opal. We laughed and talked and made bets on who would lose which game. The alcohol had seeped into my veins until everything was a blissful haze—my questions and unease fading away.

Even in my altered state, I couldn't help but notice Kieran's eyes rarely left me. They had practically sparkled with happiness even though I never saw a drink in his hand. His laugh had echoed through the room all night long while we watched Sebastian lose at almost every game he played. And when I at last grew too unsteady on my feet, he walked me to my room, carefully unlacing the boots I was unable to do myself.

I wiggle my toes now, savoring the warmth, surprised at how well I feel—no lingering effects of our revelrous night.

Sighing, I drag myself from the comfort of my bed and pad to the armoire, selecting a gray suit. The scales on this one lack that characteristic opalescence, but are so intricately patterned I spend several long moments admiring it.

Moving through the motions of readying for the day, I finish, and slip quietly out of my room. The Citadel is usually quiet at this hour—save for the early supply runners—and I'm grateful for the solitude.

I make my way quickly down the few corridors connecting the housing wing to the mess hall, and smile when I find Sebastian and Opal already sitting at one of the tables.

Snatching a muffin from the food table, I plop myself down in front of them.

Sebastian groans groggily as he squints against the sunlight streaming down from the high windows. A half eaten muffin and singular piece of untouched sausage sit on his plate. His dark brown hair is unusually fuzzy, poking out in every direction as he hunches forward. Opal doesn't even react, eyes bloodshot and sullen as she stares at the empty spot in front of her.

I stifle a smirk, thoroughly enjoying my own breakfast.

"Rough night?" I ask.

Sebastian looks up at me, his face void of any emotion aside from the irritated squint of his eyes. A giggle creeps out of me, at which he looks slightly offended but remains silent.

I push his plate closer toward him. A glance at it and his dark skin seems to take on a grayish hue.

Kieran appears, taking a seat beside me. One look at his friend and he snorts. "Rough night?"

Sebastian turns that deadpan stare on him. "Really?"

We both chuckle as he rises from the table and shuffles away—now a decidedly green shade.

Opal grimaces. "I think I'll… be at home today."

I offer her a sympathetic smile as she drags herself to her feet.

Alone, Kieran's nearness permeates the air around me. My stomach flutters, but I don't know if I should mention the way he looked at and touched me last night… or his father.

So instead, I stuff another bite in my mouth.

"Where do you get the skins for the uniforms?" I hold up a gray-scaled arm for his inspection.

"Dragons shed," he shrugs, his mouth full. "Our ancestors asked if we could use the skins for our clothing."

"Didn't your mother teach you it was rude to speak with your mouth full?" I swat at his arm.

He swallows. "Obviously, they obliged. And good thing, too. Dragonhide lasts way longer than traditional fabrics and is far more comfortable. Plus, they look better." He pokes me in the ribs with an elbow.

I hiss, my ribs still bruised and sensitive.

"Sorry," he winces.

Absentmindedly picking at my muffin, I let my gaze rove up and down his body, appreciating the skin-tight quality of the suit.

"I don't have supply runs today" he says. "Do you want to go to the Field?"

Go see Boreal and be… free? Lose the confusion and churning and sorrow in the wind?

"Absolutely," I grin.

***

Kieran's thumb strokes the top of my hand as we head from the direction of the Supply Field, finished with our day in the Field of Stars. My hair is tangled and wild from our flight, my smile stretching over a face tight with a pink sunburn.

"I don't think I could ever get used to this." I say.

"To what?"

I savor his soft touch, the safety of his hand around mine. "To all of this. The magic, the dragons, the lifestyle." *You.* "All of it."

He glances down at me with a questioning expression but doesn't break his stride. "Oh, yeah?"

"Yes, it's—"

My voice dies in my throat as Lucielle, Verenathia's Talebearer, steps into the corridor. Kieran stiffens and grips my hand tighter. My heart immediately starts to beat with panic, and foreboding's vice-like grasp crushes the air from my lungs.

He looks just the same as he did that day in the Court of Elders. His milky blue gaze swirls as he gazes ahead, seemingly looking at everything and nothing all at once. The folds of his white robes flow noiselessly along the ground, giving him the appearance of gliding across the smooth stone. Every bit of the black, scrolling tattoos on his head are covered by his hood—pulled low enough that only those unsettling eyes are visible above a mouth held in a perpetual unfeeling line.

A mouth that's swollen with a split lip.

It's only when I see the figure following behind him that the room, the rest of the world around me, goes distantly silent. It's as if my surroundings lean in, focusing on the scene before me; I don't even know if I'm breathing.

There's no expression on the face of the figure behind Lucielle. No concern, no curiosity, no fear.

I gape at the swelling, the black eye and disheveled clothing. There's a split across his cheek and red marks all over his arms and neck.

And his eyes. There's… *nothing* in his eyes. Just a blank, almost mindless obedience as he follows Lucielle through the corridor.

"Ashden," I choke out.

The realization hits me. Hits me like a kick to my ribs, knocking the breath out of my lungs as it sends my mind reeling. My heart starts to beat impossibly fast, too fast as I try to rein it in. The walls are caving in, their massive windows are shattering, being blown in from the outside. It has to be that weight that's pressing in all around us, crushing me. It has to be—

"Easy, Rae," Kieran's voice is low and soothing, but there's an underlying threat of darkness in it.

The Culling. I've been so distracted that the thought hasn't crossed my mind since my first day here. I haven't seen a single Goramalan servant anywhere.

Anywhere.

Raimy. Along with the image of the kind baker—the Warbearers, and the feeling that emanates from the Inner Sanctum; that sense of dread and foreboding. The niggling worm of something amiss now has a name—and is writhing in my gut, churning into nausea.

Ashden doesn't even so much as blink as they near us, his face void of any emotion—of anything at all. Lucielle stares straight ahead, but there's the slightest shift in his usually unshakeable exterior.

I want to scream. I can already feel it building in my throat, roiling up from my lungs, from my soul. Kieran places a steadying hand at the small of my back, urging me forward.

They pass directly beside us—Ashden's gray eyes hollow as they stare straight ahead.

"Ashden," I breathe. My voice is something hoarse and foreign as it rasps out of my throat, and I clamp a hand over my mouth to stifle a cry. There is no reaction from my brother, even as Lucielle stiffens—but keeps walking.

One numb foot in front of the other, Kieran's hand reassuringly against my back, we finally come to the end of the corridor and turn directly into the next one. My heart beats wildly and I force my breaths to steady.

In through the nose. Out through my mouth.

"Kieran," I whisper, willing my voice to steady. I already know the answer, know it with every panicked beat of my heart, but I ask anyway. "What was that?"

He inhales a long breath before blowing it out through pursed lips. I'll slap him if he tries to dance around the question like he did with his father, but he says quietly, "The Culling."

The dread sinks further, roiling in my core. I can't control my breaths now. They're coming too rapidly, my heart is beating too fast, the walls are collapsing around us—

"Rae," Kieran faces me, placing his hands on my shoulders. "Breathe." There's so much concern and fear and pain in his expression. "Breathe." He breathes in slowly through his nose and out through his mouth.

I follow, staring into his eyes as I force my body into submission. Instead of the usual glimmering emerald, his eyes are a green tempest.

When I've finally calmed myself enough to speak, I demand, "What did he do to my brother?"

He flinches, removing his hands from my shoulders. "Lucielle puts a binding trance over them when they arrive." He pauses, swallowing. "So they don't try to run."

"Run from what, Kieran? From the life of luxury and honor we're promised?" Each word is clipped with anger. Cold.

He doesn't say anything but I can see the guilt in his eyes—guilt and something else I can't place.

"Why haven't I seen any of my people here, Kieran?" Anger laces my words now, thinly veiling simmering panic. He still doesn't answer, his chest heaving.

My voice rises to a cry. "Where are they?"

He steps forward, abruptly closing the distance between us as he brings a finger furiously to my lips. "Do you want everyone in the Citadel to hear you?" He asks in a coarse whisper.

I'm taken aback. His face is so near to mine, every single speck of guilt and rage is on full display.

Rage, yes—that's rage.

"Where are they?" My voice is a choked whisper, threatening to break.

He straightens, running a frustrated hand through his hair. "Here," he says, his voice softer now.

No. I close my eyes, shaking my head in disbelief. *No, no, no.*

"Show me where they are."

His face is tight, pinched with pain. "But, Rae—"

"No," I demand. "Show me." My mind is whirling with so many questions and my heart won't stop its ceaseless drumbeat against my ribcage.

He nods, resignation settling over him like a blanket. "We'll go after sunset, once people have gone back to their homes for the night," he says quietly.

I don't respond, my stomach sick.

"And Rae," he continues. "You cannot tell a soul what you are doing tonight. You can't tell anyone you even saw Lucielle. No one. Not even Sebastian and Opal." His tone is so insistent that I mutter a numb agreement.

We head back. To where? I don't know. I think we're walking to give ourselves something to do. I think I might shatter, otherwise.

The light filtering in through the floor to ceiling windows signifies it's late afternoon.

Sunset will be here soon.

CHAPTER 33

My love, the anguish I have from this is almost too much to bear. I know they will soon be old enough, but it is breaking me

I cannot calm myself as we near the Inner Sanctum.

My brother.

My *brother.*

My brother is here, and no matter how hard I try to convince myself otherwise, I know something is wrong.

Our final argument has been playing over and over in my mind as Kieran and I have waited until sunset—until the Citadel has emptied for the night—to make our way to the Inner Sanctum. The last words that were spoken to my brother, done out of anger and hurt, pound themselves deeper into my heart. They burned like acid then, and are eating away at me as such now. I would do anything, *give* anything to go back to that night and ensure that it never happened.

I should have gone back. I never should have left.

Our footsteps echo solemnly through the empty corridors. The Warbearers, Kieran informed me, don't actually reside in the Inner Sanctum, but rather, have their own private wing of the Citadel. The Inner Sanctum, it turns out, is used for 'other activities.' I don't know what those activities are, but now, as it looms ahead of us, I can't help but feel that overwhelming sense of something… off.

There's never been a reason to question the Culling—never a need to. It had never occurred to me what actually happens on the other side; I just blindly assumed that what we were being taught was the hard and fast truth. But after learning of the magic barred from us… I should have known.

I should have known.

That day in the library when I had asked Kieran where my people were, he told me they were in the Inner Sanctum. It makes sense; the Warbearers rarely leave that place, so it would stand to reason that's where their servants reside. Yet still, the memory of Ashden's vacant, unseeing gaze doesn't leave my mind. And Kieran's response?

Wrong. Something is so wrong.

We turn into an intersecting hall that's smaller than the usual corridors that checker the Citadel. The only light drifting in comes from the ceiling height windows running along the upper edge of the walls. Right now, I don't even want to think about how Kieran knows the route—why he seems so familiar with it, as if he's been here many times before. And maybe he has; maybe he's spent more time watching his father than he's led me to believe.

A shiver snakes its way down my spine. That thick heaviness that seems to permeate the corridors around the Inner Sanctum are suffocating me. If those corridors are veiled by that weight, then our nearness—this sensation—is a thick, winter-proof down blanket.

We stop at a massive set of onyx doors. There are no hinges, no handles. Nothing but the smooth, polished plane of stone as it sits flush with the wall; seamless, reaching almost all the way up its marble face. I can see my reflection on their surface—my lips a tight line.

The doors stand so tall, so formidable; their bodies are a stark black hole against the white surrounding us. Gaping at us, waiting to swallow us whole.

Kieran looks at me. There is such heaviness in his eyes. So many emotions swirl with such intensity that I look away.

His voice is raw, resigned when he asks, "Are you sure you want to do this?"

No. I'm not sure. I have no idea what lies beyond these doors, but with his display of uncharacteristic uncertainty, I'm left questioning if I've made a mistake in telling him to bring me here. I breathe deeply, trying to settle the beginnings of nausea.

"Yes." My voice is strong but I know he hears the note of fear, hard as I try to mask it.

He gives me a long, guilt-ridden look. I don't balk even as I feel the terror rising.

"Show me."

He hangs his head, shaking it as he places both palms on the dark stone and pushes. "The doors…" he murmurs. "They're keyed to the blood of the Warbearers. No one can get in… Or out. " His throat bobs. "I think the only reason I can open them is because I share my father's blood."

His rambling—maybe a tell of his nervousness—seems like some foreign, distorted thing; as if I'm laying at the bottom of the ocean and he's shouting from the surface.

The massive door glides easily backward, revealing a staircase underneath chiseled from the same onyx material. A soft orange glow emanates from somewhere deep within.

Kieran starts to descend, checking over his shoulder to see if I'm following. My body is screaming at me to turn around, to not go down and see what lurks beneath the Citadel, but I follow.

Once we're both on the ground at the base of the steps, Kieran reaches a hand up and presses on the underside of the stone slab, pushing it back into place. I don't have time to question the mechanics of such a thing as he quickly leads me forward into the dark hallway.

The air is cool and damp, with a noticeable metallic tang.

We come to the end of the passage and I blink while my eyes adjust to the low light. A massive chamber sits before us. Torches line the circular walls all the way around, no doubt kept alight by the same magic that keeps our own fires in Ra'goramal. There are no sounds except for my own heartbeat as it beats itself to death. I wonder if Kieran can hear it too… wonder if his sounds the same.

Unlike the onyx, this room is made of gray stone; as if it was carved straight out of the ground itself. And there are… *Author above.* I clasp a hand over my mouth to stifle the scream that tears up my throat.

There are people in here, all deathly silent.

Unmoving.

Every one of them rests within a ring of stones inlaid in the ground. The stones themselves are intricately engraved, pulsing with a soft white light that emanates from the markings. Like a heartbeat.

They're all slumped shoulders, bowed heads, and half-closed eyes as glowing white tendrils slowly seep from their bodies, feeding into the ring of stones around them.

My feet are rooted to the spot. I can't think, can't breathe. I feel a steady hand on my shoulder and follow the length of it to its owner.

Kieran, his face heartbreakingly gentle, just stares at me. I cling to him, tethering myself so I don't get sucked under by the wave of horror rising within me. I take a tentative step forward, then another, and another until I'm walking between the rings, my eyes burning. None of the people stir. They don't even seem to acknowledge our presence.

What is happening?

One of the figures is on his side, his body curled in on itself. I can't stop the cry that tears out of me as I race to the edge of his ring.

His eyes are sunken deep in their hollows, with ashen skin that sags loosely. The fullness of his face is gone. His once strong, capable hands are nothing more than bone. He's still wearing the same thing he would have worn for a long day in the bakery, though now it hangs limply on his emaciated form.

"Raimy," my voice is barely a breath.

There is movement, the faintest of movement, as his eyes slide beneath his eyelids.

"Raimy."

He opens his eyes a fraction, then lifts a hand centimeters off the ground. His eyes, once a rich brown, are dim now, almost faded; like the color has been drained right out of them. His dry, cracked lips begin to move slowly, as if it costs him great effort. There's no sound, but they form the same word over and over.

"Rae. Rae. Rae."

My heart shatters. The kind, lovely baker that I've always known is now nothing more than a shell.

"Raimy," I choke. Darting a frantic gaze to Kieran, I demand, "I can't hear him. Why can't I hear him?"

I don't give him a chance to respond before turning back to the baker. "I'm sorry," I breathe as tears brim in my eyes. Reaching a hand tentatively toward him, I'm stopped by an invisible hard wall between us. My throat tightens. I feel all the way around the base of the ring, working my way up to the top.

An invisible dome, sealing him in.

I have to do something.

"You can't," Kieran says softly. "And even if you could…" he trails off, gesturing to Raimy.

I stand, eyes locked on the baker. I hadn't realized I said the words out loud.

Kieran's right. In this state, he doesn't have much time left.

There's nothing I can do. I can't do anything. I have to do something. Surveying the room through bleary eyes, waves of nausea roll through me.

And then I see him.

Ashden sits in his own ring, head down and shoulders slumped—those glowing tendrils leaching from him and into the engraved stones. With eyes barely open and trained on the ground, he doesn't see me as I race toward him, feeling as my hands again meet that invisible hard wall.

My frantic movement draws his attention, and he lifts his head. His eyes widen in shock—pure, unadulterated shock—as he looks at me. Some animalistic noise escapes me as I drop to my knees in front of him, separated by the barrier. His lips are moving—saying something I can't make out.

He shoots to his feet, only to slam his head on the invisible ceiling. He raises his hands to feel above him, then hand over hand he moves down the curved wall of the dome. His movements become faster, frantic as he feels around the base at the floor, all the while those glowing tendrils pouring from him.

He drops to his knees behind the wall in front of me, and the tightening of my throat threatens to suffocate when I see understanding dawn on him—see the silvery wet lining his eyes.

I can see what he's saying now, face to face only mere inches apart.

"You're alive. You're alive. You're alive." Over and over.

"Yes," I cry, placing my palms against the wall as I kneel forward. "Yes, I'm okay." I blink, desperately trying to clear my vision.

"I'm sorry. I'm sorry."

"No," I cry. "You aren't the one who should be sorry." I pound against the wall with my finger, pointing at him. "Not you, I'm the one who needs to be sorry." My voice is a strangled cry as I keep pounding on the wall between us. "Not you—me. I never should have left," my hands are fists now, beating against the wall as if I can break it. "I should have never left."

"I'm sorry," he says again.

"No!" I shout, fully hysterical now as I relentlessly beat the damned wall. He's going to die in here, I know he's going to die. "This is my fault, not yours." I cry. "I'm going to get you out of here."

Warm, steady hands grab my shoulders and pull me away from Ashden. I struggle against Kieran as he draws me back, leading me to my feet. Ashden bristles, but I see the acceptance that washes over him, sending me thrashing in Kieran's arms.

"You have to stop," he whispers. "You're going to hurt yourself or draw the Warbearers here."

I whirl on him, fire on my tongue, but find only gentle kindness and immense pain in his eyes.

"It's not your fault," he whispers again as his hands rest on my shoulders.

Tears blur my vision afresh. "But it is," I choke. All of it—every last bit of it—is my fault. Maybe not the fact that Ashden is here, in this wretched place—but the poison lingering between us. The way I left him, everything we left unsaid.

Kieran opens his mouth to speak again, but my attention drifts to the wall behind him.

A stone slab sits, about as high as my waist, centered at the back of the chamber.

"Rae," Kieran's voice is low, a warning. As if he's trying to tell me not to look for answers to questions I don't want to ask. He won't stop me though, I know he won't.

I walk slowly toward that stone, dread making each step heavier and heavier. Its surface is a different color than the rest of it, almost as if it's stained—

No.

Standing before it, I stare in horror. Its surface is stained—a deep rust that forms in splatters and streaks. Dark, glistening red pools atop the stains before running down its sides: fresh. The metallic liquid reaches a slit in the floor that runs around the base of the stone, and into the ground beyond.

Horror, shock, fear, disgust—I don't know what to feel, what to think as everything slams into me all at once. I can't tear my eyes away from its surface. A stone drenched in blood. Human blood.

The room waivers around me. I turn slowly, unsteadily, and see every one of those broken people in their prisons as they await whatever cruel end is in store for them.

Before I even realize what is happening, I'm running. I run without making the conscious decision to leave. Tears burst from my eyes and flow freely down my face as my pounding footsteps echo throughout the cavernous chamber.

Everything writhing around inside of me reaches a fever pitch and my heart explodes into panicked terror.

Tearing through the passageway, I come to the stairway leading up out of this chamber, this hell. I take a few steps up to reach—pushing and clawing at the stone above me.

I need to get out. I need to get out. *Please let me out.*

It's not moving, it—it… it's not moving. A shriek strangles its way up my throat, and then the door glides forward, letting silvery light down into the stairway.

I fly up the steps and out into the hallway. My vision is so blurred as the tears stream that I scarcely look where I'm going. There's no sound but my pounding footsteps echoing off the stone—none except for the other set not far behind.

My breath is coming in heaving, gasping sobs as I run.

I run fast and I run far, taking turn after turn until I find myself at the front entrance to the Citadel.

I want out. I want out of this perfect, gleaming place that screams with the blood of the innocent.

I NEED OUT.

Throwing open the large glass door, I barrel onto the moonlit colonnade. The door opens a second time not a heartbeat later as Kieran emerges, panting. I make it to the railing of the grand staircase before dropping to the ground and vomiting into the hedges that line it.

I heave, over and over until my strength is completely sapped. My lungs, my throat, my legs—everything burns. I spit, trying to clear the acrid taste from my mouth.

Brushing a hand across my eyes, I sit back on my heels, wrapping my arms around myself and rocking. My chest is still heaving as I gasp for breath, my heart still refusing to calm.

Kieran's footsteps sound from behind me, coming closer.

My voice is hoarse as I ask, "Why didn't you tell me?"

Blood.

So much blood.

He silently lowers himself to the ground near me. His tone is gentle, and I can hear the note of excuse in it before he even starts, "I—

"Why didn't you tell me?" I repeat, cutting him off.

Calm down. Breathe.

I can feel his eyes lingering on me but I keep my gaze trained on the hedges.

"I wanted to," he says quietly.

"Then why didn't you?" I snap, whipping my head to him—not bothering to hide the tempest inside of me. Fresh tears blur my vision as an aching, crackling hurt ripples through my heart.

Traitor.

The name that I've labeled myself, that keeps flitting through my mind at my own actions—is now directed toward him. Toward whatever bond I'd thought we might share.

Traitor.

The blood-stained stone, freshly soaked while rivers of red drip down its sides… I suck in a breath at the realization. That will be Raimy. That will be Ashden. The blood, still so fresh—

I dive forward onto my hands and knees, heaving again. I vomit, coughing and spitting until there's absolutely nothing left—and then some, as my stomach tries to rid itself of the memory.

Kieran places his palm on the ground as I struggle to draw breath. Droplets of water emerge from the cracks between the stones all around us, slowly rising into the air while they catch the pale light of the moon.

The droplets converge to form a large orb, which then directs itself toward me under Kieran's guidance.

I wipe my mouth on my shoulder and rise, sitting on my knees. The orb retains its shape as I pluck it out of the air and hold it to my lips, drinking until it shrinks to nothing.

Reluctantly bringing my gaze to his, I can't help the torrent of confusion and rage at his expression. The pain in his eyes is so great; so deep, that for a moment, I think he might actually care.

He blows out a long breath. "If I told you right away, you would have left."

"And that would have been my decision to make," I bark.

"I know," he says quietly. "I'm not saying it was the right decision."

Why would you have cared if I stayed or not?

The quiet question filters through my anger—driving through it like a cool wind, cutting the warm, murky layers of my rage. But a darker, heavier question presents itself. Its cloying thickness suffocates the cool wind as it curls black, scrolling tendrils around it.

"Why am I here?" Panic is starting to set in again but I keep my voice deceptively low, unfeeling.

Something like fear shows in Kieran's expression—the first I've seen from him—and he swallows, but regains his composure in less than a heartbeat. "I don't know what you mean," he says. "You're here because you wanted to be here."

"Don't bullshit me," I spit. "How am I here? Your people are killing mine." The day I arrived, when he demanded to speak to the Elders and Warbearers… alone…

"What did you do?" I breathe.

Fear—real fear—lights his eyes now. His voice is edged with panic as he says, "I made an agreement with the Elders so they wouldn't kill you that day."

Something about the way he says those last two words sends a shiver through me.

"That. Day?" The words are clipped as I pour every ounce of willpower I possess into steadying my voice.

He looks at me, pleading. "I did what I thought was best to keep you from getting executed—"

"Which was?" I cry.

Moving to his knees, he kneels directly in front of me. His eyes burn so intensely I have to force myself to hold their gaze. "I told them that if they spared you that day, I would turn you over to them once you found what you wanted."

"Turn me over to them?" I ask, disbelief echoing in my voice.

His hands clench into fists in his lap. "To be executed," he says carefully.

His voice is a plea, an unspoken question—willing me to understand.

But I don't. I can't.

Traitor.

Traitor.

Traitor.

The word pounds itself in a loop through my head.

"How could you?" My voice breaks.

He grabs my hands with that same pleading insistence. "I was never going to, Rae. You have to know that. I hope that by now you know me well enough to know that I would never do that to you."

I shake my head in disbelief and snatch my hands out of his grasp. "No, I don't know. How could I possibly know?" I ask, my voice fraying with anger and the soul-cutting bite of betrayal. "You lied to me. You've been lying to me this entire time. Everything I've done, everything I've been—all that I've seen here has been built on a lie."

"Yes, but—" he runs a frantic hand through his hair. "I would never do that to you. I would never do that to anyone, Rae." His eyes glint with an almost wild sort of pain; flaring slightly, begging for understanding.

I know you wouldn't. I know. I know. The hurt and confusion and betrayal all rage within me, each screaming louder than the other as they demand to be heard.

"Please," he whispers.

"My brother is in there," my voice rises, and I wince at the way he recoils, though I can't stop myself. "Was that going to be me? Trapped until I'm slaughtered like an animal?" I'm shouting now, forcing everything he's done to me back at him, unfiltered. "Does everyone else know what's actually happening?"

I don't even have to ask. Every single side-eyed glance, every glare of hatred, all of the snide remarks, the attack… How could I have been so blind?

I abruptly pull myself to my feet. Scrambling up after me, he blurts "Rae—"

"I can't do this. I need to be alone."

CHAPTER 34

ASHDEN

Rae.

Rae was here.

Here.

Rae is alive.

In this room. This place.

Author above, what is this place?

The scent of blood and something electric, something wrong… They're all I smell.

Blood and stone and dampness. And that scent—that scent that's more of a feeling. A feeling that wars against every part of my being.

I drop my head into my hands, wincing as the bruises on my face press against my palms. I tried to fight. Tried like hell. My fading will came back with a roaring vengeance when I heard my name called in the Storehouse. Rae or no, family or no, it was the last thing I had to hold onto. My last 'fuck you' to Verenathia.

But it was wrong. Something was so horribly, sickeningly off. My mind and body didn't work—didn't work together like they're supposed to. It was like the rotting hand of a corpse had squeezed my will in its grip. No amount of struggle could break its grasp. It crushed my very being.

And Rae—I saw her in the halls here. I couldn't move or tell her I love her, couldn't fight. I saw her with that Verenathian we met that day on the loading docks. I wanted to hug her, scream at her, I don't know. But she's alive. I don't understand how or why, or why they told us she'd been executed, but it doesn't matter.

She's alive.

The barrier around me muffles all sound. I can't hear anything, save for the roaring in my head.

Punching, kicking, hitting, slamming my bodyweight into it—nothing affects this barrier. Nothing.

The people all around me, all in various degrees of decay—that's what these barriers are for. To keep us trapped while they drain us. Some, whose bodies look like nothing more than husks, no longer have anything surrounding them. Maybe they're no longer a threat.

The glowing tendrils pumping from my body leach straight into the ground, no doubt feeding whatever unholy purpose the Warbearers have us here for.

I should be surprised, shocked, outraged—something, but there's only a growing pit of cold, bitter hatred inside of me. For the Warbearers. For this place. For what they've been doing to our people, what they've done to our daily lives. The lies that are so glaringly clear now that I'm sitting here. The hatred is like acid inside of me.

But none of that matters. Rae was here, and she is alive. Still alive, even after all this time.

I have to get out of here, have to get to her. I don't know what that man is going to do to her, or why he was here with her. He seemed concerned, seemed like he cared.

But he's one of them.

I have to get out of here.

Peering around the room, I search for something that can help me get out. Every move feels heavy, as if trudging through mud. My limbs are leaden, and even slamming against the barrier as I did when I first arrived leaves me winded.

This magic is draining me so fast. Magic that I didn't even know existed like this a day ago.

It's a wonder Raimy is still here, still hanging on. I try to avoid the baker, the sight turning my stomach.

Four hooded figures emerge from the doorway in the stone wall. Three hold back as the fourth lurks through the room, stooping at one of the rings to collect a person I don't recognize—one who may as well be a skeleton wearing a sagging skin suit.

I try to tear my eyes away, but I can't. My heart begins beating a war-rhythm against my chest.

They carry the person to the stone slab at the back of the room. The stone stained with blood. Its coppery tang is all around me.

With surprising gentleness, the Warbearer sets the person on the slab, her body limp and unmoving. They step back, surrounding it, completely still, not a rustle in their robes.

Several long moments pass in utter stillness, the Warbearers' eyes all closed.

What are they doing?

As if in answer, the one that gathered the victim now moves toward the slab again, producing a wicked, gleaming dagger from his robe. The hilt is embellished with jewels and runes.

I swallow.

He stands in front of the woman's body, blocking my view of what is about to take place.

In one swift movement, the dagger flashes forward. I can't see but I know it finds its mark.

Blood begins to run down the stone slab and into the floor around it. The Warbearers only continue to stand, observing. My heart beats so fast, as if it's trying to escape my body, trying to escape this place. I press my back against the barrier behind me, putting as much space between myself and the Warbearers as possible.

They're still standing there when the blood stops flowing.

CHAPTER 35

I remember when you would race toward the door as your father came home from the day's catch, asking him to tell you stories of the sea. So small and full of wonder. I am so proud of you, little bird. You are becoming such a wonderful young woman. Never stop looking for the beauty in life, no matter how dark things get.

Anger, so much anger, and hurt like I've never known radiate from my shattered heart. Utterly betrayed, I trudge my way through stony meadows to the Field of Stars, where I know Boreal will be waiting.

Silence, so complete I can hear the whisper of grass against the rocks, stretches out before me. The land is abandoned at this hour while everyone sleeps contentedly in their homes, blissfully unaffected by the horrors taking place here.

I can't understand… any of it, try as I might. What is the purpose of killing my people, and how has it been kept a secret this long?

Why? Why are they doing this? Why have we been lied to?

Why did he lie to me?

He should have told me.

I probably *would* have left if he told me. Even though that siren song still sings to me, I would have found a way to suppress it—tamped and stuffed it down forever until it shriveled into some forgotten crumb of myself.

No you wouldn't have.

My head jerks in surprise at the words that flicker through the war in my head, quiet as a whisper—steadfast as a promise. Uttered from somewhere deep inside of me, as if it may have not been me at all.

I blink, glancing quickly around. No one. Nothing. Shaking my head, I continue on.

The thought, wherever it came from, is right, though. I wouldn't have left. I couldn't have. How could I, knowing people, *my* people, were dying right below me? And not just dying, but being mercilessly tortured and sacrificed.

I couldn't have.

But what could I have done, what can I do? I don't understand the whole of what's happening, and even if I did, I'm one person. And clearly, they will have no issue eliminating any potential threats to the tentative peace between our lands.

But now, my brother is among the dying.

***

Boreal is waiting for me near the Field of Stars, resting against a boulder in the meadow. As if she could sense my distress and knew I needed her as quickly as possible. She tosses her head and offers a soft chortle as I appear.

"It's good to see you too," I murmur, reaching up to stroke her silky scaled side. I work my way up to her neck, relishing the cool velvet of her scales. She leans into my touch, chirping quietly, before pulling away to look into my eyes.

Her wisdom—ancient and deep, passed down through thousands of years of collective existence—takes my breath away. I feel like she can see straight into my soul, baring all of my turmoil. We sit like that for several heartbeats, both a spectator to the other's inner workings. There's a deep sadness in her dark eyes, far below the surface of her youthfulness.

"You know too, don't you?" I whisper, my throat tightening. She lowers her head and utters a quiet, guttural moan.

My words are still a whisper as I force them over the lump in my throat. "I want to go home."

Even as I say the words, I know without a doubt that I can't. I can't leave Ashden here, trapped in that pit of hell.

She shuffles around until her shimmering side faces me. Kneeling, she flicks her head, beckoning me onto her back.

I don't hesitate, clambering up quickly and finding my seat. I need to get away from this place—need to feel the wind biting my skin and whipping my hair. I don't want to think or feel anything other than the sky surrounding us, swallowing us up in its enormity as we slice through its star-flecked depths.

Boreal seems to want it too, leaping into the sky as soon as I'm secure, beating her wings hard to carry us high into the night. I let each pounding break of her wings beat out the chaos whirling inside me.

Soon the ground is but a dark blanket below us. I glance over my shoulder to the Citadel, gleaming proudly atop its hill, and exhale the sour taste of nausea that arises at the sight of it.

When Boreal dives forward, streaking across the sky, the wind screaming past my ears, I do not look back. The land soon turns to the scattered rocks of the Field of Stars, and past that—the open, unending chop of the sea far, far below.

We soar for hours. All sense of time disappears as I lose myself in the bliss of freedom. I don't tell her where to go, but rather, let her fly wherever calls to her. I only need to feel her—grasp onto her calm, steady presence while we glide as one.

She takes a weaving flight pattern, plunging high before diving low again and again—sending my stomach into my throat—but I can tell she's flying with purpose, toward an unknown destination.

"Where are we going, girl?"

She shakes her head, snuffling, and continues on her flight. I don't bother to demand an answer.

Closing my eyes, I lose myself in the roar of the wind, but a sob works its way up my throat.

I don't know what I thought existed between Kieran and I. Maybe a sweet, tender friendship… maybe more. The yearning I was beginning to feel for him, the care he took toward me… all he's shown and taught me; I thought it meant something.

It was all a facade. Every word, every action, every pain shared. All of it. How can you care for someone and let them believe a lie? How can you build a relationship off of one?

But… Kieran is good. I know he's good. There's a reason. There has to be.

Maybe that's my own delusion talking in a weak attempt at self-preservation.

Whatever we shared was built on the sands of deception, distorted by my own emotion, and was only waiting for a strong wind to shatter it.

And oh, has it been shattered.

Here I am with the knowledge of what's truly happening, with knowing my brother is at death's door, and Kieran's betrayal is consuming my thoughts.

I let my sob escape, Boreal and the wind the only witnesses to my despair.

I don't know how long has passed before she stops suddenly, beating her wings softly to keep us hovering in place as we face the vast sea. She's insistent, stretching her neck forward, whimpering eagerly as if desiring to push forward.

"What is it?" I ask, swiping a tear from my cheek.

She only hovers, her body taught with insistence.

I squint into the darkness, only able to make out the glint of waves in the moonlight. Everything is watery darkness.

Nothing.

"Is there something there?" I can tell we're northwest of Verenathia, but how far, I'm not sure.

Pushing my heartbreak aside, I purse my lips and focus on the memory of the maps we have. I can't remember any of the other land masses outside of Hathswarden—the territory made up of Verenathia and Ra'goramal. Everything outside of that is a muddled blur.

"Am I really that bad?" I mutter.

Boreal snuffles, as if to say 'yes.'

I roll my eyes and pat her neck as we bob. The world is calm up here. The wind whispers through my hair, the sea churning contentedly.

Gesturing ahead, I ask, "Why don't we go?"

She whimpers and tosses her head enthusiastically, but refrains from going forward.

"Did you just want to show me?" I stroke again along her smooth scales. She exhales a long breath, and if I didn't know any better, I'd say it almost sounds like relief.

I laugh softly, "It is quite the view, thank you."

She turns her head to me then, watching me with a single eye, pleased, but there's something deeper still within my dragon's gaze; like she's communicating something to me in her own quiet way.

Sighing wearily, I close my eyes. The weight of it all threatens to crush me, pulling me under like a tidal wave. I need someone I know, someone I love to help me process this. To help me discern what needs to be done. Author knows I can't leave my brother, or any of the Goramalans, to continue this death dance.

I need Avice. Not only that, but she deserves to know what's happening.

The need to clear my head, to reapproach the situation with fresh eyes, is an overwhelming force. Anything I would have to say to Kieran right now would be emotionally charged with the memory of the blood so wet in my mind.

The familiarity and comfort of home whisper to me. I know time is very short. Who knows how long the Warbearers leave their victims before killing them, or what determines the order they choose for it. Raimy; poor Raimy, has been here so long.

As terrible as it is, the thought gives me hope that I have time to figure out how to get Ashden out of there.

Still, the clock has begun its countdown.

More than anything, I wish I could run home into my mother's arms right now. She would hold me in her comforting embrace, knowing exactly what to do, knowing how to navigate it. She always lived life with a type of assurance that I wished I possessed. Would she be afraid in the face of death? Because as much as I wish it were otherwise true, I've never been more terrified in my life.

CHAPTER 36

May the Author keep you when life gets so dark that you cannot see.

I arrived back in Ra'goramal just as the first light of dawn was streaking across the sky; having flown through the night back from wherever Boreal had taken me.

She now rests deep in the grasslands above the village. We found a valley nestled between the foothills for her to stay in, undetected.

I had waited until I knew the village would be well into the day's work, then quietly trekked my way through the swaying grasses and cattle, pausing at the bluff before slipping into my cottage—unnoticed.

I want to go into town for someone, anyone, I can talk to. Something to tether me to my old life, to the only thing that's ever been constant as everything else seems to be crumbling down around me. The silence as I wait for the day's work to be done rings like the blows from my forge-heated mallet, driving me further into madness.

It's a fool's wish, though. I'm a traitor and fugitive now. I can only hope I'll be able to sneak to Avice's cottage when she's finished working.

My stomach churns endlessly at the thought of telling her about Ashden. The Culled are given a day for goodbyes… she already knows where he is. I'm doing my best to blot out why he's there—for now, at least. I can't allow myself to unravel.

Sighing, I rest my head on my arm, looking out our window. The sun is tracing its evening path, almost sunken fully behind the bastardized isle. Brilliant pink and orange streak across the sky, signaling the near time for Goramalan workers to head home for the day.

The surf claps against the rocky surface of the beach. Several people are there, enjoying the dying rays of the sun. The weariness in which they carry themselves is the same as always… yet so drastically different from the ease at which the Verenathians live that I feel like I'm in two separate worlds.

Something though… something is different. A shift. Something lining the usual weariness. A tense look over a shoulder; a too-tight smile; arms crossed in a huddled conversation. Different from the usual tension; this feels more like an undercurrent of fear or… panic?

What is going on?

Dragging my attention away from the window, I survey our cottage for the hundredth time since returning, trying to settle myself within its familiar walls. It's just the same as when I left; the half-filled pitcher on the cabinet, the boots by the door, the trunks at the foot of our beds. It's me who has fundamentally changed. No longer do I view it through the eyes of a naive girl, only seeing the lovely things in a world that is broken beyond belief.

My bed is still rumpled, as if Ashden hadn't been able to bring himself to touch it after I left.

After I left. I squeeze my eyes shut against the tide of regret that threatens to drown me. Rubbing my temples, I begin pilfering through the cabinet, searching for something to eat. Feeling around the jars, my hand lands on something made of glass. Not quite a jar, not exactly a pitcher…

Pulling it out, I cock my head in confusion at the half empty bottle of liquor. My parents never drank. I've never drank; not regularly, at least. Ashden has never tasted a drop as far as I know. Why was this hidden?

Scanning the room again, I look for anything amiss.

I open Ashden's chest at the foot of his bed. An empty liquor bottle stares back at me, next to a silver flask. My eyes water as I reach for the flask. A swallow's-worth of liquid murmurs inside when I shake it.

No, something isn't right. This can't be Ashden's.

Just then, the front door clicks—creaking on its hinges as it swings open. I shoot to my feet, a cry on my lips as Avice appears, her arms laden with books. The second our eyes lock, she drops all of the books and shrieks, falling to her knees.

I hurry to her side, snicking the door shut behind her as I crouch to the ground. Her hands are clasped over her mouth as she gasps and sobs, her tears flowing over white-knuckled fingers.

A bolt of alarm lights into me.

"Avice?" I whisper, grabbing her arms.

Her face is so, so pale; her eyes wide and disbelieving.

"You," she gasps. "You—y-you're supposed to be… dead."

I pull her shaking form into a hug. "I know I am—"

"No," she pulls back, scanning me through tear-filled eyes. "You're really supposed to be dead." She swipes a hand across her face. "Verenathia—they-they sent a letter. You were dead," she sobs again.

Ashden acted as if he'd seen a ghost. I shake my head in confusion. "I don't understand, Avice."

She takes a few calming breaths, scrubbing her face with her hands. After a few moments, she sits back, rocking on her heels. "The Verenathian Court sent word," she hiccups. "A reminder. They said they found one of us, and that the traitor was executed."

She grabs my shoulders, shaking me. "*You were executed.*"

I blink, and then it dawns on me. They sent word when Kieran told them they could have me as soon as he was finished with me. In their eyes, the whole time, I was as good as dead—living on borrowed time.

I push past the raw ache in my chest and loose a breath. "Well," I say slowly. "I'm here."

She's still wearing her cream colored uniform, her hair in a tight topknot. Guilt tightens my stomach at the sight of the dark circles under her eyes.

Blinking a few times, she runs her hands across her face, her head, fraying her smooth hair.

"How are you here? I don't understand." And then, her face void of anything other than stricken disbelief, she whispers, "You were dead, Rae. Dead. Do you understand that?"

"I promise it gets even crazier than that," I mumble.

"Tell me," she breathes.

***

I tell her everything. The beauty and grandeur of the land; the magic it possesses; the dragons; all of the wonderful things. I tell her of the lovely little creatures and plants alive with their own magic; of floating stone islands and shattered rainbows. The memories of Kieran feel like they're splitting me in two—so raw and tainted from his betrayal, but I tell her those too.

And I tell her of the death and the blood and the wrongness of it all. The lies, the oppression. I leave out the part about Goramalans and Verenathians alike being capable of magic. It feels like too much, too fast. Too heavy, when I'm still trying to process all that it entails.

When I finish, she just stares at me. Trying to wrap her mind around everything I just shared. Still reeling from the shock of seeing that I'm alive.

I can't bring myself to look at her directly. I want nothing more than to fall to my knees and beg for forgiveness. To wrap my arms around her and tell her that everything is going to be alright, but the memory of Ashden being led through the Citadel—of him trapped under that shield—slams into me, bringing the scent of blood with it.

At this point, I think I could spend the rest of my life apologizing and it would never be enough.

"So you're saying," she finally breathes. "That everything we know is a lie? And Ashden?" The words stick in her throat.

I nod, unable to speak it out loud.

Her voice, so soft it's barely a whisper—"They're going to kill him."

There's such finality in that statement. Before, the laws were untested—no one had dared break them. The thought of treason, of execution—nothing more than legend; an exaggeration of an abstract concept.

But now, having seen the truth in all of its hideous glory, her words settle over me like a promise.

Ashden is going to die. They're going to kill him. That's what they do, what they've done since the war. 400 years, and we didn't know. How could we? Everything we've been taught, every story we've ever been told is a lie. Layer upon layer of mistruths and falsehoods. Lying by omission and outright deception.

We're just as capable of the magic the Verenathians perform and are able to produce our own Safeguards. We've been living under their thumb—oppressed, beaten down, bowed with labor when we are just as powerful. Why do we even need Safeguards? There are no obvious threats around us, and even if there were—if we were taught the same magic, we could take care of ourselves.

Kieran tried to tell me. In his own ways, without outright admittance, he tried.

They've fabricated the threat to keep us trapped. *They* need us. We do not need them.

Rage lights through me. Hot, burning fury at what they've done to us; what they are currently doing to my brother. Kieran tried to tell me. In his own ways, without outright admittance, he tried.

"No they're not." My voice is thick with rage. "I'm not going to let them kill him."

"But what can you do, Rae?" Avice looks completely lost, helpless.

"I don't know," I admit. "But I'm not going to sit around while he's dying."

Her lip trembles slightly. "Please don't leave again. Don't leave me. I already believed I lost you. I—I can't do that again. Not both of you. Please."

I wring my fingers in my lap, trying to diffuse the raging torrent inside me. "But how can I do nothing when I know there are people, our people—my *brother*—dying? And what happens if I live the rest of my life having done nothing at all? I'll have spent all of it tortured by guilt, and then the secret dies with me—with us. What do you expect me to do, Avice?"

"I don't know," she says quietly.

"He would do the same for me. And for you. You know he would. What kind of person would I be if I just"—my voice falters—"left him there. How could you expect me to do that?"

"I don't," she snaps. "But I don't want to lose both of you. After learning what you know now, going back up there is a death promise."

It is, I know she's right.

"Avice, I would rather die for my brother than live the rest of my life without him. I've already lost both of my parents…" I let out a shaky breath. "I can't go through something like that again. He's all I have left."

She looks me straight in the eye. Anger blossoms across her face in a pink spread; her usual quiet, gentle demeanor gone in an instant.

"So what happens if you die, and Ashden lives? Do you put him through the agony of that again? Does he live out what will be left of his life under the Warbearers with the knowledge that you're no longer here?"

I draw back; she may as well have slapped me.

"What happens if you both die? The Verenathians might make an example out of you, and I'll have to live the rest of *my* life without either one of you. Maybe they'll make everything harder for the rest of us to tamp down any type of would-be rebellion." She heaves a shaky breath, her eyes glinting with determination. "It would all be for nothing. Nothing, Rae."

And then I see the anger for what it is.

Pure, unadulterated fear.

"Avice," I say.

"What."

"I'm scared too."

Her furrowed brow and tight lipped expression soften. She closes her eyes, inhaling deeply before letting it out through her mouth.

"I know I'll be killed for even setting foot on Verenathia again. They could send a patrol after me and have me brought back to be put under there—I know that. I'm so scared Ashden will die before I figure out a way to get him out, because you're right, I am nobody and nothing. I was just stupid enough to go somewhere I don't belong and learn things I really wish I hadn't. But now that I do know, I can't go back to the same life I had, and I'm definitely not gambling with my brother's life."

And it's true; I wish I had never gone to Verenathia—wish I'd had the presence of mind that night to calm down and talk myself out of it.

I yearn for the person I was before. The one who was easily distracted by sunsets and flowers and bees; who could gaze at the ocean for hours on end.

"Then take me with you."

I open my mouth, ready to shout 'no,' but I close it again, biting my lip. It's not my place to take that choice from her, though my heart screams at the thought of losing her, too. I can't, not when so much has been taken from me already.

I sigh. "Fine."

"Fine," she repeats, crossing her arms.

As much as I wish for her to stay in the relative safety of Ra'goramal, I can't tell her what to do after disregarding her own wishes for me to stay. That would be hypocritical at best, cruel at worst. Ashden is a brother to her too, after all.

"I'm not going to tell you how stupid of an idea it is."

She shrugs. "It's no different than every other bad idea you've dragged me into."

But it is. My despair cuts through me. *So much worse.*

"What are you doing here?" I ask, gesturing to the books scattered across the floor.

"Oh!" she scrambles to her knees and starts to gather them together. "I needed to be somewhere quiet, and with you both gone—" her voice cracks.

"It was easier to be here… easier to feel you guys." Her eyes lined with silver, she grabs the books and rises, setting them on the table.

"I'm sorry," I whisper.

She keeps her gaze trained on the texts in front of her. "What's done is done."

Chewing my bottom lip, I wince when I taste blood. "What are these?"

"I found a book hidden in Lichera's desk."

Everything pressing in on me pauses. "What do you mean? What kind of book?"

Her eyes glint mischievously, and I almost sob at the peaking through of her usual self. "I found it while I was cleaning up an ink spill. It was hidden in a secret compartment in his desk."

"You sneaky bastard," I breathe.

"That's not even the best part. It's some ancient history account, over 1,000 years old," she swallows. "Of Verenathia. Of the Warbearers and their magic."

I stare at her, gaping.

"It acts as if it's teaching how to use the magic they possess—"

"Acts?" I interrupt.

She nods. "Some of it is written in an ancient language so I… I can't read it. But from the few parts that I could, it references another book. Maybe if we can find the other, we can translate it enough to learn how to stop the Warbearers, or… incapacitate them, at least."

An ancient book that describes the history and source of the Warbearers' magic? What would the purpose of a book like that be for?

My breath stops. Sucked completely from my lungs.

The language of the world before the War. Kieran's words to me about the ancient book he had in his room. The book written in the Ancient Language. The one he couldn't translate.

No… Please, no.

"Rae?" Avice eyes me wearily.

"He knew," I murmur, more to myself than her. "He knew."

She winces. "This… Kieran?"

He knew and he kept it from me. He was trying to figure out its purpose.

Shaking my head in disbelief, I ask, "Do you still have it?"

Her gaze lingers on me for a moment longer, but she digs around the pile and pulls out an identical tome to the one Kieran had found.

"Where did it say their magic comes from?" I whisper, gently taking the tome from her.

Her eyes gleam. "It spoke of an ancient island. It's the source. And there's"—her forehead pinches—"there's a temple. Somewhere here; something to do with the magic. I don't know."

Something strikes me low and deep. Something I can't define or explain, but a hidden part of me hears, and knows.

Unlike Kieran's book, this one feels… wrong. As if something about it wasn't made for this world. Like a pulsing darkness. A sickness.

I feel something yawning open before me. Something boundless and ancient that I can't explain. A feeling, a sensation; a thought just out of reach.

Boreal.

Her insistence last night. Her unknown path. That… *something* she was looking toward just beyond sight. And Rose. Her belief in the Author's island. Liquid starlight.

"Avice."

She glances up from one of the books she was flipping through. "Hmm?"

"I need you to find every map you can get your hands on. The older, the better."

CHAPTER 37

There are things kept hidden, little bird. One day I'll be able to share them with you, but if not, never stop searching on your own.

It's dark as I walk. I can't see where I'm going, but my feet know the way. They take turn after turn on their own accord, as if following some predetermined path.

"Where am I going?" I voice into the silent darkness.

No response. Just the sound of my feet on the smooth stone.

Stone.

Realization hits me. I force myself toward the wall I know will be beside me, feeling as if I'm slogging through quicksand. I stretch my hands out, straining as I struggle to make contact. I press harder and harder, until there, my fingertips brush the cold, slick marble wall.

The corridor before me illuminates under a phantom moon, and I gasp, clamping a hand over my mouth to stifle my scream.

At the end of the corridor stands a single Warbearer–still as a statue as if he, too, were made of the stone surrounding us. His black hood is pulled so low that I can't see his eyes, but I can feel them. They're trained on my body, unrelenting.

I take a trembling step backward, my legs screaming to run. The Warbearer starts forward; slowly at first, but quickly gains momentum until he's at a flat-out sprint down the corridor.

I force my legs to run, to move, to do something, but they won't obey.

Straining, I stand there, helpless, as the Warbearer barrels down on me.

He nears, stretching out his arm to grasp my neck in cold, bony fingers. I try to scream, but the sound is cut off as he grips my throat, squeezing. His face is still veiled in shadow, hidden beneath his hood.

White glowing tendrils appear in my peripherals. I shift my eyes, sick with fear when I see the magic leaching from my own body, right into him.

I kick, clawing at his hands as the world starts to grow muffled, my lungs screaming for air. I reach out and rip the hood from his head.

Kieran's green eyes gleam in the moonlight as he squeezes harder, as cold and unrelenting as death.

I sit up with a jolt, gasping as I pull in breath after breath; deep and cool in my aching lungs. My body is slicked with sweat where I'm trembling under my blankets.

I look around the room. *My* room; *my* cottage. Avice is sleeping soundly in Ashden's bed next to me. Soft, milky-white light filters in through the window, propped open to let in the fresh night breeze. The sky is obsidian beyond, flecked with glittering stars.

I take measured breaths—in through the nose, out through the mouth. Closing my eyes, I will my heart to steady its frantic pace.

It was a dream. A dream.

A sob works its way up my throat but I swallow hard and lay back down.

A dream.

A dream.

I close my eyes, listening to Avice's even breathing. The gentle lap of the sea outside my window caresses my mind, lulling me back to sleep with each break over the shore.

***

I wait impatiently for Avice to finish work. She assured me she would leave as soon as possible and, hopefully, with the maps I requested.

Per her suggestion—more like lip-quivering demand, I don't leave the cottage.

Except to visit Boreal.

Unable to leave her alone, I snuck out at dawn and made it back to the cottage before the sun had broken over the Pulchram mountains bordering the grasslands.

She'll go back to Verenathia—to the Field of Stars—until I need her again. It's not safe for her here and I can't spend my time worrying about her. Not that I even have to worry. She's a dragon. She can incinerate anyone for simply looking at her wrong.

Everything Avice said has been running through my mind on a nonstop loop. A secret book speaking of an ancient magical land, instruction on the magic the Warbearers use, an ancient language—it all sounds like the stories our mothers would tell us at bedtime. And yet, I can't get the memory of Boreal's wayward journey, nor her understanding, out of my head.

Shortly after breakfast, boredom becomes my companion. I busy myself with magic practice, too anxious to sit still. I'm again awed by what we have the power to do,what we've never been shown we can do, although it's different here. Whereas the energy flows freely on Verenathia, it's stunted here; almost as if the streams of energy are frozen, unable to flow in the solid ice they're suspended in. Isolating each one is a task in and of itself, and moving it at all takes more energy than I possess at the moment.

I squint at one of the sluggish streams. Blinking a few times, I make out a dark, broken current flowing alongside it.

No. Not flowing. I cock my head, reaching out to feel it.

Cold. Empty. So heavy and overbearing and—

The Safeguards.

The dark currents are a sickness, an infection encroaching on the lovely magic. They're what's stifling it. What has been put in place to keep us safe. To protect us. What we so gratefully repay them for with our lives.

I groan, blinking away the sight of it all. Tired, so tired, I chew my lip and turn to the chest at the foot of my bed instead and rifle through my belongings, trying to find my sense of me.

I hold up a pair of worn leather pants, pockmarked with burn holes, and glance at my dragonhide-clad arm. I can't bring myself to take the shimmering suit off. It feels as if the foreign clothing is an outward indication of the change within myself over these past weeks—the comfort and ease of movement are just a bonus.

I find my mother's journal at the bottom of my chest where I last placed it after I couldn't bear to read any longer. I had found it so soon after she died, the wounds still too raw to flip through the memories she had so carefully recorded for me.

I peer into the chest at the brown, canvas-bound book. Simple, scrolling engravings cover the bottom corner, where my mother's name is inscribed.

Rosalynn Bryorfall.

A lump forms in my throat but I swallow, picking up her journal gently and run my fingers over the inscription.

Sitting with my back against the chest, clothes strewn about around me, I open it—not bothering to find a particular page.

My mother's delicate handwriting greets me as it fills both pages from top to bottom. I thumb through several more, admiring the neat strokes in their perfect lines. Her artist's touch shines so evidently in every single jot and tittle.

One of the passages catches my eye and I stop flipping.

"You scare me, precious daughter, and oh, how I do love you. I know you will do great and terrible things some day. You are adventurous and downright reckless, but the love you carry for life and beauty is that of no other. You inspire me daily to be more courageous. Your view of the world changes my own, and I don't think you will ever know how grateful I am for that. Do not bow to the confines of this world, but break them and shape them into something better. And never forget, my little bird with raven black hair, you will always fly."

"Oh, mama," I whisper, tears burning my eyes.

The door flies open and Avice bursts into the room, heavy laden with tomes, her eyes bright and cheeks flushed.

She pauses, shifting the stack of documents to peer over them.

"You okay?"

I smile at her uncharacteristically disheveled appearance; the wisping hairs that have sprung free from her tight updo.

"What?" she asks, still standing on the threshold.

"Nothing," I laugh, relishing the fact that I get to talk to my best friend again. "Yes, I'm fine. Now go set those down before you faint."

Tossing me a heavily unamused expression, she does so, setting the load down with a thunk. I rise, gently placing the journal in the bottom of my chest.

I will return to you. I promise.

Brushing one last loving finger against the canvas, I turn my attention to the clothes scattering the floor. Bundling them together, I toss them unceremoniously into the chest.

Avice snickers, and I find her standing against the table with her brow raised. "Find what you're looking for?"

"Oh, hush," I say as I brush past her to the spread of documents on the table.

She pivots, hovering over the materials. "I managed to find some of the oldest maps our library holds. I had to convince the librarian they were strictly for work-related use. Since most like this were destroyed, they don't let just anyone have them."

I cast her a sidelong glance.

She only shrugs. "I didn't know how else to get them."

I nod. "What are the rest?"

"Every book we have on Verenathia and the War—also the oldest I could find. They hold a lot of the original maps from some of the first cartographers."

"Perfect," I breathe.

Eyeing one of the more modern renditions of our world map, I grab the scroll and unroll it across the table,pushing the other books and documents aside.

I trace my finger along the western border of Brolithar where Ra'goramal and Thrunall sit. There, miles off the coast, lies Verenathia, and past that…

Confused, I squint at the map. Beyond the western edge of Verenathia lies… nothing. The Sea of Ashwaroth stretches on for thousands of miles, stopped only by the continent of Liathryn far to the north.

Dragons are the fastest mode of transportation we possess, but they're not that fast. We may have flown for hours under the stars, but not long enough to make it as far as Liathryn. I know there was something there, amongst the sea, so why isn't it on the map?

"What is it?" Avice asks, watching me carefully.

"Do you remember the name of the island in Lichera's book?"

She cocks an eyebrow at me. "Edrealle."

I nod and pick up another rendition of the map—this one much older. "Edrealle," I mutter distractedly, rolling out this one on top of the last.

The likelihood of Boreal's odd behavior pointing toward the mysterious island is low, laughably low. But still, any hope, even the smallest glint, is enough to keep me going. I don't know what I'll do, otherwise.

I find Verenathia and look in the general direction of the mystery island. Still, nothing. Grabbing the next map, I do the same, and with the same result.

I blow out an exasperated breath. Maybe I'm looking at it all wrong. Maybe what Boreal showed me isn't an ancient mystery, but rather something new—something undiscovered and unmapped.

But, no, that wouldn't make sense. Though extremely far and few between, I know ships have arrived here from Liathryn, bearing all manner of exotic spices and fruits. I can recall, faintly, being a small child and smelling the rich, earthy scent of something unfamiliar as it wafted through our cottage—rising gently from a simmering pot above the fire.

I close my eyes, rubbing my temples. Surely one of those ships would have discovered it throughout the millennia.

"When are you going to tell me what you're doing?" Avice asks from beside me, having taken a seat at the table.

I squint at the map again, as if that will make the island appear.

"After Kieran took me to the Inner Sanctum, I left with Boreal. I let her fly wherever she wanted, and she took me…" I let my words trail as I search for the location on the map. Finding the empty spot of ocean in the general direction, I place a pointed finger on it. "Here."

Avice's brow is furrowed as she looks from the map, to me, and back to the map again. "What did you see?"

"Well," I start, faltering. "Nothing, actually. But Boreal was acting as if something was there."

Her eyes are bright with excitement as she gazes at the stack of documents on the table. "And you really think it could be Edrealle?" she whispers.

"I think it's wishful thinking," I say quietly. "But I want to know for sure."

If it is Edrealle—if such an island exists, and is truthfully the one that our magic originates from; maybe there's a chance that the answers I'm looking for might reside there.

She reaches for one of the books on the table—an aged manuscript with a leather bound cover that has been patched in many places. I read the title as she pulls it near her: *Verenathia 800 p.w.*

"Eight hundred years before the war?" I ask, eyebrows raised.

"Yes," she says reverently. "Not quite as old as Lichera's, but it should have some original renditions of the maps."

She opens the book, flipping to the section we need. Stopping on a map that spans both pages, her eyes rove over it hungrily. I turn my attention back to the pile of parchment on the table as I decide which to study next. Very quickly, she gasps, staring wide-eyed at the map in front of her.

"Look," she breathes, her eyes sparkling. She slides the book along the table to me.

I scan the page quickly. This map is hand drawn in careful lines with neat, precise handwriting; rather than printed by the cartographers as the others are.

My stomach bottoms out. For there it is—right where I had guessed it should be. Northwest of Verenathia, standing alone in the midst of the Sea of

Ashwaroth, is a mass of land; barely more than a speck.

"Erytaria," I mutter under my breath, vaguely aware of Avice moving beside me. The unfamiliar name knots my brow in confusion.

"I think its name was changed," she breathes, pushing another, even older book my direction. I take it gently in my hands, careful not to put too much strain on its fraying binding and cracked parchment.

I gape at the tiny island—in the same spot as the previous map. Directly below it, in faded writing, rests its name.

Edrealle.

"What?" I breathe. "How?"

Not only is there a mystery island that exists—to this day—but it is the very land that all of the magic in our world originated from. Why would it be recorded here, but not in our current maps? They're copied from generation to generation, with newly discovered lands added and shifting borderlines accounted for. The only logical explanation is that it was intentionally removed.

Erased.

"Do you think anyone knows of it?" Avice asks quietly.

I contemplate the question. Rose only mentioned legends and stories, never any specifics. Never a name. The only information that would lead to its discovery is found in Lichera's book, which is kept tightly hidden. Does Lichera know? Is that why he wants no one else in possession of it?

The Culling—We've been lied to for hundreds of years; could there be some way these two things are connected? There's no reason to remove the existence of a known land from common knowledge. The only thing repeating itself in my mind is why.

Why?

"I—"

The door flies open. I shout, leaping upright, and my stomach coils in dread at the figure standing in the doorway.

Lichera sneers at us—two men I don't recognize at his heels. My blood turns to ice when I see their dragonhide uniforms and daggers sheathed in the belts around their waists.

"Well, well," Lichera's cold, snake-like voice hisses through the room. "It looks like we have a traitor on our hands."

CHAPTER 38

You and your brother came home today a wreck. Imagine my horror when you limp through the door with Ashden's shirt tied around your broken leg as he helps to support you. I know you will remember this well when you read these words. We took you to the healers and you are prescribed a full recovery, but you mustn't get ahead of yourself, little bird. Watch before you step. Listen before you speak. Pause before you act. If not for your sake, than for your mother's.

Words and thoughts leave me as Lichera eyes us, his voice dripping with venom.

"Imagine my surprise when I happen to see sweet little Avice barge into your cottage in such a hurry." He narrows his eyes. "When we all know, very well, that Mr. Bryorfall is no longer here."

His black uniform is as polished as ever, with every button, every fold—even the threads in the seams the embodiment of perfection. He curls his lip in distaste. "I found it odd that she needed to be here, in an empty residence, so I took it upon myself to make sure things were moving as they should."

I don't dare look at Avice, who has gone silent as death beside me.

He was watching her. Did he know I was still alive? That I was here? Known I would return?

One of the Verenathians shifts behind Lichera, and something about him strikes a chord of recognition within me. Something about that mousey brown hair and brazen demeanor—I peer at him from under my eyelashes and stifle a cry when I realize.

Barrett.

The memory of the blow to my ribs stings as I bring my gaze directly to his, staring defiantly. His eyes are glued to me; full of pure, cold hatred. A smile twitches on his lips when our eyes meet, and my stomach lurches.

Lichera strides confidently into the room, leaving the two men in the doorway—no doubt to block our exit should we try to make an escape. I don't have time to question why they would be under Lichera's command as he nears me. Leaning down until he's mere centimeters from my face, icy, cruel delight glimmers behind his spectacles.

"While it is such a delight to see you here, treason is an executable offense, dear Bryorfall." His rancid breath tickles my nose but I hold my chin up, forcing myself to meet his gaze.

Abruptly, he rises to his full height, leering over me. "Restrain her," he calls sharply. Dread wraps itself around my heart, my lungs, and squeezes tightly, suffocating me.

The two men instantly glide into motion, striding toward me. Barrett smiles as his calloused grasp meets my arms, and he jerks them behind me, no light or kindness in his hazel eyes. I wince at the bite of the thick leather strap as he tightens it around my wrists.

I freeze when the sharp, unmistakable edge of metal digs into the skin on my back.

"Move," he snarls, urging me forward.

Lichera glances down at the table with all of our maps spread across it. "What happens to be so interesting that you'd need our oldest maps, ladies?" He shuffles through the tomes, leafing through some of the books Avice brought.

I don't think I'm breathing. Avice isn't either, from the look of her.

Lifting one of the maps and setting it aside, he pauses, staring at one of the documents, his hand mere inches from the table.

"Oh, my dear Avice. What have you done?"

Unmitigated fear flows through me at his quiet. He's too calm, too cold. Not the coldness of hatred; the coldness of one who simply does not care. Complete indifference and apathy.

Dangerous.

His gaze is hard as ice as he snatches up his book, tucking it under his arm. Avice, pale and drawn, flinches when he stalks over to her.

"While I do hold a slight partiality to you, little Avice—it is quite nice having such a well-trained dog around the office—that little dog doesn't seem to be so obedient any more, does she?"

Avice presses her lips into a thin, tight line.

"Respond when I speak to you," Lichera snaps.

Her voice, soft and defiant: "There's only one animal in the office, and we both know it's not me."

He chuckles low in his throat before lashing out and striking Avice, open-palmed, across her face. A stinging red handprint appears in its wake. Avice clutches her cheek, her eyes smarting, but says nothing.

"Grab her, too," Lichera says nonchalantly. Within heartbeats, Avice is restrained in the same way, her cheek bright red and swelling.

I don't fight as we step out into the fading sunlight. I've seen the way the Veranathians train for this, have seen the way they're taught to use the weapons at their disposal. I know I don't stand a chance, so I cooperate, reserving my energy.

Ra'goramal rarely has any crime. If I recall correctly, I've only seen the brig used two, possibly three times in my life. I don't know if I'll be held and given trial, or if Lichera will take me straight to be executed. These are untested waters.

The thought sends a wild sort of panic coursing through me, and I fight the urge to surge forward as hard and as fast as I can.

As if reading my thoughts, Lichera snickers, though the sound holds no amusement. "You're both going to the brig for the night. My wife, I'm sure, has a lovely dinner made for me, and I can't be bothered with blood on my hands tonight."

I swallow hard, hatred sitting heavily in my gut. We pass by Raimy's bakery. The windows reveal a dim, empty interior. No scent of fresh baked goods. No fire burning in the oven. No steady kneading of bread.

"You'll be given a fair trial before the Synod, but treason has its consequences. Personally, I feel that it's an impertinent waste of time, but," he waves a dismissive hand. "Procedure and all."

Death. The consequence for treason is death.

"We'll figure out what to do with you later, little Avice."

I fight the fear, fight the panic, fight the overwhelming surge of terror that casts my brain into a haze. If I'm executed, there will be no one to save Ashden. He'll die a tragic death up there. Alone, with so much left unsaid between us. Avice would try—I know she would, but she's on the path to the same brutal end as I am.

No. I can't die. I won't die. I'll find some way out.

Surely there has to be a way out.

People milling about town pause, eyes wide as we pass. Children scatter, whispers are shared behind covered mouths, chasing me.

"Isn't that the Bryorfall girl?"

"She's alive."

"They must've got their information wrong."

"She's the reason they're up our asses."

"She's a deserter. Poor Markell."

"Traitorous bitch."

Traitor.

Everyone gives us a wide berth, no one daring to come near the traitor, as if my rebellion will rub off when I brush past them.

I should be angry at them. Should be angry for how quickly they've turned against one of their own, but they are not the enemy.

They're deceived. If anything, I feel a pang of sympathy. I want to shout the truth; I want to shake their shoulders and scream at them until they understand. Until the truth is so deeply ingrained that there is no room for lies.

The words are bubbling up inside of me, roiling, until nothing but the knowledge of my immediate death if I open my mouth keeps my teeth clenched.

I keep my head high as we pass by the Head Loadmaster's office, then the Storehouse, and eventually come to a stop at the Meeting House—empty now due to the workday being over.

Lichera stalks to the door, opening it in one smooth motion. It's unlocked, like all of the others in Ra'goramal.

I had never questioned it before. I had always felt a sense of comfort in the fact that, though we're under the continuous oppression of the Verenathians, we have enough to sustain ourselves, the threat of theft or violence is low.

That simple comfort is a crumbling facade in the face of what's been stripped from us.

Lichera moves into the dark building, snapping his fingers at his two cronies to follow. Barrett prods me in the back with his dagger, so close I can feel his hot breath on the back of my neck.

I've only been in here twice before: once, when I was assigned my duty, and the second, after my parents died. Ashden and I were required to come before the Synod as they signed over titles and property; putting it under both of our names.

I hated it then and I hate it now as we move through the dingy room, my eyes slowly adjusting to the dimly lit space, courtesy of the oil lamp now in Lichera's possession. There are no windows; only the stuffy, suffocating scent of wood and old men.

We're led through rows of wooden benches before passing the elevated platform at the back of the room. A long desk sits on it, with enough seating for the entirety of the Synod while they face the assembly.

Between the dim, windowless space and my racing heart, breathing starts to become immensely difficult. Lichera continues, striding briskly to a door at the back of the room.

Barrett's breath tickles my ear as he whispers. "What's wrong, Goramalan? Not used to consequences?" He chuckles low in his throat. The other follows suit and shoves Avice forward.

"Enough," Lichera barks from up ahead. He reaches the door and, with a bit of a heave, lifts up on the wooden board holding it shut. It takes him a good deal of straining before the latch breaks over and lifts. Grunting, he shoulders the door open. It creaks noisily on its hinges as if it hasn't been used for a long, long time.

Dust-filled cobwebs line the corners of the room, and I suppress a cough as our movement stirs up the motes now floating in the haze of the oil lamp.

I stare and stare at the grate that lines the back wall of the small room. A single iron door breaks its impenetrable surface.

Unlike the rest of Ra'goramal, this one is locked.

Lichera reaches into his coat pocket, producing a set of jangling keys that he uses to open the heavy door.

"Get them in there," he spits.

Barrett sneers, low enough that only I can hear, "A place fit for a pig."

He releases his grip on my wrists and kicks, sending me flying into the cell.

I stumble, slamming my shoulder into the wooden wall at the back. Cursing under my breath, I turn to face them just as Avice receives the same treatment. More graceful than me, she catches herself before blasting into the wall.

Lichera slams the door shut, panting slightly. The grating sound of metal on metal clangs through me while he locks the door, pocketing the key again when that damning bolt clicks into place. He turns toward the two standing near him.

"Go back now. Your work is finished here," he snarls.

With a uniform dip of their heads and a final sneer from Barrett, they make their way out of the tomb-like room. My heart stutters when they take the lamp with them. Lichera follows, turning one last time in the doorway.

"I'll have more questions for you ladies in the morning. Rest well—I've heard execution is tiring."

The wooden door shuts behind him, and my stomach sinks when I hear the board thud into place, sealing us in.

The darkness is so thick, so complete, that I can feel it around me—like I'm swimming through ink. It's suffocating, this pitch blackness, and I draw deep breaths to calm my heart as it continues on its death march. It does little, though, in the stagnant air.

The muffled sound of wood on wood reverberates from the meeting room when Lichera slams the final door. Now we're truly sealed in. Trapped. There's no one who can help us.

No one.

If there's one small comfort, it's that Lichera is arrogant enough to leave us unguarded. There are no sounds or movement coming from outside the door.

We have to find a way out. We have to. The alternative is not an option. Although, where would we go if we do manage to get out?

Maybe being delivered up to the Warbearers… maybe that wouldn't be a bad thing. Being trapped with Ashden as we die—albeit slowly—would at least mean neither were alone. He would know I tried.

The thought brings a small sense of relief to my rapidly despairing heart. If things weren't broken between Kieran and I, maybe he would have come to help.

But no… he wouldn't. It's just a pretty hope to hide the agonizing truth. The lies were so thick—almost as thick as this darkness. Everything I know about him could be false.

It's funny, these truths. They have the ability to enlighten and break and shape who you are. Maybe it's because of that; we almost always choose to live in their shadows.

He never cared about me. He couldn't have; you can't care about someone and do that to them. It doesn't matter what the reasoning was.

"I don't know how to pick a lock," Avice says flatly from where she rests on the floor.

"That makes two of us," I mutter.

CHAPTER 39

Ashden–your steady, calm nature entails that you do things by the book. It is one of the things I love most about you. But, don't forget that rules are made to be broken–just a little bit.

I run over all of the ways to get out of this damned room over and over in my head. There's no way to tell how long we've been in here, and the never ending darkness is starting to chip away at my sanity.

Several hours, at least. I know it's been that long. I've tried and failed, several times, to use the magic around us to bend the bars; to break them, melt them—but to no avail. The Safeguards are a stifling weight, making magic near impossible.

Can I pick the lock with no tools? Absolutely not. Can I squeeze through one of the gaps between the iron bars? Not a chance. Could I figure out a way to summon Boreal and have her blast this entire building to ash? Also no, although it's starting to sound like a viable option.

Avice and I don't bother talking. We both know there's nothing to be done, and unless one of us has a revolutionary idea, talking only wastes what little air there is.

I sigh, resting my head on the cool metal and close my eyes, savoring the chill of it against my stress-flushed skin.

Eyes open, eyes shut—there is no difference. The darkness is so thick and all-consuming that I force myself to take measured breaths, even as I feel the weight of such darkness pressing in on me.

A scuffling sound issues from the meeting room. I stiffen, straining my ears in the deafening silence.

Movement—somewhere in the assembly room, slow and deliberate.

"What was that?" Avice hisses.

I swallow. Lichera is gone for the night, and the two Verenathian brutes along with him. If any one of them decided to come back, they would have comfortably—and noisily—made their presence known. No, these movements are careful, intentional.

Until a shuffling thud issues from the room, followed by a muffled grunt of annoyance.

"I wish these walls weren't so thick," I breathe.

A faint light emerges from the small gap under the door, only detectable by it being the blackest of nights in this room.

My stomach churns with apprehension.

Why would someone be in here at this hour? Who would be here? The meeting house is used strictly during daytime hours.

A man's low voice floats through the room. The sound is familiar; something about its depth, its cadence. I strain, wishing my melodramatic heartbeat wasn't roaring in my ears.

The murmuring continues and I make out two distinct voices.

My blood freezes in my veins.

That deep voice; the voice I had known so well—had loved listening to—as he taught me; showed me things I never could have dreamed existed; who gave an ear to my heavy heart.

He's here. Kieran is here.

But how? Why?

The murmuring bounces back and forth. I strain to catch even a word but the wooden walls are too thick, the darkness between us too impenetrable.

Kieran's voice grows sharper and then finally, finally, that dim glow under the door brightens as someone nears. I can make out the shadow of the iron bars now; I can see my hands in front of my face. A tiny sigh escapes Avice.

The door swings carefully open. And there is Kieran, his beautiful face lined with tense sorrow. A moment later, Sebastian appears behind him. I feel as if I've been punched in the gut for how quickly the air is sucked out of my lungs.

Kieran eyes me warily. The warm glow of the lamp shifts with him as he scans the small room.

"Hi," Sebastian offers.

Relief, irritation, outright anger course through me as I stare at Sebastian, his warm umber skin gleaming in the lamplight. He lied to me just as often and as deeply as Kieran did.

"What are you doing here?" It comes out more of a biting demand rather than a question.

Sebastian winces. "I guess I deserve that."

"Yes, you do. What are you doing here?"

He opens his mouth but it's Kieran's voice I hear, and I don't miss the mild reprimand in his tone.

"Rae, it's not his fault."

Sebastians holds his hands up defensively. "It's true. This one," he jerks a thumb toward Kieran. "Threatened me within an inch of my life to keep quiet. Not that… not that I really wanted to say anything anyways. That's not exactly something to be proud of."

"You?" I ask incredulously, turning a glare on Kieran.

"It's one of those things," Sebastian offers. "You know what's happening, but it's easier to turn a blind eye to it than actually face it. It's easy to grow complacent when it doesn't affect you. Plus, the Warbearers are so secretive about it—it's not like they're parading magic-bound Goramalans through the Citadel on their way to be sacrificed. Out of sight, out of mind, you know?"

Everyone… everyone knew. The hatred, the disparaging words, it all makes so much sense. I can't tell if that's relieving or equally as infuriating.

Tucking his words away for a later conversation, I wave a hand. "Avice, this is Sebastian. Sebastian—Avice."

He sketches a bow. "Sebastian Alaman at your service."

A small smile tugs at her lips. "A pleasure."

"And Kieran," I add.

She nods briefly at him.

Kieran looks annoyed; uncomfortable, even.

I've made the confident, commanding son of a Warbearer uncomfortable. Good.

He moves to the door in front of me, eyeing the lock.

"Don't bother, Lichera has the key."

"I can open it," he says quietly.

"How?"

He doesn't respond, only turning to Sebastian before he says, "Let me see your knife."

Wordlessly, Sebastian hands it to him. I fight the urge to step back toward the wall, away from Kieran. He may be here now, attempting to pull me away from certain death, but I don't feel as if that instantaneously qualifies him for my forgiveness.

Inserting the knife into the keyhole, he begins meticulously working it up and down; back and forth. The metal lock clicks and ticks as he works his way through it.

"How did you learn how to do that?" Avice blurts.

Sebastian answers for him. "We're trained in lockpicking. In the event of another war, we need to be able to escape if we're ever imprisoned."

Avice casts me a sidelong glance; I only shrug in response.

A couple minutes pass. Avice shifts nervously on her feet, darting a look to the door every few seconds. I watch, in spite of myself, with growing apprehension as Kieran's face is pinched in concentration. My inner lip is bleeding from where I've gnawed it raw.

The lock shifts, metal on metal clicks, and it opens. We all breathe a collective sigh of relief as Kieran wipes the slight sheen of sweat from his brow and pulls on the large door. The ancient hinges grate with each fraction of movement—the sound seeming to ricochet through the too-quiet building.

I step through the now-open space and give Kieran a terse nod, feeling like an asshole. "Thank you."

He offers a curt dip of his chin. The uncomfortable tension lingers between us until I ask, "How did you know we were in here?"

Both Sebastian and Kieran shift, as if neither want to answer.

"The Court ordered two soldiers to Verenathia for 'peacekeeping.'" Kieran says. "I knew your presence was detected as you crossed the Safeguards and it was only a matter of time before Lichera found you."

"And if I was executed immediately?" I demand.

"I got here as soon as I could without drawing attention," Kieran grits out.

"Forgive me, I forgot attention was more important than my life." The words are bitter and acidic, but his admission cuts. Deeply.

"That's not what I said, Rae."

"You two can do this later," Sebastian interrupts. "We need to leave."

Avice's expression is laced with fear as she asks, "Where do we go?"

I can see the helplessness in her eyes. I've always loved her for her timidity; for the uncertainty that has sometimes led to quiet determination. But now, that restraint sears me with guilt.

"Boreal, Cinder, and Stoney are here," Kieran says quietly.

Boreal. I probe through my inner workings for her presence, and my throat tightens when I feel her nearness. An opalescent warmth meets me, calm and expectant. My thoughts must have been too loud to hear her arrival.

"Where do you expect us to go?" I ask.

Kieran's eyes meet mine, so bright and full of pleading. "I don't know," he admits. "But we can go to the grasslands for now, until we figure out what to do."

He's right. We need to go—need to get away from the very real threats plaguing us here. The grasslands are only a short trek away, and will likely be the first place searched in the morning. But it will buy us some time; at least for now, while we figure out our next steps.

I brush my hand along Avice's arm. "You can still plead innocent. You're not at threat for execution."

I know she can read my plea. *Please stay. Please don't put yourself in any more danger. I'm sorry.*

She gives me a shaky smile. "Accomplice is still just as bad. I don't really feel like facing trial in the morning."

I purse my lips. "You will never be able to go back." Not to Ra'goramal. Not to the life she has. Not to who she was before. If she follows us to Author-knows where, there is no going back.

"I know," she whispers.

A soft thud comes from the room outside of our door. The hair on my arms and the back of my neck prickles as ice sleuths through my veins.

Kieran slowly moves a finger to his lips, beckoning us to remain still. Footsteps sound on the wooden floorboards, slow and deliberate—as if their owner is sauntering down the beach on a comfortable stroll. I press my lips into a tight line, my blood roaring, certain of who possesses those arrogant steps.

They draw closer. It doesn't matter how quiet we are; if we run, if we don't. There's no escape.

Avice's eyes are wide, and I place a steadying hand on her trembling arm.

"I'm sorry," I mouth.

As if on cue, Lichera's voice booms through the deathly quiet.

CHAPTER 40

Fight for what is right, for what is true, my little bird.

Where do you think you're going?" Lichera's large frame fills the doorway. Even at this hour, he's still wearing his uniform. His narrow, hateful eyes sweep over us. "Did you really think I was foolish enough to believe you wouldn't try to escape?" He raises the watch on his wrist to eye level. "Ah— right on time, too."

Foolish enough to come alone. I glance to the empty room behind him. No light, no more footsteps. Only Lichera.

That cruel gaze travels up and down Avice's shuddering form. "Disappointed is an understatement, Breckenwater. I truly didn't wish to kill you," he sighs. "Yet here we are."

"And Trymera," he turns his attention to Kieran. "I do admit I was mildly intrigued when I felt your arrival. I would have hoped, under any circumstance, it would have been to keep young Bryorfall contained—but I can see that doesn't seem to be the case. And you've brought your friend; what a delight."

Breathing becomes a little more difficult. He felt Kieran's arrival?

"What do you want, Lichera?" Kieran's deep voice is low with warning.

Lichera rubs the bridge of his nose. "I want everyone to follow the rules and expectations that we have upheld for hundreds of years. It really throws a wrench in my routine when I have to oversee an execution."

I've never truly hated anyone. I've been angry, bitter, vengeful, yes—but have never genuinely hated someone the way I do this man before me. I clench my fists at my sides to keep from throwing one into his face.

"Wouldn't it have been so easy, Bryorfall? So easy to simply do as you're told, just like everyone else? So easy to not question." His sneer is something sick and twisted. "And maybe, just maybe if you had, your brother wouldn't be up in the clouds right now."

The ground shifts below me. He watches me—a wide, satisfied grin plastered across his face. I force myself to hold his gaze, force my breaths to steady even as icy silence fills my head.

My voice is low, lethal—a demand. "What do you mean."

"I mean," he answers, his tone a song of cruel, arrogant pleasure. "That maybe a suggestion was slipped to my dear friend Lucielle. That maybe your brother's selection for the Culling was more than mere coincidence in order to teach a lesson." His voice drops to a whisper. "Such a poetic turn of events, isn't it, young Bryorfall? But a waste, truly, if you'll be dead in the morning anyway."

The room is spinning, my blood roaring.

This is not my fault. It's not.

It can't be.

Faster than I can blink, Kieran reaches out and punches Lichera, connecting with his jaw. I press a hand to my mouth as the sound of flesh and bone collide. Avice gasps, and Lichera falls heavily to the ground, unconscious.

We freeze, staring at the unmoving heap at our feet. No one dares move. Several long moments pass before Kieran looks at Avice and I. His jaw is a hard-set line—urgency written in every feature. He turns a guarded gaze to me. "We need to leave. We can't be caught here."

As if he even needs to say the words. I try to go, but my feet are frozen to the floor, disobedient. My mind is reeling, and that coiling pit of anguish is squeezing tighter, tighter, tighter, until I can't breathe.

Kieran's voice cuts through my panic. "Rae, we need to go. Now." I snap my head up, finding Sebastian and Avice already on the other side of Lichera, heading out the doorway.

I don't have time to dwell on these things right now. I command my body to move, and force one foot in front of the other. One step at a time, I urge myself on, casting one last look at Lichera's unconscious form.

We make our way quickly through the assembly room, the feeble light of the lamp guiding our way. Sebastian sets it by the door as we arrive, snuffing it out.

"We'll go to the dragons," Kieran whispers. "Stick to the alleyways and shadows. No one speaks until we're there. Most should be sleeping but you don't want to draw the attention of anyone who isn't. And be quick; Lichera won't stay down for long."

There's no shortage of command in his tone. The command of someone who, though gentle in nature, has spent his life training for moments like these. That punch—quick, calculated, brutal—is proof.

I nod, not bothering to hide the distrust that I'm sure is written all over my face. The quiet pleading flashes in his eyes again, but I look away. There are no other options right now; I'll demand explanations later.

I can feel his sharp pang of disappointment as he turns to Avice for confirmation. She nods meekly, her face pale.

"Let's go."

Kieran opens the door slowly, carefully. The night is still, the moon high in the sky, bathing everything in soft white. He scans the area before darting out the door and slipping into shadow to the left of the Meeting House. Avice goes next, then myself—Sebastian taking up the rear. We creep along the perimeter of the Meeting House until we reach the slope leading to the grasslands. It's too steep to climb here, so we stay in the shadowed alley of the buildings that line the wharf.

Though I'm grateful for the sounds of the sea, I jump at every break of the waves along the shore. Each crunch of the cobbled path underfoot sends me scanning between buildings to the moonlit wharf.

Kieran's lithe, muscled form takes up the view in front of us. With head back, shoulders squared—an air of calm urgency radiating from him—he halts when the footpath leading up to the grasslands begins. Beyond the start of the footpath, the rows of cottages stretch, their thatch roofs and unlit windows dozing peacefully.

A soft sea breeze floats up from the beach as cows roam lazily beneath the star-flecked sky. The scene is so peaceful; serene, and again I have that strange feeling that this may be the last time I see it.

Maybe… maybe if I'm lucky enough to walk through these lands at the end of all of this, I will have again shifted into a different person entirely. Maybe the weight of what I've done and learned will have crushed me between now and then, twisting me into an unrecognizable husk. I can already feel myself fracturing when I allow myself to think too far.

Shaking the thoughts away, I scan ahead. I've been up and down this path more times than I could possibly count, but I've never considered how utterly exposed it was. Nothing lies between us and the grasslands ahead—or the town below.

Silently, Kieran beckons us onward. We step out of the shadows and into the moonlight.

My foot catches a rock on our trek up the footpath. I stumble forward, but Sebastian catches me before I fall flat on my face.

"Thanks," I mutter. He winces and offers me an apologetic smile.

Several long minutes pass in tense silence as we head, single file, up the footpath. The cows and sheep graze peacefully, raising their heads and blinking sleepy eyes when they catch wind of our whispering footsteps.

This is taking too long—we're too exposed. My body is aching to burst into a sprint, to find my dragon as quickly as possible to get out of the openness. Swaying grasses stretch far and wide, eventually meeting the Pulchram mountains.

Even if I tried, there's nowhere to hide.

Finally, finally, a rocky outcropping appears, peeking up from the ground through the grass. I can feel Boreal's nearness, like the warmth of a fire radiating deep into the cold.

I can't help it—I break into a run, stumbling past Avice and Kieran as I bolt toward that outcropping.

Safety. Her nearness—her presence—is a lifeline in this undulating unknown.

Arriving at the rocks that border the cleft, I look down, panting—right into the eyes of my dragon. She and Cinder are pressed firmly up against one another, wings tucked in tight to their sides. Stoney presses himself as far into the wall as possible, his body rigid, as if trying to escape the females. The sight would be laughable if I had any capacity for joy right now.

Our arrival snaps whatever tenuous leash restrained them to the cleft, and they simultaneously leap into the air, their wings pounding mightily as if to shake off their confinement. Puffs of dust begin to cloud around us, sending Sebastian into a sneezing fit. Having satisfactorily rid themselves of the cleft, they sink back down, the earth shuddering with the impact of their landing.

Cinder's attention is fixed on Kieran, who gives her a pat and strokes her snout. Boreal's chirp of indignation has me snapping my gaze to her while she eyes me, annoyed that she hasn't received any attention yet.

"Impatient," I coo, moving toward her and running my hand along her neck. She chortles softly, shuffling her snout all over my body, making sure I'm okay.

Avice coughs as the dust settles around us. Her face is white as the moon above, her body trembling slightly.

She's never been this close to a dragon before. Oops.

"They won't hurt you," I say softly, angling Boreal's head in her direction. My dragon narrows her eyes and stalks to Avice, nostrils flaring as she scents her.

Avice flinches at Boreal's nearness, but doesn't balk as Boreal leans in closer. She tentatively stretches out her hand. All it takes is one gentle sniff, and Boreal's nudging her snout into Avice's chest, almost knocking her off her feet. A breathy laugh escapes my friend, and I can't help but grin. Boreal chirps, then sneezes in Avice's face.

"Gross," Avice mutters, chuckling, as she wipes her face with her sleeve. Wipes the soft bruise that has appeared from Lichera's hand.

Kieran is eyeing us wearily from where he stands at Cinder's side, arms crossed. "We need to get out of here."

And just like that, the moment of levity is gone.

"Where do we go?" Avice asks, not quite meeting his eyes.

"I'm getting my brother," I say flatly, leaving no room for argument.

"No," Kieran says with equally as much command.

I whip my head to him, rage lighting through me. "What?"

His eyes burn. "They'll kill you."

"And why should you care?" I snap. A muscle in his jaw ticks.

"Rae," Avice says quietly. "He's right. If you go straight there, you'll die."

"What do you expect me to do?" I demand, unwilling to flinch away from the temper in Kieran's gaze. "I can't leave him there."

"No, but you can at least think through what's in front of you before rushing into something that's going to get you killed."

"Don't," my voice is soft, cold. "Condescend to me."

"I just want you to be safe," he says mildly.

"How interesting that my safety has to be at your convenience."

"Okaayyy!" Sebastian interjects. "Let's all take a breath.

"You," he points at me. "In through the nose, out through the mouth." He turns to Kieran. "And you. Same thing. Deep breaths." He watches us both for a moment. "Good? Good. Okay—let's think about this rationally.

"Kieran is right, Rae. They'll kill you the second you show your face." Glancing at Kieran, he adds, "But she can't leave her brother. You would tear the world apart to get Opal back, you can't fault her for doing the same."

"I don't," he clips.

The two men stare at each other in silent challenge—wordless thoughts and emotions flowing between them in the way that only a brother's bond will allow.

Kieran relents. "Like I said earlier, we need to go somewhere safe until we figure out what to do. None of us are welcome here."

"We could go to Edrealle," Avice offers, her voice barely a whisper.

"How do you know about Edrealle?" Kieran asks, too sharply to be conversational.

I raise an eyebrow at him. "How do you know?"

He meets my gaze evenly. "Do you remember that book you found in my room? The Covenant?"

My heart squeezes. "You told me you couldn't translate it."

"I couldn't, but—"

"But what, Kieran?"

"But some of the parts I could translate, Rae, documented the source of the world's magic as originating from Edrealle."

I chew the inner corner of my lip. Why had he gone looking for that information? Was it a coincidence that he happened across it, or is there another, deeper reason? So many questions, and I'm left with the sting of betrayal all over. Had I really known so little of this man in all the time we spent together? Had he really hidden that much from me?

"What is this book?" Avice asks, her eyes burning.

"I just told you—"

"No," she interrupts. "How did you find it? Was it mentioned in a class you took? Did your dragon tell you?"

He cocks his head at her. "I found it hidden deep within the library. What little I could read speaks of these things." His eyes dart all over her expression. "You found its counterpart," he breathes.

"Accidentally," Avice stammers. "There was much I couldn't read because it was written in an ancient language that—"

"That only its counterpart, along with books on the Ancient Language, can translate," he finishes for her.

"So what does this mean?" Sebastian asks, glancing nervously between the three of us. "Do we go to this island?"

"No," Kieran says simply. "We need both books and the manuscripts on the Ancient Language. Now."

"Why?" I demand.

"Did Avice not tell you what was in that book?"

Sebastian pipes up. "I don't know what's in either one of these books, so if someone would kindly enlighten me."

Kieran casts him a sidelong glance. "The book that we have on Verenathia is half of an ancient guide to the magic the Warbearers use. It was used from the beginning, even before the war, to teach the Warbearers. The one we have… it's full of information on how to create. How to build and grow. The way it references the other," he blows out a breath. "I've questioned if it's the second side to the same coin. Not to create, but how to destroy."

"Why don't they use it anymore?" Avice asks.

"I think they do."

"But why leave it here? Why not Verenathia?" she presses.

"That's what I've tried to figure out from the moment I found it. I assumed the other was here—I couldn't find any trace of it in the Citadel. If it contains what I suspect, it would make sense why it's been hidden."

To keep the knowledge of how to kill, how to destroy, hidden from magic wielders. Not the Warbearers, but the Verenathians. To keep any would-be power out of their hands.

My stomach churns. "Well we're going to have to figure out a different plan, because the book is gone."

"What do you mean, the book is gone?" Kieran says coolly.

I inhale sharply but Avice interjects, "Lichera took it when he threw us in the brig."

"Damnit," he runs a hand through his night-dark hair.

"Okay," Sebastian drawls. "Now all we have to do is figure out where he put it."

We all level equally deadpan looks on him. His eyes widen innocently. "Not an easy task. Noted."

"If I know Lichera…" Avice murmurs. "I think he would be foolish enough to take it back to his desk."

I snort. "Maybe not foolish, but arrogant enough."

She nods, as if trying to convince herself more so than us. "The Loadmaster's office."

"Are you sure?" Kieran asks.

I glare at him. "Have you paid attention to any of this conversation?"

"I mean," he snaps. "That we don't have time to spend the rest of the night searching for the book."

"Funny, I seemed to have forgotten my impending death. Thanks for reminding me." I give him a saccharine smile.

Avice eyes us warily. "It's the most likely spot. If it's not there, then we'll figure out another way."

"What do you plan to do if we can find the book?" I ask, unsure if I want to know the answer.

His eyes bore into me with the force of a raging tempest. "Believe what you want about me, but I've spent the past seven years trying to learn of a way to stop what the Warbearers are doing. If we can find that book, it might contain the information we need—or at least point us in the right direction."

I drop my gaze as we fall silent, weighing the implication of such words.

"Sebastian," Kieran says. "Go back to Verenathia and get the other half, along with the other manuscripts. Really old books on my desk, can't miss 'em. We'll stay here."

He salutes Kieran. "Yessir."

"Don't come back here. When you leave, head south down the coast. They'll scope out the grasslands first."

Sebastian inclines his head. "Don't die."

"I don't intend to," Kieran growls.

Sebastian turns to Avice and I, offering a wink. "Find that book, ladies. And don't mind him," he waves at Kieran. "He's in a bad mood."

With a running leap, Sebastian swings himself onto Stoney's back. The dragon pumps his powerful wings, and a few heartbeats later they're in the sky, fading into nothing against the clouds gathering over the stars.

CHAPTER 41

We went far down the shoreline today. I'm sure you could tell, but I missed your father dearly the whole time. Yet, that didn't diminish our time together, my little bird. Racing home to beat the approaching storm was thrilling, and the way you and your brother laughed made our saturated clothes worthwhile.

Arms crossed, I don't hide the distaste in my expression as I stare Kieran down.

"Why are you helping us?"

A muscle in his jaw feathers. "Why wouldn't I?"

"Why all of a sudden? You've known about this for how many years? Why care to do anything about it now?"

His throat bobs. "I've always cared, but I couldn't do anything about it."

"Bullshit."

Avice brushes a hand softly against my arm as Kieran's expression hardens, determination glinting in his jeweled gaze. "What did you expect me to do? One man against four who wield otherworldly power? Not to mention the politics—the war it would start."

My body starts trembling, but I force my voice to remain steady. "As if you don't wield that same power."

Avice whips her head toward me. Confusion—confusion and a single question burn in her eyes.

"I may have left that part out," I mutter.

"What part?" she demands.

"The Verenathians all possess magic—just like the Warbearers, though a little different." I avert my gaze, hating how small my voice sounds. "And so do we."

Her eyes widen. "And you didn't think that was worth sharing?"

"I'm sorry." The words are empty, futile.

Her lips form a tight line as she crosses her arms. Wordlessly, she shakes her head and wanders off, eyes raised to the night sky.

Always. I'm always the cause of pain to those I love. I don't know if there will ever be a day I don't hate myself for it.

Kieran watches me with a raised eyebrow, judgment written all over his face. As if he can see the hypocrisy practically oozing from me.

Gritting my teeth against the venom trying to work its way up my chest and into my words, I take a cleansing breath. "I felt you, Kieran. I don't know if it's something you've learned to do, or if it's just… you. But I felt your magic the first day you showed me how to use it."

He stiffens. "You felt a shield. I've taught myself how to shield myself so I can't be affected by others' magic."

"And the power I felt running beneath it?"

He shakes his head. "It's not enough, Rae. Not against them and what they possess."

My eyes fill with tears. "You didn't even try."

"You don't understand—"

My anger flares into something bitter and explosive. "I don't understand? *I don't understand*? I saw what they're doing up there. I saw the altar. I saw my brother—you know, the brother that is going to die if I don't do something about it? I saw Raimy, and the others, and… all of it.

"And now? All I can see in front of me is someone who knew. Someone who's known what's been happening since he was eighteen years old and hasn't lifted a finger to do anything about it. Your opinions and beliefs about it mean absolutely nothing if you're not willing to act on them."

Anger dances in his aura, reaching out a hand to my own.

"So maybe you're right, Kieran. I will never understand how someone can sit by and watch innocent people die. Watch an entire population be deceived and oppressed and sacrificed, and not even try, when he very well may have been the only soul who was ever given the chance."

He inhales, but I hold up a trembling hand. "No. We need to get the book."

I don't give him a chance to respond. I start down the trail toward the town, my heart aching. Uncaring if I'm spotted right now.

Let them come. Give me something to take this anguish out on.

Kieran's soft footsteps fall in line behind me. The raging torrent between us is palpable. The bond we shared, broken and festering, lingers in the air like stale smoke.

I don't know what to think, what to believe. It's all a jumble of thoughts and memories, hurt and anger… and regret. Always so much regret. And like a secondary heartbeat pounding the words into my core:

Traitor.

Hypocrite.

Liar.

Part of me knows if I would give Kieran a moment to explain, really explain, maybe I would understand. I know he's good. I can feel that he's good. There's not a touch of cruelty or malice in him—nothing like the darkness I've felt.

Right now though, it's easier to be angry with him then face the roiling voices in my heart. The wound is still too fresh, too new—still bleeding from his betrayal.

After a few moments, Avice quietly slips in beside me, her hurt carefully concealed beneath a blank expression. A brisk wind whips through the grasslands, chilling the night air as she sighs. "I think Lichera will have sent a search party out by now."

I exhale a pent up breath. "We just need to get in and out of the office without being seen."

She nods, not needing to say that if the book isn't where she expects it to be, we're all as good as dead.

We reach the end of the trail, the cobbled road of the town stretching out before us. No voices, no light. Keeping to the shadows, we duck behind the bakery and dip into the alley running along the back of the street.

Tucked between the bluff rising high to our right and the wall of buildings to our left, I start to breathe easier.

That is, until a murmuring begins floating toward us. Light from lanterns dances ahead, near the Meeting House.

Shit.

We pause in the alleyway. Kieran says, quiet as death, "They're going to assume we tried to get out of here as soon as possible and send patrols to the grasslands first. I doubt they'll search the town at all."

"Unless Lichera knows we're after that book," Avice whispers.

Kieran absentmindedly strokes the stubble along his jaw. "I think I can get in the office from back here. That way we don't have to go out into the street."

Following his line of thinking, I interject, "The Safeguards."

Something like guilt flashes across his face. "I can break through them."

Of course you can.

"I don't like how close they are," Avice says, looking in the direction of the Meeting House, her face pinched with worry.

"I thought they would have been sent off by now," Kieran muses. "Maybe Lichera took longer to wake up than I expected." He falls silent as a cacophony of voices rises quickly, reaching a fever pitch, then falls back to a hushed murmur.

"We stay right here until they're sent off," he whispers.

I nod, but Avice, *Avice* says, "Or we could get in now while we have their noise to disguise us. Maybe we could be in and out by the time they disperse."

Go now, when our sounds will be drowned out by the crowd, and risk being found if they decide to start searching. Or, wait until we're sure they're in the grasslands, leaving the office safe, but making our journey back risky at best.

"They'll see Boreal and Cinder if they get to the grasslands before us," I breathe.

Kieran considers. "I have a feeling they'll be able to stay well hidden. I like your thinking, Avice."

She nods. "We should hurry, then."

Kieran steps in front of us, leading the way on feline-quiet feet. The Loadmaster's office is four buildings down from where we are, and we're at its back in a couple tense minutes. We're close enough now to the crowd gathered outside of the Meeting House that I can pick out individual voices—Lichera, Arundraya, and Markell among them.

Kieran steps up to the damp wooden wall of the office, placing his palms on it.

Silence. Then heavy footsteps on the cobbled street.

"Hurry," I hiss.

The wall beneath Kieran's fingertips begins to shimmer, wavering in the moonlight.

I watch, breathlessly, as the wooden planks dissolve one by one, creating an ever growing hole in the wall. Avice's eyes are wide with disbelief.

I listen carefully for the sound of footsteps heading toward us, but so far, I think we're safe.

Soon the hole is just big enough to step through. Kieran stops, removing his hands and steps back, gesturing for us to go through.

Moving in front of Avice, I sidle through, not willing to chance her being the first one in if there's a threat on the other side. But when my feet land on the wooden floorboards of the office, the place is dark and quiet. Little moonlight seeps in through the small windows dotting the space, just enough to make out the desks lining the room.

Avice comes in next, blinking the darkness away. Kieran quickly follows, and the hole closes in behind him. I reach out to feel the wall, but my hand falls into the humid outside air.

An illusion.

"Where do you think it'll be?" He whispers.

Avice glances around the room, swallowing. "Follow me."

She leads us to Lichera's desk and crouches. Pushing his chair aside, she reaches into the desk and feels around the back of it.

"There's a little lever…" she murmurs, probing around almost blindly in this dark. "Ah."

A click sounds, and then the soft thud of wood. I squat beside her, peering at the hidden shelf that's dropped down from inside the desk.

The dragonhide-bound manuscript rests on the shelf, safe.

I breathe a sigh of relief, thanking the Author that Lichera is just as arrogant as we thought he was.

"…office first—we'll go down from there."

Voices sound outside the door to the office.

I freeze. Avice's eyes widen in terror. Kieran remains calm, but his hands move to the daggers at his hips. A lethal edge hardens his expression.

"I'll get it." A man's voice sounds from right outside the door.

We're all gathered around Lichera's desk—nowhere to go, nowhere to hide.

"Get behind a desk," Kieran hisses.

I don't argue, bolting behind a desk to the right. Avice remains at Lichera's, tucking herself into the space where his chair sits.

The door swings open, just as Kieran crouches behind another desk, his hands still resting on his daggers.

Light from a lantern sweeps the room. My heart beats furiously, my breaths coming in shaking pants. I pull myself in as tight as possible to the hollow in the desk.

Footsteps.

Shit.

Slowly, the footsteps roam through the room as their owner scans the office. They grow nearer, walking the perimeter.

My heart threatens to fly out of my chest as they grow nearer. I don't dare peek around the side of the desk to see who it is.

The light from the lantern grows brighter, brighter. Closing in on me and my little desk. The wall in front of me is cast into stark relief, bright enough that I can trace the grain of the wood. The desk feels like a coffin, holding my soul for all of eternity.

Closer, that light grows. The footsteps louder, until whoever it is is near enough that I can make out the swish of fabric as they move.

And then I'm being blinded by the lantern. I want to flee, but I'm frozen in place. A man's face appears, illuminated by the light.

Markell.

He looks tired, even more so than the last time I saw him. New lines have appeared on his forehead, beside his eyes, and the invisible weight that bowed him before looks like it's primed to press him into the ground.

His eyes widen, his gaze darting around the room before returning to me. We stare at each other for several too-tense moments.

"Please," I breathe.

"Everything clear, Arman?" A man's voice calls from the office's entrance. Markell glances at the door, back to me. The call of discovery, to apprehend, to sentence—it seems stuck in his throat.

"Please," my voice breaks.

Another glance to the door. Relief and anger and confusion and… pity war across his face.

"Arman?" That gruff voice demands.

He gives me a long, long look. Casting one more glance about the room, he swallows.

"All clear here," he calls, heading back to the doorway. I hear his voice a moment later. "Not a trace."

The men leave, slamming the door behind them. I can't stop trembling, my lip quivering too hard to form words.

Peeling myself out from the safety of the desk, I almost jump out of my skin when I find Kieran standing beside it.

"What are you doing?" I hiss.

His hand rests casually on his belt. "I assumed he was going to sound the alarm."

"Would you have really harmed him?" Avice asks, crawling out from under

Lichera's desk, the book held protectively against her chest.

"Yes. They wouldn't hesitate to harm us, so yes—if necessary," he says grimly.

For me. *Because* of me.

"Can we leave," I whisper. "Please."

Kieran's eyes soften. "We should. Sebastian is probably halfway to Verenathia now. Maybe we'll beat him."

I can't bring myself to smile at the halfhearted attempt to lighten the air, so instead, I brush past him to Avice. She's clutching the book tightly against her chest, her face pale.

"You okay?" I murmur as a soft, drumming roar begins outside the office.

"I'm fine. We need to get out of here like… yesterday."

I nod, moving toward the illusionary wall. I can't help but admire as Kieran steps straight through it, the bricks unwavering. Avice follows, and I take up the rear, stepping through it.

Straight into the driving rain. Lovely.

My braid is soon hanging heavy against my back while tendrils of hair stream down my face. But my body is warm, dry, and I find a newfound appreciation for the dragonhide.

We trudge through the alley, the water soon turning the dust coating the stone into a thin layer of mud.

Lightning flashes. Avice is thoroughly soaked and miserable looking, but there's no sign of movement ahead in the brief light.

We reach the footpath leading to the grasslands. Without the moon or a lamp, the route back is essentially black, wet, nothingness.

Kieran pauses at the edge of our safety, and I stumble into him.

"Sorry," I mutter, wiping the rain away from my eyes.

It's too dark. The sheets of rain are like a thick blanket distorting our view. We step out of the alleyway and begin making our way blindly back up the footpath.

After stumbling into Kieran for the third time, he says, "I can make a light but it will give us away to the patrols."

"Then don't," I snap.

"Your griping will likely give us away too," Avice grumbles.

I ignore them both, plodding onward—my boots starting to squelch uncomfortably with each step.

I've been up and down this path so many times that I can feel how close we are to the cleft. I can also feel, with no small amount of urgency, Boreal beckoning to me.

I'm waiting. Hurry. Her insistence tugs at our bond.

Lightning arcs overhead, illuminating the plain in a flash of daylight. There, ahead and to our left, is the cleft with the dragons. The lightning flashes again, but something else catches my eye before we're cast back into darkness.

A few tense moments, then another flash.

Avice cries out, pointing at the group barreling toward us. Their lanterns must have been put out by the rain, leaving them invisible. About halfway across the plain, I can only assume they've spotted us as they head this direction, fast.

"Kieran?"

"I saw them. Run like hell for the dragons."

I grab Avice's hand and pull her with me as I break into a sprint toward the dragons. Avice knows these paths as well as I do, and flies across the mud. If anything, Kieran should be at a disadvantage, but years of training keep him steady and light on his feet.

Hurry, hurry, Boreal calls.

I can't see my hand in front of my face or hear anything other than the rain and wind. Lightning splits the sky, revealing the group running; their having found us now not even a question.

Close, they're too close.

"Faster!" I shout above the noise of the storm.

Avice hits a patch bare of grass and almost loses her footing in the slick mud, but I haul her upright.

Night is illuminated once more.

The cleft is close.

But so are our predators. With each flash of lightning, they gain on us. My lungs are burning, my legs aching, but I frantically push forward.

If they take us back there, back to that room—I know that, this time, we won't get back out.

So close.

A soaked body slams into me, knocking the breath from my lungs as Avice's hand is ripped from mine. My assailant and I tumble into the mud, his body on top of mine. There's a wet thud as my head connects with the ground. The pain comes a moment later. Blinking against the crackling ache, I scramble to get my arms free, trying to shove him off of me. The mud and grass is as slick as ice beneath us, smearing in my suit, my hair. He grunts, fumbling for something while keeping me pinned by sheer body weight alone.

I pull my legs up and lock mine with his. He's caught off guard, distracted by whatever he's trying to get to. I twist, throwing all of my weight into the movement. He tilts, sliding off of me enough so that I slither out from under him, grasping for anything to help in the muck around us.

Another flash of lightning. Avice is on the ground but her attacker is much larger than mine. Kieran grapples with another man, the glint of steel in his palm reflecting the electricity in the sky.

I lunge for Avice, stumbling when my foot catches a root. My knees slam into the ground but I brace myself enough that I don't faceplant. I dig my fingers into the mud, grasping wet stalks of grass, trying to pull myself up as my legs slip.

Something drives into my back, pressing me into the sludge. My cheek is cold and gritty where it's forced into the sodden earth. My arms are wrenched painfully behind me and I feel the unmistakable bite of a rope around my wrists. I twist and thrash, nothing more than a writhing earthworm as my foot is still caught in a tangle of roots.

The ground reverberates underneath me. A warning.

Deeper than the thunder, the roar of the rain, it sounds as if the earth is awakening.

I pause my thrashing. No, that sound is coming from inside me.

Boreal is growling—a low, ominous tone that carries through the ground. The noise fills my head, drowning out the sounds of the storm, and I realize it's Cinder's growl too—intertwining with Boreal's that causes the ground to shake beneath us.

A torrent of flame erupts. I cringe from the heat from the blast, but the flames don't touch me. Or Avice. Or Kieran.

That stream of fire is directed toward the men attacking us. The weight at my back disappears, the scent of singed flesh and hair following its retreat. One of the men falls back, scrambling to push himself as far away as possible, his eyes wide with terror at the dragons now towering above us. The other two don't get so lucky, caught directly in the path of that deadly heat. In the glow, I can see the fourth man sprint back toward the safety of town, practically sliding down the path.

The flame recedes; the twin roars of fury with it. I swallow the bile rising in my throat and look away when the lightning breaks overhead again.

None of them were Markell, that much I know.

I scramble up the slope, kicking until my boot is free. Carefully pulling myself to my feet, I breathe a sigh of relief to find Avice and Kieran alive.

We don't waste any time, bolting to the dragons before anyone else arrives. Boreal sniffs me cautiously as I clamber up her side, checking for injury.

"I'm okay," I breathe. She chuffs indignantly as if she's not ready to believe it unless she's determined for herself.

Avice doesn't hesitate when I reach down to help her up.

"Are you okay?" I can't tell if there's any wounds on her.

"I'm fine," she grits out. I breathe a little easier. She may be a little banged up, and uncomfortable, and angry. But she's alright.

The rain increases from driving to a barrage. I shout above the roar when Avice settles behind me. "Do you still have the book?"

"Do you really think I'd be here right now if I didn't?" she shouts back. I smile grimly. More lightning tells me Kieran is ready atop Cinder.

I lean close over Boreal's head. "Let's get out of here, girl."

She launches in a single bounding leap, her wings beating powerfully against the storm. Avice grips my waist tightly, the book pressed between us as we pitch upward.

Higher and higher we go, pushing into the rain as it meets us in dagger-like drops. I tuck my head low into Boreal's neck, trying my best to protect my face from the cutting sheets.

Finally, she levels out, flying partner to the thunder and lightning. Hard and fast, she pushes up the coast—away from Ra'goramal.

And this time, I know I will never be able to return.

CHAPTER 42

Patience has never been your strong suite, little bird. Your early years were strained by that hot temper and readiness to be anywhere else but where you were. Learn to rest, learn to subdue the storm inside you. There will be a time and place for it.

Dawn breaks over the mountains, the sky beginning its climb to lavender. A dark line over the edge of the sea is the only sign of the storm we weathered, aside from the mud caking every inch of me. And the grass tangled in my hair. And Avice's muddy body behind me.

Cinder and Kieran fly evenly alongside us. Kieran's legs are coated in mud, his hair completely disheveled and matted, but… otherwise unharmed.

I can't deny the relief that floods me every time I look at him.

When the sun is beginning to reveal itself over the Pulchram mountains, Kieran urges Cinder into a descent. Boreal follows closely, making for the strip of beach below. Avice's grip on my waist tightens and my stomach rises to my throat as we drop.

The black rocks of Ra'goramal's beaches have given way to a coarse, light-colored sand that blurs as we race by in our descent. What looks to be an old fisherman's hut rests where the beach meets hinterlands.

Along with a green dragon and its rider.

In spite of everything, the sight of Sebastian and Stoney brings a smile to my lips.

The dragons kick up a spray of sand as they land, forcing Sebastian to duck behind Stoney's flank for protection. Stoney gives a displeased chuff and shakes the grains off in protest.

"Sorry," I croon.

My amusement is cut to the quick when I dismount. My bones groan, the dried mud caking my body having formed a shell that cracks when I try to move. Avice looks equally as miserable, wincing as she lands in the sand.

Kieran, damn him, lands gracefully, as if our night hasn't affected him at all.

We must be a sight to behold. Sebastian watches us with a mixture of shock and confusion. "What the hell happened?"

"Patrols," I grit, attempting to stretch out my calf.

"Oh… right."

I switch legs, groaning with the effort. "You better have that damn book."

"Whoa," he holds a hand up. "Of course I do." He pulls a pack from his back that I hadn't noticed. Reaching into it, he begins pulling food out of it. Food. And fresh uniforms.

I could kiss him.

"I figured you guys would probably want something clean. Didn't expect you to look like that," he gestures to Avice and I. "But these things get uncomfy when they dry, and when the deluge started…"

I throw my arms around him, stopping his rambling. "Thank you."

He wraps his own tightly around me. "Couldn't let my third favorite friend stay like this."

Rolling my eyes, I head toward the waves lapping gently at the beach. The water rushes against my ankles as I step into it, lukewarm and comforting. Heading deeper into the surf, it embraces my tired body.

With the sea lapping at my chest, I flip onto my back and float. My eyes flutter shut as the early morning sun warms my face.

Moments later, splashing breaks the tranquil water, and I crack an eye to find Avice wading toward me. Kieran and Sebastian sit side by side on the beach, talking as they gaze over the sea.

I offer a small smile as she dives forward, cutting easily through the water before resurfacing and floating onto her back. We lay like that for… I'm not sure how long. Until my fingers are wrinkled and the dirt from my hair and body is dissolving into the water.

The water is so lovely, but I force myself up and begin scrubbing. Running my fingers through my grimy hair, I pick little bits of grass out, wincing when my fingers snag in the tangles.

"I hope we find something that will help," Avice says quietly, moving to her feet. Her gaze is dark as she watches the sky. She hasn't bothered to scrub the dirt from her body yet; a soaked, muddy mess.

I begin untangling her braid, running my fingers through the encrusted strands. "You said so yourself that Lichera's book contains information on the Warbearer's magic. All we need is to learn how they do what they do, whatever they're doing. Or something to counteract it." Gently tipping her head back, I rub the dirt from her scalp, watching it bleed into the sea.

"What if it's not enough," she whispers.

My heart clenches. As if I haven't asked myself that same question countless times.

"Then we'll keep going until it is. Even if we have to go to the source itself."

Edrealle. That mysterious island Kieran's mother spoke of. The source of the Warbearer's magic. They're one and the same, I can feel it in my bones.

"And if they kill us before then?" Avice turns when I finish rinsing the muck from her head. Her eyes are haunted, dark circles shadowing the skin beneath them.

I swallow. "Then all of us will die. Ashden will die. But maybe it won't all be for nothing. We wouldn't have been able to change anything in our lives, but maybe our deaths would serve another purpose. People might start asking questions, might see that there's something wrong, that there's something more. Maybe we would be enough of an example to prompt questions. Questions that could lead to something, anything. The knowledge… it's what they're afraid of. They don't want us to know the truth."

The Warbearers. Knowing the whole truth means being unable to believe a lie. A deceived population is one easily controlled. They know that. They know that and they're afraid of us learning the truth.

You can't sell safety if someone doesn't know they're in danger.

Even if that safety is the very thing killing them.

And I do believe what I'm telling Avice, I do. But a dark, empty part of me whispers that it's all for naught. A fool's errand. Our lives to be forgotten in the tide of history, our people forced to spend the rest of theirs not knowing what they're capable of or what's being done to them.

"Maybe," she says listlessly.

"Hey," I splash water into her face. "Let's go get dry. Imagine if you're all muddy and nasty when we get Ashden."

She shakes her hair out like a dog as pink tints her cheeks. But she smiles, splashing me back. "And imagine what Kieran must think, seeing you all crusty."

I huff. "He's probably thinking he's made the biggest mistake of his life." The words are more bitter than I intended when they come out.

"I think he is," she muses quietly, watching the two men on the beach.

I don't allow myself to consider her implication, and instead drag my water-heavy body up the surf. Sebastian tosses us the uniforms as we reach them, pointing to the fisherman's hut up the beach. "Don't worry, I scared all the crabs away."

I avoid Kieran's gaze. "Thanks."

Side by side, Avice and I head toward the abandoned hut, listening to the gulls cry overhead.

The steps leading to the deck of the dilapidated hut creak under our weight. The wooden slats are weather-grayed and falling from the hut in some spots, providing for several gaps in the walls. Glancing at the sagging roof, I decide it's not going to cave in on us, and step into the dim interior. Sand dusts the slatted floor, coating the single bucket and fraying net that rest inside.

I undo the clasps at my back and peel the uniform off of my body. Avice does the same, shrugging her blouse off and tossing it to the ground. I wince at the ribs I can now count down her sides and the hollow plane of her stomach.

She catches my eye, her own softening. "I haven't been able to eat very much since you've been gone."

Her words suck the air from the hut. "I'm so sorry," I breathe, tears pooling in my eyes. "Truly. For what I've done to you and Ashden. I am so, so sorry."

"We've always known this day would come, Rae. All of us. Yourself included. Keeping you contained to a life that's mediocre at best is like chaining a dragon to a fishing pole. Something is going to break at some point, and we both know it's not going to be the dragon." There's no anger, no animosity in her expression. Just gentle truth, and a little amusement.

I laugh even as the tears spill over. "Way to make me feel better."

She shrugs, but offers a sly smile. Eyeing the gray dragon scale uniform in her grasp, she steps into it, sliding the slick material over her hips and torso. "Help me get this thing on."

I spin her around, buttoning the clasps up the back, forcing the memory of Kieran doing the same deep, deep down. Finishing, I slip into my own and turn for her to do the same for me.

The memories come anyway, ignoring my best defenses. The feeling of Kieran's fingers brushing against my back; the way his body curled over mine while we slept. Our darkness shared. An ear given to the other's anguish. Contentment and delight in each other's presence.

The memories come, and take my breath with them.

***

Kieran and Avice pour over the texts. Sebastian and I offer input when necessary, but I let the two who know these things better take the lead.

Kieran was right, the two books each act as a key to the other. The one from Verenathia is full of knowledge on how to create, how to heal and bind and nourish. The other makes my stomach turn. Magic on how to destroy, to rip apart and fray, to oppress and siphon and poison.

Good and evil.

Two sides to the same coin.

But why? Why do they exist? Where did they come from? And why, why was Lichera in possession of one?

So many questions, too many questions to keep track of. My head is spinning by the time the sun begins its decline over the horizon.

Avice taps a finger against her pursed lips.

"What is it?" I ask for the tenth time.

"A temple," Kieran answers for her.

"A temple?" Sebastian and I ask simultaneously.

"There's the island—Edrealle—and there's a temple. Well, more than one, but…" Avice muses vaguely.

"What, exactly, is this temple? And where is it?" I ask.

She turns wide eyes to me after scanning the pages a heartbeat longer. "Here. It's here on Ra'goramal."

I blink, her words floating around in my head with no meaning, no understanding.

"Impossible."

"There would be no way to know that without both books," Kieran adds. "Almost like both belong there, in said temple—together. One can't divulge the truth without the other."

"Or maybe it's to prevent the wrong people from finding this temple if the books are separated," Sebastian offers.

Avice nods emphatically.

"We're not sure what this word translates to, exactly," Kieran admits, pointing to a section of text. "But, roughly—life, creation, something to that effect."

"A temple of creation," I breathe.

He eyes me warily, nodding.

"Why here? When was it built and what was it built for?"

Shaking his head, he hands the book in his hands to Avice, picking up the other before scanning a few more pages. "I'd have to spend more time translating. There's only vague mention of both the temple and the island from what I've gathered."

"Wait," Sebastian interjects. "Doesn't the book tell us what the Warbearers are doing? Can't we just learn how to do that and use it against them?"

Both Avice and Kieran distractedly shake their heads no. Something heavy and cold settles in my stomach.

"We're missing something," Avice whispers. "All of the knowledge on the wicked magic the Warbearers are using is here… it's all here. But not how to use it. Only that it exists."

Helpless panic begins rising inside of me. "So what do we do?"

They look to each other. A confirming nod from both. "We need to go to the temple."

"You're telling me we have to go back?" Sebastian groans.

Kieran raises an eyebrow. "The books speak enough about it that it has to be important. What for, I'm not exactly sure. But if it can show us how—I"

"These books were supposed to show us how to get my brother," I cut him off, anger and panic giving bite to my words. "That's why we risked our necks to get them—they were supposed to contain the answers and we were supposed to be on our way back to Verenathia right now to save him."

"Rae," Avice's voice is soft.

"No." The tide inside me is rising higher, higher, doing its best to take me under. "What happens if we go to this temple and it doesn't give us what we need? What if this ends up being some wild chase that never leads us to the actual answer and Ashden dies up there?"

I'm unable to stop the trembling that's taken over my body.

"If this doesn't show us what we need, then we'll go back to Verenathia and I will personally see to it that Ashden gets out of there alive," Kieran's tone is gentle, but firm.

"Pretty words from someone who's sat by all these years and said so himself he's powerless against them."

I hate myself—absolutely, utterly despise myself when something like devastation flashes across Kieran's face.

"I–I didn't mean—"

"No," he rises to his feet, a muscle in his jaw flexing. "You're right. And I'm sorry." He turns, and begins down the beach on silent feet.

Sebastian pinches the bridge of his nose, rubbing. "If we're going to stand any chance of getting your brother back, you two are going to have to get your shit together."

Avice gives me a look as if to say he's right.

"Well I'm glad to see you two are getting along so well," I gesture in Kieran's direction, glaring at her.

She glares right back, unflinching. "People lie, Rae. People make mistakes. Author knows you and I have made our fair share. But there's always a reason. Always."

"Unless you're a Warbearer or Lichera," Sebastian adds.

I drop my gaze, staring at the grains of sand on my legs. Avice watches me closely.

"Talk to him."

CHAPTER 43

ASHDEN

My head feels heavy, muffled—like it's stuffed with cotton. The noises around me sound like they're being filtered through water. I try to move my arms, my legs, but they feel like lead.

What is going on?

I open my eyes, blinking against the grit and burning. The stone beneath me is like ice against my body, and a violent shiver wracks me.

Where am I?

It all comes back in a rush.

Lucielle. My name on his scroll. The magic-bound ride on the back of his dragon. My wordless trek through this place. This shield around me, doing… *something* to me.

Rae.

The thought is like a blow to my chest. She was desperate. I remember her pounding on this shield, screaming. I wish I could have heard her. I wish I could have spoken to her. I need to make things right with her. I have to make things right.

I drove her to this. Drove her here. I will fix it.

There are people all around me. They're all on the floor like I am, surrounded by these same shields. If we could just talk to each other, maybe we could figure a way out.

I try to move, but it seems to take more energy than I possess.

Why am I so tired?

This shield around me acts like it's attached to my body. White streams of something flow from it, from me? Connecting us.

Anger rises up within me. Anger at these people. At this mess I'm in. I told Rae they were cruel, not worth our time—and here we are.

But still, I love her. None of this is her fault. It's mine.

She has no family left; I can't leave her, too.

No. I will get out of here. I will find her and I will make things right. I have to.

It's too cold in here.

CHAPTER 44

You are more intelligent than you realize, Rae. I know you'll be able to find your way out of anything, and if you can't, there's a possibility that the challenge before you was meant to be.

The crunch of footsteps coming up the beach announces Kieran's return long after the sun has set and stars fleck the sky. Choosing a spot at Avice's side before the texts, he produces an orb of light—much like the one Sebastian created for Avice earlier—and avoids my gaze.

Maybe it cements my worthlessness, but I can't bring myself to talk to him. Not yet, anyways. And not even out of my own anger, but simply because there's too much to do, too much to plan for and figure out. My own emotions can wait.

The summer evening is thick and warm, the breeze blowing off of the sea easing some of my anxiety. My mind has been racing since Avice was able to translate the names of the manuscripts, and part of me wishes I didn't know them now.

The Covenant, and the Oathbreaker.

A promise, and a betrayal.

According to Avice, too, the Covenant is much, much older—the original design and purpose of the magic. The Oathbreaker's presence feels like a sickness, an infection rotting away at something beautiful.

And why a temple? Religion hasn't existed in our realm of the world for as long as our history books allow. References are made to collections of beliefs upheld by other territories and peoples, but we've never subscribed to any such thought process. Any mention made of the 'Author,' is simply a folktale, much like the story Kieran's mother shared with me; passed down from generation to generation. For these texts to speak of a temple—let alone as if this temple was their birthplace—is nothing short of baffling.

My entire being recoils at the thought of returning to Ra'goramal to search for it. The fact that we will because we're following the roughly translated words of ancient text makes me want to throw up.

Exhaling a long sigh, I stare up at the stars. Always steady, always unchanging. Sebastian leaves the books to the other two and drops down beside me. We lay in silence for awhile, the ocean ebbing and flowing quietly along the beach.

"Try looking at the magic," he whispers.

"I'm tired."

He gives me a sidelong glance. "Just do it."

Sighing again, I close my eyes. I envision the stars; the light and energy they produce. The sea—its constant lapping and crashing a steady force of energy. I feel my friends around me, and the pure light of the moon.

I open my eyes, and I can't even breathe at what I behold.

Energy from every single star in the sky streams in a glittering, iridescent band. Toward each other, toward the moon, flowing and swirling through the sky; cascading down to us.

Everywhere.

The moon is so white and so pure it hurts my eyes, but I can't look away. Dark bands of strength reach up from the sea, gravitating toward it as the moon's energy pulls the tide. The two forces flash in glittering bursts where they meet.

And nowhere is the rotting, dark tendrils of the Warbearers' power. No weight or oppression. Only freedom and breathtaking beauty. As it should be.

"Thank you," I whisper.

Sebastian only nudges my shoulder in response.

***

"Where do they say the temple is located?" I ask.

"It doesn't say…" Avice chews her lip.

"Of course it doesn't."

After hours of discussion, we've decided to wait here until we can return to Ra'goramal under the guise of darkness the following night.

Sebastian uncrosses his legs, stretching them out in the sand. "If I were a temple, where would I be?"

Flicking a shell into the foamy edge of the waves, I watch as it gets pulled back into the ocean. "Probably in the center of everything—up on a hill so everyone could see you for miles."

He concedes. "Beauty attracts admirers."

"Well I don't think 'beauty' is what we're looking for."

"The temple is old, at least a thousand years if these books are any indication," Kieran muses. "Which means it's lost to time. Most likely built over, since there's no sign of it anywhere."

"So we're looking for the *site* of an ancient temple?" I flick another pebble. It flies so far out into the water it vanishes from sight.

"Underground," Avice cocks her head. "I think we need to be thinking underground."

"Unless it's in the cliffs," Kieran adds.

Hopeless. This is utterly hopeless.

"Should we split up?" Sebastian suggests. "You know—divide and conquer and all that. Two take to the cliffs, the other two scour the town?"

I suck in a sharp breath. "And risk getting caught?"

"Going back to Ra'goramal is risk in and of itself," Kieran says mildly.

"I'm aware."

He looks away after a few heartbeats. "Sebastian, you and Avice go to the cliffs. Rae and I will search the town."

Bastard. I don't know if I can stand being alone with him right now.

"What do we do if either of us finds it?" Avice asks.

"The dragons," Kieran, Sebastian, and I say simultaneously.

Chapter 45

The day you were born gave me purpose. I had Ashden already, of course—but having a daughter, a human who will watch so closely for the rest of her life, gave me a reason to better myself. Ashden has your father to be an example, but you, my dear, you are the apple of my eye. The weight of expectation to impart to you the knowledge you will need to succeed, while keeping your spirit free, is a challenge I'm willing to accept. For you, my little bird.

Ra'goramal is silent when we land in the grasslands. No lights, no voices, no evidence of patrols, only the crash of waves against the shore. The gnawing anxiety in my stomach lets up a fraction at the silence. I know they haven't given up in their search, but maybe now they've lessened the intensity.

Avice clutches Sebastian tightly as they leave us in the grasslands, making their way for the cliffs at the town's edge.

I follow Kieran's lead, guiding Boreal down to the cleft where the dragons will again hide while we search. Both of them give a grunt of disapproval as we nudge them into the tight quarters, but dutifully tuck in their wings and fall silent.

"Where do you think we should start?" I whisper, shoving aside my own roiling emotions as we start the trek back to town.

The gnawing in my stomach grows when he doesn't answer immediately. I can't help but glance at the moon, already halfway through the night—signaling the fact that we don't have enough time.

"I think if I was part of your leadership," he says finally. "I'd try to assert my own power over whatever previously existed. If I knew it existed."

My heart sinks. "The Meeting House?"

The seat of the Synod.

He blows out a breath. "I think it's as good a place as any."

The thought of the Meeting House—that stolid, weathered building—placed over ruins in order to claim ownership and power seems… childish.

I toss my hands up in the air, a hysterical laugh working its way up my throat. "What do we have to lose?"

He glances sidelong at me with more than a touch of concern.

"Don't answer that," I mutter.

Everything. We have everything we've ever known or loved to lose.

A pinprick of blood springs to my finger where I've been picking at a loose piece of skin. Kieran's nearness is almost as disruptive to my sanity as the situation we're in. Part of me—a bigger part than I'm willing to admit—yearns to lean into his warmth, to wrap my arms around him and breathe in his scent. For things to be as simple and easy as they were.

As if sensing my thoughts, Kieran says, his voice barely more than a whisper, "I didn't want to lie to you. Each day it continued made me even more sick than the last."

"I know," the words lodge in my throat, unable to make it past the emotions stuck there. *I know I know I know.*

But do I? Do I really? Or would I rather believe that than face the truth of utter betrayal?

He inhales as if to continue, but I stop him, not yet ready to rip off the precariously placed bandage and bleed out all over again. "Let's find this temple… if it even exists. Everything else can wait."

Another thread of me dies when his eyes darken, revealing the deep grief I've seen peek through only a handful of times.

He nods. "Don't be afraid to use magic if necessary. Remember, they won't hesitate to kill you." His voice is hoarse.

"I can't. The Warbearers… the Safeguards. I can't get through them."

"That's what they want you to think." The whispered words hold a level of fervor that causes me to lean in, despite the weight between us. "That's what all of it is—all mind games. If they make you believe you can't do something, how are you supposed to show them any different?"

"I'm not following."

His emerald gaze bores into mine. "The magic they've overlaid through the Safeguards is real, yes. But they want you to *think* it's impenetrable, unbreakable."

"My people don't even know magic exists as it does. I doubt the Warbearers are concerned about what we think."

He shifts closer. "Something tells me they do. The Warbearers tell you they're protecting you by providing Safeguards. You believe it. They tell you that taking your people is an honor and a privilege. You believe it. They tell you that you're incapable of magic and—"

"Let me guess," I bite down on the lip trying to tug itself into a smile. "We believe it."

"Don't be a smartass."

I roll my eyes, grateful for the levity, however temporary. "So you're telling me, that as real as the stifling magic in the Safeguards is, I can break through it if I… *believe* I can?"

"It sounds stupid when you put it like that, but, essentially. They want you to believe you have no choice but to be complacent. Think of the Safeguards not as protection, but as a cage. A suggestion from them, a little 'field of protection,' and you're in the cage they've built for you. Some, when caged, do nothing but accept that it is now their lot in life. Others"—a suggestive glance—"will fight and scrape and claw their way out. So it's easier for everyone to not know. But that's what it is, Rae, and you can break it.

"They don't want you to know the power you possess; because if you—if all of you knew, you would no longer be their slaves."

I swallow, my mind buzzing at his admission of the conclusions I've already come to.

"If that's the truth," I say, finally. "Then why didn't you use that same power to do something before?" Before all of this. Before Ashden.

Before me.

The silence stretches long enough that I know he's not going to respond. I clench and release my fists at my sides, anger heating my blood.

"If you…"

A small white light flickers in and out of my peripherals, and what I was about to say freezes in my throat.

I squint in the direction the light came from.

"What is it?" Kieran follows my line of sight.

There, a little white light near the ground flickers—longer this time before disappearing again.

"That," I whisper, already moving toward the mysterious light. It winks in and out again.

"Rae," Kieran's voice is low with warning.

"What?" The light appears again, staying longer this time. Pure white and almost like a flame—it flickers.

Come.

Wisps of light, like tiny arms, reach out, as if beckoning me.

"Have you ever read of the Ignistulti?" I jump at the sound of Kieran's voice.

The little creature blinks out of sight, and I stifle a groan. "No. What is it?"

He eyes the space the little light occupied with undisguised suspicion. "Beings of light and fire. Clever, mischievous little things. Magical. Legends say they appear only to lead people to their doom."

It appears again, a step further away this time.

"That doesn't make sense. I've spent my entire life in these grasslands and I've never seen them before. Why now?"

"You mean why now that you've learned of the magic that flows through our world, can use it yourself, and are looking for a way to stop the most powerful people in our lands? You really want to ask why now?"

"Oh, hush." Those tiny, flickering arms are reaching toward me, pulling me in.

Follow me.

I take a step toward it but Kieran gently reaches out a hand, stopping me.

"Are you sure?" His expression is open, but wary.

The little creature blinks in and out. It appears again, further away than the last time, still beckoning, clearly leading… somewhere. Pure white. Bright. No darkness or wickedness that I can detect.

"Yes."

He lowers his hand, sighing. "Then let's go."

The Ignistulti continues to flicker in and out of view, leading us further away from town. I look over my shoulder at every whisper of grass, each shifting rock, but no patrols appear.

Each time I think I'm close enough to reach out and touch the Ignistulti, it disappears, and I swear I can feel it laughing at me.

Deeper and deeper we go into the grasslands, chasing the blinking creature one appearance at a time. The ground begins to grow rocky and uneven as we near the foothills that border the Pulchram mountains.

Yes. It's safe. Come.

The fiery little creature leads us into the foothills. It winks into view several feet in front of us, and I gape as another appears behind it.

And another.

And another.

A trail of Ignistulti blooms into view, leading directly toward a cave entrance between two boulders, so cleverly hidden I doubt anyone could find it unless they knew what they were looking for.

Each one of the creatures is a different color—a path of rainbow flame for us to follow.

Come.

I glance at Kieran. "Shall we?"

He snorts, beginning toward the cave entrance. "I would say ladies first, but I don't think it'd be proper sending you into the face of danger."

I roll my eyes. "Always a gentleman."

"Always," he winks.

The teasing rubs salt onto my gaping heart. If only things could have been this easy, this effortless forever.

One by one, the Ignistulti blink out of view as we approach, and, this time, they don't reappear. I can feel them dancing just beyond sight, as if I peered through the veil that separates us, I'd find them twirling and laughing.

We reach the mouth of the cave. Peering into its depthless face, I'm unable to see past where the light of the moon stops.

Kieran forms a glowing sphere, its light illuminating the walls of the cave, and hands it to me.

"Thanks."

He inclines his head and forms another. We stare into the cave together now, spheres of light in hand, and begin our descent.

Gravelly stone crumbles underfoot as our feet slide down the sloped ground. The light reveals nothing but gray stone all around us. No rivers, no animal remains, not even a cobweb. Nothing but this empty cave as it tunnels deeper. After a few minutes, I look back to find that the entrance is nothing but a dot in the distance, far above us.

My foot begins to slide on a loose patch of gravel, and I stumble back before catching myself. The momentum thrusts me forward, slamming my head into a low hanging jut of rock off the wall.

Shit. The impact jars me as a bolt of pain shoots through my head. Tears spring to my eyes, blurring my vision, and Kieran is at my side instantly, helping as I clumsily pull myself upright.

"You alright?" He scans me, landing on the spot I can now feel a trickle of blood run from. The sharp pain throbs, and I run my finger tenderly along the split on my forehead.

"I'm fine," I grit, wiping away the blood leaking toward my eye.

He watches me with such intense concern that I avert my gaze.

"Can I help you?"

I blow out a breath, my heart stumbling. "Fine."

He brings his hands to my forehead. Gently, he touches his fingertips to the wound, his eyes meeting mine for a second before focusing again. I swallow the tightness in my throat.

Warmth begins to spread across my skin, tingling, taking the sting away. Bit by bit, the swelling recedes as flesh knits back together.

A few moments later, he drops his hands, regret lurking in the air around him. I prod along my head gently, but feel nothing. No split, no knot.

"Thank you," I whisper.

His throat bobs, his voice hoarse. "Of course."

The cave seems to listen, expectant, finding us standing almost nose to nose. Silence stretches as the air crackles between us.

"We should keep going," he whispers.

I nod, unable to find the words.

***

On and on and on. The path levels out and continues onward.

"We have to be nearing the mountains now," I muse.

"If not already underneath them," Kieran adds.

I squint into the darkness beyond the light of our orbs. "Wait."

Breaking into a sprint, I tear down the path until I reach a solid wall of stone.

And a door.

Kieran reaches my side, panting.

Ancient and splintering, the door is hanging on hinges falling away from the crumbling stone. Kieran gives it a shove and it begins to shift and creak open, revealing an empty passageway.

Stone on all four sides, as if carved out of the underbelly of the mountain, the passageway extends deep into the earth. Cracked in some places, roots protruding through in others, a thin layer of dirt coats everything. There are no doors or rooms that I can make out, only this passageway.

"Do you really think this is it?" I ask a bit breathlessly.

Kieran gives me a look as bewildered as my own and begins down the passage.

"Shouldn't we—" I pause as faint noise floats to us along the dust motes.

Whirling, I peer down the opposite end of the passage, stretching my arm out to cast the light from the sphere further.

Nothing.

But there, again—voices.

My heart begins hammering as dread blooms in my core. If Lichera knows this place exists, he may have decided to extend a search party.

Would he be willing to risk uncovering this place just for the sake of law and vengeance?

The air around me grows tight, and I fight to steady my rapid breathing.

A faint glow appears far down the passage. With each second that passes, that glow grows stronger and nearer. Kieran moves to my side, angling himself toward it.

Do we run? Do we stand and face whatever is coming? Where would we run to, if we decide to go? We have no idea where we're at, or where this leads.

Stronger, stronger the light grows until finally, as if turning a corner, an orb appears.

And two faces behind it.

Avice and Sebastian halt, blinking at us.

"How did you…" I begin.

"Little fire creatures," Avice says, eyes bright. "They led us here from the cliffs. There was a tunnel that kept going on and on until it turned into this," she gestures around us. "We figured we'd probably find you sooner or later."

"The Ignistulti," Kieran says quietly.

"The what?" Sebastian's brows knit together.

I grin. "Ignistulti. They led us all here. They seem to be tied to the magic—the good magic," I add quickly.

"Ah, well, let's keep going," Sebastian says, scanning the passageway. His eyes dance with curiosity as he practically bounces on his feet.

We move, Kieran producing another orb, and continue further down the passageway. Deeper underground.

Cracks spider web across the stone in places, and, aside from the uneven floor, the passage is surprisingly well preserved. The air grows cooler the further we go, smelling like damp earth.

"Do you think there'd be any traps?" Avice asks, picking her way across a crumbled patch of earth and stone.

"Considering the nature of the magic," Kieran's steady gate doesn't falter. "And the use for the temple, it doesn't seem to be the kind of place they wanted to keep people out of."

Life-giving, beautiful magic, open and free for all to use and be taught. What has gone so wrong that it's been erased from history and our people enslaved?

"Who is *they*?" Sebastian asks.

"Whoever was before," I offer.

"Likely," Kieran murmurs.

Images, so faint they've almost been lost to time, begin appearing along the walls as we walk. Flowers, trees, the sun, the sea. Images of nature, and as they progress, depictions that almost resemble the beams of energy radiating from everything.

"Whoa," Avice breathes, trailing her finger across an image of the sun bringing forth life on barren ground. The colors are murky, faded with time and dirt, but it's easy to tell they were once vibrant pieces of art.

Illuminating the images with my orb, I follow the streams of magic on the wall and stop short when they reach an image of an island. A lone, small island, but very clearly bursting with life and foliage. The waters around it are calm, empty, looking once to be brightest blue. Bands of magic reach from the island, stretching out across the wall, touching each and every depiction of land—encompassing every image. Streaming and swirling and embracing, the magic ebbs and flows around it all.

Swallowing, I step back until my back presses against the cool stone of the opposite wall. When I behold the entirety of it, my breath catches in my throat.

This wall… it's a mural. A depiction of many lands and aspects of life; all of the elements—here. One by one, the others reach my side. Silent, reverent, taking in the sight before us.

"Incredible," Avice whispers.

We stand for several long moments, drinking in every line, every image; the story this mural seems to be telling.

And then the darkness beyond the orbs begins beckoning, tugging me toward it. Stepping over a fallen chunk of the ceiling, I make my way toward it, my heart pounding painfully against my chest. That feeling, that sensation is so like what drove me to Verenathia that my mouth goes dry.

Come. Yes, come. My legs are trembling as I pick my way across the stone.

You're so close. Almost home, it seems to whisper, tugging at those invisible tethers on my heart.

I pick up my pace, tripping over roots and crumbling sections of the floor.

Yes, yes.

But I pause, something at the foot of the mural catching my eye. Avice, nearly at my heels, almost stumbles into me as I stop completely, unable to take my eyes off of what lies on the floor.

Jars of paint and paintbrushes, dirty cloths and other, empty jars. A section of the mural has been wiped clean and meticulously repainted. Only a thin layer of dust and dirt covers the newly bright colors, unlike the thick layer of grime over the rest. As if someone was in the process of restoring the artwork.

I sink to my knees in front of the jars, knowing what I'm going to find before I can even see them clearly.

My mother's paintbrushes. I would know them anywhere and in any lifetime. As a child, I had seen them in her hands more times than I can count, almost as much a part of her as us.

The brushes are stuck to the jars—now stiff and flaking with dried paint. Prying gently, I pull one out of a jar of blue. Her initials, R.B., are engraved in the handles. An anniversary gift from my father, she had once told me.

With trembling hands, I reach up toward the mural, tracing my fingers along the careful strokes.

Beautiful, so beautiful.

The colors before me blur as longing and questions crest over me like a wave. How did she know about this place? Why had she never told us? And if she knew about this, did she—did my father—know about what's been done and taken from us?

A soft hand rests on my shoulder as a single tear falls into the chalky paint. "Look what she was doing," Avice whispers.

Dazed, I look up at her, but her eyes are on the newer paint. Rising to my feet, I stand beside Avice, taking in the whole of what my mother was in the process of restoring.

Great, green, grassy plains, backed by magnificent mountains. Cliffs rising high to its northern side, a little coastal village rests along a rocky beach. There are the Loading Platforms, dragons atop them. And there, across the sea and high in the sky, is the great floating isle.

The lands are fresh and vibrant, the sea still a half muddled mix of a work in progress.

"Why?" The noise is small and broken when it comes out of me.

Slipping an arm around my shoulders, she rests her head against mine. "I don't know, but I think we owe her to find out."

Yes, that presence seems to say. *Yes, come.*

Kieran and Sebastian are quiet, watching from near the opposite wall—giving me the space I need. Catching Kieran's eye, I find his lined with sorrow.

He offers me a small, tight-lipped smile. But instead of sadness, anger begins to well inside me. Hot and sharp, it builds into a raging torrent.

Why had she kept this from Ashden and I? What was she doing repainting it?

I will never be able to ask her, to learn why. And Ashden? Ashden is gone. If we can't get him out he'll never be able to see this, to ask these same questions.

I might not be able to see him again, but I will *never* see my parents again.

The grief cuts through my anger like a hot blade, igniting it, honing it into something deadly.

I won't let them kill him. Not after everything they've already taken from us. I will go to the ends of the earth to learn how to render their magic useless and get my brother back.

Come.

The paintbrush slips from my hands, dropping into the dusty jar with a clatter. Kieran and Sebastian begin making their way into the darkness, allowing a moment of solitude—the orbs in their hands lighting the way. Avice remains by my side as I take in every detail of my mother's work.

I don't know how long we stand like that, side by side.

"For her," I whisper, pulling myself away. Avice nods.

"For her."

A few minutes later, we reach Kieran and Sebastian where they're stopped at a wall with a shut door—large and wooden and solid, no cracks or decay belying its age. Both of them take turns trying to open it; straining against the latch that seals it. They pry at it, even going as far as to try and kick it in—but to no avail.

A very shut door.

So close. So close.

Avice tries, but with the same result. Whatever we're looking for, whatever the purpose for a temple like this, lies behind this door. I know it. I can feel it.

Placing my hands on the door, I can't help but gasp when I find it alive with magic. Warm, pulsing with energy, it fills me with joy and pain and love and loss. Crisp blue seas burst across my vision. Peaceful, swaying grasses. Babies laughing; crinkled eyes on a time-worn face. The sky after a storm.

I jerk my hands away, heart racing.

"What?" Kieran demands, looking for all the world as if he's about to slaughter someone. "What is it?"

"I don't—" I stammer. "I don't know."

But I do, I just don't know how to put it into words.

Tentatively, I reach for the latch again. That same magic surges through me when I make contact with it. I pull up, up, muscles straining, my body filling to the brim, and then—

A click. The latch releases.

I don't pull the door open. Instead, I turn to my friends. Kieran, wide eyed, watches me with something akin to awe. They all do.

"Do it," Avice whispers, seeing the question on my face.

Trembling, I reach again for the latch, and hesitate. What if the answer is not what we want it to be? What if it's only another clue? What if it will take more than we're willing to give?

"Rae." Kieran's voice is low, almost guttural. I turn to face him.

"I never did anything," he pauses, his throat bobbing. "Because I was afraid."

I close my eyes, allowing his words—his confession—to wash over me. And I understand, I do.

I really do.

So I turn toward the door for the final time. And for my mother and father, for my brother; for what Kieran has endured, and for what has been taken from my people, I will not be afraid.

CHAPTER 46

My love, how I miss you so. The children are content, believing you to be returning from your fishing trip soon. I know, one day, this will be easier.

With a heave, I shove the door open. Inhaling deeply to brace my quivering legs, I step through the doorway and go slack at what lies before me.

I'm standing on a balcony that overlooks a massive underground cavern several stories deep. A cavern carved into the center of a mountain, if the rough-hewn walls are any indication. From the floor far below, marble pillars stretch up and past the balcony, reaching all the way to the top of the mountain—the center of which is entirely open to the night sky. Moonlight filters in, bathing everything in soft white.

I'm shoved forward as my friends barrel in behind me. Stumbling toward the railing, I freeze when I see the bottom of the cavern. The floor is smooth, made of the same white marble that is so prevalent on Verenathia; browned with time and disuse. Stairways made of the same material descend from either side of the balcony, running along the length of the wall behind us before finishing their descent down the side walls.

The Verenathian marble, the scale of it, the fact that this is here—that it exists. I… I can't comprehend this. But it's the magic everywhere—magic that I can see without trying—that has me breathless. Currents of swirling, glittering light flow throughout the entire cavern.

Down below, at the head of the room, four different bands, brighter and thicker than the other delicate streams of magic, flow between stone conduits. A milky white one, one of various greens, a band of purest blue, and one that resembles a pillar of fire—its orange and red hues are so bold. The conduits themselves rest atop a dais—the magic reaching between them and another set that seems suspended high in the air.

"The elements," Kieran whispers, gaping.

A soft murmuring whispers through the cavern, and I quickly locate the stream that flows down from the stone behind the dais. It runs through a channel in the marble floor, disappearing below; beyond the vantage point of the balcony.

Kieran holds his orb of light over the edge of the balcony and crushes it into a million, glittering pieces before tossing them into the air before us.

Like liquid starlight, the shards of the orb dissolve into the air, igniting this underground world. The whole room illuminates, bright as day, as the energy from Kieran's orb transfers itself to every single particle of magic. Sparkling light flows everywhere, warm and twinkling.

Welcome home.

The energy this room holds—like stepping into the first ray of spring sun after a long winter—fills me entirely.

"Damn," is all Sebastian says.

Come.

Like an embrace, that sensation tugs on me, pulling me forward. Not daring to question if anyone else feels it too, I begin tentatively down the stairs.

Not a trace of the necrotizing darkness from the Warbearers touches down here. As if this magic—this energy—is too light and pure, forcing that darkness away.

Pausing on the landing, I follow the trail of the stream until it disappears into a cleft in the wall below the balcony. A large doorway fills that wall—what lies beyond hidden in darkness, leading deeper into the mountain.

Step after slow step, I continue downward, drawn to the magic at the head of the room. Those elemental streams pulse with life. Every thought leaves my head as I draw closer and closer. I need to be near it, to feel it, let it flow through me.

Breathe me in. Feel me.

It seems to want it just as much as I do.

I descend the last of the steps. The starry night sky hovers far above me, yet feels so close I could pluck a star right out of it.

Reaching the dais, the bands of raw energy seem to glow brighter. Air, earth, water, fire. All of the magic at its base. Undiluted. Untampered with. Pure. Good. Nothing about this feels wrong or dark or oppressive. As if the magic itself is simply a force, shaped to the will of the wielder.

I can't help it, I reach out into the stream of air.

Images and emotions and sensations. A newborn's first gasp, the final sigh at the end of a long life.

Weightlessness fills me, as light and free and endless as the wind. My skin tingles, the hairs on my arms and legs standing on end. If I jump, I'm sure I'd float away.

I snatch my hand away, gasping.

"Rae!" Avice shouts, at my side in an instant. "What is it?" Her eyes are wide.

"Magic," I breathe, already reaching for the next.

The smell of dirt and damp leaves fills me. Lush, green, living things. Warm earth and crisp tree bark and driftwood. Intoxicating color. Adrenaline. My blood sings with it. Flourishing and vibrant and so… alive.

I don't snatch my hand away this time, instead letting the sensation wash over me. Letting it fill me to overflowing.

And I reach for the next.

Dark and deep and cool. Deafening and murmuring and trickling. I'm weightless and sinking all at once. Drowning… borne along a wave. A warm bath drawn by a lover. Tears of sorrow. Of joy. It streams through my very veins until I'm fluid. Uninhibited and powerful and effortless.

Finally, I reach out and touch the last.

Roaring flame devours me whole. Heat and light and insatiable hunger. Anger. Passion. Unquenchable, untamable, it burns me alive from the inside out, leaving kindled embers in its wake.

Slowly, I remove my hand and hold it before me. The soft, pale skin is undamaged and gleaming.

Everything is suddenly crystal clear.

"This temple is for everyone," I whisper, not sure if my friends can even hear me. "For whoever wants it. Access to the magic—raw—magic. To… life. Freedom. So much power at our fingertips… and it's free."

This magic, these individual elements, the frequencies of life—it doesn't take. It gives. Unlike the dark, siphoning magic that the Warbearers possess, this magic flows through us all, through every living thing, connecting us in ways we don't fully understand. Giving us power and freedom.

This is a gift; from who or what I'm not sure, but so clearly a gift.

My body starts to tremble under the weight of this knowledge. The Warbearers… what they've done, what they've taken and stolen and corrupted, it's unbelievable.

We're forced to provide for them with no choice, no say. Our whole lives are spent toiling under the weight of their demands while they take and take and take. The very blood of my people pays for their dark magic. Or strengthens it, at least.

All the lies we've been fed, all of the truth that's been buried and destroyed… it's all too much. We've been stripped of our power without knowingly giving it up.

The Verenathians have access to power because their isle is rife with it. Would Ra'goramal be the same if it weren't for the Safeguards?

The answer settles in my stomach like a stone.

Kieran, Avice, and Sebastian are all standing beside me, silent as they come to the same realizations.

"Are Verenathians taught the full scope of magic?" I ask quietly.

"No," Sebastian and Kieran answer simultaneously, but it's Kieran who continues. "Mainly party tricks, like imbuing things with light. Smaller magics, but never the full scope."

"And you?" I glance at him even though I already know the answer.

"Everything I've learned, I've taught myself. They've kept the knowledge out of easy reach. There, if you search for it, but not easily obtainable."

The healing, the physical manipulations—both things the Warbearers want hidden from the Verenathians.

Two things hit me at once.

The Verenathians, though capable of manipulating magic, have also been deeply deceived. The Warbearers don't want anyone holding that much power—none other than themselves..

And, it takes a lifetime of knowledge and practice to reach the level they've attained.

A lifetime we don't have.

My parents… My parents, damn them, they knew. And Ashden—

Ashden. My breath starts coming quicker, matching my increasing heart rate. I try to fight back the overwhelming surge of panic.

Kieran was right. It's not enough.

Sebastian reaches into the bands of power and I slip away, trying to calm my breathing. Running my fingers through my hair, I move to the doorway under the balcony. A large room appears, along with a hallway leading ever further into the mountain. I squint, trying to adjust to the low light.

My stomach hollows.

Endless bookshelves. Rows and rows of them. Every single one of them empty. Nothing but dust and cobwebs.

My steps crunch on something amidst the dust of the marble floor. Something long and brittle. Stooping, I pick up the object, choking out a gasp when I realize what it is.

A human bone.

I scan the rest of the room, as dimly lit as it is, but it's enough.

Human remains scatter across the floor.

The empty shelves, the bones… I can only guess what took place here, and it has the Warbearers written all over it.

All of the knowledge held in this room, gone. They've removed all traces of it from Ra'goramal. Removed the language surrounding it and rewrote our histories to hide it

This magnificent place is suddenly too cramped, too stifling. I need fresh air. I need room to think, and to figure this out.

I'm drowning.

I leave my friends to their exploration and wordlessly head back up the stairs to the passageway.

CHAPTER 47

Ashden, the time we spent together while your father and sister were away has filled my soul in ways I did not know I needed. You are a treasure, and your presence is not something I will ever take for granted.

Stars flicker limitlessly above me.

After leaving the mouth of the cave, I scaled up one of the taller foothills, finding a comfortable ledge to think on.

My mind is a jumbled mess, my emotions are a tangled web, and my soul is continuing to fracture under the ever-growing weight of it all.

Footsteps scrape behind me. I turn, expecting to see Avice having found my hiding spot, but it's Kieran's emerald gaze that meets mine.

I can't even summon the energy for a snide comment.

"Mind if I join you?"

My gaze travels listlessly out over the rolling foothills as I gesture to the empty spot beside me. He settles down, close enough that our arms brush.

We're silent for long minutes, listening to the wind whisper through the grass.

"I don't know what to do," I admit.

A moment of silence. Blowing out a breath, he says, "All we can do is take the next step."

"Which is?"

He stares up at the starry sky. "We're going to get your brother."

"You said so, yourself," my voice is empty. "We're not powerful enough. Not against them. Not like this."

"I know, and I'm sorry."

Another beat of silence.

"When I learned the truth about the Warbearers; about my father"—he swallows—"I was afraid, Rae. For the first time in my life, I didn't know what to do, which direction to go, anything. I knew something like that couldn't be allowed to go on, but I…" a crease forms between his brows. "I began researching everything I could about the magic and I taught myself things that none of the rest of my people knew. But I was so lost."

In a different life, I would reach out to rest my hand on his and tell him I understand, but I remain quiet and still.

"I still am," he adds softly. "And maybe that makes me weak or pathetic—hell, it does. I just—"

And maybe it's the uncertainty of what's to come, or maybe it's that slight crack in his voice, that almost imperceptible slip of his strong exterior that forces me to swallow the hurt and bitterness and say, "Tell me everything. From the start."

A long, bone-tired sigh escapes him. "I haven't been able to eat. Hardly been able to sleep. I've only been able to keep enough water down to keep from dehydrating."

"Why?"

"Do you remember the first day we met, on the Loading Platforms?"

Of course I do. I could never, will never forget the way he looked at me. But the betrayal, the lies he wove—the pain cuts deep all over again.

"Yes."

His throat bobs. "When I first saw you, it—I… I can't explain it. There was nothing and no one else that mattered. It was like getting tunnel vision, but I was completely out of control, and you were the only thing I saw." He runs a hand through his hair, and I would laugh at how unkempt he looks right now if we weren't in this situation. "I don't know if it was your magic or what it was, but I just—I couldn't…"

I've never seen him at such a loss for words.

"You know me now, Rae. You know I'm not like that—the kind of person I portrayed. But I couldn't think straight, I didn't know who I was or who to be—all logic and reason left."

The cocky bastard. Not just because of me, but because of the boy that was abandoned. That strong, unwavering, arrogant exterior—the facade to hide his brokenness.

"I still couldn't think straight for the rest of the day. I delivered supplies to the wrong locations and screwed up the information on an order so bad that they gave me the rest of the day off. Told me to go home and get myself together.

"I told Sebastian that night I met this girl. 'This girl' was the only thing I could call you, the only thing I knew you by. You were all I could think about. I kept rambling and pacing like a lunatic until he eventually told me to shut up."

That night is so clear in my mind. The night my emotions were so conflicted and out of control. He was the catalyst that night—the catalyst for my undoing. I realize it now, and finally understand what Ashden meant; what he was trying to keep me from even if he couldn't express it properly.

"When I saw you in the commons, after Laurel had dragged you in there, in front of everyone. It took every ounce of self-control I possessed to keep myself from throttling her."

He shakes his head. "I couldn't believe it was you. Here I had only met you the day before, and there you were. It felt like the Author himself dropped you into my path and it was so selfish—probably the most selfish thing I'd ever done—but I had to find a way to keep you with me for as long as possible. I had to get to know who this strange girl was; I couldn't live with myself if I didn't. It's almost like," his voice falters. "It's almost like our magic collided. I couldn't let you go. That fast, you were a part of me. I would have gone insane if I tried."

I can't stop my hands from shaking. Closing my eyes, I draw my knees in close to my chest, taking even breaths.

He cuts me a glance, his eyebrow raised questioningly. Blinking, I nod for him to continue.

"So…" he sighs. "I told the Court and the Warbearers that they could have you. Because that's what they would have done immediately, if no one intervened. They would have taken you the moment Laurel brought you in or they found you. I'm not sure if it would have been on sight or if they would have taken you to the Inner Sanctum to be siphoned like the rest.

"I begged them to let you stay. I'm not proud of it, but I couldn't let them harm you. I couldn't handle a world with no more… you. Even though I then only knew your name, the thought of this clever, brave, beautiful woman at the hands of the Warbearers was too much to bear. None of them were aware I had discovered the truth of their wickedness, so they agreed to let you stay until I was… finished with you, and then I was to return you to them. My father was the one who ultimately swayed the decision. I still haven't been able to wrap my mind around why, but he did."

Unshed tears burn my eyes.

His deep voice waivers now. "I was never going to let them take you, Rae. Never. I was going to get you off of the isle before they realized you were missing—tell them you fell to your death or something so they wouldn't go looking for you on Ra'goramal or alert the Synod. I would have ended my own life before letting them have you."

I swallow against the tightness in my throat. "When you brought me before them, you did it knowing that it could have ended with my execution?"

"Your being on the isle was grounds enough for execution. Me bringing you before them was a gamble, yes, but I wanted it to be on my terms. If I hadn't been in the commons when Laurel brought you," his throat bobs again.

"Why didn't you just tell me?" My voice cracks. I'm struggling to wrap my mind around it; trying to understand.

"I wanted to—" his own voice breaks, his eyes lining with silver. "I wanted to," he repeats. "When I came out of the Court and saw you sitting there, I panicked. I felt so stupid for what I had done. I felt like you would think I was equally as stupid and laugh in my face before demanding to be taken home." A single tear rolls down his cheek. "I thought there was a chance you would want nothing to do with me, that you wouldn't want to speak to me again, and I wouldn't even blame you. I couldn't bring myself to tell you just then. It was selfish and immature and—

"After that, it had gone too far. I was still going to tell you, I was just looking for the right moment." His shoulders tremble. "I couldn't let you go."

He leans forward, burying his face in his hands. "I'm so sorry."

Seeing him like this—so broken, so vulnerable, I want to wrap myself around him. Someone who was only entering into adulthood when his whole life was shattered.

Losing my parents has broken me thoroughly, but what would I have done if they had abandoned Ashden and I for unimaginable darkness?

As I watch his shoulders shake with regret, I see him now for who and what he truly is.

Lost. Broken.

Yet unlike me, he hasn't let that brokenness turn him into a pit of rage and despair. He's trying to find his way, trying to hold onto the good in a world that is so, so dark.

Was what he did selfish? Yes. Impulsive? Absolutely. But who am I to cast judgment? How can I hold that against him? I've made more than my fair share of poor decisions.

That wounded part of me is still bleeding, but understanding is slowly beginning to staunch the flow.

I don't want to hold it against him. The bitterness and hurt is a poison. I want the gentleness and liveliness and ease that we had before. I want the camaraderie and listening ear. My partner in adventure and… I just want him, whatever and all that entails.

"Kieran." I rise and kneel beside him, peeling his fingers away from his face. Red-rimmed eyes meet mine, as vibrant and beautiful as ever.

"It's okay," I whisper.

It will take time to fully heal. But for him, for this; I want to try.

He pulls in a shuddering breath. "I have never regretted anything more in my entire life. The thought of anyone hurting you makes me sick, and that's all I've done."

"I know," I whisper again, kissing his fingers.

"As soon as you left, I knew I lost you. No one in their right mind, especially not someone like you, would accept what I had done."

"I was hurt, but I didn't want to leave. I… I just needed space. And time to think."

He pulls his hands away and scrubs at his face. "When we saw your brother… that was it. I decided right there that if I lost you, I would learn to accept it. I couldn't keep you from him, and I couldn't keep what was happening hidden any longer. If I had… that's too much, too far. There's no coming back from that. I would have jumped off the Edge."

"I know," I say quietly.

His nearness, his vulnerability, breaks something in me. Without thinking, I lean forward, drawn in by the magic sparking between us.

My lips find his; softly, tentatively. He tenses, but when I brush my lips against him again, he deepens the kiss, bringing his hands to gently cup my face.

Light and color and bright, beautiful things dance through me. His cheeks are wet, and I inhale his scent. Like salt air and fresh rain and something I didn't know I needed. I never want it to stop; never want it to end.

Reluctantly, he pulls himself away, searching my face.

"I'm still here," I whisper.

"So it appears," he murmurs, a corner of his mouth tugging upward.

I flick his cheek, grateful to see a small part of him peeking through. He grips my other hand and presses it to his lips.

I lean back as he shifts, leaving us sitting knee to knee on the ledge. The stars twinkle overhead as a warm breeze brushes the waist high grass.

"I'm so sorry," he breathes.

"I know." I cock my head. "I've never had a man so captivated by me before."

He rolls his eyes. "Don't let it go to your head."

"Too late," I smile sweetly.

Watching me intently, he ventures, "Would I be a fool to hope the feeling is reciprocated?"

I grasp his hands in mine, absently running my thumb over his skin. "Oh, don't flatter yourself."

"I'll take that as a yes."

My face warms and I avert my gaze to the stone beneath us. My heart feels as if it's a butterfly that might flutter away at any moment, alight on the warm glow flowing through my body.

I would have given anything to hear these words days ago—a lifetime ago—but now, everything has changed.

"I think there could be something beautiful between us," I say carefully, not missing the flash of worry that crosses his face. "But after all of this, I don't know if now is the right time."

And, oh, how I wish it was. I wish we had the freedom to talk, to work through things, repairing what needs to be repaired. To do it slowly, sweetly; taking all the time in the world to fully explore what's at our fingertips.

"Rae, I only need you; in whatever capacity you're willing to give. And if you're not willing right now, that's okay."

I get lost in the depth of his eyes, seeing the tempest that still rages, letting everything unspoken pass between us. "Thank you," my voice is raw.

"Don't thank me," he whispers.

I drop my gaze to our hands clasped over our knees. "What else is bothering you?"

Letting out a long sigh, he says, "My father."

I close my eyes against the ache in my chest.

"Pain for pain?"

A sad laugh escapes me. "Sure."

"I don't know the best way to explain it," he says. "I hate him—hate him more than I've ever hated anyone. How could he leave us? My mother? My *grieving* mother? And his children?" His voice drops to a whisper. "How can he kill so easily? I've tried, for years, to understand, and I still can't."

My hand finds his and I give it a gentle squeeze.

"But he's still my father," his voice cracks. "Nothing will ever change that fact or that bond, however broken it is now. He's my father," he repeats, more to himself than me.

"The things he's done—does—they're horrible. All of the Warbearers need to disappear, wiped off the face of the earth; not even worth a memory. And when I think of my hatred toward him, the pain he's caused my family, the thought of destroying them is… satisfying. But when I think of him as my father, as the man who taught me how to shave and sat by my bedside telling me stories, it gets… confusing."

"I can imagine," I whisper. I don't have the words to offer him. Nothing I say can fix what's been broken. Only he can figure out the best way to move forward, and it's a position I don't envy.

So I do what he's done for me so many times. I sit in silence, pressed against him, not letting go. Giving him the space and safety to process and share if he wants, or needs, to.

We sit like that for several long minutes, side by side, until he says, "Pain for pain."

I chew my lip, closing my eyes against the tears burning them. "Ashden very well might die, and it's my fault."

"It absolutely is not and don't you dare tell yourself that." His tone is commanding. Hard. No room for argument.

"You heard what Lichera said."

"Lichera is a weak rat of a man and likes to throw empty accusations to give him a sense of power," he spits.

But why *did* Lichera say that? He's a Goramalan, at the mercy of the Verenathians just like the rest of us. What gives him the power to suggest their next victim?

I don't complete the train of thought. That's another level of complexity for a different day.

"He could've been chosen at any point for the Culling," Kieran says quietly.

And he's right; I know he's right, but…
"I just happened to expedite the process."
A soft squeeze. "You can't think like that, Rae. You'll drown."
Maybe he doesn't realize that I already am.

Chapter 48

ASHDEN

So cold.

Everything is cold. It's like the blood isn't reaching every part of my body. My hands are stiff. My legs are stiff. I can't feel my feet.

Something is wrong.

More than the coldness and numbness. Something I can't put my finger on. Those white bands feel like they're pulling everything from me. My thoughts. My blood. My warmth.

Pieces of home come floating to me every now and again. Memories. Images. I think they're being sucked away.

By what? How?

Oh, yes. These bands. This magic.

What is this magic?

It doesn't matter though; not really.

It does. It does. It does matter. It does it does it does it does.

Something rises within me. Anger? Desperation? Regret? It's deep, deep within me. Almost out of reach. It's like it's pounding on a door far away and the sound is muffled.

I need to fight. I need to get out of here. I need to think.

Why can't I think?

I ball my hands into fists, but my fingers barely clench together. Slowly raising my hands above my face, I would cry out at the sight if I had the strength.

They're pale and withered and I can see my veins through the skin.

What is happening?

The cold stone floor is leeching all of the warmth from my body. I need to get up, I need to move; to do something.

Rae.

I have to. Damn it, I have to. I can't give up this easily.

My legs don't move. I pull and heave until I'm panting, but my knees only bend a few degrees.

Whatever this magic is, it works fast.

Help me. Help me.

Anger? Panic?

Yes. Panic. I can't move.

Yes I can. I can and I have to. I have to. I can. I can.

But I can't.

Help me.

There's no one to help me. I lost that when I estranged the only part of my family I had left.

Rae.

A cold sweat breaks out across my brow. I force my body to do something, I don't care what.

All I manage is to roll from my back to my side.

Swallowing, I wince at the grittiness in my mouth and throat.

It's so dry, it's sucking the moisture from my body;from the inside out. My lungs are burning, burning.

I can't breathe.

Those white bands continue flowing, flowing.

Move, damn you. Move.

Twin tears trace paths down my face and drip to the ground.

CHAPTER 49

The Author has placed you in this world for a purpose, little bird. Know this. Cling to it. Hold fast to this knowledge when everything falls down around you. Life will push you to the point of breaking, and you may. But never stay down, never let it win.

Kieran and I return to the temple hand in hand, where Sebastian is suspended between all four elemental bands—laughing his ass off.

Avice is standing in front of the dais, arms crossed and grinning widely. We reach her side, and I can't help but smile as Sebastian rotates within the magic like meat on a spit.

Noticing our return, he, rather ungracefully, withdraws himself from the magic and flops to the floor. His tawny skin is radiant and there's a feral gleam in his eyes.

"'Bout damn time," he declares, looking pointedly at mine and Kieran's intertwined hands.

"What are you doing?" I barely restrain my giggle.

He flourishes dramatically. "The magic appears to be as fond of me as I am of it."

Cocking my head at the bands of light, my curiosity piqued, I let go of Kieran's hand and step onto the dais.

Reaching both into earth and water, I'm immediately met with a crashing waterfall over stone and moss. The smell of a forest after a rain. The dirt on one's knees after they hit the ground, begging in desperation.

I stretch until my left arm is touching both elements, and pull my other free, reaching for air. Immediately I'm filled with the sensation of wind whipping through the grass; of a breathless laugh. Grit-filled eyes and the stinging nose from a dusty wind. The ocean—tossed into an uproar. A gasp of delight. A flame fanned.

And that hollowness inside, as if all the air in the world has been sucked away when you hear those dreadful words: they won't be coming home.

My body is filling, filling—every nerve taught. It beckons to me, overwhelms me, and I press forward, welcoming the intensity.

I lift my foot into fire.

A scorching wildfire. The heated words of an argument. Earth collapsing, giving in to the inferno's demand. The give and take between water and flame. Tears of rage. Peaceful crackling that warms a home. A tangled web of limbs and heavy breathing.

I've never felt so whole, so full and complete and alive. Emotions; sensations; real and raw and powerful, flow through me unabashed. Life and death—two parallel lines, forced to run alongside each other for all of eternity, each unable to exist without the other.

All of this at my fingertips to move and manipulate how I wish.

A wild laugh tears through me. This is more than the freedom of the open air with the dragons.

This is ecstasy.

This is what we've been created for.

Without warning, all-consuming, overpowering rage fills me. Rage for what we've lost, and for what's been taken. Hot and sharp and unreasonable, I can't think beyond the hate now coursing through my veins.

I will kill them. I will kill every single one of them for what they've done.

Someone grabs my hand and pulls me out of the magic's embrace. My foot hits the dais, and I stumble, gathering myself before I fall into Kieran.

"Easy," he murmurs.

Instantly, that poisonous rage is gone. Exhaustion and a… normal amount of anger are left in its wake.

Panting, I try to orient myself within the room. Avice's eyes are wide with concern, and the color in Sebastian's face has drained a bit.

"Did I…?"

"Let the magic overwhelm you?" Kieran suggests. "Yes."

I nod slowly. It would have been so easy to let that rage consume me.

A gift, yes; this magic. But not one to be taken lightly.

Heavy silence settles over us. Expectant silence. The silence of having come to the temple and learned what we can in the short time we have, knowing what comes next.

"Well," Sebastian blows out a long breath. "Where do we go from here?"

My vision blurs as I stare at the ground. "Verenathia," I whisper.

Sebastians crosses his arms as shadows flicker in his warm eyes. Avice shifts, her hands worrying at the hem of her shirt. None of them will say it, though I know we're all thinking it.

"We don't know how long Ashden has left," Kieran says quietly. "It would be best to get there as soon as possible."

"Even with what little we've learned?" The hem of her shirt is stretching as she begins to wring it.

I know she cares just as much as I do about Ashden, but the question—the doubt behind it—sours my stomach.

"Did you expect some grand revelation? Maybe a handbook on how to eradicate the Warbearers' magic?"

Hurt flashes across her face. "No. I wanted to give Ashden the best possible chance, though. I know we don't have time to learn the ins and outs of the magic, but what good is it if we go up there unprepared and get ourselves killed?" Defiance gleams in her eyes. "No one makes it out in that scenario."

Irritation has me biting my tongue so I don't lash out again. "Kieran can show us all he's learned—"

"And we just hope for the best?" She interrupts.

"No." Yes?

"I don't know about you, Rae, but I'd much rather spend another day or two soaking up all we can, learning everything we have access to, before going back up there." She straightens, keeping her gaze locked on me.

"What happens if we spend that day or two, and we find him dead already by the time we get up there?" I challenge.

Time. The only thing we're unsure of, while always needing more.

"Both are valid points," Kieran cuts in easily. "You could spend a lifetime studying the magic and learning how to manipulate it, but Rae's rightwe don't have that kind of time." He cuts me a glance. "But we can't go up there carelessly, either—"

"I'd be very curious to know what part of this feels careless to you," I demand, trying to ignore the sting of his words.

His eyes soften, stripping me bare as he peers right into the terrified furor beneath. "It won't take long to show you all that I've learned. Another day, at most."

"Will it be enough?" Avice asks, avoiding my gaze now.

His throat bobs. "It's going to have to be."

Another day. Another day as Ashden gets weaker and weaker. Another day for Lichera to decide his life is no longer valid.

"Will he still be there?" I hate how my voice cracks, but this fear is breaking me apart piece by piece.

Kieran brushes a finger across my cheek. "I can't make any promises, but I think Lichera won't order his execution until he has you. The Warbearers would use him until there's nothing left, otherwise."

Horrible words, but the truth, at least.

"We'll stay here to practice, then head to my family's home—"

"What?" Sebastian asks sharply. He's been uncharacteristically quiet, watching each interaction with a taut mouth and forehead lined with worry.

Kieran cocks an eyebrow. "I'm going to say goodbye to my family before we go. I won't do that to my mother."

Sebastian narrows his eyes. "And you're going to tell them?"

"I'm tired of it, Seb. I'm so tired of this shit."

Sebastian begins pacing. "If you tell them what we're doing they'll demand to come with."

"And that would be their decision to make," Kieran snaps. "I'm not going to leave my family like my father did. They're going to know, regardless of the threat to them, and that's it."

"Kieran," I whisper.

I see the pain and bitterness. The brokenness we share. I've been selfish to only consider myself at the biggest risk here.

It's become too personal—intensely personal for him.

"I don't know about this, Kieran." Sebastian's voice is low with warning, more serious than I've ever heard him before.

"It's my family," Kieran barks. "I respect the fact you want to protect them, but I was the one who was there when my mother would sob and scream through the night because of my father and brother."

Avice's eyes go wide, but she remains silent.

"As if I wasn't right there with you," Sebastian snarls. "Don't play like that with me."

"They're going to know, and I'm done talking about it."

Sebastian casts a glare to the ground, shaking his head before walking away, his arms crossed tightly over his chest.

I study Kieran carefully, wondering the depth of pain that has pushed him to this. The Kieran I've grown to know would do anything to keep his family safe, even if it meant withholding the truth.

Yet, is safety without the unadulterated truth worth it? Is it worth losing the ability to make a knowledgeable decision for yourself?

My heart breaks for Rose, though, and all she's endured. I don't blame Kieran for being unwilling to put her through that again.

"Do they know what's happening?" I ask.

"No."

Avice shifts uncomfortably beside me before wordlessly heading off in the direction Sebastian went.

"They deserve to know though, Rae." He shrugs. "They deserve at least a goodbye."

"Don't say that," I fight the panic-edged pitch in my voice. "Don't act like we've lost before we've even tried."

He offers me a sad smile. "Just being realistic."

"I know…" I blow out a long breath. "You know they're going to come if you tell them."

Opal and her bold, fiery personality… there's no way she would stay away. And Rose, well, I can't imagine she'd let her children charge off into the face of death alone.

"And like I said, that's their decision. But I have to tell them."

Relenting, I nod. It's his family; if that's the decision he's made then I'm not going to question it any further.

"What do you think it's gonna look like up there?"

A muscle in his jaw ticks. "No doubt it's an all out manhunt. There's no way Lichera was going to let us go that easy. He's probably got patrols scouring both territories up and down."

I drop my head into my hands, rubbing my temples against a growing headache. "Great."

Kieran steps closer and gently pulls me into a hug.

"One moment at a time, okay?"

I relish the warmth of his arms around me, breathing in the salt air scent on his chest. His steady heartbeat is soothing, driving away the panic with each beat.

"Okay," I whisper.

CHAPTER 50

I know I've been absent a lot, my little bird. I know you miss me, although you don't mind the freedom to wander the shore and grasslands as you please. One day, though, you'll understand. All of the knowledge will settle into your being, and you'll realize you've always known.

We lead the dragons hard and fast, the approaching isle looming menacingly before us.

We spent the daylight hours in the temple, listening to every word Kieran shared as he taught us how to wield the magic.

The problem is that the magic is simply the force of life at its base—elements and frequencies—and is shaped to the wielder's will. Most of what Kieran knows is life-giving and protective in nature. Which is necessary, I know—the knowledge of how to protect ourselves from the Warbearers is important—but they are wicked and cruel. We need something just as dark to combat them. And even with Kieran as our guide, I can feel it in my bones—it's not enough. Nowhere close to enough. Having conjured up every ounce of grief and rage and hurt spooling inside of me, I was able to turn it into something dangerous. Not deadly, but enough of a defense to fight back, maybe.

The other problem is that it's hard. It takes so much focus to hold the magic to your will. Certain things get easier each time I open myself to it, but I don't have the experience, nor the time to acquire it. Not enough to utilize it to its full capability.

The realization sends fear, cold and heavy, filling my body.

My gaze roams over the boundless sky, the Citadel beginning through the clouds. I've come to the conclusion that I will kill the Warbearers, if the opportunity presents itself, and I don't think I would regret it. What they've done is sitting like lead in my soul, festering and hurting and poisoning me.

"Are you with me?" Avice shouts above the wind buffeting us.

I snap my gaze back to the isle as we near, so close now that I can count the houses lining the outer ring.

"I'm here," I shout back.

Kieran and Sebastian explained how the land patrols would work, having been trained in them, themselves. As long as we remain hidden, we should be fine.

The dragons are alert, but at ease, which serves to lessen some of the tension pulling my body taut. They can sense things we can't—if they feel it's safe to land, it likely is.

Closer, closer the isle draws, and then we dive, streaming toward the Edge.

Halting their plummet, they each pull up with a powerful thrust of their wings, leaving us hovering at the Edge of the isle. Without giving myself a second to reconsider, I jump from Boreal's back. My knees buckle as I land, and I roll, knocking the air from my lungs. Kieran follows, then Sebastian. Avice pauses for a heartbeat before leaping. She lands about as ungracefully as I did, dirt and grass stains streaking across her suit.

She stands, swiping at the loose blades of grass peppered across her legs and gapes at the rolling lush plains stretching out around us.

"This is unreal," she breathes.

"It really is something," I admit. How I wish she had been given the opportunity to see what I've seen and experienced all the wonder this place has to offer.

The last ring of houses sits across the open expanse before us. If a patrol flies over before we make it to the shelter of the houses, there's no hiding.

I don't allow myself to continue that line of thinking.

"Let's go," Kieran orders, having dawned the mask of a soldier—all hard lines and taut command.

We don't argue. Slipping into motion, we quietly pick our way across the grass. No words, unless it's an emergency. Silence and speed are the only things we're afforded.

***

We make it to Kieran's home quickly—mainly due to its position near the outer ring—and the conversation with his family goes about how I expected it to.

"Absolutely not," Rose's tone is adamant, fresh trails of tears wetting her face.

Rose—throwing her arms around Kieran in relief the moment he walked through the door—stands face to face with him; the latter a whole head taller as he towers over her small frame.

And now, as Kieran concludes the story of our journey, what we've learned and what must be done, Rose is beginning to cry; pleading with us to stay, to not put ourselves in danger.

Opal doesn't say a word, face drawn and sallow where she sits at the table. Sebastian hovers near her, his arms crossed protectively over his chest. Avice has tucked herself into a corner of the room, quietly observing with fear-filled eyes.

"We have to," Kieran's deep voice is gentle, more tender than I've ever heard it.

She cups her hands around his face. "No, you don't have to do anything. This isn't your responsibility, Kieran."

"It's not," he agrees. "But who else is there to do anything about it?"

She only shakes her head, tears coursing down her weathered face.

"They can't keep doing this. We can't let them. I'm sorry, mom," his voice falters. "But we're going."

"Please," she whispers.

His eyes brim with emotion. "I have to."

"I'm going with," Opal says numbly. "You're not dying without me."

Kieran offers her a tight-lipped smile, even as Sebastian looks like he might combust.

"Have you even considered the war you will start by doing this?" Rose holds her fingers to quivering lips.

"Yes," Kieran nods. "There's not another way around it. This has gone on for too long. No more are innocent people going to suffer."

She wears an almost wild sort of grief now, her eyes bright with terror. "The Citadel is on lockdown. They've been looking for you all for days. Patrols have been running nonstop, and the Court has issued a warrant for your arrest on sight if anyone finds you."

Breaking the treaty between our lands, uncovering a long buried secret, escaping prison, assaulting the head of Ra'goramal's synod and fleeing the territory… Sounds about right.

"Damnit," Sebastian mutters.

"We already knew this was likely happening," Kieran reminds him. Turning back to his mother, he puts his hands on her shoulders. "I love you. You've given everything for Opal and I, and I will never be able to pay that back. I'm going to do this…" he swallows. "I'm going to try to make things right."

Rose is fighting an internal war as she looks into her son's eyes. After several moments of tense silence, she lets out a weary breath; a sad smile beneath tearful eyes. "You're a good man." She gestures to all of us. "All of you. And clearly, I won't be able to talk you out of it.

"Tell me what you need me to do."

***

We spend the next day pouring over diagrams of the Citadel, planning. With it being the central hub of Verenathia and the entire population trained to defend it, it's apparently not uncommon to have a full-scale map of the place.

Over and over, we drill into each other the best way to get there from here. How to remain hidden; what sections to avoid; making sure everyone knows where the Inner Sanctum is—and the quickest way out.

We go over all the patrol routes; the areas that will be guarded the heaviest, and the ones that will be the least.

"We'll need to split up," Kieran says, fingers tapping his mouth contemplatively as he paces the small room. "A bigger group is easier to spot—too hard to remain hidden."

Sebastian does a quick head count. "We'll go in pairs. Avice, you're with me. Rae, go with Kieran. Opal and Rose," he inclines his head toward them.

I glance quickly at Opal, who nods her agreement—tossing a tentative grin at her mother. Her body is lean and strong due to years of training; her hands well calloused from hours spent wielding all sorts of weapons. I know, too, Rose had the same training before she chose the path of a healer. They're more than capable of handling themselves. Avice and I will be the drawback.

"And," Kieran says quietly. "Unless they've been given orders otherwise, they won't hesitate to kill you. It's part of our training."

His words sink heavily in my stomach. In other words: kill them before they get the chance to kill us.

"We're going to avoid the patrol routes as much as possible, but it's inevitable that there will be some overlap. We want to avoid casualties, but if it comes to it…" his voice trails off. He casts me an unreadable look.

Are we really discussing this? Is this truly what this situation has come to? A month ago I didn't even know what was happening to my people on Verenathia, and now I might very well have to kill them in order to get my brother back. It feels like some kind of fever dream.

How can I, how can Avice—how can any of us be expected to end someone's life? I suppose if it came down to a matter of survival, instinct would kick in. Maybe it's easier for my Verenathian friends—having spent their lives training for things like this. Maybe neighbor and friend and colleague mean nothing in the face of survival.

I will do it, if it becomes necessary. For Ashden, I will do it.

"What about Black Protocol?" Sebastian asks in a low voice, giving them a knowing look.

My heart leaps to my throat but Avice beats me to it, a slight quaver to her voice. "What's Black Protocol?"

Kieran blows out a long breath. "If the Citadel is under attack, anyone patrolling can issue Black Protocol. If called into action, a massive ward is placed over the Citadel. It was woven by the first Warbearers after the war, and is fed by the magic of the land. It's never been used.

"Once it's there, no one gets in, and if you're already in, you don't get out." There's a note of finality in his tone that makes me shudder.

"How do we avoid it?" I ask.

"Don't get caught," he shrugs.

Sebastian and Opal nod their agreement. "Get in, free the prisoners, get out."

"And if it does get enforced?" Avice's voice is so small now, too small.

Opal answers, equally as quiet. "Only the Warbearers know how to break it."

"And," Rose starts. "Magic is dampened once it's engaged. Still doable, but weak. It won't be any help against the Warbearers."

Kieran nods. "There's an underground tunnel, too. Its entrance is hidden in the wall near the Supply Field. If Black Protocol is engaged, we can get out through there."

And he just now mentions that? "I thought you said no one could get out?"

He cocks an eyebrow at me. "Only those who aren't supposed to be there in the first place. It wouldn't be very 'tactically defensive' of us to trap our own people in the Citadel where they won't be of any use until the threat is disengaged."

"Maybe lead with that next time," I snap.

His gaze softens as he strides to the seat next to mine and eases himself into it. My view is blocked by his broad shoulders as he leans forward, so close I can smell the sky and sea on him. He says quietly, "We're going to get your brother out of there, okay?"

I swallow the tightness in my throat and return my attention to the diagram spread across the table.

After running through the plan—the layout of the Citadel, everyone's role, worst case scenarios—we practice manipulations. Manipulation after manipulation; shields, bindings, cloaks, tethers, even a bit of siphoning.

Hours later, unable to focus any longer, we all bathe and change into clean clothes. Opal is taller than Avice and I, but nothing a little rolling of the legs can't fix.

Rose makes us all some tea. I breathe in the calming blend of aromatic herbs and spices, but it does little to help my fraying sanity. As we sip, with nothing left to do but wait, I pace the room.

I need space. I need air. It's too cramped in here; my chest is tight with anxiety and too many bodies around me. But I do my best to calm my breaths one heartbeat at a time, knowing that we'll have fresh air soon enough.

CHAPTER 51

ASHDEN

Cold.

Weak.

Confused.

What am I confused about?

I don't know…

I try to move, but… everything is heavy… so heavy.

Why? Why are these… these things attached to me so angry? How long has it been?

How long has what been?

Yes, these things. So, so cold. So angry. I don't know why. It hasn't been this bad before. No, this is worse. Whatever this is—it's hell.

I want to move, I need to move. My legs… they don't work right. Nothing is working right.

Why do I feel like this? What is going on?

I hear something now. *What is that?*

I force my eyes open, using every last drop of energy. They're so heavy…

What are those? Tall, dark figures move through this place.

A word floats through my mind. I try to grasp it. I'm trying so hard…

Warbearers. Yes. Those are Warbearers. And I'm on Verenathia.

Is Rae here? Why hasn't she come back to me? I don't know if I can handle this much longer.

Weak, so weak.

My vision is blurred. I try to focus on the figure near me. They're…picking something up off the ground, I think.

No, picking *someone* up. Good, maybe they'll help them out of this place.

Does my body look like that?

Rae. I miss Rae. I want to see her, talk to her.

The figures are moving, going away; hopefully going far, far away.

Oh, they've stopped.

This is too cold. I'm too cold.

What are they doing?

What is who doing?

The Warbearers.

I don't know. *What is happening to me?*

A scream rings through this room. And now, silence. Red stains that odd stone.

Something wet slides down my face. Slowly, so slowly, I reach my hand up, up…

Tears.

Something isn't right.

Please, someone come get me out of here.

Someone.

Anyone.

Please.

I'm so afraid.

CHAPTER 52

Night has fallen. The rings of houses, shops, and restaurants are quiet now, though dragons soar in pairs overhead, scanning.

Back at his home, Kieran showed us how to form a different sort of cloaking shield around us in case the Warbearers placed a field over Verenathia in an effort to detect our presence.

"You ready?" he whispers to me as we slip unseen from shadow to shadow toward the Citadel. Sebastian and Avice are one step—one shadow—behind, with Rose and Opal taking up the rear.

"No," I admit.

"Me neither."

His words hang heavily between us as we slip through the rings. The gleaming white structures surrounding us in perfect lines feel like a graveyard amidst the stillness.

Dread coils in my stomach with each footstep, tighter and tighter as the Citadels draws nearer.

I probe for Boreal's shimmering presence in my mind—our unspoken bond. I know she'll be at the wall to the Supply Field right where I need her, just as well as I know she can sense every thought and emotion running through me right now.

We arrive at the base of the grand staircase leading to the Citadel and skirt around its side, hugging the slope of the massive hill the Citadel is built on. Lush, rolling hills stretch out all around us as we leave the residential sectors behind.

Staying in a single-file line to maximize the shadows, we pick our way across the base of the hill. Several minutes pass, and the wall surrounding the Supply Field begins, stretching high above us. I swallow my fear and push forward.

A soft chortle comes from ahead, around a bend in the hill, and I smile softly as Boreal, Cinder, and Stoney appear. Their characteristic shuffling impatience has been replaced by a solemn stillness, as if they understand the gravity of the situation.

"Hey girl," I whisper as I approach, patting her nose. She snuffles against my chest softly, resting her head for a moment before looking up to meet my eyes. Again, I pause at the wisdom and knowledge in her gaze.

"Let's go," Kieran whispers.

I look around at my friends, family. We all nod in silent agreement. Taking a collective breath of preparation, we mount.

Avice wraps her arms tightly around my waist. Rose sits behind Kieran, and Opal rests her head against Sebastian's back as she grips him tightly.

Glancing up, I swallow at the sheer hillside reaching high into the sky, and the impenetrable stone wall atop it. It would be impossible to get to the Supply Field without dragons—as it's designed. Easily two hundred feet high, and a borderline vertical wall—save for the gentle slope at the base of the hill.

If someone had the proper equipment, they might be able to scale it. But it wasn't made to defend against dragons, against Verenathia's own, and we're about to slither in like snakes.

The dragons begin climbing their way up the face of the hill. Comprised mainly of dirt, it makes little noise as they sink their claws into it.

We had discussed this earlier. At the risk of being heard by the dragons' wingbeats, which are surprisingly loud, climbing the hill seemed like the safest option. The Supply Field is the least guarded section of the Citadel—due to it being borderline impenetrable, but we wanted to take no risks.

Too soon, we reach the base of the wall. With a powerful bunching of her haunches, Cinder leaps, her strong legs propelling us up and forward. Using only one beat of her wings to help with momentum, she grips the edge of the wall.

Clinging precariously to its edge, I don't dare look down as I let go and scramble up her body and onto the top of the wall. Avice follows closely behind, along with the rest of our party, and we're soon teetering on the edge.

"Wait for us," I whisper, holding Boreal's face for a moment before turning toward the others.

Kieran has moved to the front of the line, leading us toward that set of steps I remember well.

The last, and only, time I was on this wall, I had considered abandoning everything and everyone I had ever known for the possibility of a life that was, on the surface, exponentially better. But that possibility had never been, had only been a carefully crafted facade.

The magic of that night glows bittersweet in my memory, aching in its temporary beauty.

As expected, the Supply Field is empty. We arrive quickly to the steps and file down.

The marble pillars supporting the ceiling rest all around us, the wall with the entrances to the corridors stretching ominously to our right.

Though the Inner Sanctum is near the Supply Field, it would be dangerous to head straight there. We'll need to get to an armory because, although we'll have magic at our disposal, little can be done against a trained warrior with a steel blade.

"Remember your routes," Kieran says quietly. "Keep an eye out for extra patrols. If it goes to shit, get back to the dragons as fast as you can. Be safe."

And with that, we move to the corridors with nothing but the sound of our heartbeats to break the silence.

Sebastian and Avice head down a separate entrance while Rose and Opal follow on our heels. With a quick dip of their heads at the first intersection, they branch off in the opposite direction.

Alone, Kieran and I proceed carefully down the corridors. Pausing at each intersection to listen for passing patrols, their footsteps seem to echo all around us.

My heart beats wildly. I feel like an animal trapped in a cage, and one wrong move or misstep will have me quickly meeting my end.

Kieran notices my jumpiness and briefly places a comforting hand at the small of my back. Not daring to speak, I give him an appreciative glance before turning my attention back to the moonlit corridor.

Silent as serpents, we make our way down each corridor until suddenly, Kieran is shoving me forward. I almost trip as he bundles me quickly into one of the alcoves. My heart leaps into my throat. I hadn't realized a group of footsteps had grown closer, turning down our corridor. Thankfully, he's not as distracted as I am, pushing us out of view just as they entered.

Forcing down the rising dread, I inhale deeply, preparing myself for what I know is coming. The patrols are trained to scan every alcove as they pass; surprise is our only advantage.

The clip of their boots on the marble grows louder. I quiet my breathing, noting their individual cadence and weight. Three people, just as I'd been told.

Kieran will need to be fast, so fast. Even my best attempts will be no match against a group of honed weapons.

Too soon, they're almost even with our alcove. Kieran nudges me, and before I can talk myself out of it, we jump out from its safety, directly into the path of the patrol.

I blink and one is down, having taken a precise blow to the side of the head. The other two widen their eyes in shock, and I throw myself at the one furthest toward the opposite wall.

The man grunts as my full body weight slams into him. Panic takes over as I punch and kick blindly,

In a matter of seconds, the man has me on the ground, arms behind my back, pinned. Unable to move, I watch the woman Kieran was engaged with fall unceremoniously to the ground.

The weight suffocating me is abruptly thrown off, freeing me, but the man is down before I can even get to my feet.

I grip Kieran's proffered hand and he pulls me up. Shuddering, I glance at the felled bodies. All it would take is one slip from Kieran for us to end up the same way.

"How long will they be down?" I whisper as I help him move the bodies into the alcoves.

"Normally, probably ten minutes. But with a little bit of magic…" his quiet voice trails off. "Maybe an hour, hour and a half at most."

His words hit me like a gut punch. The moment they wake up, they'll alert the other patrols, or worse, engage Black Protocol.

The clock has started, and every second counts now as it ticks down.

As if reading my thoughts, Kieran nudges me. "Don't go down that path. One moment at a time."

CHAPTER 53

Kieran's memory of the patrol routes serves us well, and we arrive at the armory without encountering another group. Sebastian and Avice are already at the door when we arrive; no sign of Rose and Opal.

"How many?" Kieran asks.

"Two," Sebastian responds, his voice grave.

"No issues?"

Sebastian shakes his head. "I ran into Trenton; bastard put up one hell of a fight, but no issues thanks to Avice here. I think she's been holding out on us."

I cast a questioning glance at my friend. Her cheeks flush pink as she ducks her head and turns her attention to the armory door.

Following Kieran into the dimly lit room, I gape at the menagerie of weapons. Shelves and hooks plaster the walls, brimming with swords, daggers, maces, clubs, mallets, throwing knives, and several others I don't know the name of.

Many of the weapons are Markell's work, some even my own. I exchange a knowing look with Avice, her face a mirror of my own.

After this is over, Kieran and I are going to sit down and have a very, very long talk.

He hands me a belt, fashioned with several spots for daggers. I palm the smooth leather, hesitating for only a moment before strapping it on. Scanning the wall, my gaze snags on the row of daggers, their blades polished to a mirror finish. Foreboding grips my body.

Three sheaths on my belt. Three daggers that I may or may not have to use. Three opportunities: a choice I'll make each time I reach for the cold metal. The potential to end a life as complex as my own.

Carefully selecting each one, I weigh them before sliding them into their sheathes. I know these blades, these hilts. Shaking my head in disbelief, I slip the last one in.

Kieran selects two shortswords that he straps across his back. He fastens a belt of daggers similar to my own around his hips, and completes the ensemble with two small blades in each boot. My breath catches at the sight of him.

Beautifully lethal.

I've seen what he can do alone, with no weapons; the strength, speed, and power he possesses. Now, with muscles outlined by the skin-tight black suit and steel glinting across his back… Deadly.

"We need to go," Sebastian says. Equipped with a single broadsword at his back and a twin belt of daggers, he flashes Kieran a concerned glance.

Time is rapidly counting down. I can feel each second pressing in on me as it ticks away. One second closer to being discovered, one second closer to Ashden's death.

Or, perhaps, both.

"Any sign of mom and Opal?" Kieran asks hurriedly, handing Avice a final knife to slide into the baldric she selected.

"No," Sebastian chews the inner corner of his lip. "But they'll be alright. They're fast, and good fighters. There's been no sign of our discovery yet so all we can do is keep moving forward."

Kieran gives him a pert nod before turning to me. "Let's go."

With that, we exit the relative safety of the armory and head down opposite directions in the corridor; our footsteps silent.

We pass through several more corridors, listening to the passing patrols, until I begin to feel the dark weight that looms near the Inner Sanctum. We're close. After this intersection, only a couple more—

A patrol turns directly into our path, coming from the adjacent corridor. Terror laced adrenaline flashes through me like lightning. They must have adjusted their routes, or we're not—

One of them lunges, wrapping strong arms around my head like a vice. A broad hand claps itself around my mouth, stifling my scream.

I thrash, willing the panic away, but the arms around me are like solid steel. The other two are locked on Kieran.

I try to pull in a breath, to cry out, but the hand around my mouth is merciless.

"You afraid your boyfriend is going to get himself hurt?" A familiar voice says in my ear.

Cold, icy dread sleuths down my spine at the hot breath on my ear, and I jerk my head away, straining against his arm. I hadn't been paying attention. Too surprised by the patrol's appearance, I didn't note the hateful sneer.

A sickening chuckle reverberates against me. "That's right, pig. Surprised to see me again?"

Barrett.

I can hear the loathing in his tone, in the tightness of his arms around my head. With one easy movement, he could snap my neck. Kieran has shown me how to do it, and it's terrifyingly easy.

Fear unlike anything I've ever known bolts through me.

Kieran knocks one of the guards down, his body slumping on the floor. Horror works its way up my throat when the second pulls out a dagger, angling it toward Kieran's side.

"A shame," Barrett growls in my ear. "I always hoped I'd be the one to slip a dagger into him."

He's taller than me, and far heavier. I snap my gaze away from Kieran and thrust my hips backward, pivoting to the side in one fluid movement. A hiss of irritation escapes him as he staggers—caught off guard. I grab one of the daggers from my belt, its weight formidable in my palm, but he lashes out again and grips my neck in his meaty hands.

He's squeezing hard enough that air becomes a chore to drag into my lungs. My heart beats wildly, threatening to burst through my chest. My lips start swelling, my head pounding.

A feral look of delight dances across his hateful face. "Oh, I'm going to enjoy this."

Spots dance in my vision. I'm going to pass out.

Then why don't you just kill me already, you bastard. Anger begins to burn, hot and thick through my veins—eating away at the terror coursing through me until I am nothing but fire and fury.

I am *done*. Done being treated as an inferior, as if my life is worth less than theirs. Something to be used and discarded.

Not giving myself a chance to reconsider, I thrust my arm backward, plunging my dagger into his stomach.

His enraged cry fills the corridor as he releases me. I gasp, spinning to face him as the sounds of Kieran and the other guard ring behind me. Cool air fills my lungs, stroking my raw throat. Blood again begins flowing to my head.

Barrett's face is a twisted mask of fury as he stares at me, wide eyed. Blood oozes between his fingers where they're pressed against his abdomen.

I can't rip my eyes away from the ruby droplets as they puddle, stark against the gleaming marble. They seem to stare back at me, taunting me, standing as a defiant display of what I've just done. Nausea roils in my stomach.

"You *bitch*," he snarls, the veins in his forehead bulging

He lunges forward, but rage and pain make him sloppy. I jump to the side, ducking as I jut my leg out. His foot catches mine and he topples forward, landing with a grunt on the ground.

I throw myself on top of him, pulling out another dagger and pressing it to his throat.

"You will never touch me again," I spit, even as some fundamental part of me withers.

He grins an icy grin, his face hideously contorted with hatred.

Faster than I can react, he squeezes my hips with his thighs—rolling over and pinning me underneath him.

Thrashing and kicking—I realize immediately I can't move. My arms are pinned under his knees, and I cry out as his full weight digs in sharply, grinding my bones into the marble.

"I'll touch you wherever and whenever I want," he sneers. His blood is still seeping from his dragonhide suit—the red blossoming around the wound like some sort of macabre flower and dripping onto my stomach.

He runs a bloody hand down my side, my waist, and rests on one of the daggers at my hips.

I buck, trying to twist away and out from under him, but his weight is planted firmly on me. Air again becomes a struggle as his significant weight drives it from my lungs.

Slowly, he removes my dagger from its sheath, dragging it up my stomach and across my breast. I swallow a scream of panic when the cold metal presses against my throat.

I'm going to die. This man is going to kill me.

His face, mere inches from mine now, bears a savage look of satisfaction.

"I've wanted to do this since the day you showed up," he whispers near my ear, his hot breath making me sick to my stomach.

My shoulders feel like they're about to slip out of their sockets as I fight to get out from under him, but my arms are thoroughly stuck. A sheen of sweat pricks my brow as I strain to pull myself away from the blade at my throat.

Suddenly, he shudders, and I hear the unmistakable, nauseating sound of steel through flesh. A flicker of confusion crosses his face as his eyes widen in pain. He convulses, then slumps forward—directly onto me.

I kick and writhe, trying to free myself from the dead weight on top of me, but he doesn't budge. Sickened panic takes over and I begin flailing wildly.

I need to get away, I need out, I can't do this.

The heavy warmth slides off of me; onto the ground, and I'm left staring at Kieran's grim expression.

"Are you okay?" he asks, scanning me from head to toe as he offers a hand. I take it, pulling myself up and surveying the area around me.

The first guard is slumped on the ground, but breathing—no visible wounds anywhere on his body. The second doesn't seem to have fared so well. A large, dark, wet patch spreads across his chest as he lays on the ground, staring up at the ceiling—unmoving.

And Barrett.

Barrett.

He's facedown on the ground, one of Kieran's daggers buried in his back to the hilt.

I glance down at the blood spilled onto my suit and swallow the bile rising in my throat. I try to brush it off, but it smears. Wiping and wiping, it just spreads further across my body. Swiping at my suit frantically, I try desperately to get the blood off of me.

Blood. So much blood.

Kieran reaches out, grabbing my shaking hands and holding them in his. My chest is heaving, and his face blurs when I look up at him.

"What have we done?" I whisper.

The misery in his gaze hollows my stomach. "We're getting your brother out of here." He lets me go, retrieving his blade from Barrett's back.

CHAPTER 54

The suffocating darkness of the Inner Sanctum presses in around us as we head down the corridor that leads to its massive onyx doors.

Time… We're running out of time. I can sense it; feel it with each breath, each heartbeat. Not only for us—those first patrol groups will be waking soon, and we still run the risk of the dead ones being discovered—but for Ashden. He's been in here too long already. I can feel him waning.

Hurry. Hurry.

Opal and Rose round the corner at the opposite end of the corridor and hurry on silent feet toward us. Kieran almost sags with relief at the sight of his mother and sister.

I do a quick once over, but they seem unharmed—save for the spray of blood across Opal's thigh. Its pattern tells me it's not hers.

They meet our gazes, faces grim. I can't even begin to imagine the impact this will have on them. The horror of what lies beneath this Citadel and the part they'll play in putting a stop to it. The death that is likely to come.

Maybe it's my fault, what they're enduring—the undertaking before us.

It *is* my fault, though, in a convoluted way. I should have stayed home, should have swallowed my despair and carried out my duties like every other person I've ever known.

No one I love would be in the positions they're in right now if I had.

No. Not here. Not now. There's too much at stake. If I think about it any longer, the guilt will swallow me whole—dragging me down, down, until there's no air left and I am nothing but a shattered soul, borne along its waves in a sea of torment.

"Three groups," I hear Rose say, and I drag myself out of my mind.

Kieran flinches. "Is that why you weren't at the armory?"

"Yes," Opal says. "We got held up right off of the Supply Field and mistimed the route."

The sound of uniform steps rings through the corridors, approaching our spot in front of the Inner Sanctum.

Kieran pushes us through the opening of the corridor and into the hall that acts as an antechamber to the Inner Sanctum. The looming, black doors stand commandingly in the center of the wall.

The patrols' steps are smooth, unhurried.

Good. They still don't know we're here.

We wait until the sound of their boots on the stone is a distant memory, then move forward out of the shadows.

"Where are Sebastian and Avice?" I whisper, my stomach working itself in knots while we wait for our friends.

"We don't know." Opal's tone does little to ease my fraying nerves.

"We can't wait for them much longer," Kieran's voice is strained, as taut as every line in his body.

"We can't," Rose concedes. "If worst comes to worst, Rae—you can free the prisoners while we hold off the Warbearers. Three against four doesn't sound too bad," she attempts a smile, but it comes out as more of a grimace.

I nod, my mouth dry. The seconds move past at lightning speed, taking my sanity with them. Opal bounces from foot to foot while Kieran watches the outer corridor, his jaw ticking.

What could be taking them so long? Did they run into more patrols than expected? Did they mistime the patrol routes? Or worse… I don't let myself dwell on the alternative.

"We can't wait any longer," I breathe, giving in to the tensing panic—that connection with Ashden that is screaming to hurry.

"You're right, we need to go," Kieran's gaze softens when he meets mine, though cold determination radiates from him.

Rose exhales a sharp breath, worry creasing her brow. "Author keep you," she whispers in the direction Avice and Sebastian should have been coming from.

Inclining his head, Kieran says quietly, "Go."

We make our way to the doors towering before us. I meet Kieran's gaze for a heartbeat. Sorrow, apology, and the softest bit of warmth. He places his palms on the glass-smooth stone, the wards woven into them recognizing something within his blood that allows them to be unlocked.

I wonder if he's remembering that night. The time he brought me here, when everything I thought I knew had crumbled down like sand around my feet.

With a heave, the stones slide out of the way, revealing the dimly lit tunnel underneath.

My body begins trembling, and I clench my fists at my sides, squeezing tight enough that my nails bite painfully into my palms.

Silently, we file down the steps. The tunnel is dark, suffocating. Sandwiched between Kieran and Rose, I want to scream as step by step, we move closer to the end. To Ashden.

We turn right at the end of the tunnel and the vast, domed cavern opens up before us. Robed figures stand at the edge of the room, their backs turned to us.

I fight back the nausea swirling in my gut. They're standing at the stone slab—the stone that ran red with fresh blood last time I was down here.

Looking past them, my world narrows to a single point as I see the body on the slab—see the person lying prone.

I clasp my hands over my mouth, stifling the sob that tears up my throat.

Ashden.

Kieran sees it too, and immediately breaks into a run toward the Warbearers. Toward his father. Rose and Opal follow; faces so, so pale.

I sprint after them, seeing nothing and no one but my brother, unmoving on that stone.

The Warbearers jerk their hooded faces to us. Confusion, then shock register in their black, soulless eyes. As one, they raise their hands. Their fingers move, waving and twitching as they perform some type of manipulation. I don't know what they're doing but I don't want to find out.

"Kieran!" I shriek as a wall of blinding light appears in front of the Warbearers, closing us off from them.

Even as I scream his name, he's already working. A shimmering web of crystalline blue emanates from Kieran's hands, spreading throughout the room. It coats everything it comes into contact with, like a blanket of starlight over the room. As it meets the Warbearers' wall of light, I watch in horrified awe as it clings to it, dissolving the light into mist.

The wall shrinks, eaten away by Kieran's shield, until it is nothing more than vapor in the air.

Their faces are all mirroring images of hatred and fury. Again, they begin moving as one, but Kieran's shield moves to them, coating them in the crystalline blanket.

As the shield envelops them wholly, it disappears, entwining itself and weaving into their dark magic. Their strange hand movements slow, then stop altogether.

Icy wrath twists their faces, emanating from them in a force so heavy it could press me into the ground if I let it. Wrath and… *panic.* They're still not moving. I dart a glance to Kieran, straining to hold his shield in place.

They *can't* move.

Rose steps beside Kieran, casting her own shield out over his; a soft, yellowed glow to his icy blue. Kieran's shield appears, lifting from the Warbearers before grasping Rose's. The two shields fuse into one, overlaying everything in the room, and sink back into the hooded figures.

"Get the prisoners," Kieran says tightly, his voice strained. His hands are taut, his body rigid as he concentrates, binding the shield to them so he can release it when we leave.

My body is leaden as I step around them—my insides quaking at being so near to the Warbearer's all-consuming darkness.

Ashden's eyes meet mine as I race to the edge of that hideous stone slab. A relieved sob chokes out of me as I see the life—though waning—but life nonetheless, in his gaze. His breaths are shallow, but steady.

"Rae," his voice is barely a whisper.

"Ash," I choke out, reaching for him—feeling for him to make sure he's really here and he's alive. His skin is so cold. "I'm so sorry," I breathe.

He shakes his head faintly. "No. Not right now. My arms. My legs."

I nod, swallowing the boulder in my throat, and move to his wrists and ankles. Though I can't see it, I can feel the same hard wall as the domes over the prisoners.

"Shit," I mumble. "Hold on."

I close my eyes. Energy moves about the room—swirling here, pulsing there; ebbing and flowing and pulling.

I visualize that energy, all of it, and let it seep into me, into every pore and vein in my body. The dark magic in the room threatens to drown out the good, but I take it all in. Once I can feel it flowing freely, I begin to separate it. Pulling on each strand individually, I move it, bending it to my will.

Black and broken, the dark magic curdles around the currents of golden energy. Like a rot, it pervades and creeps into every tendril, wrapping its presence around it.

Opening my eyes, I see the bands around Ashden's wrists. Those broken, black shards of energy. I focus on tearing it apart in my mind—forcing the energy around me and in me into those wicked bands.

A pulse like lightning shatters through one and it fractures, the strands of energy fraying. I push again, harder. Another pulse. Pushing one more time, the band shatters in a flash of light, disappearing into nothingness.

I don't give myself time for satisfaction and move to his next wrist. Opal arrives at my side, her face impossible to read, and begins working on Ashden's ankles.

He stiffens, and I can see the hatred and fear in his eyes as he watches her closely.

When the bond around his ankle dissolves, she moves to the other side, brushing against his leg.

"Don't touch me," he hisses weakly.

Opal blinks, shrinking back.

"Ash," I say softly. "She's here to help."

He gazes at me intently. A wave of emotions too complex for me to decipher washes over his face, but, finally, he nods.

Gently, Opal finishes dissolving the bonds and wordlessly moves to one of the prisoners.

When the last bond is dust in the wind, I whisper, "Can you walk?"

He grunts. "I think so. Those things…" he trails off, breathless. "Whatever they are. When they're on me, I"—another pause—"everything is hard. But, even just now, it's easier." He swallows, taking shallow breaths. "I'll be okay."

My heart breaks for him as I help him sit up, easing his legs over the edge of the slab.

The Warbearers still haven't moved—bound completely by Rose and Kieran. The weight of their wrath and hatred bears down on me, an almost physical presence in the room.

Ashden's bare feet meet the ground heavily, his knees buckling under him as they struggle to bear his weight. He leans on me, panting.

"Give me a second," he breathes. Fear coils itself like a snake around my lungs, squeezing the air out.

He gains his footing, supporting himself, but still leans heavily on me. "Come on," I whisper.

I lead him away from the stone slab. Wet blood squelches underfoot as we make our way out from behind the Warbearers to the vulnerable openness of the room.

Rose and Kieran stand side by side, fighting to finish their shields. A sheen of sweat coats Kieran's face, and Rose is beginning to tremble.

It shouldn't be this hard.

Another thought slams into me so hard it knocks the breath from my lungs.

Where is Lucielle?

Opal has gotten one of the prisoners out, and is working on another. The man—one who looks vaguely familiar, though I don't have time to place—is strong enough to stand on his own. He stares, frozen, in a haze of shock at the scene before him.

He hasn't been here very long, then.

The other, much like Ashden, is weak—barely able to hold herself upright. I can only hope that she's functional enough to walk out of here.

Opal moves to another and begins working on the bindings on him, quickly undoing the shields around him Thankfully, he can walk on his own.

"Kieran." My voice echoes uncomfortably through the room.

"I'm almost there," he replies through gritted teeth.

"Hold on," I whisper to Ashden. Releasing my grip on his arm, I ease away from him. He sways a bit, but manages to stay on his feet.

Closing my eyes, I open myself to the energy again. When I open them, I can see Rose's and Kieran's shields over the room, and that creeping rot beginning to encroach on the delicate tendrils of their magic.

I cast my own energy over the two shields like a glue, anchoring it to the Warbearers. Using my hands, I wrap the bands of my magic around the Warbearers' hands, arms, and torsos like a vice. A bead of sweat trickles down my temple with the effort. I weave one more band around and around Kieran's father, then let go.

"Wait," Opal calls from across the room, rising to her feet as the final prisoner crawls out from that siphoning circle.

"Let me do it too," she breathes, moving to my side.

She closes her eyes, her body going taut as she, too, casts her own shield over mine.

"Okay," she gasps. "Now!"

With a groan, I watch as Kieran's and Rose's bodies loosen, slumping with release.

The Warbearers are frozen to the spot, bound by the invisible magic.

"We need to go," Opal's voice quavers slightly.

I nod, turning to my brother, but pause. Rose is standing, her arms wrapped tightly around her middle, gawking at Kieran's father.

Something inside me fractures at her tight-lipped, tearful gaze. Her husband, lover; the father of her children. I can't begin to fathom what emotions plague her right now.

I swallow the tightness in my throat and slip an arm around Ashden. "Are you okay?" I ask quietly, guiding him toward the entrance.

"I'm alright," he rasps.

"That won't hold them forever," Kieran says as he slings the weakest woman's arm around his shoulders, doing more than his fair share of carrying her weight.

I open myself to the magic and shudder at the darkness eating away at our bindings.

"Which is why we're going to get the hell out of here," Opal grits. Her face is pale—a cold emptiness in her eyes that wasn't there before. She stoops, helping one of the prisoners to her feet. The other two are strong enough to walk by themselves. Rose collects herself and moves to their side, but not before casting one last glance at her husband.

"The guards from the patrols…" my voice trails off. "They'll be waking up soon."

The ones that aren't dead.

Kieran nods. "We're running out of time. I have no idea what Sebastian and Avice have gotten themselves into, but I really fucking hope they're still alive."

The edge of panic in his voice pushes me onward, one step at a time out of his horrible place.

CHAPTER 55

We move slowly through the tunnel; painfully slow. The prisoners are all weak, and we help them along at a crawl when everything within me is screaming to run.

Ashden is so heavy at my side. With my arm wrapped around his waist, his arm slung over my shoulder—each step drags as most of his weight remains unsupported. My heart breaks with each stumbling step.

This is my fault. I've done this to him.

"How are you doing?" I whisper, quietly enough that the others don't hear.

"Okay," he pants. "Like I said, my mind is coming back quicker than my body." He stumbles, almost taking both of us down, but I catch him. "I'll be okay, don't worry."

Worrying is all I can do when I look at his sallow complexion; at arms and legs that seem to have had the life sucked straight out of them.

We come to the steps leading out of the Inner Sanctum. My body screams with impatience as Rose helps Opal and the woman—substantially weaker now from the trek across the Inner Sanctum. The other two, strong enough to carry themselves, follow behind us.

Kieran goes next, supporting the weakest as she tries—and fails—to carry herself up.

"Let's get the hell out of here," Ashden mutters as we shuffle up the steps and emerge into the corridor.

We all pause, taking stock of the Citadel.

Silent as death.

The hair on the back of my neck prickles. It's too quiet. Unnaturally quiet. Where are Avice and Sebastian? How much longer until the guards wake up?

Where is Lucielle?

"The tunnel is only a few corridors down." Kieran darts a glance at me, but I remember the maps. I practically burned them into my memory. "We need to get there, right now."

We start limping down the corridor. This one—this sole corridor outside the Inner Sanctum—is the only one that feels even remotely safe. With only one wide entryway in its center, it's closed on both sides. The thought of being so encumbered and visible from all angles in every other corridor has my stomach turning over.

Pausing at the entry, Kieran deems it's safe and leads us forward. No sounds echo off the marble around us, save for our soft, shuffling footsteps.

We pass safely down the corridor and make it to the next intersection. Again, no signs of life stir around us, and we continue forward.

With each step forward, the dread inside me screams louder.

On the third corridor, one of the the prisoners—whose breathing has grown increasingly shaky as we've made our way—barely supports herself against Kieran. I watch in horror as she begins to gasp—quiet, wheezing sobs, but the noise makes me jumpy as it echoes down the corridor.

"I can't do it," her voice is barely a breath between each cry. Her sunken cheeks are tinted an awful gray, while purple dusts the circles under her eyes. Her arms and legs are shriveled into nothing but bone, her skin hanging loosely.

"I can't do it," she says again.

Kieran moves quickly into an alcove and gingerly sets her down against the window. His brow is pinched, his gaze heavy; at a loss for words.

We all gather in a tight semicircle around the alcove, faces grim. The prisoner suspended between Rose and Opal sags.

I wish I knew their names. My people—born of the same land and blood.

Kieran kneels before the woman. "You can do it," he says softly, looking into her tear-filled eyes.

"No, no, no," she chokes. "Too weak. Too much."

He takes her hand in both of his and continues to meet her gaze. "The tunnel that will take you out of here is down two more corridors, do you think you can do that?" There's no condescension in his voice, only gentleness.

She continues to shake her head, silent tears streaming down her hollow face. Ashden slumps even further beside me, watching the woman with such sorrow that I want nothing more than to take the memory from him.

The tears continue to stream even as her breath begins to slow. Kieran doesn't move, doesn't let go of her hand.

Moment by moment, her breaths wane, until I'm counting the seconds between each one. Still, the tears fall.

She takes one last shuddering inhalation, and stills.

"Author keep you," Rose whispers.

"We can't leave her here." I don't recognize the woman, but I know she has someone back on Ra'goramal who cares about her—who deserves to know. A friend, family member, anyone—I don't care.

"We're not leaving her here," I repeat, borderline hysterical.

"No, we're not," Kieran says softly, eyes still trained on the woman.

He stands, tenderly releasing her hand and turns to one of the others—now slumped against the wall. "Are you okay to keep going?"

He nods, his eyes vacant.

Kieran inclines his head to his mother and sister, "Good. They'll help you."

I watch—shocked, grateful—as Kieran stoops to pick up the lifeless woman. Cradling her in his arms like a child, he motions us forward.

The silence blanketing us now is a different sort. A heavier, sorrowful silence; one that seeps into your bones and weighs on your soul.

We're almost there. Almost there.

Taking the next turn, we step into the abandoned corridor. My stomach leaps to my throat as I see a heap of black bodies near the opposite end.

"They're dead," Opal says flatly. "We took this route when we came in."

I wonder how long it will take for her to recover from this—from everything she's witnessed today. All the lies and deception. Of witnessing the darkest secret a people could hold.

I can't tear my eyes away from the bodies littering the ground ahead of us. A spray of blood peppers a section of the floor near one of the bodies—twin to the one across Opal's thigh.

Not daring to touch them, we carefully pick our way over the tangle of limbs and torsos as we come to the end of this corridor.

And then I hear it.

Footstep. But not the steady footsteps of a patrol.

My breath stops.

Two sets of footsteps. Running, sprinting, pounding the stone floor with no regard for secrecy.

I whip my head toward Kieran, knowing the panic is evident in my face—as evident as the tone of those footsteps.

His brow is creased, a worried line running down the center of it while his jaw tenses. "It's coming from the direction of the Inner Sanctum."

He looks around our group, at Ashden and the other three, and I know what he's thinking. All too weak to run. Defenseless.

"Get in the alcove," he demands, shoveling us toward the one on our right.

I lead Ashden over, almost tripping over his feet in my haste, and help him to the ground.

The footsteps are getting louder, faster, closer.

Sebastian and Avice round the corner at the end of the corridor. I gape at them. Their clothes are sprayed with blood, loose and wrinkled in places they shouldn't be. Sebastian's cheek is bruised—a bleeding gash running across it. Avice's hair is wild, falling down around her neck and face—her characteristic topknot hanging loosely to the side of her head. Their faces glisten with sweat as if they've been running, or fighting, for a while. Their eyes are wide as they sprint toward us.

And then, as Sebastian opens his mouth—terror coating every note of his voice—my heart drops to my stomach.

"Lichera!" he screams.

Chapter 56

A sickening, sizzling energy crackles through the air. I can feel it begin at the topmost part in the center of the Citadel and creep down over the entirety of it like some kind of acid rain.

The energy continues to move down, doming around the Citadel—trapping us beneath its dark, rotten tendrils.

And in one instant, I can feel the energy that flows and moves through me; the air and sun and sea and every beautiful and horrible thing I've ever seen or done, crack. That light, that driving force—it shatters, pressed beneath the weight of something that should have never been borne.

Black Protocol. I can feel it in my bones.

"Go!" Avice shrieks, still pounding down the corridor toward us.

A voice snakes from behind us, at the end of the corridor we're dangerously close to.

"If it isn't Miss Bryorfall and her band of traitorous degenerates."

Lichera steps into the corridor slowly, deliberately—completely unbothered by the group that stands before him—and saunters forward.

Sebastian and Avice pull to a stop next to us, gasping for breath but never taking their eyes from the snake in the corridor with us.

Lichera's long, rat-like nose is distorted into some horrible remembrance of the feature—crunched in places it should be smooth, grotesquely swollen in places it should be full. A trickle of blood runs from it, lining his snarled lips before continuing in a trail down his chin.

Even with a face twisted into otherworldly wrath—it's his eyes that I can't look away from. Like the Warbearers, they are now wholly black; soulless. All of the life within them fully withered into a festering darkness.

I don't understand. Terror slows my thoughts; taking my mind on a trudge through mud.

Like Avice and Sebastian, his uniform—the all-black ensemble of the Head Loadmaster—is disheveled. A slice through the fabric across his bicep reveals a deep bleeding gash.

A crooked smile plasters itself on his face when his eyes lock on mine. Cruel; so sickeningly satisfied it feels like I've swallowed oil.

"Such a valiant effort, your little escapade," Lichera spits, eyeing Kieran and I. "If you truly thought you would get out of here—get away with this–you're more foolish than I ever would have thought possible. Idiots and traitors, every single one of you." Small flecks of frothy spit fly from his mouth. Deranged.

"You're the fool," I fire back, unable to help myself. "If you think something like this could go on without consequence."

Lichera chuckles low in his throat. "Oh, my dear Rae, you thought you could come in here with your little friends and rescue your people—your brother. And then, you would return home the hero, a sort of savior." His depthless eyes narrow on me. "Or maybe the public recognition isn't something you desire. Maybe the praise for your heroic deeds is second to the guilt you're seeking to assuage. If you had only listened and done your part, none of this would have happened. Sure, you or your brother could have been chosen for the Culling at any point, but it wouldn't have been solely because of you, now, wouldn't it?"

I open my mouth but no words come.

"Just like your parents. I don't know why I expected any different." He shakes his head. "Rest assured, this bit of nonsense will soon be extinguished. Your people will know that you broke the laws in the treaty and receive the just punishment for your actions. They will not question, will not know any different, and things will return smoothly to how they should be."

The world shifts beneath my feet, my blood beginning to roar in my ears.

"What did you say?" I whisper.

He cocks his head at me, cruel amusement shining in his eyes. "Oh," his words are dripping with delight. "Oh, you didn't know, did you?"

My nails are digging so hard into my palms I feel the skin begin to break.

"Your parents were both much like you, dear Bryorfall. Poking their noses where they didn't belong, learning things they shouldn't have. They were beginning to ask too many questions, to pry into our histories a bit too closely. You see, we just can't have that. Things run beautifully when everyone does their part. And your parents, well… they were becoming a threat to the design we have put in place. So as a preemptive measure, we had them erased."

Such silence in my head. Such roaring, neverending silence.

"You might be wondering why I'm telling you these things. But it's simple, really. You are all going to be executed—after my Warbearers study you, of course. We need to learn what runs through your veins that makes you so sensitive to the magic. As for you," he thrusts a bony finger at Kieran. "Treason, espionage, attempted anarchy," he counts the accusations off on his hand. "Despicable. You had so much potential, yet you've sold yourself and your people for this worthless girl."

That roaring silence shifts.

Erased. As if my parents' lives were worth less than the dirt on his shoes.

Killed. Not lost in a storm. Killed in Author-knows what way. Dead, at the hand of this man. This whole time; out of spite, oppression, control. This whole time, and I did not know.

My loving father. My beautiful, gentle mother. They knew the truth; they were trying to find a way out, I know it, and they lost their lives because of it.

Because of this man.

That roaring silence quiets, then cracks, bursting the dam to a well of light and fury and power I thought Black Protocol had severed from me completely.

"You," I stare and stare at Lichera. "You did this." Rage and power build within me.

His mouth twists into a horrible, crooked smile. "Yes, yes I supposed I did. And I will do it again, gladly."

Everything that has been taken from me, everything that has been taken from my people; every lie I've ever believed crushes me.

"YOU DID THIS," I shriek.

Without thinking, I throw myself at him, bright magic pulsing from me, forcing back his darkness.

Our bodies collide, the momentum knocking Lichera to the ground. I'm instantly atop him, using his shock to my advantage. Crushing his arms beneath my knees, I begin slamming my fists into his face, his chest—anywhere I can access. All I see is his hideous face, the shock and fury in his eyes.

Where my fists connect, skin splits. I know my knuckles should be screaming at me, but I don't feel it. I can't feel anything aside from the shattering inside of me. Can't think over the all-consuming rage.

"RAE!" Avice's terrified voice cuts through the murk. I glance up at her, barely half a heartbeat, but it's enough. Lichera throws me off of him. The breath is knocked from my lungs when I land in an ungraceful heap.

While Lichera pulls himself to his feet, ungodly fury darkening his face, I look to the end of the corridor, at what caused such horror in Avice.

The Warbearers. Unbound from our magic by Black protocol.

Kieran's gaze locks on mine. So much emotion crosses his face, making it hard for my adrenaline-soaked mind to comprehend. Longing and desire. Resignation. A depth of feeling so intense I can't breathe.

And because I'm not sure what's going to happen, I burn that image into my head. Him—standing there, onyx hair piled haphazardly on his head, a few tendrils falling messily into his eyes. Eyes so full of the raging complexity of life and regret and… love. Love shines in his eyes. For me.

My throat tightens.

Beautiful. The most beautiful thing I've ever seen.

Oh, for more time.

"Get your brother out of here," he breathes. "Go."

Faster than I can process, he sprints at Lichera, daggers in hand. I cry out as their bodies collide and I hear the sickening crunch of bone, but I don't watch to see whose it is.

Dashing to the alcove, I lean down and frantically help Ashden to his feet.

Grunts and metal on metal ring through the marbled corridor. And while it feels so wrong to press forward without Kieran, I refuse to let this sacrifice be in vain. I know I'm no match for Lichera; Kieran has given us the only fighting chance.

Light on his feet, he thrusts at Lichera with those deadly daggers but the older man dodges the blows. Kieran's muscles ripple and bulge under his black suit as he thrusts and ducks, kicking out at Lichera's feet. The kick connects, sending Lichera careening to the floor.

I don't watch any further.

Sebastian and Opal help a prisoner each while Avice and Rose support the weakest between the two of them, leaving me alone with Ashden. He's moving as fast as he can, I know he is, but I want to shout at him to hurry, to go faster. Every second we're in here is one closer to death.

He's drained. I can see it in his eyes. A sheen of sweat coats his face. The stress and quick pace have taken a toll on his already weakened body.

"I'm okay," he says quietly.

A cacophony of footsteps begins to sound through the Citadel, growing louder with each passing second.

"GO!" Kieran roars as he struggles to throw a panting Lichera off of him.

Feeling like my heart is being torn in two, I press forward with Ashden leaning heavily on me. The sounds of struggle continue behind me.

I can't leave him. I can't.

Releasing Ashden, I whirl, pulling one of the daggers from my belt. In one fluid movement, I hurl it as hard as I can at Lichera's hulking form. With a squelching thud, it embeds itself into his thigh. He falters, shrieking in rage, but that moment of weakness is all Kieran needs.

I turn, reaching for Ashden again. "We're almost there," I whisper; as much to myself as to him. "Almost there. Almost there."

We're at the edge of the corridor when four robed figures materialize in front of us. Simply appearing out of thin air, they block our path out of the Citadel—having somehow spirited themselves from the end of the corridor.

Avice stifles a cry as she and Rose stumble with the abrupt stop before catching themselves.

Dark, empty eyes watch us with unrelenting intensity.

A voice, like one and many—both real and not, pierces the air.

"You should not interfere with things you do not understand."

I gape at the Warbearers but their mouths… their mouths aren't moving. Like they're speaking straight into my head.

Something leaden settles in my bones. They don't give any time to respond before moving toward us. I try to grab Ashden tighter—to flee, to fight, I don't know—but, to my horror, I realize I can't move. My body, my limbs, all are frozen, barred by whatever dark magic they've placed over us.

Ashden pulls from my grasp, eyes wide with shock.

The prisoner suspended between Avice and Rose slumps to the ground, unable to support herself. Sebastian, Opal, Avice, Rose—all of us are frozen, stuck to the spot.

The other two prisoners, now without Sebastian and Opal's help, dart their gazes around frantically. I can see it in their eyes as they look between us and the Warbearers; at Kieran and Lichera engaged behind us.

Don't do it, I want to scream. *Don't do it.*

A heartbeat of a glance between them, and they take off down the corridor, as fast as their weakened bodies can carry them.

NO. I want to scream, want to cry, but my mouth is as useless as the rest of my body.

They don't make it more than ten feet before one of the Warbearers raises his hand. His palm starts to glow—hot, white energy building and arcing along his fingertips. I stare and stare at that energy, willing it to vanish, as something within me begins to build.

A fiery white orb shoots from his hand, blasting into the prisoners. The impact sends a shockwave through the corridor. I'm knocked back by the force of it, but the magic binding me holds me upright. Ashden, already weakened, flies backward, stumbling to the ground.

The prisoners' broken bodies are thrown, slamming into stone. A sickening thud crunches as they land, sprawled and unmoving. Bile rises in my throat at the sight of the charred flesh bubbling over bone, sagging in shredded strips from their limp bodies. Their clothing is little more than a dusting of ash.

Tears are running down Avice's face. Sebastian looks as if he might be sick, and Rose—oh, Rose and Opal—their expressions are numb. Haunted. The emptiness and horror has sucked away any remaining light, for that was their husband and father who shot that fiery sphere of death.

Fighting the overwhelming terror, I close my eyes, feeling around for the bands of darkness around us.

Not enough time. Not enough time. Not enough time.

The energy is broken and festering. I dig deep—probing; searching for something, anything.

There. I latch onto the decrepit magic and don't let go.

I open my eyes. The broken strands of blackness surround us. It grips our arms, legs, wrists, mouths, everything it can—sealing us in.

Daring a glance at Sebastian, I find him locked onto me. His easygoing and lighthearted demeanor is gone, his shoulders leaning inward, his eyes dark. Deject and utterly hopeless. I offer him a beseeching, sympathetic glance, hoping he can read it in spite of the paralyzing magic.

Scanning Rose's and Opal's haunted gazes, I pause. Another look at

Sebastian.

None of them are even trying to fight the encroaching darkness.

I keep probing around, and then I see it—the faintest band of glittering red around the magic restraining them. Not on me, but on them. The bands around me are wholly black.

I throw myself at that tiny band of red, delving into it. It hardens itself, throwing me back with an untameable vehemence. Like an invisible barrier of knives, it cuts into me, trying to force itself onto me. Pushing, pushing, pushing.

I throw myself into it, pushing back, sweat beginning to prick my brow. The air grows tighter as I struggle to get shaking breaths down. The Warbearers are going to see at any second what I'm doing, but their attention is temporarily held by something out of view.

A fresh wave of dark resistance hits me along with the realization of what I'm fighting.

The Warbearers don't know Kieran has taught me how to use the magic. They don't know I've been to the temple, that I've had the raw elements coursing through my veins. That I know the full, unadulterated truth. They think I'm a useless Goramalan, incapable of what they've corrupted. Avice too—her bands are black, just like mine. The red must be some kind of specific binding over Verenathians to render their own magic unusable.

They don't know. Trapped by their own ideals.

As fast as I can, I set to work breaking the bonds around me. I find the strands and sever them, one by one. Like taking a dull knife to a fraying rope, I cut them off. Golden light begins to flow around me, taking over the rotting magic of the Warbearers.

I free my hands first, then my arms, legs, and mouth. My heart races, my breath coming in trembling gasps.

Freed from the Warbearer's grasp, I throw everything that I am into breaking those glittering bonds around my friends.

I let go of the magic when I see Lichera stalking toward me, bloodied and snarling.

Kieran.

I gasp, whirling to find Kieran wholly still—the same invisible restraints on him now. Panic lights through me, splitting me in half. Faster than I've ever done before, I probe through the magic until I find those damned red bonds. But unlike the rest of my friends, his soft golden light is spreading through and around it.

I breathe a quick sigh of relief. He'll be able to find a way through. He's stronger than they realize.

"You bitch," Lichera spits, reaching me and wrenching my arm behind me before twisting my other. His claw-like grip digs into the soft inner flesh of my bicep, and I cry out. Thrashing and writhing, I try to escape his grasp, even stomping down onto the arch of his foot—but to no avail. His grip is unfaltering.

"I was going to have you all taken to the Inner Sanctum," he snaps. "Such a poetic ending for a band of traitors, but because of your insolence, you've forced—"

A deep voice booms from behind the Warbearers, cutting him off. "You have committed a grievous offense against Verenathia and her people."

CHAPTER 57

A white-robed figure strides toward us.

Lucielle.

The Warbearers part to let him step between them. He stops before us, eyeing the scene with disgust, his eyes darkening with disappointment when they land on Lichera.

"We'll have to find a new Bearer," he muses nonchalantly.

Lichera sputters, his grip tightening on my arms as the blood drains from my head at Lucielle's words. And then a cold, black wave is blasting toward us. A scream begins tearing its way up my throat at that wave of black death, but it doesn't touch me.

No—reaching us, it seems to bend around me, focusing itself into a spear—like point, and pierces straight through Lichera's chest. A spray of blood peppers my hair as a wet gurgle rasps from him, his grip loosening from my aching arms. He slumps behind me and I whirl, just in time to see him stagger back a step before thudding, lifeless, to the ground.

A clean, gaping hole bores right through his heart.

"You," Lucielle sneers, glaring at Kieran. "How disappointing."

I swallow the bile rising in my throat, swallow the panic that's rising with death on its heels.

Lucielle points at Kieran. "End him. Take the rest to the Inner Sanctum; alive."

"NO!" I shriek. A strangled noise erupts from Rose's frozen mouth but the Warbearers are instantly moving. Kieran's father reaches me, gripping my arms the same way Lichera did. I try to fight but I feel like I'm moving through mud. My arms and legs don't want to obey.

"You're not like anything we've seen before," he breathes in my ear. "We're going to enjoy finding out how you managed to break through Black Protocol."

As he utters the words, a suffocating, black weight settles over me. Panic rises up my throat when I realize it wasn't just my fear that made my limbs feel foreign.

Everything is so heavy. So dark. So wrong. Two of the Warbearers reach my friends, one grabbing Sebastian and Avice; the other, Rose and Opal.

My friends' bodies begin shifting in movements that are wholly not their own. Their arms twitch in odd directions, their legs rising and falling with slow, jerking movements, pulling them forward step by hulking step.

Pain sears into me, lighting every single one of my nerves. As hot as the fires in my forge and as sharp as a dagger, it tears me apart. Blackness blinds my vision and leaks into my veins, filling me from the inside out. It's seeping into every pore and I can't breathe. I can't breathe. It's flooding my lungs. It's all I can see, all I know as the pain doesn't stop. It doesn't stop.

A scream tears out of me, ragged and piercing.

Somewhere through the blackness, I hear a roar of wrath to my cry of pain.

"LET HER GO!"

Kieran.

I force breath after breath into my lungs, trying to push back the darkness overwhelming me.

Breathe.

Breathe.

That tiny force within me, nothing more than the flicker of a star, holds, unyielding to the torrent of darkness flooding me.

Breathe.

That tiny light stays flickering. I fight my descent into the blackness with every breath.

Something slams into us from behind, and I fly out of the Warbearer's grasp. Pain and darkness immediately evaporate, and I'm thrown back into the hell of the corridor.

Thudding to the ground, I spin on my hands and knees. Kieran is standing behind his father, a dagger in his hand.

He slides it deep into the robes at his back.

Kieran's face is a war of emotion. Rage and guilt and a hollowness that has never been his guise. With tears streaming down his face, he grits his teeth and pulls the dagger back out, his father's blood gleaming on its blade.

A blast of power from Lucielle sends Kieran flying to the ground. His father sags, his breathing ragged, but remains standing; his face too veiled from his hood to see.

"Remove. Them." Lucielle commands, each word clipped.

Kieran fights to pull himself up, but whatever force Lucielle hit him with has left him weakened, his legs trembling with the effort.

I fight, willing my body to cooperate, straining against the magic binding it as Kieran's father struggles toward me. Another web of invisible bands falls over me and I cry out in desperation. I'm not fast enough, not experienced enough to fight their magic.

It's not enough.

Not enough.

My friends continue their jerking movements, slowly making their way out of the corridor. Ashden slumps on the ground, cast aside as if he's not worth the air he breathes.

The final Warbearer remains where he stands and raises his hand, holding it toward Kieran the same way Kieran's father did to those prisoners.

Everything stops. Everything simply stops.

His hand begins glowing, emanating that same deadly energy.

Kieran's father shoves me down the corridor, away from Kieran. Away from his son.

"Kieran!" I scream.

I can feel something simmering in my veins. The culmination of my life—all the pain, the joy, the heartache and ecstasy. I can feel it twisting together, writhing and thrashing—fighting against the dark magic around me.

I don't know what Lucielle did but Kieran can't get up. He's kneeling, his breath heaving as his head hangs over his knee. He pulls his head up, silvered resignation lining his eyes.

"Please forgive me," he whispers. "I love you."

No. Don't say it. Not yet. We're getting out of here. None of the words in my heart make it into the open air.

That writhing force inside me breaks some of my bonds, allowing me to crane my neck around to face Kieran's father.

"Do something!" I cry.

Something, something in the depths of his soul flickers for a heartbeat, shows itself through the pain evident in his labored breathing, but he forces me onward.

"NO!" The sensation inside me is growing, growing. An unearthly tempest of pain and energy. It fractures more of his restraint on me.

I thrash wildly, trying desperately to free myself.

Ashden turns wide eyes to me.

"Go!" I cry "Go home! Get out of here!" Hysteria pitches my voice as I fight with every ounce of rage I possess.

Kieran's father jerks my hair, forcing my head forward but I turn toward Ashden again.

"I love you," I can barely get the words out.

A bright, fiery flash lights the corridor.

CHAPTER 58

ASHDEN

I don't know what's happening. The Warbearers possess magic I never even thought possible. Everyone seems to possess magic, although I don't have the luxury of time to question it.

My mind is free now, though sluggish from whatever siphoning force they had on me.

I can move. I can move when none of the others can. They don't think I'm a concern. Probably going to die on my own if I can get out of here.

But Rae, I don't have the words for how good it is to see Rae. She came back for me, she's risking her life to get us out of here. She's too good. Too pure for this awful, dark world.

Even now, as she's fighting to free herself from the Warbearer at her back, I can see it. She was frozen like the rest. I don't know how she freed herself; that's beyond the scope of my understanding. All I know is she did, and I know it's a testament to who she is.

And I can see, too, the way she's looking at this man. Kieran.

I don't know him. I've only ever spoken to him on the loading docks.

But he's here, and so are these other Verenathians. I can tell he's been integral in helping Rae get to this point. He's sacrificing everything. They all are. Which is a testament to his own character; he's at just as much risk as Rae,

Verenathian or no.

And he's going to die.

When I look at my sister, I can see it. Whether she understands it herself or not, I can see it. I see the fear for his life, and the tentative love. Young, unsure, still just a bud daring to break through the surface; but it's there.

I remember the way my mother looked at my father, the gentle care he always took toward her. I've always wanted the same for myself—hoped I would find it someday.

But Rae, with her ability to see the light in a world that is so dark, has gone and found it. I can't let them take that away from her. I can't let them rip it away when there's still so much left to grow, to be done, to be experienced. So much hope and vibrancy and joy still yet to shine.

She deserves it. She deserves it more than anyone I know.

And because she is who she is, I know she'll get there. She'll seek beauty until it's staring her in the face.

As I look at Kieran, his own face raw with panic—panic, and acceptance—I can see that same tenderness reflected in his own eyes.

Maybe someday I would find someone who ignites that same light in me. Maybe I would find someone to grow old with. Someone who would care for me in that same way. But I can't dwell on that, not now. Rae has found it, and she deserves to keep it.

She was right about everything, but I'll never get to tell her that.

She's wonderful; she always has been, and she deserves it.

She deserves it.

CHAPTER 59

Press onward, my dear. Always press onward.

No.

The Warbearer lunges forward and that heinous sphere of fire is free. I can't tear my eyes away as Ashden throws himself onto Kieran.

NO.

I keep thrashing, thrashing, trying to get to my brother.

A blinding impact, that same shockwave of heat and energy. Then stillness.

I can hear screaming but I don't know if it's mine. Something is tearing my throat and lungs, but is that sound… is that really me? My body is floating away from me, as if in a dream. Or maybe that's me leaving my body, leaving this wicked, cruel world.

This isn't happening. I know it isn't. Like that dream I had of Kieran killing me—this is a dream. It's a horrible, awful, sickening dream and I'm going to wake up.

I still hear the screaming. I can still feel something shredding my insides.

I'm not waking up.

Why am I not waking up?

My brother's body, now melted and broken, lies on top of Kieran. Kieran is roaring, cursing, pinned beneath Ashden, unable to shift my brother off of him.

This isn't a dream.

My body is writhing and fighting of its own accord now, that glowing tempest inside me reaching a fever pitch, threatening to tear me apart as Ashden, throwing himself over Kieran at the very last moment, flashes through my mind on a loop. The Warbearer who did it looks vaguely surprised, as if my brother's life is a mild inconvenience that got in the way of his target.

I shut my eyes tight at the overwhelming surges within me—at the pain from my parents, from the wrongness of this world, and now this gaping, shattering fracture tearing through me as I look at Ashden's broken body.

My overwhelm meets with the golden energy twisting in me and they coalesce. The collision is too much for my body to contain. Magic meets magic in a cacophony of energy and beauty and pain.

I erupt.

Blinding white light breaks from my body. As if radiating from my skin itself, it illuminates the corridor, casting it into brightest daylight.

A web of golden filigree flies from my hands and spreads throughout the corridor. Everywhere those dark, broken bands of magic are—they disintegrate when my magic meets them. Everywhere the magics collide results in fracturing explosions that burst across my sight.

It breaks the bonds on my friends, on Kieran. Flooding the entire corridor, it continues to spread as it fills the Citadel. The oppressive weight of Black Protocol breaks, leaving emptiness in its wake.

My body is on fire. Heat and light and ice rush out of me.

An overwhelming surge floods from me as the power stretches even to Ra'goramal. I can feel it shattering the Safeguards, shattering every hold these wretched people have ever cast over us. One band of magic at a time, it overrides and breaks that dark net, until only emptiness remains. Not the emptiness of loss, but the emptiness of something inviting newness into its midst—inviting life.

Light and free.

All the writhing, tearing, and fracturing inside of me recedes, settling into calm.

A Warbearer, eyes wide with fear, releases Sebastian before spiriting away. Gone in a blink. The remaining Warbearers exchange frantic glances before following suit. Using whatever semblance of power they have left, they disappear, vanishing into thin air. Lucielle pauses, not bothering to hide his hatred nor his shock, and gives me one last damning glare. A curse and a promise. And then he's gone.

Kieran's father remains the longest, watching us with an expression unreadable from underneath his hood. Then he's gone too.

I race to Kieran's side and drop to my knees. "No, no, no," I whisper through the welling tears as I gently roll Ashden's body off of Kieran.

His shirt is ash across his burned back. I swallow a cry as the smell of burnt flesh singes my nose; his back a charred mass. Raw, exposed skin peaks through the burnt pieces, sagging from his ribs.

Kieran summons the strength to pull himself up and helps me roll Ashden onto his side. His eyes are still open slightly, and there's a faint rise and fall to his chest.

"Ashden," I choke. "Ashden, please." I can't think of any other words as tears begin dripping onto the marble while I kneel beside him.

"Please," I whisper.

I can hardly make out his voice as he murmurs, "Rae."

Gently, I take his hand in mine. "I'm so sorry," the words barely make it past the tears clogging my throat.

"Rae," he breathes, his face contorted in pain.

No, no he needs to stop. He needs to conserve his strength.

"Rose!" I cry.

Kieran's mother rushes to my side in an instant. Her face is pale and drawn, her lips pressed into a tight line as she surveys Ashden.

"Please help him," I whisper.

Her lips press even tighter as she begins to shake her head.

I shake my own in response, unwilling to hear it. "No. Please, help him."

"Rae," her voice is achingly gentle. "It's more than just surface wounds. The magic—it does things… it's not something I can heal." Her eyes brim with tears. "I'm sorry."

"No, no, no," I breathe. Over and over again, it's all I can think—all I can feel.

Ashden's mouth is moving again, his eyes having closed. I crouch down until his breath tickles my ear.

"Find the life you deserve," he croaks.

"Ashden—"

"Mom and dad would be so proud of you."

I take his hand in mine, gripping so tightly, trying to hold onto the life seeping out of his eyes. "Please," I whisper. "Don't leave me."

"I love you," he breathes.

"No, don't talk like that. You know I love you too, but we're going to get out of here. I'll take you home," I choke.

He only sighs, the corners of his mouth lifting the tiniest bit.

"Please," my voice is a broken thing. "You're all I have left."

His eyes open a crack. "You…" he pauses, drawing a weak breath. "Have… everything you… need. Don't give… up, little bird."

His chest falls one more time.

Then stills.

Pain unlike anything I've ever felt shatters my heart so far that, in this moment, I know I'll never be whole again.

I press my head into the cold marble floor as a guttural sob wracks my body. The tears break free in a rush, streaming hot down my face, pooling below me.

This wasn't supposed to happen. We were supposed to be out of here right now, on our way somewhere safe.

Not this.

Not this.

A warm hand rests itself on my shuddering back.

Kieran.

I throw myself at him, into his accepting arms, and he holds me tight.

"This… wasn't… supposed… to happen," I heave between gasping sobs.

His arms tighten around me, pressing me further into his chest. "I know," he murmurs into my hair. "I know."

Another set of hands begin stroking my back and I turn to see Avice, devastation written across her face.

"I did this," I cry.

She wraps herself tightly around me, pressing her cheek into my back. "You didn't do it. He did it. For you, Rae."

Her words send a lightning bolt of agony through me, and I dissolve again into Kieran's chest.

"Rae," Kieran's deep voice is soft. I feel Avice's warmth at my back retreat. "We're not safe here, not yet. We need to leave."

"But," I glance to my brother's still form beside us, panic starting to take a foothold. "But, Ash—"

"We'll take him with us," he gently cuts me off.

"Where do we go?" I ask, hiccupping. Uncaring where I go; whether I live or die.

He strokes my cheek with his finger. "Back to the temple, we'll be safe there for now. It will give us time to…" his voice trails off.

Why do we need time? What is there, anymore? None of it matters.

I nod numbly, roughly swiping the back of my hand across my eyes.

Rising to his feet, Kieran pulls me to mine. I feel as if I'm floating—not really inhabiting my body. As if this really, truly is a dream.

Opal, Sebastian, and Rose all watch me with haunted, sympathetic gazes.

Kieran stoops, carefully scooping Ashden's body into his arms, and we make our way through the corridor and toward the waiting dragons.

CHAPTER 60

KIERAN

"*This wasn't supposed to happen.*"

No. It wasn't.

I can't get Rae's broken voice out of my head. I can't forget the look Ashden and I shared as he threw his body on top of mine. One look, but it said everything.

Love her. Protect her. Take care of her. Everything my soul has been bent on doing since the day I met her—everything a look can convey, man to man. But that last gleam in his eye is what's destroying me.

I forgive you.

Me, of all people, for what I've done. My people for what they're allowing to happen. He saw, he experienced it himself—he knows, and yet, that gleam conveyed his final intention. His last act—one of sacrifice, of love—and he did for me. For Rae, I know. But it was *my* life that he saved with his own.

That he thought me, belonging to a people that have done nothing but destroy the lives of his, worthy of saving is a weight almost too much to bear. And as much as I wish it were otherwise true, there's no bringing him back. Not even the magic is capable of resurrection.

I don't know where the Warbearers fled to, but they and the Court will no doubt do their best to cover up what happened. They'll try to push it off as an attack from a foreign land or something equally as ridiculous. They'll do their best to force everyone back into the routine of normal life—but they can't. Nothing can erase the stain of genocide. The Goramalans will likely revolt when they learn the truth, and good for them. If nothing else, the Culling will likely not continue without a fight.

Even if one life is spared, maybe what we've done is worth it.

And my father.

Oh, my father.

The pain that accompanies the thought of him will be my undoing, if I let it. That darkness clings like a blanket, stifling me. The questions, the abandonment, the hurt—I can't escape it.

I was only a boy when he left. An adult in years, but I still needed my father—I still do. How do you ever stop needing something so integral? But I didn't have a choice. The phantom weight of my dagger, covered in his blood, is haunting me. I can feel it there no matter how hard I grip Cinder.

My stomach is a mess of knots and numbness. My cheeks are raw where I keep swiping at the liquid whipping free from the wind. Ashden's lifeless body seems to weigh Cinder down, her wingbeats heavy as we soar back to the temple.

Rae is beside me, lagging behind a bit. Maybe to keep an eye on Ashden, to make sure his body doesn't fall to the sea. But I don't intend to let him go. I don't intend to let her down again in the way I've done the whole time I've known her.

I can't explain what that woman has done to me. I've never had anyone affect me so completely, so quickly and deeply before. I can hear the song of the wind in her laugh, and the way her eyes burn… I can't escape it. I know we've not known each other for long, but in that time, she's engrained herself so deeply in me it's as if she's become a part of me. As necessary to life as the air in my lungs.

I glance behind me, at the sight of that beautiful face. Her eyes are puffy and raw, her face pale. The dark eyes that are usually so clever, burning with an inner fire, are now hollow. Bottomless depths of an unfillable void. She keeps her gaze trained straight ahead, not bothering to wipe the tears that run down her face. Avice is clinging to her tightly, her own face wet with sorrow.

I drag my own back to the horizon. I have to. I don't want her to see the mess that I've become. I need to be there for her, need to be a rock that she can throw all of her rage and grief onto. She has Avice, but her family… Rae has no family left.

Cinder chortles softly, sensing my distress.

"It's okay girl," I soothe, patting the side of her neck. She chuffs, and I know she doesn't believe me.

"It will be," I promise. "Let's just get to the temple, okay?"

***

Stepping over loose stones, I carry Ashden's body to the door of the temple. I block out the feeling of his ruined back against my hand, trying not to be sick as we pass by the mural. The fresh paint from Rae's mother glows softly from the light in my own mother's hand.

We come to the door to the cavernous temple still pushed ajar; just how we left it. Everything else looks the same too. Nothing has been touched or tampered with since we were last here. Lichera's infectious presence hasn't spread down here, then. Maybe he didn't realize we found it, or maybe he didn't care. We were never anything but walking corpses to him anyway.

Sebastian steps ahead of me, his face solemn, and opens the door wide. The magic in the room beyond pulls me in, lightening the weight of Ashden in my arms as I step through the door. Gingerly, I pick my way down the balcony stairs.

I told Rae we would come here because it was safe, but really, I don't know what to do. It is the safest option right now, as both Rae and Avice are fugitives. Stepping foot into town will get them imprisoned—but Ashden deserves a proper burial. He's worth more than an unmarked grave in the grasslands… So here we are.

My chest tightens as I near the base of the steps. Swirling streams of magic move closer, as if they're peeking at us, inspecting. The energy of the room pulses, active and alive and seeking. It's tranquil, though.

Setting Ashden gently on the dirty marble floor, I pause, crouched, trying to collect myself before facing Rae. I feel her at my back as they all file down the stairs.

Rising back up, I turn to her. The emptiness in her face shatters something inside of me and I grab her, pulling her in tight to my chest.

She feels so small, so fragile. As if one wrong breath could have her taken away. And I suppose it's true; the death clinging to us testifies to that fact.

"What do we do?" She whispers, pulling in a shuddering breath.

I don't know.

I'm smart. Not in an arrogant sort of way, but I've worked my ass off to learn as much about anything and everything as I can. I saw what a lack of knowledge did to the Goramalans, and I told myself I'd never let that happen to me. But that knowledge—the power and problem solving that it brings—can't do anything right now. I don't know what to do.

"What do we do?" She repeats, her voice pitching upward slightly.

I've never been one to panic, but the body lingering behind us and the fear in Rae's voice sends a jolt through me. My body feels like it's teetering along the thin edge of a glass pane—one wrong move will send me careening over the edge and shatter it entirely.

"Kieran," she pulls back, her eyes darting behind me. "What do we do?" Her breaths come faster now, her body beginning to tremble.

Avice is at her side in a heartbeat, pulling her into another embrace. The look she gives me over Rae's shoulder is beseeching—a plea to figure this out so Rae won't have to endure any more trauma.

I don't know.

Author, help me.

Opal draws back, a hand pressed to her mouth. She stumbles back another step, almost tripping over Sebastian, before hurdling up the stairs to the door atop the balcony. Sebastian chases after her, and a moment later the sounds of her retching fill the cavernous space.

My mother stands with her arms wrapped tightly around herself, watching Rae and Avice with watery eyes.

Please.

Stepping toward Ashden, I pause, my own stomach churning at the sight. His skin has taken on the sallow pall of death while angry red wounds web across his skin. Thankfully, the mess of exposed, raw flesh on his back is hidden as he lays, his eyes closed. If I didn't know any better, I'd almost say he's sleeping.

Help me.

The swirling magic in the room halts its dance, as if the entire temple holds its breath—listening. Then slowly, like creeping fingers, the magic begins probing about the room. Like shimmering smoke, the bands lower, searching for something. Lower and lower they descend, leaving the openness of the air, and come down to us.

Rae jerks out of Avice's grasp as a brush of golden light feathers across her back. They weave and undulate between us. A sense of warmth and peace settle as they continue in their exploration.

I don't think I'm breathing. I've never seen the magic behave this way—even as I've spent hours and hours diving into it, searching for a way out of the darkness on Verenathia.

The elements between the conduits on the dais begin radiating particles of light. That light spreads through the room like an effervescent blanket, meeting with the smoke-like magic as it rises in response. The forces converge and coalesce before lowering again.

They find Ashden's body. The bands of magic gently brush against his lifeless skin. As soft as a lover's touch, as gentle as handling a newborn babe, they travel along his skin. His arms, legs, and face all begin gleaming with golden light.

Like coils of rope, the magic begins wrapping around his body. They wrap until he seems entirely bound, but…

I swallow. That's not what this is.

First, the damage across his body fades. Those red lines get pushed back, receding as if being reabsorbed into the impact that initially caused them.

The tendrils wrapped around him carefully pull taut, and his body begins lifting into the air. My mother gasps from behind me, and Rae cries out, taking a step toward her brother.

His body continues lifting until it's suspended in the air. He looks completely at ease, like he would if he were floating in the sea. Taking on a golden shimmer, his skin begins to glow.

More of the magic wisping through the upper part of the mountain lowers. It reaches Ashden in probing strands, descending on him the way a mother would over a hurt child. Brighter and brighter his skin glows as the magic weaves in and around him.

Now above us, his back exposed, the wounds there waver. Like the hands of a surgeon, the magic knits them together until the skin is unmarred. And still he grows more illuminated.

Rae is shaking uncontrollably now as she stares at Ashden's body. Stepping forward, I wrap my arms around her shoulders. She brings her hands to mine, gripping so tightly her knuckles turn white.

I want to take this from her. All of it—even as an otherworldly serenity has settled over the temple.

I squeeze her tight, feeling as her tears drip onto my arms. My mother and

Avice move to our sides, eyes wide. Shuffling footsteps behind us signal Opal and Sebastian's return.

"Author above ..." Opal breathes.

The magic shifts around Ashden urgently, yet theres's a tenderness there, almost like it has a mind of its own—some form of consciousness. I don't understand it. Every touch is concerned and careful, but insistent, as if it knows what must be done.

Glittering mist begins floating around Ashden's body while he rests, now fully repaired and luminous.

The edges of his skin waver, shimmering in the light of the magic. But, no... That mist is coming *from* his body.

It *is* his body; turning into iridescent particles and joining the cascade of elements as they swirl about the cavern. Like ink in water, his body diffuses into the air. All the while the bands of magic wrap and probe around him.

A sob shakes Rae's body, and she sinks to the ground, pulling me with her. I drop behind her, easing her descent as she falls to her knees, her eyes locked on Ashden.

Bit by bit, he disappears. Wavering, shimmering, then turning iridescent. Glimmering particles are streaming from him now, as if the magic is absorbing his soul.

The peace in the cavern—a calm I can't explain—feels like something usually reserved for the solitude of the grave. An almost reverent sort of calm—the only sounds in the temple are of Rae's overflowing grief.

Slowly, Ashden's body becomes translucent as the magic takes it, until there's nothing left but a faint outline.

And finally, that outline fades as the last bits of him are diffused into the force of magic. Like a galaxy of stars and color, a rainbow of opalescence spreads throughout the cavern.

The wisps of magic move faster now, joyfully almost.

"Look, Rae," I whisper. "They're dancing."

A bright flash, as if all the rainbow colored particles turn into nothing but light, and the cavern is cast back into its characteristic warm glow. The magic lowers again, twining between us. It takes special care toward Rae—surrounding her, brushing against her before dissipating.

The elements retract, returning to their streams at the dais. The magic floats back to its place in the air, and everything settles.

No one speaks, all too astonished at what we just witnessed. Rae continues to shake in my arms, her tears falling silently.

I pull her into my lap, curling my body around her as if I can protect her from her grief. She sobs into my chest, soaking my suit.

We sit, wrapped tightly around each other for an indefinable amount of time. But I won't leave her. Never again will I let her go. Never again will I hurt her the way I have.

Never again.

Finally, she pulls herself up. Glancing at everyone gathered behind us, she pries herself out of my lap and sits back on the floor in front of me. Pulling her knees in tightly to her chest, she watches me with swollen eyes.

Author above. She's so beautiful I can't even breathe.

"Thank you," she whispers, her voice raw.

My entire chest restricts, and I force back the burning in my eyes. "Of course."

She offers me a sad smile. "Where do we go from here?"

The weight of that question threatens to drag me under, but I hold her stunning dark gaze.

"We'll keep going—one moment at a time."

"One moment at a time," she murmurs.

"Just one," I whisper, pulling her hand to my lips and pressing a kiss into it.

I choose to believe that there is hope. I have to. Though darkness and the unknown linger outside the safety of this temple, I'm not letting go of it. For her—I will not let go of it.

I will fight for that choice—the decision to choose hope. I don't know what the coming days, weeks, or months will look like, but I know there's a reason for this darkness. There has to be. Hope is tentative; disappearing when despair rears its ugly head.

If I let it go—if I let that lifeline to the knowledge that some day, things will be right again—I'll drown. But I can't, there's still too much that needs to be done—too much to live for.

Because even with this darkness, I know if we never had the night, we wouldn't need to search for hope. And without the night, we would never learn to appreciate the warmth of daylight.

My father taught me that.

www.ingramcontent.com/pod-product-compliance
Lightning Source LLC
LaVergne TN
LVHW100506110826
845146LV00002B/539

* 9 7 9 8 9 9 5 1 7 7 1 1 1 *